FIRST KISS

"You feel my tutoring of you has been a waste of your time then?" Julian asked stiffly.

"No! Of course not!" Samantha said fervently. "You taught me how to be a lady, Julian." She turned his hand over and pressed the palm against her cheek. "But who will teach me how to be a woman?"

She moved closer and wrapped her arms around his neck. "Who will hold me . . . like this?" She pressed her body against his. "Who will . . . kiss me, Julian?"

Julian's body had turned completely traitorous. His pulse was racing, his blood drummed through his veins, and an ache had settled in his loins. And the only possible answer to her questions seemed to be . . .

To kiss her.

THE PERFECT GENTLEMAN

DANICE ALLEN

AVON BOOKS ◆ NEW YORK

THE PERFECT GENTLEMAN is an original publication of Avon Books. This work has never before appeared in book form. This work is a novel. Any similarity to actual persons or events is purely coincidental.

AVON BOOKS
A division of
The Hearst Corporation
1350 Avenue of the Americas
New York, New York 10019

Copyright © 1997 by Danice Allen
Inside cover author photo by Steve Ducher
Published by arrangement with the author
Library of Congress Catalog Card Number: 96-96479
ISBN: 0-380-78151-4

First Avon Books Printing: January 1997

AVON TRADEMARK REG. U.S. PAT. OFF. AND IN OTHER COUNTRIES, MARCA REGISTRADA, HECHO EN U.S.A.

Printed in the U.S.A.

RA   10 9 8 7 6 5 4 3 2 1

Prologue

Montgomery Manor
Hampshire, England
December 25, 1816

"**I** knew Amanda Jane would make a beautiful Christmas bride," Aunt Prissy said, sniffling into her lace-edged handkerchief as she sank into a chair by the fire. "The wreath of holly in her hair was sheer inspiration! And how clever of Jack to have the aisle in the family chapel lined with potted poinsettias. The entire affair was lovely . . . just lovely!"

"Indeed," Aunt Nan agreed, blinking her teary eyes as she stood in front of the fire with her arthritic fingers splayed and stretched to the blaze. "It couldn't have been a nicer ceremony. I especially liked the intimacy of it, with just the immediate family present. Though, under the circumstances—with Jack's last wedding being canceled like it was—it was only proper. What did you think, Samantha?"

Samantha wasn't sure what she thought. The logical functioning of her brain was playing second fiddle to the feelings in her heart. She sat on a

1

footstool by Prissy's chair, her ungloved hands stretched to the warming fire. But she felt no more comfortable now than when she'd been standing outside in the damp cold, waving good-bye to Amanda. . . .

Having prided herself on being the unsentimental sort, Sam was disconcerted to find herself on the brink of tears. While Amanda's elderly aunts waited for an answer to Nan's innocently posed question, Samantha struggled with her emotions. Not more than ten minutes ago, a half sister whose existence Sam had been entirely ignorant of two months before, had driven off in a carriage for the coastal city of Dover, then on to the Continent for an extended honeymoon. Sam hadn't had the slightest suspicion how dear that newfound sister had become to her . . . till now.

"Samantha?" prompted Nan.

Sam looked up. Her throat had constricted too tightly to squeak out a single word, and she knew as she watched Nan's watery brown eyes soften with understanding and sympathy that she had to get out of that room immediately or embarrass herself. *She* was no sniveling female, ready to weep at the drop of a hat or the absence of a sibling!

Sam rose abruptly from the footstool and picked up her froth of silvery pink skirts. "Samantha, where are you going?" Prissy called out in alarm, as Sam ran past her chair.

"For a walk," Sam managed to croak in a strangled voice.

"But why don't you wait for Julian, dearest? Julian will be down presently," Nan called after her, but Sam couldn't wait . . . not even for Julian. She flew through the double doors of the elegant drawing room, into the hall, past the ever-present footman, and out the front door.

Blinded by a distorting curtain of tears, Sam instinctively turned in the direction of the small stone family chapel that had been set apart from the edifice that the wealthy Montgomery men called home. The cobbled walkway was slick from a morning shower, but Sam hurried heedlessly on, intent only on getting away to a place where she could be alone.

Inside the church were sepulchers that held the mortal remains of past Montgomerys . . . the noble forebears of Julian Montgomery, the present marquess of Serling, and Jackson Montgomery, Viscount Durham, Amanda's bridegroom and Sam's new brother-in-law. The more ordinary family members, however, as well as several longtime servants, had been laid to rest in the tiny cemetery behind the church, their graves marked by tombstones . . . some rather handsome and ornate, others much more modest.

Sam gravitated toward the simplest tombstone in the small, green graveyard, tucked away in the farthest corner, where an overhanging gable of the church sheltered a patch of grass near the grave. She sank to the damp ground, her skirts billowing about her, and for several minutes gave vent to her unhappiness.

"What's wrong, Sam?"

Startled, Sam looked up . . . way up . . . into the face of Julian Montgomery, Jack's older brother. He stooped and threw her cloak about her shoulders, then straightened and hovered over her. With the gray, leaden sky as a backdrop, Julian's cool, golden beauty shimmered like the winter sun.

As blond as a Viking and with eyes the icy, silver-

blue of an Alpine lake, Sam thought Julian had the
bearing of a prince and the noble mien of a saint.
His features seemed carved from the finest marble,
carefully chipped and smoothed to classic propor-
tions by an obsessive artist. Sam searched those
features now for a hint of what he was thinking,
what he was feeling, but she soon dropped her gaze,
frustrated by the impenetrability of his expression
and embarrassed by her own out-of-control emotions.

"I'm . . . I'm just missin' Zeus and Neptune,"
she mumbled, wiping her face with the back of her
hand. "I wish't we didn't have t' leave 'em at
Darlington Hall."

Julian remained silent, and Sam darted a glance
at him. He had raised one finely arched, tawny
brow in obvious disbelief.

"It's the truth!" she blurted defiantly. She did
miss her dogs, but that certainly wasn't why she
was blubbering like a babe. However, she'd no
intention of telling Julian the real reason for her
unhappiness.

Julian shook his head. "You expect me to believe
you're crying over those large, unruly curs you call
pets?" he said disdainfully. "Do you take me for an
idiot?"

She'd be a fool if she did. Julian was far from an
idiot. His intellect surpassed even his astonishing
physical beauty. And this paragon of brains and
tautly muscled brawn was her "teacher." Yes, the
acknowledged arbiter of good taste for the *haut ton*
had vowed to turn *her*—a sow's ear—into the
proverbial silk purse. And this miracle was to be
wrought in plenty of time for Sam to be presented
next April at a coming-out ball as Amanda's "cous-

in," instead of what she truly was . . . Amanda's bastard half sister.

Conveniently, Amanda had an uncle and aunt on their father's side who had lived and died in a remote village in Cumbria without producing offspring. Since the uncle, a genteel clergyman, as well as the aunt, were long dead now, apparently having left behind no close friends or neighbors to tell their tale, it seemed safe to claim Samantha as their orphaned daughter, who had been taken in several years ago by Amanda's parents. Mr. and Mrs. Darlington were also conveniently deceased and couldn't refute the fabricated explanation for Sam's existence.

A man who was a stickler about a woman's pedigree would blanch at Samantha's obscure background, but with the patronage of the marquess of Serling, as well as Amanda's respectable connection and the generous dowry she'd settled on her sister, Sam would have no trouble attracting suitors. But she sometimes wondered if it would be entirely ethical or wise for a woman to enter into marriage with a man who didn't *really* know her. Such a woman would have to remain, in part, a stranger to that man for as long as either of them were alive.

While Sam continued to be miserably silent and immersed in distressing thoughts, Julian reached down, caught her hands, and pulled her to her feet. Painfully aware of her swollen eyes and reddened cheeks, Sam balked. "I won't go back to the house lookin' like this, Julian. I don't want no one thinkin' I'm some sissified waterin' pot."

"We're not going back to the house," Julian said calmly. "At least not yet. We're going inside the chapel. It's warmer and much more cheerful in there. Warming up and cheering up is exactly what you need, my girl."

Sam didn't want to go, but she went anyway. Julian was not a man accustomed to being denied. And that's precisely why he was her teacher instead of a bevy of assorted tutors. Amanda had engaged tutors at the beginning, but she'd soon learned that Julian was the only person who could prod, bully, tease, and order her little sister into acquiring the basic education and accomplishments required to establish herself comfortably in society and snag herself a husband.

Amanda would have been surprised to learn that obtaining Julian as her sister's one and only teacher was what Sam had intended and connived for all along. She'd been purposely stupid and incorrigible with the tutors Amanda had hired, holding out for the only person whose opinion truly mattered as far as she was concerned. But Amanda did not suspect, nor did anyone else, that Sam not only cared for Julian's opinion . . . she cared for Julian, too.

Desperately.

In fact, Sam fully intended that her unsuspecting brother-in-law, the man who made her knees go weak and her heart beat as fast as a hummingbird's wings the minute he entered the room, would be the husband everyone was so eager for her shackle.

Because of being kept virtually a prisoner on remote Thorney Island off the West Sussex coast, as per her father, Simon Darlington's orders, and for the first seventeen years of her life dressing and behaving like a wild boy, Sam's knowledge of the world was woefully limited. And the only men she'd met were Jack, Julian, and the servants at

Darlington Hall and now Montgomery Manor, but Sam knew instinctively that there was no one on the earth more to her taste than Julian Montgomery.

Inside the chapel, Julian guided Sam to a pew. The candles were still lit from the ceremony, and the air was redolent with the scent of melting wax, flowers, and garlands of scottish fir. They sat down and Julian let go of her hand, then tilted her chin with the touch of his forefinger. "Now tell me what's really troubling you, Sam," he ordered.

"What makes you so sure somethin's botherin' me?" she mumbled.

"First off, you're crying. You *never* cry. I know how you disdain what you perceive as a weakness, and I can only conclude that something really bothersome has brought on this torrent of tears."

"It ain't no torrent of tears, Julian," she retorted. "I just weeped a little weep, that's all," she added sulkily.

"I see," Julian replied thoughtfully, his penetrating blue eyes keeping relentless track of every fleeting expression on her face. The way he watched her and—nine times out of the ten—managed to read her thoughts and feelings, gave Sam gooseflesh. It was not, however, an unpleasant sensation. . . .

"So what brought on this 'little weep'?" he asked. "Could it possibly be because your sister has gone off on a honeymoon and won't be back till the spring?"

Sam clenched her jaw, willing away the fresh wave of sadness and fear that washed over her.

"She hasn't deserted you, you know," Julian said gently.

Sam turned startled eyes to his. "I'm not—"

"Don't try to tell me you're not worried," he advised her. "I won't believe you."

Sam swallowed back a lump of raw emotion and impatiently dashed away new tears. "I'm no idiot, neither. I know she's just goin' on a honeymoon. I know she'll be back."

"Do you?" he inquired coolly. *"I* know she'll be back. But since your mother died giving you birth, your sanctimonious father banished you from his life to an isolated island so that no one would know he'd 'sinned,' and even your caretaker deserted you when the money quit coming after your father died . . . isn't it possible, Sam, that Amanda's going away frightens you?"

"You don't beat about the bush, do you?" Sam gave a huff of breath that was half exasperation, half relief. "All right," she admitted crankily. "So maybe I *am* a little nervous about Amanda's goin' away. My head says she'll be back"—she touched a hand to her head, then to her heart—"but in here, I've got a *squeezed* feelin'."

Julian smiled, and Sam couldn't help but smile back. Genuine smiles from Julian were rare, and they always made Sam feel like she was basking in sunshine.

"A *squeezed* feeling, you say? Well, what do you suppose we could do to relieve you of that particular disorder of the heart? Will a chocolate bonbon do?"

Sam's brows knitted in a frown. "A chocolate *bonbon?* Julian, you treat me like a child! There's a big difference between a skinned knee and a troubled heart, y' know!"

"I understand the difference in maladies, brat," Julian replied. "But, after all, you *are* a child. I'm nearly twice your age and was already a fully grown adult when you were born."

This was just the sort of talk that raised Sam's hackles. "If I'm such a child, why are you and Amanda so bent on findin' me a husband in the spring?" she asked testily.

"By the spring, I shall have turned you into a woman, Samantha. A lovely, accomplished woman." He eyed her critically. "The transformation won't be overnight, of course. You will consider me a harsh taskmaster at times, but I hope we'll still be friends when the season finally comes round. The task is rather daunting, I grant you," he added wryly, flicking her cheek. "But not beyond my powers."

"Why do I need a bloody husband?" Sam demanded to know, goaded by his patronizing attitude into cursing. "Priss and Nan don't have husbands."

"Watch your tongue, brat," Julian reprimanded, then continued in a lecturing tone. "Marriage will guarantee you a secure home and unquestioned respectability. Amanda and Jack and the aunts and I only want you to be happy."

"Will marriage make me happy, Julian?" Sam crossed her arms and stared hard at her mentor. *"Will* it?"

Julian frowned down at his troubled, troublesome student. Her blue-gray eyes were narrowed. She held her chin at a belligerent angle, and her soft, pink lips had thinned to a grim line. But with a wayward golden curl bobbing over her smooth white forehead, she looked like nothing so much as a peeved cherub. It was hardly an intimidating picture. In fact, it rather tickled Julian's fancy when she got all puffed up like a pigeon guarding her nest.

"Well, Julian?" she demanded. "Don't I deserve to be happy?"

"If anyone does, you certainly do, Sam," Julian admitted. "But, unfortunately, no one is guaranteed happiness in marriage. Security and respectability, yes . . . if one marries wisely. But happiness . . ." He debated about how honest to be with her. Finally he sighed and said, "Happiness in marriage is rather a matter of chance, I should think."

She looked incredulous. "Are you sayin' that marriage is a gamble?"

Julian gave a rueful smile and countered her question with another. "Why do you suppose *I'm* still a bachelor? I'm not a gaming man, Sam."

"But if a man and a woman love each other more than anyone else in the whole world, why wouldn't they be happy?" Sam persisted.

Julian was charmed by Sam's naïveté, but saddened by it, too. "Such love is rare, Sam. Your sister and my brother found it, but they're exceptions to the rule. Most people who marry aren't in love. They marry for different reasons altogether . . . usually worthy enough reasons, you understand. Generally, one can only hope to find a certain compatibility in a marriage partner, mutual respect, and sometimes friendship."

Sam clutched Julian's arm. "Oh, but that's not enough! I want to love my husband *madly,* Julian! And I want him to feel the same way about me."

Julian was silenced.

"Julian, you're not saying anything."

He shook his head. "I don't know what to say."

"I'll tell you what to say," she began, her expression earnest, almost fervent. "You can promise me

something. You can promise me that you . . . and Jack and Amanda and the aunts . . . won't make me marry a man I don't love!"

"Well, *I* certainly won't force—".

"Or a man that doesn't love *me* as much as I love him!"

"But Sam, in finding a life's mate there are many other considerations to take into account—"

"Promise me, Julian. Promise me that the man I marry will be the right man, the one and *only* man for me, the man who will make me the happiest woman on earth!"

Julian was only too aware that keeping such a promise would be far more difficult and carried far more responsibility than turning a rough-cut jewel like Sam into a diamond of the first water. But with her eyes fixed on him so imploringly, the lashes still wet and spiked from her recent crying, he didn't have the heart to refuse.

He heaved a beleaguered sigh. "I promise, Sam."

She glowed with happiness and trust, and Julian knew at that moment that he'd taken on much more than he'd initially bargained for . . . much more than was prudent.

"Now what about that bonbon, Julian?" she reminded him.

He rose and tucked her arm in the crook of his elbow. "I don't see why not," he conceded. "But let's turn this treat into a lesson. There's a proper way to eat chocolates, Sam, and it's one of the many things you must learn before April."

Sam skipped alongside Julian, her worries seemingly forgotten. "I certainly hope there will be a *few* fun things I can do that won't have to be done 'properly,' " she complained with a saucy grin.

"There will be," he assured her.

She squeezed his arm. "Promise me, Julian."

He laughed. "I promise, brat."

Chapter 1

❧〜〜❧

Montgomery Town House
Queens Square
London, England
April 1817

"**C**hin up! Shoulders back!"

Samantha lifted her chin and rolled her shoulders into proper alignment with her hips. While Priss and Nan watched nervously from the sidelines, Julian slowly circled her, inspecting through his quizzing glass every detail of her person. To her credit, Sam held her head high and withstood his scrutiny without batting a lash.

The gown was perfect. It was traditional white, and demure enough to satisfy the stiff-rumped matrons who would attend Sam's coming-out ball, but the cut showed off her figure to great advantage and was guaranteed to capture the interest of any red-blooded buck who happened to glance her way. Having overseen the design of the gown himself, Julian had made sure that the modiste had used a modicum of ruffles and furbelows. The simpler the better was Julian's opinion. Better to see the girl

13

instead of the dress . . . unless, of course, the girl was nothing to look at.

This was not the case with Samantha. From top to toe she was perfection . . . he'd seen to that. And though Julian couldn't take credit for what nature had endowed her, he could certainly congratulate himself for showing off her natural charms in the most effective and tasteful manner possible.

Sam's charms were considerable. She was of medium height and lithe, with a tiny waist and small, high breasts. Her shoulders were gracefully sloped, her neck was long and slender, and her face was heart-shaped and delicately featured. She had enormous long-lashed blue eyes and a crop of blond curls—cut daringly short in a gamine style—that was sure to be noticed and admired.

Looking closely for any slight defect, Julian was satisfied that her appearance was everything it should be. But now, half an hour before the first guests were to arrive at Sam's coming-out ball, he had to make certain that she was prepared in every other way to take London society by storm.

He ended his inspection, tucked away his quizzing glass, and positioned himself in front of her, peering down his aquiline nose. He clasped his hands behind his back and spread his legs slightly in a military pose. She stared up at him, her eyes wide, her gaze steady and serious and understandably apprehensive.

"How would you address Lady Jersey should she deign to speak to you?" he suddenly barked, making the aunts jump.

"I would address her as 'Madam' or 'Lady Jersey,'" Sam promptly replied with a slight quiver in her voice. "Never 'My Lady' or 'Your Ladyship.'"

"Because?"

"Because that is how the servants address her."

"Who is the current president of the United States?"

"Mr. James Madison," she answered loud and clear, the quiver gone as she rallied her courage.

"When using a finger bowl, do you dip the fingers of both hands in at once, or only one hand at a time?"

"Only one hand at a time." She paused, then grinned. "And I must *never* use it to bathe my face or feet."

Priss and Nan chuckled, but Julian raised an imperious brow and Sam and the aunts abruptly sobered.

"How many glasses of wine are you allowed with dessert?"

"Only one. And I must sip it with delicacy and moderation."

"Are you allowed to curse?" he asked, then added in a beleaguered murmur, "A habit which has been the very devil to cure you of."

"No, I mustn't curse." She sighed and rolled her eyes. "Not under *any* provocation."

"What will you say if someone asks you about your parents?"

"Simply that they are aunt and uncle to Amanda and they died several years ago in Cumbria. My father was a rector."

He nodded. "Very well. Now . . . let's see." His gaze drifted upward, seeming to search the ceiling for inspiration. Then his head lowered abruptly and his eyes narrowed. "Miss Darlington, do you approve of Lord Byron?"

She lifted her chin defiantly. "Yes."

"Incorrect, Sam," Julian snapped. "When discussing the poet in polite society, you cannot approve of Byron. He is a profligate."

Sam pouted. "But I *do* like his work. *The Prisoner of Chillon* was inspired. Besides, polite society is hypocritical, Julian. Many of *them* are profligates, too."

"Of course they are, but that is beside the point. Now on to the next question. How often should you use a French phrase?"

"Frequently. But only if I am perfectly sure it applies to the situation or I would be committing a *faux pas.*" She raised her brows inquiringly. *"N'est-ce pas?"*

He nodded perfunctorily. *"Oui.* Well done, Sam. *Très bien."*

Sam risked a small, satisfied smile, which escaped Julian completely because he had begun to pace the floor and thoughtfully stroke his chin. Suddenly he stopped and turned to Priss and Nan. Caught unaware, they snapped to attention.

"Her sewing . . . has it improved?"

"Tremendously, Julian," Nan said, nodding eagerly, the little lace cap she wore on top of her snowy white hair bobbing up and down as she moved to pick up a pillow from the sofa. She held it up for him to see. "She made this cover. Isn't it delightful?"

Julian gave the hodgepodge of colorful flowers and birds of paradise a cursory once-over, then barked, "What about her painting?"

Priss rushed to an easel standing near the window and came back with a canvas splashed with watercolors. "It's called *Kitten in the Ric-Rac Fern.* Nan and I thought it rather clever. Isn't it clever, Julian?"

Julian's brows knitted as he stared at the painting. He took out his quizzing glass to better inspect it, then sniffed and said in a dampening tone, "It will do. And her playing of the pianoforte and singing?"

Nan and Priss glanced uncomfortably at each other, then shrugged helplessly.

"We can only hope no one asks her to perform," Priss admitted.

"However, she *speaks* beautifully now," Nan pointed out, trying to look on the bright side. "Quite like the lady she was born to be!"

"I only had three months to learn to sing and play on the pianoforte," Sam quickly added. "Considering that, Julian, I don't think my singing and playing are *too* awfully bad!"

"Nor too awfully good," Julian retorted. "She rides well and she dances excellently," he continued, ignoring Sam's piqued look. "We can only hope she dances just as well with other partners besides myself."

"You are an exceptional dancer, Julian," Priss said with a fond smile. "I'm sure you make all your partners look as though they're dancing on air."

"Don't flatter him, Aunt Prissy," Sam said, crossing her arms. "He's already insufferably sure of himself."

And for good reason, she reluctantly admitted to herself. She stood in the middle of the tastefully appointed drawing room, waiting for Julian's reaction to her teasing remark. Predictably he disappointed her by showing no reaction whatsoever. She'd never met anyone with more self-control or reserve.

For the past three months Sam had spent the greater part of every day in Julian's company . . . and she was more in love with him than ever. But she couldn't say that familiarity had diminished her awe of him. She stared at his imposing figure standing out in stark contrast against the velvet drapes that hung in golden folds at the window behind him. She wanted to make this man proud of her. She wanted his approval more than she wanted her soul's salvation. But she wondered . . . was it truly possible to impress such a paragon?

Tonight Julian was dressed elegantly and properly from top to toe in black. Not a speck of lint marred his superfine jacket and sleek, muscle-hugging knee breeches. Not a scuff dulled the mirrorlike shine of his patent slippers. Not a hint of dust dulled the glitter of his golden fob and diamond stickpin. Not a suggestion of a wrinkle ruined the artful arrangement of his brilliantly white cravat.

And not a flicker of emotion passed over his patrician features. . . . But Sam knew Julian had emotions, deep and abiding ones, and she was determined to be the woman who brought them to the surface.

Her emotions were certainly at surface level these days. Besides being nervous about the ball that was to start in a matter of moments, where all the skills she'd learned over the past three months would be put to the test, she was missing Amanda.

"She couldn't help it, you know."

Sam startled. She stared into Julian's penetrating gaze. He'd read her thoughts again, but she wasn't about to admit that fact. She'd just be stroking his aristocratic ego, and the aunts already did plenty of that. "What are you talking about, Julian?" she said, pretending to be smoothing a wrinkle out of her skirt.

"You know exactly what I'm talking about," he

said succinctly. "You're missing your sister . . . and I don't blame you. However, I hope you understand that she had a very good reason for absenting herself from London at this time."

The emotions Sam had been trying to keep under control broke to the surface. "I don't know why Jack had to get her pregnant so fast . . . and on their honeymoon, too, when they're supposed to be having fun!" she burst out.

Priss "tsk-tsked" and Nan couldn't help a secret smile behind a plump, neatly gloved hand.

"Many brides get . . . er . . . with child on their honeymoon, Samantha, darling," Nan explained. "And precisely because they *are* having fun! But no one could have known that she'd be prone to miscarriage and ordered to bed for the duration of her breeding period. You read her letter, dearest. She wishes she could be with you at your come-out ball as much as you do. I know you don't want her to jeopardize her health or the baby's."

Sam sighed and plucked self-consciously at her skirt. "Of course not."

"And while we are only her aunts," Priss interjected, "and yours, too, if you will only think of us as such—though we aren't actually related, coming, as it were, from Amanda's mother's side of the family—we love you *dearly,* Samantha. Never fear, we will stick to your side like mending plaster. And who better to have as your sponsor and mentor for the season than Julian? No one could have a more splendid introduction to society than the marquess of Serling!"

Sam grimaced. "That's just the trouble, y' know."

"What can you possibly mean by that, brat?" Julian inquired icily.

Sam continued to pluck at her skirts and divert her gaze. "I've been taught by the best. So if I accidentally curse, or use poor grammar, or slurp my soup, or trip over my feet in the middle of the dance floor, I'll have no one to blame but myself. And, worst of all, I'll mortify *you,* Julian!"

"I'm not so easily mortified," Julian assured her, giving her hands a light slap. "Now stop plucking your skirts, or you'll ruin the fabric."

Obediently she clasped her hands behind her and looked up at him with a woeful expression. He smiled and shook his head, then placed his hands on her shoulders. Sam got warm all over when Julian touched her. And she enjoyed the strong feel of his long fingers through the thin material of her puffed sleeves.

"Don't worry, Sam," he assured her, still smiling as he gazed steadily into her eyes. "I have complete confidence in you. You're a beautiful, bright, accomplished girl. And you've learned in three months what most wellborn simpering misses take years to learn." He raised his brows. "And, who knows, maybe tonight you'll meet the young man who will become your husband."

Sam smiled back, buoyed by his praise and sure she could fly to the moon if Julian told her she could. As for her future husband . . . well, she had already met *that* particular fellow. Compared to Julian, she was sure that all the other men she'd meet at her coming-out ball would be dead bores.

"What do you suppose she's saying to them?" Julian wondered, standing beside Nan and Prissy's chairs where they sat on the sidelines of the ballroom, keeping a sharp eye on their charge. Sam was several feet away, the center of a group of gentle-man, all of whom were laughing and smiling at whatever it was she was saying.

"I don't know," said Nan, frowning and chewing her lip. "But they all seem to think she's prodi-giously entertaining."

Prissy wrung her hands. "She's had so little experience with men."

"You mean none, don't you?" Julian grimly interjected.

"Yes," Priss agreed. "And so it makes one won-der how she can manage to amuse them so easily." She looked up at Julian, worry etched on her face. "You don't think she's being . . . er . . . vulgar, do you?"

"Not on purpose," was his unreassuring reply.

Now even Nan was wringing her hands. "You'd better go, Julian, and find out what's going on. Claim her for a dance or something."

"Her dance card is full to brimming," he re-vealed with a wry edge to his voice. "I would have to usurp the place of some moonstruck young fool who would then become tragically miserable for the rest of the night."

"That can't be helped," Nan said fretfully, alarmed by another burst of laughter coming from the cluster of admirers surrounding Sam. "You must find out what the child is saying!"

Julian agreed. He strode toward the jovial assem-blage where Sam's shiny blond curls bobbed ani-matedly in the middle of a veritable sea of men. Her instant success had probably already incurred the intense dislike of every mama with a marriagea-ble daughter to get rid of that season. Now he only hoped she wasn't giving the *ton* something juicy to chew on by way of behaving outrageously. But she wouldn't do that, would she? Hadn't he taught her well enough to guarantee her best behavior?

His mere approach was enough to scare away some of the more timid devotees, but by the time he reached Sam she still had half a dozen men hanging on to her every word. Hovering a little behind a young man he knew as Ninian Wentworth—a foppish dandy if ever there was one—Julian listened and braced himself for the worst. But Sam, who seemed totally unaware that Julian was eavesdropping on the conversation, was only talking about . . . her dogs.

"But Zeus is even worse than Neptune," she was saying, her expression vibrant and her eyes bright. "He's this great, vicious brute with giant teeth"— she bared her own small white teeth to demonstrate—"but he's afraid of mice! I caught him once hiding behind a butter churn, shaking like a tree in a storm! You'd have thought he'd been charged by an elephant rather than a silly little mouse!"

As the men laughed, Julian studied their faces. None of them were smiling sardonically or exchanging knowing glances. They weren't patronizing her or egging her on to make a fool of herself. They were genuinely enchanted by Sam's artlessness.

"You miss Zeus and Neptune a great deal, don't you, Miss Darlington?" said Nathan Ford, in his nasal American twang. Nathan was a rich plantation owner from Virginia.

"Oh, you can't imagine how much," she said with a breathy little sigh that was sure to stir the protective instincts of every man present. "But my guardian, Lord Serling, says London's no place for

them. They're a rowdy twosome, I must admit."
She got a dreamy look in her eye. "But sometimes I
just wish I could romp with them awhile, or snuggle
up to them for a snooze by the fire."

There was complete silence while Sam lost herself in the pleasant picture she'd created in her
mind, and every male eye in the group was fixed
adoringly on her.

"By Jupiter, I think it's dashed shabby of Lord
Serling to keep your dogs in the country when you
so obviously miss the little bounders," Ninian
Wentworth finally burst out, reddening clear to the
roots of his blond hair. "What kind of an ogre is the
fellow, I ask you? I always thought he was toplofty,
but I must say I'm downright boggled to hear he's
that cruel to you, Miss Darlington!"

Amused by Ninian's gallant outburst, Julian decided that this would be the perfect moment to
make his presence known. "Are you boggled indeed, Mr. Wentworth?" Julian drawled, stepping
into the circle of bachelors. There was a collective
gasp.

Ninian's beardless, boyish face went ashen and
he stuttered, "Oh! My . . . my lord!" He managed a
weak smile. "Didn't know you were there, sir."

"Obviously."

"P-pardon if I've offended," he stuttered. "I only
thought it a dashed shame Miss Darlington doesn't
have her dogs in town. She's been telling us all
about them, and it's obvious she misses them
tremendously."

"No offense taken, Mr. Wentworth," said Julian,
who didn't take pleasure in terrifying harmless
fribbles like Ninian. Poor sport, that. "But, in
defense of my behavior, I must tell you that Miss
Darlington is not exaggerating about the size of her

pets. They are bounders all right, but hardly 'little' ones. And they are the most ill-mannered ruffians you can imagine. If they were a smaller breed and trained . . . or at least trainable . . . I might not have objected to her bringing them to town."

No one dared argue with Julian, and as his presence had put a damper on the jovial mood of the group, he bowed briefly to Samantha and bade her in a whisper to "Carry on your court, brat." She smiled archly at him, her face and eyes aglow.

As he walked away, Julian congratulated himself on creating such an enchanting creature. He was sure he'd be weighing marriage offers in a matter of days. His business soon to be concluded with Sam, Julian allowed himself to consider for the first time in months his own matrimonial business.

After Julian assured Priss and Nan that all was well with Samantha, he looked toward the door just in time to witness the entrance of Charlotte Batsford and her parents. As always, she was the essence of elegance. Her midnight-blue gown was tastefully simple but alluring. Her auburn hair was artfully arranged, and her head was held high with just the right amount of self-assurance.

Some people—men in particular—complained that Charlotte was too reserved. Cold, even. But Julian disagreed. Ever since Charlotte broke her engagement with his brother so Jack could marry his true love, Amanda, he'd become very well acquainted with the lady. Although he certainly couldn't claim to "love her madly," as Sam desired to love someone and be loved in return, he did find her company easy and comfortable.

Of good family and fortune, she was gracious, circumspect, kind, compassionate, and moral. She had feelings, but she kept them carefully controlled. She would make an excellent marriage partner, someone with whom he could enjoy a serene, stable, and sensible existence.

In short, she was exactly Julian's cup of tea. He had decided last November that he was going to marry Charlotte, but he'd put the actual proposal on hold until he got Sam launched in society. He had, however, visited the lady several times in the interim, but had not made public his intentions. That would soon change.

She turned and their eyes met. He smiled and walked toward his future bride.

It was nearing midnight, and Sam's feet were killing her. She had danced every dance and had been surprisingly well entertained by all the men vying for her attention. But though she hadn't found them to be dead bores, as she'd expected, Samantha hadn't met a man that came close to measuring up to Julian in her estimation.

Finally the country dance ended and Sam's partner, Jean-Luc Bouvier, bowed low over her hand, kissing it gallantly. According to Priss, who had whispered the information into Sam's ear during a break in the dancing, Jean-Luc was half-English, his mother the daughter of a viscount with a huge estate in Derbyshire. At seventeen, against her father's wishes, she'd eloped with a member of the French aristocracy—a marquis, no less—giving birth in Paris less than a year later to a little boy.

Jean-Luc had been raised in France till the revolution brought an end to his idyllic childhood. His French father was killed during the uprising, and his mother had brought him home to Derbyshire. All was forgiven by the English relatives, and Jean-Luc was raised in the bosom of their family.

Grandparents and parents now all deceased, Jean-Luc had a considerable fortune, a certain continental flair, and a romantic history that made him very interesting to women, young and old, married and unmarried alike.

"This has been the most *celestial* experience of my life, Miss Darlington . . . to dance with an angel," Jean-Luc said solemnly and with just a suggestion of a charming French accent that no amount of English tutoring had managed to browbeat out of him. But as he straightened and looked at her, there was a teasing gleam in his eyes and a roguish grin on his handsome face.

Sam had already grown used to Jean-Luc's grandiose compliments, delivered playfully and with the full knowledge that Sam understood and was amused and entertained by his flirtatious ways. She smiled, and with an equal portion of playfulness, coyly tapped Jean-Luc's arm with her fan. "You're going to turn my head with all your compliments, Mr. Bouvier," she warned him.

Jean-Luc laughed appreciatively. "I don't think so. You are too modest and unaffected . . . rare qualities in a beautiful woman, I assure you. But it is a challenge I will continually address myself to . . . to turn your pretty head, Miss Darlington. I suppose you would not believe me if I told you that however exaggerated you might think them, I really meant every one of the compliments I've paid you tonight?"

Sam might have been imprisoned on an island for seventeen years, but she recognized a flirt when she saw one. She merely smiled and shook her head reprovingly, saying, "A 'celestial' experience, Mr. Bouvier?"

Jean-Luc threw back his head and laughed again,

and Sam couldn't help but laugh, too. She looked him over, acknowledging him to be quite handsome despite the fact that he was not blond and blue-eyed, a color combination she was inordinately fond of in a man. Jean-Luc was as dark as a gypsy and had chocolate-brown eyes. He dressed very well, too, with just a little more jewelry and ruffles than the simple style started by Beau Brummel and espoused by most wellborn English gentlemen. But however handsome, however dashing and amusing he was, he had one unsurmountable defect. He wasn't Julian. Which reminded her . . .

"As much as I enjoy talking to you, Mr. Bouvier, I must look for my next partner," Sam said, beginning to edge away through the crowd.

Genuinely surprised, Jean-Luc caught her hand. "Look for your next partner? How is this possible, Miss Darlington? Shouldn't he be looking for you? A man would have to be a fool not to be waiting at your elbow at this very moment, eager to hold you in his arms. The next dance is a waltz, as I recall."

Sam gently tugged on her hand till he reluctantly released her. "He's no fool, Mr. Bouvier," she assured him with a wry smile. "He simply doesn't know I saved a dance especially for him."

Jean-Luc raised his brows in a speculative expression. He was probably correctly construing Sam to mean that she considered her next partner someone special. But Sam couldn't be bothered with wondering what Jean-Luc would think when he saw her dancing with her guardian. She had to find Julian.

Sam turned away from Jean-Luc and quickly scanned the room. She'd caught a glimpse of Julian's golden head above the crowd now and then, but she hadn't been able to see with whom he'd been talking. He definitely hadn't been dancing. But she was about to change that.

Spotting him near an alcove in the far, quieter end of the long ballroom, Sam approached. Her heart was pounding and she had butterflies in her stomach just thinking about dancing with Julian. Over the last few weeks he'd taught her every dance she was expected to know, but the waltz had always been her favorite. With his hand on her waist, their thighs skimming and his chin brushing her hair, it had been a thrilling experience every time.

Although she had only a rudimentary idea of the mechanics of the physical intimacies between men and women, Sam imagined that making love with Julian would be very similar to the bliss of dancing with him. Certainly, nothing she'd felt while dancing with other men that night had come even close to how she felt gliding across the floor in Julian's arms.

Within a few feet of Julian now, Sam noticed that he was talking with a tall, ginger-haired woman in an elegant dress—just the two of them. That "squeezed" feeling came over her heart again.

The woman noticed her first, and smiled. "I believe this is your lovely charge . . . am I right, Julian?" she said.

Julian turned and raised his brows inquiringly. "Sam! What the deuce are you doing here? Some distraught young man is probably looking desperately for you. Isn't a waltz about to begin?"

Sam hesitated, feeling suddenly shy under the kind but unnervingly steady gaze fixed on her by the older woman. "Shouldn't you introduce us, Julian?" the woman said finally, lightly touching Julian's arm in a possessive manner. Some invisible cord around Sam's heart cinched a little tighter, squeezed a little harder.

"Of course," he murmured, recovering his manners. "I was just concerned that Sam might miss the next dance. Charlotte, as you guessed, this is my ward . . . temporarily . . . Miss Samantha Darlington. Samantha, this is Miss Charlotte Batsford."

Sam and Charlotte said their "how-do-you-do's" and nodded politely. *So this is Charlotte Batsford, the woman Jack was going to marry,* Sam thought to herself. She was torn between pity for the cruel trick fate had played on Charlotte when she had to call off her wedding the very day before it was to take place . . . and gut-wrenching jealousy. Was Julian acting on some chivalrous notion to pay attention to Charlotte because Jack had broken her heart? Would he be so gallant as to marry the woman just to undo Jack's wrong?

As Sam's heart beat wildly and her mouth went dry, she told herself not to get carried away with silly, unfounded notions. Julian was going to marry *her,* not Charlotte Batsford or anyone else. But first he was going to dance with her.

"Pardon me, Miss Batsford," Sam said at last, having recovered her courage along with her determination. "Would you mind if I spoke to Julian alone for just a moment?"

Charlotte looked surprised, but only said, "Why . . . no. I don't mind. I'll just wait for you over here, Julian." Then she retired into the alcove, some ten feet away.

"That bordered on rudeness, Sam," Julian admonished her when Charlotte was out of earshot.

"Well, I'm very sorry," Sam said, lifting her chin defiantly. "But she made me nervous."

"What *do* you want, Sam?" Julian said in a beleaguered tone. "In a matter of seconds the orchestra will play the beginning strains of the waltz and your partner will be wanting you. Who the deuce is the fellow, anyway?"

Julian caught Sam's wrist and read her dance card. Again his brows arched in surprise. "Me? But I don't remember writing on your card. Besides, I've engaged Miss Batsford for this dance."

Now Sam felt foolish . . . and childish. Miss Batsford darted an occasional discreet look their way, making Sam feel even more embarrassed. She had mistakenly assumed that Julian wouldn't dance the entire night . . . except with her. She had spent so much time with him over the last three months, she had begun to think of him as entirely her own. She had even convinced herself that as desirable as Julian was, he was not sought after by other women, nor did he seek out any of them. She had assumed that he had no intention of marrying, and that she was the only woman who could turn his opinion around.

But now Sam saw that she'd been terribly wrong. As Julian stared at her, his gaze puzzled and a little irritated, she thought she finally understood what she truly was to him. Despite all the womanly accomplishments he'd taught her, he still considered her at best a child and at worst simply a well-met challenge, a clump of clay he'd molded to his expert specifications. She was a sow's ear ingeniously transformed into a silk purse, good enough for other men . . . but not for Julian.

"My dear girl, I should have thought you'd danced more than enough with me," Julian suggested with a bewildered chuckle. "It was good of you to save me a dance, and I must assume you did it out of respect, but I assure you I'll not be the slightest bit offended if you ignore me for the rest of the evening. As soon as your multitude of admirers see you are without a partner, you'll be inundated with entreaties to dance."

Sam recognized a sort of kind patronage in Julian's tone, mixed with impatience. It was the tone he'd use with a child. Mortification rose in Sam's throat like bile. She felt her face heating up and her eyes burning with the start of tears. But she was saved by pride.

Willing away the unwelcome emotions and forcing a carefree smile, she said cheerfully, "Very well, Julian. I *will* ignore you." Then she abruptly spun around on the toes of her slippers and headed for Priss and Nan. Halfway there, however, Jean-Luc claimed her for the waltz, and she was whisked away.

I'll show you, Julian Montgomery, Sam vowed, holding back her tears and smiling brilliantly as Jean-Luc whirled her around the ballroom floor. *I'll show you I'm not a child anymore. I'll make you as jealous of me as I am of you. Because now it's my turn to be tutor, and as each day passes you're going to learn to love me more than your soul's salvation. . . .*

Chapter 2

❧◦◦◦◦◦❧

The morning after Sam's coming-out ball, the entrance hall of the Montgomery town house was filled with flowers . . . a definitive proof of Sam's social success. As Julian walked down the stairs at his usual hour, he saw his protégé standing amongst the hothouse blooms, dressed in a daffodil-yellow gown and looking like spring itself.

Julian couldn't help a slight swelling of the chest. He'd worked hard over the past three months to turn a neglected child-of-the-mist into a darling of the *ton*. Certainly if Sam hadn't been so bright and beautiful, the job would have been much more difficult, but he couldn't help but feel he'd been the consummate tutor. And now the poor girl would be able to attract a respectable young man, marry, and settle down to a respectable life.

In this self-congratulatory mood, Julian greeted Sam with a smile. "Good morning, brat. I'm surprised to see you up so early. After your late night and all your dancing, I hardly expected you to have breakfast with me as usual."

Sam's nose was buried in a bouquet of forget-me-nots, her long lashes shuttering her eyes. She looked up at him, then carefully laid the flowers on a nearby rosewood table. "As you frequently remind me, Julian, I'm quite young. I don't need the amount of sleep to keep up my stamina as perhaps people of *your* age."

Julian raised a brow. At first he thought she was playfully ridiculing him, but her accompanying smile was so open and sweet, he quickly changed his mind. She was simply being honest and artless.

"I am not so long in the tooth yet, my girl," he assured her in a teasing manner, "that I need to sleep half the day away after a ball."

"I'm very glad of that," she answered seriously, turning to the mirror above the table to arrange a curl at her temple. "I do so want you around to watch my children grow up. *Uncle Julian* has such a nice ring to it."

Julian didn't think so. His smile and his good mood faltered. *Uncle Julian* sounded so avuncular, so stodgy. Did she really consider him so close to being a relic? He'd never got that impression from her before. . . .

"Shall we go into breakfast?" he said, offering her his arm, ready to forget the unflattering image of a tottering, decrepit old man with a cane and yellowed teeth, that Sam's words had conjured up.

She glanced at his angled arm, her pert nose going up just a notch, then announced, "Thank you, but no. I've already eaten."

Julian was surprised, then surprisingly disappointed. "I see," he murmured, dropping his arm to his side. "Well, I shall miss your chatter at the table, Sam. We've eaten breakfast together every morning for months now."

She picked up another bouquet of roses, and, as she looked at the card, casually said, "I know, but I thought it would be a good idea to be ready for visitors early this morning. The aunts said it was very likely I would be besieged with young men paying their respects."

"The aunts are quite right," Julian agreed. And having said as much, he knew there was no reason why he shouldn't excuse himself at this point and go and enjoy his quiet breakfast. But something seemed wrong . . . something about Sam. He couldn't precisely put his finger on it, but she was somehow different this morning, more remote, more . . . *complicated.*

He found himself looking at her, his gaze traveling over her figure, but this time he wasn't looking at the lines of her dress or analyzing the effect Sam's appearance would have on others. He was feeling her effect on *him*. And he was surprised to learn that he thought she was more than a little fetching. . . .

While Julian impatiently reminded himself that despite her womanly curves Sam was little more than a green girl and closer to being a younger sister to him than a sister-in-law, Sam picked up another bundle of flowers—this one a rather unusual jumble of assorted blooms—and read the accompanying card. "I should have known this colorful bunch would be from Nathan," Sam said with a smile. "Americans are always so original."

"So you like Mr. Ford?" Julian inquired, arrested by the delighted look that had come over Sam's face.

"Very much," she said.

Julian frowned. "You just met him, you know, but you already . . . most improperly . . . refer to him by his Christian name. I hope you aren't precipitously forming an attachment when there are so many young men you could choose from. Mr. Ford would assuredly drag you away to the wilds of Virginia, hundreds of miles from . . . er . . . your sister."

Sam chuckled. "Oh, I haven't absolutely settled on Nathan, Julian. In fact, I don't even know if he has serious designs on me . . . although he was awfully attentive last night and made a special point of telling me he was coming by early this morning with a surprise."

"Indeed?" Julian murmured.

"But then so did Mr. Ninian Wentworth and Mr. Jean-Luc Bouvier." She gazed into the middle distance for a moment, her brows puckered and her mouth set in a contemplative line. "When it comes time, I am determined to choose my husband from the three gentleman I've just mentioned."

Julian gave a shout of laughter, half-alarmed, half-amused by Sam's sudden pragmatic attitude toward marriage, an institution she had previously viewed with highly romantic notions and even fear. "Just a few weeks ago you were asking me why it was necessary for you to marry at all," he said, unable to keep the incredulous tone out of his voice. "And you made me promise not to allow you to marry except to the man that 'loves you most in the world.' If you are limiting your choice of a husband to three men you just met and hardly know, I can only assume you were not as earnest in your request as you sounded at the time."

"Were *you* earnest when you made the promise? Did you intend to keep it?"

Julian was cornered. Sam stared at him, her gaze keen and questioning. "I always keep my promises, Sam. But I expected you to change your mind. You're a bright girl. Once you were out and about in

society, I knew you would eventually realize that
marriage just doesn't work the way you have been
imagining it. I knew you would temper your expectations to more reasonable standards."

"As you have?"

"I beg your pardon?"

"Priss and Nan told me last night that they
expect you to marry Charlotte Batsford. Have *you*
had to temper your expectations to that which
is . . . reasonable?"

Julian felt his face warming. "You have no business discussing my personal life with Priss and
Nan," he said acidly.

"But you discuss *my* personal life with Priss and
Nan," she pointed out.

"You very well know the difference."

Sam shrugged and turned back to her flowers.
"Do I?"

Julian was constructing in his mind a suitable
lecture to repress the precociousness of his ward
when the door knocker sounded. "Good God, who
could that be at this hour?" he complained, check-
ing his timepiece. "I haven't even had my breakfast!"

Sam caught Julian's arm as Hedley, the portly
butler, sailed majestically past them to the door. "If
that's a visitor for me, Julian," she breathed in his
ear, sending an unexpected shiver down his spine,
"please don't feel obliged to stand in as chaperon
for Priss and Nan."

"Where *are* Priss and Nan?" he asked, alarmed.

"They went to the Women's Shelter early this
morning."

"The deuce you say, and with all these callers
expected!"

"It doesn't matter, Julian. I'm sure I will be quite

safe alone in the parlor with my callers. They are refined gentlemen, after all, and not savages."

By this statement, Julian concluded that Sam didn't know anything about refined gentlemen and of what they were capable. But then how could she? He'd taught her how to be a lady, but he suddenly realized that he'd been woefully negligent in instructing her on how to fend off amorous advances from randy dandies in sheep's clothing.

"Thank you for dismissing me from the arduous chore of safeguarding your virtue and reputation, brat," Julian growled. "But you must know it is essential that you have a chaperon at all times."

Sam clicked her tongue. "Well, if you *really* think it necessary. But I'm quite sure you're starving for breakfast!"

Now that she'd mentioned it, Julian did feel rather hollow where coffee and kippers and eggs ought to be about now. And going without his breakfast too long always made him cross.

"Why did Priss and Nan have to go to the Women's Shelter to do charity work this morning of *all* mornings!" he grumped under his breath, as Hedley opened the front door to reveal the expected Mr. Nathan Ford. But the tall, sturdy American held in his arms the *un*expected. Apparently Mr. Ford's surprise for Sam was . . . a dog.

"Sam!" he shouted, squeezing past Hedley into the hall, trouncing unawares on the butler's shoe in the process. "Aren't you the prettiest thing that ever set foot on God's green earth!"

"Nathan!" Sam responded with enthusiasm, as the stoic Hedley limped away, wincing. "So good to see you! Pray, what's that darling creature wriggling in your arms?"

Since the moment the door was opened, Nathan

Ford had had eyes for no one but Sam. Julian might have been a lamppost for all the attention being paid him. He was not used to being ignored, and it irked him. But he remained tight-lipped and silent, watching with a jaded eye the delicate dance of courtship being performed in front of him.

"This little fellow is for you, Sam," Nathan announced with a wide grin, displaying a healthy mouthful of glinting white teeth and dangling the dog from his large, rough hands.

Obviously of indeterminate parentage, the pup was snub-nosed, had shaggy, sandy-colored hair, and sported a lolling, toothy dog grin. The grin and the dog's hair color were very similar to Mr. Ford's, and Julian couldn't help being amused by the fact that Sam's American suitor had chosen a dog that looked so much like himself. Was this a romantic tactic of some sort? He secretly snickered.

But when Sam quickly took the dog and cuddled it against her bosom, pressing her cheek against its head and murmuring endearments, Julian's amusement vanished.

"He's just a puppy, so he's trainable," Nathan said eagerly. "And his paws are small, so I don't expect he'll get very big. Do you think Lord Serling'll let you keep 'im?"

"Why don't you ask Lord Serling?" Julian drawled.

For the first time, Nathan turned with a surprised look and noticed Julian's presence. "Oh, Lord Serling!" he said, laughing nervously. "I was so caught up in watching to see if Sam . . . er . . . Miss Darlington liked my surprise, I didn't even notice you standing there!"

"Obviously," Julian observed coldly. "But now that all that are present are accounted for, I propose we quit standing in the hall and retire to the drawing room." He lifted his arm and indicated the way. "After you, Samantha . . . Mr. Ford."

Julian followed the pair into the drawing room at a sedate pace, far enough back to notice the swagger in Nathan Ford's deportment. The fellow swung his arms and legs so freely, Julian feared for his Ming vases. Americans always seemed to take looser, longer steps than the English, he mused. He supposed it was a result of the United States being such a large country and its citizens having to walk great distances to get from one place to another.

In the drawing room, Sam and Nathan sat on a sofa together and Julian sat in a wing-backed chair opposite them. He steepled his fingers and observed the couple with a frosty glare that would have intimidated most men. But not Nathan. No, indeed. Once again, he seemed hardly aware that Julian was even in the room.

Julian cleared his throat, but Sam continued to fawn over the whimpering, panting little pup, allowing it to lick her face and paw her gown. Nathan simply watched, fascinated, looking as though he wished for the same license as the pup to display his affection so openly.

Julian cleared his throat again and finally Sam looked his way, her face aglow.

"Well, Julian, what do you say? You *can't* say no! I *adore* him. And I've already decided what to name him." She turned back to Nathan. "I'm going to call him Madison, after your American president. Don't you think it fitting, Nathan?"

"I'm sure President Madison wouldn't mind, even though the dog is only a mutt," Nathan replied. "But it's my experience that mutts make the best pets. A mix of breeding brings out the best in dogs. Inbreeding over time makes animals lazy and dim-witted."

"I hope your theory does not apply to people, as well, Mr. Ford," Julian said dryly. "The English aristocracy would not take kindly to such a description. They, after all, have been inbreeding for centuries."

Nathan looked horrified. "Lord Serling, I certainly never meant to imply— That is, I—"

"Oh, don't mind Julian," Sam said dismissively. "He's just trying to make you feel uncomfortable, Nathan. It's part of his job as chaperon to terrify young people. Now what about Madison, Julian? I may keep him, mayn't I?"

Julian was still pondering Sam's lightly delivered comment that he liked to "terrify young people." He eyed Nathan Ford, estimating that the man was pushing thirty if he was a day. Julian himself was only five-and-thirty. Just how old did Sam think he was? Fifty? *Sixty?*

"You're silent, Julian," Sam said with a sigh. "That's not a good sign. But I know one way to convince you to let me keep Madison." She stood up, crossed the short distance between the sofa and the chair, and plopped the puppy into Julian's lap. "If you hold him a moment, I know you'll decide you want him here at Montgomery House as much as I do."

Julian did not dislike dogs, but he was of the firm opinion that they belonged in the country and not in town. He scowled down at the pup. Large, frightened puppy eyes stared back . . . and then Madison promptly and thoroughly peed on Julian's leg.

"Good *God!*" Julian rasped. And Sam giggled.

Twenty minutes later, hungrier and more irritated than ever, Julian descended the stairs after quickly changing his clothes. He had left Hedley in the drawing room with strict orders not to leave the room or take his eyes off Sam and her suitor till he returned. Now, as he crossed the hall he could hear an unusual commotion coming from the drawing room. Not just Nathan Ford's, but several raised male voices could be heard . . . and the excited barks of more than one dog!

When Julian entered the room, he could hardly believe his eyes! Nathan Ford, Ninian Wentworth, and Jean-Luc Bouvier were nose to nose in the middle of the room, arguing.

Sam was sitting on the rug in front of the fireplace, romping and laughing with Madison and two other dogs—one a French poodle and the other a Welsh corgi.

Hedley was down on his hands and knees wiping up a suspicious-looking puddle, and when he glanced up and noticed Julian, a pained, apologetic look spread over his red face. Hauling himself to his feet, he said, "My lord!" in such a loud voice he could even be heard above the bickering.

The three gentleman immediately became silent and turned in Julian's direction, their complexions still ruddy from the heat of the argument.

"Good morning, gentleman," Julian intoned with quelling austerity. "What is the meaning of this vulgar display of shouting in my drawing room, and in the company of my ward?"

His affronted dignity was a little compromised when Sam chose that moment to laugh out loud at one of the antics of the pups, but Julian forged on. "And what is the meaning of turning my house into a kennel?"

Naturally, all three men started to talk at once,

making it impossible for Julian to make any sense of their explanations.

Above shouting himself, Julian simply raised his hand to demand quiet, and the shamefaced men complied.

"One at a time, if you please," he said. "Mr. Ford, you begin."

"Well, it's like this, sir," he began in his straightforward way. "I brought Sam—"

"Sam?" Julian looked daggers.

"I mean . . . I brought *Miss Darlington* a dog so she wouldn't miss Zeus and Neptune so much. I was the first one to show up with a pup, so I think she ought to be able to keep mine, not one of theirs!" He jabbed an accusing finger in the direction of the other two men.

"It's just like you *colonials* to think that being first makes you the best. But your dog has no breeding. My corgi is a purebred," Ninian sniffed, tugging on the sleeve of his puce-colored jacket.

"*Mon Dieu,* how can you *dare* speak of breeding?" Jean-Luc demanded to know, his French accent more in evidence as he appeared to be thoroughly enjoying the row and playing his part to the hilt. "Compared to your dogs, *my* poodle has the purest blood of all." He raised his nose in the air, his eyes gleaming with mischief. "Just as, compared to you two commoners, *I* have the purest blood!"

"Now see here—!"

"I *beg* your pardon, you—!"

Again Julian raised his hand and the arguing stopped. "I haven't given Samantha permission to own another dog at all, so there's no point in squabbling over which one of the three she'll keep."

"But Julian!" Sam exclaimed, rising from the floor and carrying all three wriggling pups in her arms as she moved to stand in front of him. "You *must* give me permission! They're pups, so they can be trained to be obedient. And they can stay in the stable till they're absolutely housebroken, then only come inside on very rare occasions."

Julian scowled. He was sure Sam's three suitors were transfixed by the appealing picture she presented, her hair attractively tumbled from romping with the pups, her large eyes fixed on him with such melting supplication. And the puppies already adored her . . . that was obvious by the way they snuggled against her chest, licked her face, and wagged their tails.

It was hard to resist her. . . .

It was hard to resist her *request,* Julian corrected himself. Additionally, all three of her suitors were staring at him, waiting for an answer. Nathan looked belligerent, as if ready to resort to fisticuffs to make sure Sam got to keep her "Madison." Ninian looked anxious. And Jean-Luc threw him an arrogant challenge through narrowed eyes . . . while managing at the same time to look as though he were about to laugh out loud.

However, it was obvious to Julian that there would be a scene if he refused to allow Sam to keep one of the puppies, and although he didn't fear a scene, at present he had no time or patience for one. He was hungry, and the idea of delaying his breakfast any longer was unacceptable.

"Very well, Sam. You may keep one of the pups," he told her, then added sternly, "but I want you to give whichever of the three pups you choose to the footman to be taken to the stable yard immediately.

Madison has already ruined a pair of my best trousers, and I do not choose to replace my Persian rugs at this time."

Instead of the grateful smile Julian expected, Sam's face became crestfallen. "Oh, Julian," she lamented. "You don't really expect me to choose just *one,* do you? I already love them all, and . . . and they're *gifts!* Isn't it rude to return a gift to the giver?"

Julian should have seen this coming. "Good *God,* Sam," he rasped under his breath. "You don't really expect me to allow you to keep all three of them, do you?"

But by the timorous smile on her face and the pleading expression in her eyes, it was obvious that that's exactly what Sam expected.

By noon, Sam had been hostess to a dozen gentleman callers. As Julian had been compelled to be constantly in attendance as her chaperon, he missed breakfast altogether and, after the last caller had reluctantly left, he'd stomped away toward the kitchen in a decidedly foul mood.

Satisfied with her work for the morning, Sam went upstairs to change for a carriage ride in Hyde Park, humming to herself. It would be her first appearance in the park during the "Grand Strut," when all of London society came out to see and be seen. In fact, all her morning suitors had promised to see her there. Sam hoped that Julian was finally beginning to realize that although she was an innocent, she wasn't a child. And that if *he* didn't want her, lots of other men did.

Her strategy—the strategy she'd lain awake last night developing—was to make him think she perceived him simply as her much older guardian and mentor. Her open adoration and awe of him previously had undoubtedly been perceived as childish worship. Now she would pretend that she didn't adore him and that he didn't awe her in the least. A good trick, that, but she was up to it.

As well, she would pretend that she fully embraced the idea and institution of marriage. She would make him think she had begun to regard matrimony as her duty, and that her intention was to make a sensible, respectable choice in a lifelong partner . . . romantic love be hanged.

She found it quite amazing that while Julian was very *astute* in recognizing her feelings in general, he was extremely *obtuse* when it came to realizing that she was in love with him . . . that it wasn't just a childish gratitude or worship she felt for him, but a real and very womanly tenderness in her heart and yearning in her body.

But all that was going to change. He was not only going to realize how she felt about him, but he was going to realize that he felt the same tenderness and physical yearning for her . . . despite Charlotte Batsford.

Last night before bed, Sam had discreetly questioned Priss and Nan about Miss Batsford. When they assured her that all of London was wagering that Julian would eventually take the young lady to the altar, Sam's resolve to win Julian for herself had only strengthened. Obviously she had no time to lose. Drastic times required drastic measures, and Sam was prepared to do whatever it took to become Julian's one and only.

Entering her bedchamber, Sam found her abigail, Clara, waiting for her. Clara had been employed by Julian three months ago when she and the aunts had moved into his town house. A daughter of

Julian's majordomo, Hedley, Clara was a bright, pretty girl, but she suffered the usual disadvantage of a female of her status . . . she had no formal education. So it turned out to be rather advantageous for her that Sam was required to study every night to keep up with her schooling. They helped each other, and both girls ended up acquiring a whirlwind education.

Trouble was, because she didn't have the connections Sam had, Clara was doomed to remain a servant forever, or marry as best she could. To Sam, however, Clara would always be a dear friend and a confidante. Like Hedley and the housekeeper, Verla, Clara was privy to Sam's real connection to the Darlington family, but the three loyal servants would sooner cut out their tongues than reveal the secret of Sam's illegitimate birth to anyone. Even the underlings at Montgomery House were kept in the dark about Sam's true antecedents.

Clara crossed the room, grasped Sam's hands, and swung them excitedly. "Miss! My, but you were a wondrous success today! I ran to the balcony every time I heard someone at the door, and I watched as each gentleman strutted through the hall to the drawing room. So many handsome men in fine togs!"

"Yes, many more than I expected," Sam admitted modestly. "I just hope Julian took note and is beginning to see me as more than his childish pupil."

Clara put her hands on Sam's shoulder and gently nudged her to a full-length cheval mirror, then stood behind her and began to unbutton her gown. "How could His Lordship not take note of so many men bearing gifts?" She peered over Sam's shoulder, meeting her gaze in the mirror's reflection. "And three dogs, too! I thought I'd die when I heard that the American's pup dampened His Lordship's trousers!"

Sam smiled at Clara's laughing face in the mirror. She looked quite lovely, her dark hair and brown eyes so striking next to the pristine white of her mobcap and apron. Sam often reflected that it seemed so unfair that just because you were born into the servant class, you could never aspire above it . . . at least not in England.

"Did you know he let me keep all three, Clara?" Sam asked her.

Clara slipped the sleeves of Sam's dress off her shoulders and pulled it gently down to her waist, then straightened and grinned. "Yes. I heard Papa ranting about it in the kitchen. *He's* not very pleased, of course. But I think it means you can pretty much get his lordship to do whatever you want, miss."

Sam raised a brow, observing her bared shoulders in the mirror and the roundness of her breasts in her low-necked chemise. "Do you think so, Clara? Well, I'm not so sure. He might have given in about the pups simply because he was hungry for breakfast. Or perhaps he felt pressure from Nathan, Ninian, and Jean-Luc . . . although that seems unlikely. Possibly he was just feeling generous, much like a doting old uncle might feel toward his favorite niece. I want him to be influenced by my *feminine charms!*" She plumped her small breasts with her hands and sighed. "Clara, what can I do to make him see me as a desirable woman?"

Clara eased the dress to the floor and Sam stepped out of a billow of yellow skirts. "Don't ask *me,* miss. I'm still an innocent maid, too," she said, walking to the armoire and hanging the dress on a hook. "I expect the best person to talk to about that sort of thing would be his mistress!" she joked, turning with a wry smile on her lips.

But Sam didn't consider it a joke. Something inside her chest twisted painfully. She turned abruptly away from her reflection in the mirror and faced Clara. "His mistress? What are you talking about, Clara? Julian doesn't have a mistress, does he?"

Immediately perceiving her mistake, Clara's face turned crimson. "I . . . I don't know, miss."

"But you said—"

"I was only teasing, miss," she said, averting her eyes. "I just assumed that since most highborn gents have ladybirds tucked away for their pleasure, and the practice being so generally accepted, that His Lordship might—"

"Clara, are you telling me that people don't condemn men like Julian for having a mistress?" Since her father had been ashamed of his mistress and resulting bastard child, the idea that it was perfectly all right . . . even expected . . . for an aristocratic gentleman like Julian to keep a woman on the side seemed amazing to Sam. Even unfair.

Not to mention the fact that she abhorred the very idea of Julian holding another woman in his arms, kissing her, touching her. . . . At this point, Sam always got confused. How *would* he touch her? *Where* would he touch her? How *did* men and women make babies together? A niggling voice inside Sam's head taunted her, saying, *if you don't know the answers to these questions, maybe you really are a child.*

"I misspoke, miss," Clara said, peering anxiously into Sam's distressed face. "In fact I'm sure His Lordship couldn't possibly—"

"Don't *you* treat me like a child, too, Clara," Sam said sternly. "Go ahead and admit it. You don't just suspect Julian of having a mistress, you know it for a certainty . . . don't you?"

Clara bit her lip and reluctantly nodded. "It's true, miss. All the servants know about it. He's got a lady who used to be an opera dancer set up nicely in her own little house. A fine place, I've heard. He's not stingy with her, I'm told . . . and that speaks well of him, miss."

When Sam remained silent, crossing her bare arms and staring at the carpet, Clara put her arm around her shoulder and said soothingly, "Well, you can't expect a man to ignore his natural urges, can you, miss? The fact is, if His Lordship *didn't* have a mistress, I'd wonder about 'im!"

Sam looked up into Clara's sympathetic face. She smiled wanly. "It seems, Clara, that there's still a lot of gaping holes in my education."

"Oh, no, miss," Clara assured her. "Proper females aren't supposed to know about mistresses and such. And if they know about them, they aren't supposed to talk about them or even think about them."

Another unwelcome idea popped into Sam's head. "Do gentlemen keep their mistresses once they're married, Clara?"

Clara winced. "Sometimes," she admitted.

Sam clenched her jaw and shook her head. She pulled away from Clara and moved to stand in front of the mirror again, wearing only her chemise. She stared at her reflection and mused aloud, "I expect men keep mistresses because so-called proper women are made to think that enthusiastic lovemaking is vulgar . . . that variations on the usual are forbidden. That's not going to happen to me, Clara. Julian will not need a mistress once he's married to me!"

Clara laughed. "You don't even know what the 'usual' is when it comes to lovemaking. How are you ever going to learn the 'variations'? Miss Priscilla and Miss Nancy don't know about such things."

Sam smiled smugly. "I'll just have to have a little chat with Julian's opera dancer, won't I?"

It took Clara a moment to realize that Sam was serious, then she was appalled. "Now, miss, that's not what a proper lady does. You'd better get that notion out of your head this very—"

But in the midst of Clara's lecture, there was a knock at the door. She startled a little at the interruption, coming as it did in the middle of a discussion on mistresses, but she collected herself and went to see who it was. While Sam sat on the bed and waited, there was a terse, low-voiced exchange at the door between Clara and her father, Hedley. Sam noticed that Clara didn't have a very warm relationship with her father. In fact, she often seemed even a little frightened of him. When she ended the conversation and came back into the room, Clara's eyes were large and worried.

"Papa says you're to get dressed immediately and go to the library. He says your aunts came home a few minutes ago all in a twitter and they're behind closed doors with His Lordship gabbing up a storm. Papa says Miss Priscilla has nearly wrung her hands raw!"

Sam jumped to her feet. "Oh, dear. What can the matter be, I wonder?" she exclaimed. "Hurry, Clara. Help me get my dress back on! And don't fuss with my hair. I'd better go as quickly as possible!"

A sudden horrible thought entered Sam's head. "I hope nothing has happened to Amanda or the baby!"

Sam and Clara exchanged stricken looks, then hurried even faster.

Chapter 3

As Sam half ran down the hall toward the library at the rear of the house, instead of a mere footman waiting to open the door for her, she saw Hedley. In Sam's estimation, such consideration did not bode well. And when she thought she detected a bit of sympathy in Hedley's usually haughty expression, she entered the library trembling with fear.

The scene that greeted her did not lessen her fears, either. The aunts were sitting on the sofa, their faces white and drawn. Priss was wringing her hands as if she were imagining some villain's neck. Julian stood with his back to the fire, his arms crossed over his broad chest, looking as sober as a minister presiding at a funeral. *Whose funeral?* thought Sam. *Please not Amanda's!*

Hedley closed the door, leaving her alone with Julian and the aunts. But they all simply stared at her, saying nothing.

"Don't leave me in suspense," she pleaded. "It's Amanda, isn't it? Something's happened to Amanda!"

The aunts began disclaiming at once, and Julian came forward and grasped Sam's hands, chafing

52

them between his two. "Nonsense, my girl. It's nothing of the sort. By last report, Amanda is doing excellently, and we've no reason to believe her situation has changed."

Sam sighed with relief, squeezing Julian's hands gratefully. "Oh, I'm so glad to hear it. When I was called to come so urgently, and with Hedley looking so sympathetic and all of you appearing so concerned, I assumed it was bad news."

Sam noticed Priss and Nan exchange looks. She peered up at Julian, demanding, "It *is* bad news, isn't it? Why won't you tell me what's wrong?"

Julian guided her to a chair and urged her to sit down. He straightened and looked down at her with a serious expression. "It is news of importance, certainly, though it remains to be seen whether or not it is bad news. It is unfair and cruel of us to keep you in suspense, I know, Sam, but the truth is, it's very hard to know where to begin."

"Why not at the beginning?" Sam suggested, trying to smile even though her heart was beating so fast it was difficult to breathe.

"An excellent suggestion," Nan said, nodding enthusiastically. "Excellent, indeed." She paused, then turned to Priss. "Er . . . *you* begin, Priss."

"But I wasn't the one who found the diary," Priss protested. *"You* found it!"

"Whose diary?" Sam asked, confused. "And what has a diary to do with *me?"*

"The diary belonged to Clorinda Darlington, Amanda's mother," Julian explained, leaning his shoulder against the mantel and keeping his steady gaze trained on Sam.

"Yes, unbeknownst to us, our sister kept a diary," Nan continued, pulling a handkerchief from her sleeve and sniffling into it. "And it appears she had a much worse life with Simon Darlington than we ever suspected . . . the sanctimonious brute! She was *very* unhappy."

"Am I to gather that you only recently found this diary?" Sam inquired.

"Yes, we found it this afternoon when we were going through a trunk of old clothes belonging to Clorinda, looking for suitable apparel to donate to the Women's Shelter. Amanda Jane had given us permission long ago to give the clothes to the poor, and so we finally had the trunk brought up from Darlington Hall last week and sent directly to the shelter. We found the diary hidden on the very bottom under a taffeta petticoat!"

"Had no one gone through the trunk before?" Sam wondered.

"No," said Priss. "Amanda Jane hadn't the heart to do it at first, you know, and so much has happened in the past few months. . . ."

Sam's heartbeat was beginning to slow to a reasonable speed. She certainly sympathized with Priss and Nan's distress about finding the diary and reading unpleasant revelations about their sister's life with her "sainted" father, but why had *she* been sent for with such urgency? What could any of this have to do with her? Nothing that could be revealed about her father's cruel nature would surprise her; *she* ought to know better than anybody of his insensitivity and indifference. But was there more to this than they were telling her?

The aunts had sunk into another uncomfortable silence. Sam looked questioningly at Julian. He sighed, then pushed off from the mantel and actually knelt beside her chair in the manner of a man proposing marriage. Sam's heart tripped into a fast rhythm again. "I can see that I'm going to have to tell you what Priss and Nan discovered in the diary, Sam, and perhaps I'm the person who should do it, anyway."

He took her hand, which would have been a very wonderful thing under other circumstances, but now Sam was growing fearful again. The look in his silvery blue eyes was intense, his brows were knitted, his mouth was stern. "As you know, in the letter your father left for Amanda after he died," he began, "he explained that your mother—whom he never named—died when you were born. But from the writings in Clorinda's diary, we have reason to conclude . . . that your mother is still alive. At least, she was alive a year ago when Clorinda made her last entry in the diary just before her own untimely death."

Sam had never been hit in the chest with a cannonball before—and, God willing, she never would—but at that moment she knew exactly how such a dreadful thing would feel. Her heart seemed to stop beating completely. She couldn't breathe. Everything at first was too bright . . . then all went black. The next thing she knew, she was stretched out on the sofa with Julian hovering over her, his stern mouth softened with concern, his eyes darkened with worry. At first it was quite pleasant to have his face so close to hers. Then she remembered . . . and felt her eyes fluttering shut again.

"Oh, dear!" exclaimed Prissy, from somewhere in the background.

"Perhaps another sniff of restorative?" Nan's voice suggested.

Sam forced her eyes open. "No. . . ." She struggled to sit up. "I'm not a silly, swooning female. Just a glass of water, please."

"Get her some brandy," Julian ordered, easing onto the sofa beside her and propping her against his side with his arm around her shoulder.

Again Sam lamented that she couldn't enjoy being close to Julian as much as she'd like to . . . not with such astonishing news battering her brain over and over again.

Your mother is still alive. Your mother is still alive.
She couldn't believe it. If her mother was still alive, where was she . . . and why, along with her father, had she abandoned her?

Nan handed Julian the glass of brandy, and he urged Sam to sit up. When he appeared to be going to tip the glass to her mouth, Sam shook her head and said, "I can do it myself."

Sam took the glass in a slightly shaky hand, drank the brandy in one gulp, then coughed when she felt the liquid sear her throat. But soon the liquor had warmed her numbed extremities and sharpened her thoughts. She turned to Julian and looked him square in the eye.

"Who is my mother and where is she?" she said evenly, then held her breath.

Julian paused, then answered quietly, "I don't know, Sam."

Samantha felt profound disappointment. "The diary said nothing else about my mother except that she's alive?"

"No, there was more," Nan revealed, still holding a salts bottle as she stood over Sam.

"Yes," Priss concurred, leaning over the back of the sofa. "But there was nothing conclusive. There was just enough information to worry one, I'm afraid."

"To worry—" Sam turned back to Julian. "My mother wasn't a . . . a . . . murderer or a thief or a—"

"No, Sam," Julian assured her, then added with a wry, apologetic grin, "Brace yourself, brat. It appears you have even more claim to a place in society than your father's position and respectability warranted. It seems your mother is even higher ranked than he. According to Clarissa's diary, your mother is a titled lady of the *ton.*"

"A titled lady of the—" Sam's voice trailed off as her mouth dropped open.

Julian nodded. "If such is truly the case—"

"Clorinda *always* told the truth," Nan interjected firmly.

"If you say so, I will believe you," Julian conceded. "However, quite obviously, Simon Darlington was not similarly plagued with such a virtue. He might have only told Clorinda the woman was highborn to fend off suspicion in another quarter."

"That may be," Nan said with a sigh.

"But it is reasonable to suppose, Sam, that if your mother is indeed a titled female of the *ton,* when she became pregnant with you, she must have been unmarried."

Finally finding her voice, Sam croaked, "Oh? And why do you suppose that?"

Julian glanced at Priss and Nan as if for corroboration, then proceeded. "Because—and here, my dear girl, you will be getting a little more education of the world—it is the usual practice of aristocratic females to remain faithful to their husbands at least until they provide him with an heir. Once that happy event has occurred, however, they are free to take lovers as they choose."

Sam's eyes widened as a disillusioning thought occurred to her. "But Amanda wouldn't—"

"No, Amanda wouldn't take a lover and neither would Jack. You're quite right about that," Julian hurriedly assured her. "Jack and Amanda's marriage is based on mutual affection. But, as I told you, many marriages are not." Julian waited while Sam absorbed this information.

"But if the woman gets with child the second time, isn't there a chance the babe could be someone's besides her husband's?" Sam finally asked.

"Yes, but if the purity of the line has been established through the heir, most husbands don't worry about whether or not the second child . . . or third or fourth, et cetera . . . is actually his own flesh and blood."

"It seems most unnatural to me," Sam muttered, disturbed to discover yet another hypocritical aspect of the so-called "respectable" society of which she was endeavoring to become an accepted member.

"Nevertheless, it is the way of things," Julian replied.

"So you think my mother must have been unmarried, because if she had been married she would have kept me . . . despite the fact that I was not the natural daughter of her husband," she concluded.

"You have always been quick to catch on to things," Julian observed with a world-weary smile.

Sam's head was spinning. By turns she was surprised, excited, distressed . . . but most of all, hurt. Whoever and wherever her real mother was, the fact still remained that Sam now knew she had been abandoned by not just one parent, but two. She fought back tears and shrugged, saying, "Well, whether or not she was married doesn't matter now, does it?"

"At least it gives us a clue to go on," Julian answered.

"A clue?"

"Toward finding out if Mrs. Darlington's writings are based on fact. In short, toward discovering who your mother is."

"Why even try? Why can't things simply go on as before?"

"That's quite impossible, Sam."

"Impossible?"

"It is imperative to discover her identity."

Sam gave an uncertain chuckle. "I don't understand. *Why?*"

"Because, my girl, I don't fancy the idea of accidentally marrying you off to your . . . *brother!*"

"Oh, I see," Sam squeaked out, abruptly realizing how dire the situation was.

"Yes," Julian drawled. "People might marry their cousins, but siblings are definitely out of the question. Inbreeding has its limits . . . even in England."

Sam smiled weakly. "I suppose I could avoid the possibility of—" She grimaced. *"—inbreeding* by marrying an American."

"You'll do no such thing, Samantha," Julian snapped, surprising her with the vehemence of his tone. "I'll find out who your mother is if it's the last thing I do!"

"But how do you propose to do that, Julian?" Nan ventured.

"No one is going to own up to bearing, then abandoning a child," Priss added worriedly.

"I have a plan," Julian answered.

"And I suppose you don't intend to tell us what your plan is?" Sam said.

"I do not. Discretion is imperative in this undertaking." Sam opened her mouth to object, but Julian forestalled her with an upraised hand. "Don't bother to argue with me, brat. The Season has just barely begun. I want you to forget, as well as you can, what you found out today."

"How can I possibly—"

"As soon as I find out anything, naturally I will share my knowledge with you. In the meantime, just enjoy yourself. You and I worked very hard to secure you a brilliant entrée into society, and I won't have it spoiled by inadvertently involving you in a scandal."

Sam was silenced and Julian was satisfied . . . for now. But he could tell by the stubborn set of her jaw that Sam was not going to give up on being as involved as possible in getting to the truth of the matter about her mother. He couldn't blame her, of course. He'd feel exactly the same way if he were in her situation. Although he wondered if he could be as brave and strong as she was . . . as she had been all along.

As he looked at her, at her eyes shining with unshed tears, her lips clamped tight to stop their trembling, he felt the most overpowering surge of protective affection. He just wanted her to be respectable and happy, but circumstances kept getting in the way.

"I have to change for our outing in Hyde Park," she said at last in a dull voice.

"Do you think it's wise to go out, my dear?" Nan asked, easing down on the sofa beside her.

"You must be exhausted from"—Priss waved her hands ineffectually—"all this."

"A carriage ride might be just what she needs to get her mind off things," Julian said. "But it's only two o'clock. There's plenty of time to allow her to get some rest first."

"I don't need to rest," Sam insisted, rising quickly to her feet, swaying dizzily, then sinking down on the sofa again with Julian's hands firmly at her waist. "I guess I am a *little* tired," she admitted with a weak smile.

"You've received quite a blow, dearest," Nan said, stroking Sam's arm. She turned to Julian. "Perhaps you should carry her up the stairs, Julian?"

Julian was quite willing to carry Sam up the stairs, but as independent as she was and as hard as she tried to appear invincible, he didn't suppose she'd allow him to do any such thing.

Sam looked at him, her eyes as blue and clear as a summer sky. But, despite his usual perceptiveness where she was concerned, he didn't have a clue what she was thinking. He cocked a brow. "Well, brat? Shall I carry you, or do you insist on marching up the stairs unassisted?"

To Julian's astonished surprise, Sam said in a voice as soft as silk, "Carry me, Julian. Carry me up to my bedchamber."

Julian blinked. He'd carried a goodly number of women to their bedchambers, but not for such a pure, disinterested reason as saving them from the possibility of swooning on the stairs and breaking their necks in the resulting fall. Carrying a woman in his arms had always been a sort of foreplay, a preliminary game as old as Adam and Eve, ending in sexual consummation behind closed doors. So, perhaps that was why Sam's innocently spoken request made him feel so damned . . . uncomfortable.

"Julian? What's the matter?" asked Nan.

"Nothing's the matter," Julian muttered, feeling unaccountably guilty for reasons that were completely unclear. "Er . . . are you ready, Sam?"

"You go ahead and take her upstairs, Julian," Priss said briskly. "Nan and I are going to order her a luncheon tray and mix up a little medicinal tea to help her relax. We'll see you upstairs in a few moments."

And before Julian could think of a single reason why they shouldn't desert him to the task of carting his ward upstairs all alone, they had scurried out of the room.

"Well, Julian?" Sam prompted him, looking wide-eyed at him as if he'd gone mad. Maybe he *was* losing his mind, for why else would he suddenly shirk at doing such a simple act of kindness as carrying Sam up the stairs to her bedchamber? After all, she was not his mistress or anyone he would ever consort with in an intimate manner. When he deposited her on the bed, she'd look up at him trustingly, gratefully, not with the same sultry, come-hither expression his mistress might wear in a similar situation.

Encouraged by this line of reasoning, he turned to Sam and said cheerfully, "All right, my girl. Put your arms around my neck and I'll slip my hands under your legs just so. . . ."

From his sitting position on the couch, Julian leaned over and swooped Sam into his arms, then stood up. She was as light as a feather and he easily held her high against his chest. But he still felt awkward and uncomfortable as he headed for the door.

She'd nestled her head under his chin and his nose was buried in a tumble of blond curls. He'd never noticed before how silky-soft her hair felt, how good it smelled . . . something like lilacs. And her arms around his neck were so smooth and white, her hips against his waist and her small breasts against his chest so nicely rounded and firm. Her skirts had ridden up an inch or two and her slim, crossed ankles were showing at the bottom.

He looked away. Then, for some reason, he conjured up a vision of his mistress, stark naked and voluptuous, holding out her arms in welcome. So intent as he'd been in turning Sam from a sow's ear to a silk purse, he'd neglected his mistress for three long months. But he had time now to take care of his own needs. Yes, maybe even this afternoon he would find time to visit the charming Isabelle.

Why have I never thought of this before? Sam asked herself. She was always so determined to be strong and self-reliant, scorning the swooning, simpering, tearful ways of the fashionable female. And while she could never embrace the practice of simpering and sniffling at the drop of a hat, the swooning part might indeed serve a useful purpose. She *had* been rather dizzy when she stood up in the library just now, but she could have certainly walked up the stairs to her bedchamber. Being carried in Julian's arms, however, made the giving in to female fancies worth it.

Sam was in heaven.

Was there ever a stronger pair of arms? She'd never felt safer.

Was there a broader, firmer chest than Julian's? It was so nice to lean against it.

Did all men smell so nicely of soap and some other clean, mysterious, yet deeply masculine scent? She doubted it. Julian was special.

And then all too soon he had turned the knob and pushed open the door to her bedchamber with his knee, muttering to himself, "Where are all the blasted footmen when you need them?"

He carried her to the bed and leaned over, placing her gently against the pillows. Then he let go.

But Sam didn't let go. Even while Julian pulled back to straighten up, she kept her arms firmly wrapped around his neck. Not expecting to be held on to, Julian was thrown off-balance and fell forward, landing chest to chest on top of Samantha on the bed.

"Damnation!" Julian growled, pushing himself to his elbows. "Don't you know to let go of a fellow when he lays you on a bed, Sam?"

"No, Julian, I don't," she said, staring up at him with the most innocent look she could muster. "No man has ever laid me on a bed before."

And no man besides you ever will, she vowed in that moment. She had purposely held on to him, thinking to keep him close to her as long as possible, but she wasn't prepared for the sensations that coursed through her body because of that contrived closeness. His chest against her breasts made her nipples harden and tingle. She got lost in the expression in his silvery eyes. She thought she saw anger, frustration and . . . longing? The chiseled mouth she had admired from afar was now close enough to touch, to kiss. . . .

Julian felt like he'd been picked up by a tornado, twirled in a vortex for a few hours, then dropped into a farmer's field on top of a plump, sweet-smelling stack of hay. He was dizzy, breathless, and much more comfortable than he ought to be. Hell, that's what he got for daydreaming about his mistress just minutes before! He even imagined that Sam had that same sultry, come-hither look as Isabelle always wore when she was about to draw his head down and kiss him. But that was a preposterous idea!

Julian sprang from the bed as if a bugle had sounded, alerting him to the arrival of an avenging, almighty God. And, even worse than being found in an accidentally compromising position before deity, what if Priss and Nan had walked in before he'd gathered his wits and stood up? Horrors! While Sam gazed at him with a bemused expression, Julian tugged on his vest and straightened his cravat.

"Sorry, Sam," he muttered, averting his eyes. "Damned cow-handed of me. Wasn't your fault, of course."

Fortunately, in the midst of his confused apologies, Julian was extremely relieved to be interrupted by Priss bustling into the room with a cup of steaming liquid—medicinal tea, he presumed. He quickly made some excuse about attending to papers from his solicitor, promised to check on Sam presently, and hastily exited.

In the cool of the library once more, Julian regained his composure. He couldn't imagine what had come over him just now in the bedchamber with Sam. But fortunately, she was too young and naive to even suspect that the situation had been accidentally provocative. But it was over and, he trusted, soon forgotten.

He sat down in a wing chair and picked up a book he'd been reading in odd moments of leisure, but after staring at the words for a while, he realized he wasn't comprehending a bit of it.

Feeling restless and vaguely dissatisfied, Julian stood up and moved to the window, pushed back the drapes, and stared into the stable yard. One of the stableboys was romping with the pups.

Why had he ever approved her keeping all three? he wondered, his mouth curving in a rueful smile as he watched three wagging tails and a laughing boy. Obviously he had let his fondness for Sam make him too indulgent, and now he was paying for it.

Julian moved away from the window and stared thoughtfully into the empty grate of the fireplace. There were three things he needed to do. Most importantly, of course, he must begin the search for Sam's mother. Secondly, he must propose to Charlotte.

But even more pressing than either of these tasks—should he be thinking of a marriage proposal as a *task?*—he had to see his mistress. And why he was loitering around in his library instead of fornicating in Isabelle's satin-sheathed bed was beyond him!

Julian looked at the mantel-clock. There were about two hours left before they needed to leave for Hyde Park to meet Sam's throng of admirers. He grimaced. Taking into account the half hour of traveling to and from Isabelle's house, then sprucing up for the drive in Hyde Park afterward, Julian estimated that he'd have about a half hour to pleasure and be pleasured by his mistress. Such haste was certainly not his usual style.

Julian poured a glass of brandy and swallowed it quickly, then hurried to the door. Haste was not his style, certainly, but today he had no choice. In essence, he had allowed his preoccupation with Sam's transformation and subsequent launch into society make him forget his own needs.

Now how had a sprig of a girl like Sam accomplished that? *Bloody Hell!*

Chapter 4

Although appearing outwardly plain and respectable, Isabelle's house was a veritable sensory delight from the moment one stepped over the threshold. As Julian peeled his gloves and handed them to the surprised butler, his senses were virtually attacked at the most elemental level.

The soft lighting and plush, polished furnishings, even in the hall, were designed to evoke a sensual mood. Exotic plants and scented candles added to the allure. All this, and Julian wasn't even expected . . . hadn't, in fact, been there in three months. But then Isabelle had always been his most prepared mistress, always ready for him, always eager to please.

"It's good to see you, my lord . . . if I may be so bold," the butler said with a respectful smile.

"Certainly, Powell," Julian replied amiably, although a little impatiently. After all, he was in a hurry. "Is your mistress at home?"

"Yes, my lord. She's in her bedchamber. Shall I send word that you've arrived or will you—?"

"I'll go up myself, Powell. Thank you," he added, dismissing the servant with a nod. It was impossible not to notice the relief on the butler's face.

Julian's relationship with Isabelle—the continuance or the demise thereof—would directly affect Powell's job. Certainly Isabelle would have no trouble finding another protector, but perhaps he wouldn't be as generous as Julian had been in paying the help.

Powell discreetly disappeared, and Julian quickly climbed the stairs to the first floor. The door to Isabelle's boudoir was ajar, and the hinges were apparently well oiled because she didn't hear him enter the room. Observing her while she was unaware of his presence, Julian was struck again by her beauty. She couldn't have looked more alluring had the visit been scheduled. She was curled up on a red brocade silk divan, eating an apple and reading a book. She was dressed in a matching red silk dressing gown, was barefoot, and her long black hair fell about her shoulders in wanton, but calculated, disarray.

"As tempting as Eve," he murmured.

Isabelle looked up, surprise and pleasure dawning on her face. Then, no doubt remembering that she'd been neglected for three months, she reassembled her features into an offended expression. She set down the book on a nearby table and crossed her arms, saying in a stilted tone, "So it's you at last, Julian. To what do I owe the pleasure of this most unexpected visit?"

Julian shut the door behind him and advanced. "Cut line, my girl," he drawled, smiling crookedly. "You have a right to be a bit miffed by my prolonged absence, but I'm in no mood for, nor do I wish to spend the short time I have, in explanations. Perhaps another time. . . . And don't tell me you aren't glad to see me."

Isabelle pouted, unwilling at first to relent so

easily. But when Julian shrugged out of his jacket
and threw it on a nearby chair, then untied his
cravat and started unbuttoning his shirt, her face
flushed, her eyes grew luminous, and her lips
parted in a soft pant of expectation.

"Julian, I *am* happy to see you," she admitted
breathlessly, then she held out her arms in welcome.

Wondering at the strange and unaccountable
reluctance that suddenly came over him, but determined to make up for the last three months for
Isabelle's sake as well as his, Julian shook off his
hesitancy and went to her.

The parade of carriages and elegantly outfitted
riders in Hyde Park during the fashionable hours,
between four and six, was an amazing sight indeed.
Sam couldn't see the trees and the flowers for the
people, but they were every bit as grand and
colorful as anything Mother Nature could create.
There were debutantes and dandies dressed in
pastels, gentlemen in dashing riding gear with tall,
tasseled boots and hats set at rakish angles on their
heads, and dowagers and grand ladies of the *ton*
carrying frilly parasols to shield their delicate skin
from the sun.

It was a beautiful afternoon and Sam was determined to enjoy it despite the fact that her whole
world had recently been turned upside down. She
was trying very hard not to let the news that her
mother was still alive distract her from her plan for
a lifetime of happiness with Julian. However, she
couldn't help but look at all the fancy ladies in their
carriages and wonder if one of them was her
mother.

But that was a hurtful thought, and Sam would

rather think of Julian. She could swear he'd been fighting an attraction to her when he carried her upstairs that afternoon, and that was much more important to her than searching for a mother who had abandoned her. Her mother was her past; Julian was her present and future.

Julian, however, had left the house that afternoon after depositing her in her bedchamber in the care of Priss and Nan, and returned in a taciturn mood . . . which had not changed despite the lovely weather and the many people who attempted to engage him in conversation at the park. Sam wondered if his errand had had something to do with finding out about her mother.

At any rate, Julian was brooding and silent. She hoped it might be because of her, because he'd wanted to kiss her and hadn't—for some altogether stupid reason like she was too young. Such senseless self-denial would make anyone a little cranky. If such *was* the source of his somber mood, Sam was glad, even though sitting beside him in his open barouche was rather like sitting beside a statue whose noble features had been carved into a permanent frown. But then she supposed it did not help his bad temper to be sharing the vehicle with Clara and all three puppies.

Carriages were everywhere, and while everyone was either in an elegant equipage or on a horse, no one seemed to be moving. Phaetons and cabriolets stopped alongside other vehicles so the occupants could chat, and gentlemen on horseback went from carriage to carriage paying their respects . . . mostly to the newest and fairest females in town for the Season. Sam was most gratified to enjoy a great many visitors to their chaise, despite Julian's silent and forbidding presence.

Having just bid two gentlemen good afternoon, Sam was delighted to see Ninian ride up to their carriage. "By Jove, you've brought my dog!" he exclaimed happily when he saw the corgi sitting on the seat beside Clara, panting excitedly but behaving with true British decorum.

"Yes, *George*—as I've decided to call him—is the best behaved of the three," Sam said with a smile. "As you can see, I've got them all on leading strings and have brought my abigail, Clara, along to play puppy-nurse, but George hasn't needed scolding once. He does just as he's told and doesn't bark at the horses."

"Unlike the American's mutt," Ninian observed smugly as Madison yapped furiously at his horse and strained at his leash. "Breeding will always tell."

"Not always," Julian drawled, peering from under the rim of his hat at Ninian. "Where are *your* manners, sir?"

Ninian blushed. "Sorry, Lord Serling. Meant to say 'how d' do,' but got distracted."

Julian had no chance to answer before Jean-Luc rode up. *"Bonjour,* Miss Darlington, Lord Serling." He respectfully tipped his hat at Julian, but his gaze turned immediately back to rest appreciatively on Sam. "And how does my French dog behave, Miss Darlington? Better than the American's, obviously, but how does it fare against the English?"

"How do the French always fare against the English?" Ninian said with a superior sniff. "Miss Darlington has just told me that George—named, no doubt, for our beloved King George—is the best behaved of the lot."

Jean-Luc placed his hand on his chest and intoned dramatically, "You smite me through the heart, Miss Darlington." Then he smiled teasingly. "Do not say you favor the ugly English hound over my elegant poodle?"

Sam laughed. "I really don't have a favorite. I like all three of them." She was holding the poodle in her lap, scratching it behind the ears as its eyes drifted shut in canine ecstasy. "I must admit that *Louie* is the laziest of the three. He doesn't even flinch when Madison goes into a barking frenzy, but simply likes to be held and petted and pampered. He acts rather bored most of the time."

"He has fastidious tastes, mademoiselle, and does not get excited over mundane occurrences," Jean-Luc informed her with a sly wink. "Like me, Louie is an aristocrat."

"We don't have aristocrats in the States," came Nathan's voice across the lawn as he approached the carriage on his high-spirited black stallion. "In America you decide who and what you want to be, then you work hard till you've attained your goal."

"In other words, any riffraff can be king," Ninian said disdainfully.

"On the contrary, Mr. Wentworth," said Nathan. "Any riffraff can be *president.*" Then he took off his hat and bowed at the waist, grinning from ear to ear at Sam. "Good afternoon, Miss Darlington, Lord Serling." His gaze shifted to Clara, who was trying to hold on to Madison. The mutt seemed determined to jump off the carriage seat and into Nathan's arms. His eyes gleaming with enjoyment at the spectacle, Nathan said, "Give the little runt to me, miss. He remembers our roughhousin' I suppose."

Blushing prettily, Clara stood up in the carriage and handed the pup to Nathan. Dressed in her usual uniform, minus the apron and mobcap, and with a straw bonnet tied demurely under her chin, Clara looked quite pretty, Sam thought. It was obvious that Nathan thought so, too.

"What's your name, miss?" he inquired, gazing steadily at Clara as she returned to her seat.

Clara turned startled eyes to Sam, and then to Julian. She didn't know what to say or do. Normally a servant was never noticed, much less talked to or asked her name. Jean-Luc politely looked away, and Ninian squirmed uncomfortably in his saddle. They probably considered Nathan's mistake in social protocol an indication of lack of breeding, an awkward and embarrassing *faux pas,* but Sam was pleased with his free and friendly manners.

"Clara is Miss Darlington's abigail . . . her lady's maid," Julian explained, coming to Clara's rescue.

Clara stood again and made a little curtsy, then sat down, pulled the well-behaved George onto her lap, and buried her glowing cheeks in his furry neck.

There was an awkward pause, and finally Julian introduced another topic . . . horses. This effectively got the conversational ball rolling again, particularly for Nathan, who owned a horse ranch.

Julian remained silent during the next few minutes as he closely watched the three men vie for Sam's attention, sticking stubbornly to their places by the carriage even when other men tried to squeeze in to say a word or two to the popular Miss Darlington.

Then, as the sun sunk below the trees, Julian concluded with great relief that it was time to return to Montgomery House. He perfunctorily informed Sam's three suitors that they had better be off, then he ordered the chaise to carry him and his party home.

"When we get back to the house, Sam," said Julian, "I want to talk to you."

Sam turned wide blue eyes to him and said, "About what, Julian?" She had the poodle pressed against her bosom, her chin resting on top of the pup's kinky head. She might have been the proverbial "Little Bo-Peep" with a rescued lamb in her arms. Her pale pink carriage gown and wide-brimmed bonnet with the huge bow tied under her chin at a coy angle certainly made her look the part.

Julian found it interesting that Sam managed to look demure and alluring at the same time. He caught himself staring, and he turned his gaze away to something less interesting . . . a portly man in a passing gig. "About your suitors," he finally answered her.

There was a pause, then she asked, "Which ones?"

He glanced at her and found her cheeks dimpled with amusement. "Which ones do you suppose?" he answered dryly. "The group of three from which you intend to choose your husband, of course."

She laughed, the musical sound mystically lifting his spirits, which were unaccountably low after spending a highly erotic hour making athletic love with his mistress. He felt sexually sated . . . but empty and lonely. He'd never had such a negative reaction before to good sex, and he found it odd and not a little perplexing.

"Oh, *those* fellows," she said teasingly. "But why can't we talk about them now? We'll be nearly a half hour in the chaise before we get home."

Julian glanced at Clara, who was struggling again

with Madison. She was holding the pup in her arms and giving him a stern lecture . . . as he happily wagged his tail and licked her face. George sat stoically beside her, suppressing all urges to bark at birds and squirrels he spied in the passing shrubbery.

"It's all right to talk in front of Clara, you know," Sam said. "I tell her everything anyway."

Julian sighed. "Do you?" He thought about gently reprimanding her, then decided against it. While servants couldn't usually be depended on to keep confidences, he knew Clara was more like a friend to Sam than a servant. And since Sam had no mother or sister around to talk to, he supposed it was natural that she would confide in Clara. She could certainly do worse.

"All right," he conceded. "I just wanted to tell you what I know about the three men and give you my opinion of their eligibility as . . . er . . . husbands." *The sooner Sam is married the better,* he told himself, although he didn't believe any of the three men in question were worthy of her. Most people would disagree with that conclusion, however, including Priss and Nan. They considered Sam's three favorite suitors desirable catches.

And perhaps they were right, although Julian usually trusted his own instincts over the opinions of others. In Sam's case, however, he was beginning to think his fondness for her kept him from seeing things clearly. Like a father or a brother, he probably wouldn't consider any man good enough for her.

Sam raised her brows. "You've made inquiries about them?"

"I already knew the gentlemen, but . . . yes, certainly, I made additional inquiries. It is my duty as your guardian to do so."

She nodded, studying his face in a most disconcertingly keen fashion. "All right. Please go on," she urged.

Julian cleared his throat. "Since he appears to be your favorite, we'll start with Nathan Ford." He watched for a reaction and wasn't disappointed. Her eyes lit up approvingly. Hell, maybe he *was* disappointed. Virginia was an ocean away! If the fellow didn't treat her well, how would any of them ever know?

"I like his independence," Sam admitted. "I like his open and friendly manners, too."

"He's by far the handsomest!" Clara piped up, then quickly ducked her head, aware that although she might be privy to the conversation, she wasn't invited to join in.

"Yes, he *is* handsome," Sam said reflectively. "Even though he is rather too fair for my tastes."

"Too *fair?*" Julian repeated in a tone of chagrined surprise. "But he's rather a *dark* blond."

Sam nodded. "I know. I prefer dark-haired men."

Julian's lip curled. "Indeed. Well, I never knew you had a preference at all, Sam."

"Oh, I do," she assured him with a beaming smile. "So, what do you think about his eligibility?"

Julian shrugged. "For all his talk of riffraff rising to political office and whatnot, he comes from an old and established family in Richmond, Virginia. He is young and wealthy and has no one but himself to please when choosing a wife. His father is dead, and his mother can refuse him nothing."

"He sounds eminently eligible then, doesn't he?" Sam said.

Julian shrugged again, feeling decidedly and unaccountably sulky. "In all respects except one . . . and I've mentioned it before. He'll want you to live with him in Virginia." When Sam didn't react, Julian added emphatically and rather harshly, "In short, you're wasting your time with Nathan Ford."

"What makes you think I don't want to live in Virginia?" Sam retorted, lifting that defiant chin of hers. "The more I hear about America, the better I like it."

"But it's so far away from your sister. Won't you miss her?"

"Of course. But, as you've told me enough times, it's important that I'm respectably established."

"You have other options, my girl," Julian said impatiently.

"Yes," she agreed. "Other men, you mean." She smoothed her skirts, appearing very cool and nonchalant. "Now tell me about Ninian."

"Yes . . . the dandy," Julian began caustically. "Ninian Wentworth's biggest drawback in my estimation is his deplorable taste in clothing. He's a veritable pink, a fop, a—"

"Besides his taste in clothes, Julian," Sam interrupted, "is there something the matter with Ninian?"

"Ninian comes from a good enough family, but he needs to marry for money or undertake a career," Julian said discouragingly.

"Well, thanks to Amanda, I have plenty of money," Sam reminded him, unperturbed.

"Rumor has it that Ninian wants a career in the army—"

"That's commendable of him," Sam interrupted. "I already like him better."

"But his *mama* won't allow it," Julian added dampeningly. "Ninian is the youngest of four sons, and Mrs. Wentworth tries to baby him. She doesn't think he's got the gumption for military life. She won't buy him into a fashionable regiment."

"Why doesn't he enlist?"

Julian snorted. "Ninian might pine for the military life, but not in the working army. His father is dead," he continued doggedly, "and his mama rules the world from her chaise longue and wields her hartshorn and vinegar water like a soldier wields his sword. Mrs. Wentworth is small, and her ailments are most probably imaginary, but she is formidable."

"Besides his dragon of a mother and his inability to convince her that he's got the gumption for the military, what else is wrong with Ninian? Does he gamble and wench? Does he have a bad character, Julian?"

Julian frowned. "No, but—"

"I think he's very nice."

"He might be your brother!"

"I'll keep that in mind. But until I know for sure, I certainly won't drop him from my list of matrimonial possibilities. Now tell me about Jean-Luc."

Julian shook his head. "Very well. Mind you . . . I do not hold it against him that he's half-French. But he seems more French than English."

"He seems very proud of his native country and his heritage. Is there something wrong with that?"

"No, but he's a hardened flirt, Sam. In fact, I don't think you should take his attentions too seriously. *I'm* not. He's dallied after more than one woman, I assure you. And don't let his flattery turn your head. He *does* flatter you excessively, doesn't he?"

"Other than his propensity for telling me how beautiful and wonderful I am in every way, what other reason can you give me for disliking the fellow?" Sam said with dry sarcasm.

"Nothing," Julian admitted grudgingly. "He comes of aristocratic stock—as he's let it be well-known—and when his grandfather died he left him with a comfortable fortune. However, I can't say I like him."

"But *you* don't have to like him," Sam replied, unruffled. "*I* have to like him . . . at least well enough to marry him. And if he has other points to recommend him, it wouldn't be reasonable or logical to reject him just because *you* don't like him. Aren't I right, Julian?"

Sam's eyes were wide, her expression earnest. Julian stared at her, his thoughts and feelings in a jumble. He'd been preaching reason and logic to Sam for months. Now that she was actually embracing those tenets, he felt strangely disturbed. Had he so exerted his own personality on his student that she had changed drastically from the idealistic chit she once was?

But if she had, wasn't that a good thing? After all, the ultimate thrill of creating was to make something or someone in your own image . . . wasn't it? Or was there a certain pleasant "stimulation" felt when someone challenged and even opposed your opinion?

As Julian struggled with his conflicting feelings, something occurred to right his world, to anchor it once more in sane reason and logic. Charlotte Batsford's carriage pulled up alongside his, and she inquired sedately, "How do you do, Julian? Isn't it a lovely day?"

Sam couldn't believe her bad luck! She had been making headway with Julian . . . she knew it! She believed he was jealous of her suitors—which she'd chosen simply because they were likable and persistent—and he seemed to be coming up with plenty of reasons why she shouldn't favor their suits. If he was so determined to marry her off, why was he so unencouraging?

Then Charlotte Batsford had to show up!

"And how are you today, Miss Darlington?" the lady politely continued, interrupting Sam's venomous thoughts.

Sam observed Charlotte Batsford, sitting upright in her carriage alongside her prim and most proper lady's companion, looking cool and lovely in a manilla brown carriage dress, her expression calm and friendly. Then Sam quite simply . . . lied.

"Actually, Miss Batsford," she said, lifting the back of her hand to her forehead, "it's . . . it's rather strange and has come upon me quite suddenly, but I'm feeling decidedly ill and . . . and *faint.*"

Then she collapsed against the cushions in a make-believe swoon.

Chapter 5

⌒◯⌒

Julian couldn't believe that he was carrying Sam in his arms again! She'd swooned in the carriage about two blocks from the house, and he'd had to curtail his conversation with Charlotte to rush his ward home to revive her. Concerned, Charlotte had followed in her own carriage and was close behind Julian as he hurried through the hall and into the front parlor, where he laid Sam down on the sofa.

Since this particular cozy and sunshine-filled room was where the aunts liked to sit and do needlework of an afternoon, they were present when he arrived with his armful of limp baggage and immediately flew into a flutter of nerves and excitement.

"Oh dear! Has the child fainted again?" cried Prissy.

"Has something occurred to distress her?" Nan inquired quiveringly. "Julian, did you discover who Samantha's m—"

But she did not finish the sentence when she noticed Charlotte coming through the open door not long after Julian entered the room.

"Do you have your salts bottle, Nan?" Julian

82

inquired roughly, kneeling beside Sam's motionless form and chafing her hands. He found them surprisingly warm and her cheeks quite rosy for someone who had just fainted.

"I always have my salts bottle," Nan assured him, grabbing her reticule off the table and pulling out the requested item. Julian waved the opened bottle under Sam's nose.

This was the part Sam had not been looking forward to. Just like earlier that day, she'd thoroughly enjoyed being toted about in Julian's strong arms. Her only regret was that she had to stay in character as the fainted female and couldn't wrap her arms around him and nestle her face against his warm, nice-smelling neck.

Then she'd been disappointed when he took her into the parlor instead of to her bedchamber, but she supposed he was simply concerned and looking for the quickest place to lay her down.

Reposed on the sofa with everyone fussing over her, Sam trusted that she presented an interesting and alluring picture to Julian. Such attention was worth smelling those horrid salts for . . . but only for a few seconds. Pushing the bottle away with feigned weakness, Sam blinked several times and said in a faint, pathetic voice, "Where am I?"

"You're quite safe, Sam. You're at home," Julian said shortly. "Why the devil did you faint again, child?"

Julian's terse tone was not what Sam had hoped for, and she did not like being called a child, but she was sure he spoke that way because he was worried sick about her. Running her tongue lightly over her bottom lip and lifting a languishing hand to her cheek, she whispered, "Oh, Julian. I'm so grateful to you for carrying me inside. You're so strong and—"

"You say this is the second time she's fainted today?" came the calm, no-nonsense voice of Charlotte Batsford, as intrusive to Sam's dramatic scene as a clanging bell in the dead of night. Sam looked past Julian's bent head to where the aunts hovered near the sofa and, sure enough, Charlotte stood there with them.

Sam suppressed the urge to stick her tongue out at the encroacher, but couldn't resist saying, "What are *you* doing here, Miss Batsford?"

"I was worried about you, Miss Darlington," Charlotte told her. "As we all are. If you have fainted twice today, I should think it wise to consult a doctor."

"I don't depend much on doctors, Charlotte," Julian said, his narrowed eyes fixed on Sam's face. "And in Sam's case, I don't think her fainting spells were brought on by an illness, but rather because of emotional stress. You see, today we found out—"

"Julian," Priss whispered urgently out of the side of her mouth. "Are you sure you should be talking about that?"

"Charlotte knows about Sam's true relationship to Amanda," Julian informed them. "I've told her everything."

Sam sat up straight, forgetting to behave weak and wilted. *"Everything?"* she squeaked.

Julian looked surprised at Sam's quick recovery and, recollecting herself, she slumped to the pillows and assumed her tragic pose again.

"You don't need to worry about it, Sam," Julian said, eyeing her suspiciously. "Charlotte can be trusted, and she's practically family."

"Indeed, Samantha, you may trust me," Charlotte said kindly. "And I would like very much to be your friend."

Sam didn't at all like the way things were going. Julian had almost declared his intention of marrying Charlotte right there on the spot! Practically a member of the family, indeed! He'd told her *everything!* And how dare Charlotte Batsford suggest that they be *friends?*

"We found out today that Samantha's mother is alive, Charlotte," Julian continued when Sam did not respond to Charlotte's offer of friendship.

Charlotte's brows rose, which was about as much emotion as Sam had ever seen the woman outwardly display. "Indeed?" she said.

"Yes," Julian answered wryly. "And the woman is purportedly a titled female of the *ton.*"

Charlotte's brows rose even higher. "Which titled female?"

"That we don't know," Julian revealed. "But it is a mystery we must solve if Sam is to be wed. We don't want to mistakenly marry her to a close relative."

"No. What a dreadful thought," Charlotte concurred, her brows lowering to a contemplative frown. "But how are you going to find out who she is? There won't be any church records of a birth or christening."

"I have a plan, which I will explain to you now . . . if you have a moment. I'll walk with you for a block or two while your carriage follows."

"But Julian, what about *me?*" Sam demanded petulantly.

Julian stood up and stared down at her with a thoughtful frown denting his noble brow. "You seem to have recovered with astonishing rapidity, Sam. Take a drink of water and bathe your face, and I'm sure you'll be as good as new."

"No, that's not what I mean! What about telling *me* your plan!"

"That is out of the question. As I told you before, the less you know, the better. I don't want you involved."

Sam sat up again and pounded her fists into the sofa cushions. "Julian, I'm not a child! When will you see that?"

Julian eyed his charge dubiously, then left, saying, "See you at dinner, brat."

Outside, a cool dusk was settling over the city as Julian drew Charlotte's arm in his and strolled down the walkway in the direction of the Batsfords' town house. Because Charlotte's lady's companion was in the carriage that kept pace with them on the road, it was all quite properly done.

"What do you make of it, Charlotte?" Julian asked, thoughtfully gazing at the smoky sunset.

"You mean Sam's bogus fainting spell or the fact that her mother is still alive and a titled lady of the *ton?*"

Julian squeezed her arm affectionately. "So you and I are in agreement about the fainting episode? The first one was genuine, I'm sure, but the second was an obvious sham."

"Sam is rather transparent, Julian . . . and in more ways that one," Charlotte replied.

"What do you mean?" Julian looked down at Charlotte's upturned face.

"Don't tell me you don't know?"

"Don't know what?" he returned, puzzled.

"The girl's in love with you, Julian!"

"What girl?"

Charlotte chuckled. "Can you really be so blind? You're a man of superior intellect, yet you can't see what's in front of your nose. *Samantha* is in love with you."

Julian stopped in his tracks, stunned.

Charlotte laughed again, amused by his dumbfounded expression. "Well, why do you suppose she staged that counterfeit swoon?"

"I . . . I . . ." Julian stuttered.

"So you'd have to carry her into the house, of course. It was a way of getting into your arms. As well, it interrupted our conversation on the road. She's jealous of me, you know. I've been aware of her jealousy since we met last night."

"Good *God,*" was all Julian could say at first, his mind trying to assimilate the facts and make sense of them.

"You see her as a child—and her isolated upbringing and lack of experience makes her little more than that in worldly matters—but she thinks very differently about you. She's trying to make you see her in a different light."

Julian was silent. He agreed with Charlotte that Sam was little more than a child and hardly his type of female, anyway. And even if he did feel some fondness for the chit that went beyond brotherly affection—which, of course, he didn't—he was as good as betrothed to Charlotte. And Charlotte was perfect for him in every way. Sam's infatuation for him—for it could be nothing more than that—would have to be ignored till it died a natural death.

"Be careful, Julian."

Julian looked sharply into Charlotte's face. "What do you mean by that?"

"If you don't want to marry your young ward, you had better be on the alert constantly. She'll try every trick in the book."

Julian laughed. "She doesn't know any tricks! She's an innocent."

"Tricks of an innocent are the most lethal of all," Charlotte warned him. "And she's clever, too."

"You make her sound like Delilah," Julian objected, smiling.

"I don't blame her, you know," Charlotte confessed ruefully. "How could she help but fall in love with you when the two of you have spent so much time together? Any woman would."

Julian was well aware that what Charlotte had just said was extremely flattering and tantamount to a declaration of love. And it would be entirely appropriate at this tender moment to declare his own affection and ask her formally for her hand in marriage. But after an uncomfortable internal struggle, Julian found he could not.

Instead he allowed a short silence to pass, then he returned to the original subject. "Would you like to hear my plan?"

Revealing no outward signs of having been gently rebuffed, seemingly as composed as ever, Charlotte said, "Of course. What is it?"

"It's very simple. I intend to talk to Sinclair Wallingsford, Lord Humphries."

Charlotte immediately understood. "Of course," she said decidedly. "That's exactly what you should do. No one knows more inside information and gossip about the *ton*, and has such a retentive memory, as Lord Humphries. There is so much scandal that occurs and most is forgotten over time . . . except for the truly infamous situations. But Sinclair, old hypocrite that he is, forgets noth-

ing. It takes him a little longer now to remember—
he might even need a few days to ruminate on a
given subject—but he will always remember eventually."

"That's what I'm counting on."

"You are depending on him to know which titled
ladies were with child nineteen years ago, I gather?
Particularly those pregnancies that were kept secret
for one reason or another."

Julian smiled fondly at his companion. "Exactly.
Charlotte, you are a sharp one."

She inclined her head at the compliment and
smiled. "In that way we are well matched."

Here again seemed a perfect opportunity to bring
up matrimony. But for some reason, Julian could
not. Just thinking about it made beads of sweat
collect on his brow.

"Do you go to Humphries's house now?" Charlotte presently inquired.

"Yes," Julian answered promptly, glad for another reprieve. "His house is just another three streets
away. I hope he's home. The sooner I conclude this
business concerning Sam's parentage, the sooner I
can attend to my own concerns."

Julian had been more or less thinking out loud,
but Charlotte caught his eye. Her expression
seemed to imply that she took his comment to
mean that he was postponing his declaration to her
until after Sam's mother was found. And—being
the reasonable person she was—that she accepted
this postponement with equanimity. Come to think
of it, putting off his declaration for such a very
reasonable reason suited Julian just fine. Yes, it
made perfect sense to wait.

Soon Julian was handing Charlotte into her carriage and waving good-bye. Moments later, he was

entering Sinclair Wallingsford's elegant town house.

An hour later, he was headed home no more enlightened than before. Humphries was going on eighty and, as Charlotte had implied, he was finally starting to forget. But he told Julian he would think on the matter and get back to him when he remembered something that would be helpful. Julian wasn't worried that Humphries would repeat any of Julian's explanations about Sam's predicament; the old sinner had not become privy to so many secrets without having learned to keep silent when he promised.

Besides, Humphries was in awe of Julian and would never dare cross him. But now Julian could do nothing further about the situation than read through Clorinda Darlington's diary to look for additional clues and wait for Humphries to remember.

Walking home in the cool of the evening, Julian had time to think about what Charlotte had told him about Sam being in love with him. The revelation, which he had no choice but to believe, cast Sam's recent behavior in a clarifying light. It seemed she was trying through various machinations to incite his jealousy and make him see her as a desirable woman and not a mere little sister and pupil.

Despite his good intentions to discourage Sam's infatuation with him, Julian couldn't help smiling as he wondered what she'd do next to catch his attention. . . .

Much to the joint chagrin of Jean-Luc and Ninian, it was the third day in a row that Sam had agreed to walk Madison in Hyde Park with Nathan

Ford . . . and Julian hadn't made a single objection. In fact Julian had made himself quite scarce over the past three days, and his manners were cool and remote. As she felt she'd made some progress in making him jealous at first, Sam was discouraged by this sudden turnabout.

"Don't you think so, Sam?"

Sam shook free of her galling thoughts and observed both Nathan and Clara watching her expectantly. She'd apparently been asked a question she hadn't heard, and she didn't have a clue what to answer. So she made an educated guess.

"Yes, it is a lovely day, isn't it?"

Sam was startled when both Clara and Nathan laughed out loud. Their mirth was so boisterous several people stared. Even Madison, sniffing through the grass at the end of the leading string Nathan held on to, turned and barked, adding to the commotion.

Sam couldn't help but smile. "What's so funny? I've a feeling the joke's on me."

Clara's eyes were becomingly brimmed with happy tears, and she held both hands over her mouth to try to contain the giggles that continued to spill out. "You've told us it's a lovely day three times now, miss," Clara told her, talking through her fingers.

Grinning from ear to ear, Nathan added, "Your head's in the clouds, Sam. If Clara hadn't come along with you on this walk, I'd be as lonely as a polecat."

"I'm sorry," Sam apologized sheepishly. "I haven't been very good company, have I?"

"He's had to talk to me, miss," Clara said. "And he's made me talk about myself, if you can believe it. After two days of nonstop gabbing, I've bored the poor man nearly to death."

"You've done nothing of the sort," Nathan objected, smiling down at the pretty servant girl. "The stories you tell about your brothers and sisters sound very similar to the antics of my own family. And your father sounds like the very same sort of autocrat as my own father. Pa ruled the roost with an iron fist."

"Only my father is a butler and yours was a gentleman farmer. In short, *your* family is rich and important and *mine* is of the servant class," Clara reminded him, cheerfully unembarrassed.

"My family wasn't always rich," Nathan told her.

"Only the past three generations," she retorted.

"What has money got to do with anything?"

"In England, it has everything to do with *everything.*"

"England isn't the most perfect place in the world, you know. Not everything they do here is sacrosanct," Nathan said dryly.

"Don't let my father hear you talk that way," Clara admonished him with a laugh. "He considers England the only really civilized country in the world. He refers to you as the 'rough colonial.' And since Madison has chewed the tassels off two pillows in the library and tracked stable muck on the kitchen floor time and time again, he doesn't have a very good opinion of *him,* either."

Listening to the surprisingly unrestrained and lively banter between Nathan and Clara, Sam realized that her absentmindedness and lack of conversation had not been a bad thing. Even now, the two of them were chattering away as if she weren't even there. This could mean only one thing; they were smitten with each other!

Sam's romantic nature made her instantly seize onto the idea that she would promote a match between Nathan and Clara . . . and turn it to her own advantage as well! She couldn't wait to get Clara alone to tell her her plans.

Later that night, while Clara helped her change into an evening gown to wear to the opera, Sam broached the subject.

"Clara, what do you think of Nathan Ford?"

Clara had been straightening the hem of Sam's blond satin gown, trimmed with gold, and when she stood up her face was flushed. "What do you mean, miss?" she mumbled, averting her eyes.

"I mean . . . do you like him?"

Clara's brown eyes were serious as she looked over Sam's shoulder in the mirror. "Do you mean as your suitor, miss? Are you asking my opinion of who you should marry?"

"Clara!" Sam admonished. "You know I intend to marry Julian."

Clara bit her lip. "I was wondering if maybe you'd changed your mind, seeing as how—"

"Seeing as how Julian is squiring Charlotte Batsford around and everyone expects him to marry her?" Sam finished for her.

Clara shrugged and gave her a pained look. "It doesn't look good, miss. And I don't think lowering the décolletage on that gown or pinning your curls into a sophisticated knot is going to make a jot of difference to His Lordship."

Sam glanced down at the pale mounds of her small breasts peeking above the gilded ruching of her gown. She'd never felt so naked. She blushed, but retorted, "It certainly can't hurt."

Clara shook her head and moved to the dressing table and opened Sam's jewelry box. Her voice was low and considered as she said, "Maybe you *should* give one of your suitors a chance to win your heart. And of the three you've been teasing His Lordship with, if you're asking me who I like the best . . . well, I'd have to say Mr. Ford. By far . . . Mr. Ford."

"You've certainly enjoyed his company on our walks," Sam pointed out, turning and moving to the end of the bed to watch Clara pick through the jewelry for the perfect accessories for her gown.

Clara turned, her expression guilt-stricken. "I know I've been remiss in my conduct, miss. I know I've been too chatty and free with Mr. Ford, but his manners are so friendly and easy. He's been very kind and seemed so interested in what I thought, what I liked, what I felt, even though I'm just a servant girl. Truth to tell, it was very hard not to spill out my heart like I did!"

Sam moved forward and gently took hold of Clara's shoulders. "Don't be a goose, Clara!" she said. "I'm not scolding you. I understand completely why you enjoyed talking with Nathan. I'm quite sure he enjoyed your company equally as much. In fact, I think he's in a fair way to falling in love with you."

Clara dropped the pearl pendant earrings she was holding and pressed her clasped hands against her chest. "Miss! What are you saying? Mr. Ford's a fine gentleman, and I'm just a lowly lady's maid!"

"Mr. Ford thinks nothing of such differences, which is precisely why I like him so much."

"He likes *you,* miss. He'd never prefer me over you. That's why he keeps coming round . . . to see you!"

"My guess is Mr. Ford doesn't exactly know his

mind—or heart—yet. But if the three of us contin-ue to do things together, it won't be long before he does. And if Julian thinks I prefer Nathan, he'll be mad with jealousy. I know it bothers him to think I might be whisked off to Virginia, half a world away."

Clara shook her head and looked worried. "I don't know, miss. A lot of people's feelings are involved here. I hope nothing goes awry."

Sam pulled Clara into her arms and gave her a hug. "Don't worry. I won't let anyone hurt you, Clara."

"I was worried about *you,* miss," Clara mumbled into Sam's gauzy sleeve.

"You needn't worry about me," Sam said with a confident smile. "I can take care of myself. And since there's still a few minutes before we leave for the opera, I'm going to put them to good use. I'm going to the library, Clara."

Clara blinked. "The library, miss? Whatever for?"

"To do some reading," she replied breezily, walk-ing quickly out of the room. *But not just any reading,* Sam added to herself as she descended the stairs. Julian had an extensive library. Surely he had some books that would explain the mysteries of human sexuality to her. She was tired of wondering exactly how men and women made love and ba-bies. Only a child would be so completely naive on the subject, and she was *not a child!*

"Where is she?" Julian glanced for the third time at his pocket watch and scowled up the stairs. "We've been waiting fifteen minutes."

"This is the first time Sam has ever been to the

opera," Priss said, glancing at Nan for corroboration. "I daresay she wants to look her best and is
simply taking longer than usual at her toilette."

"Yes, I'm sure you're right, Priss," Nan agreed.

Julian turned to Hedley. "Fetch Clara," he ordered.

Hedley bowed and made a barely perceptible
gesture to a nearby footman, who immediately
climbed the stairs and headed down the hall toward
Sam's room. In less than a minute, Clara was
curtsying before Julian.

"Yes, my lord?"

"What's taking Samantha so long to get ready?"

Clara's large brown eyes widened. "She was
ready a half hour ago, my lord."

"Then where is she?" Julian tried not to sound as
irritable as he felt. He wasn't usually such a stickler
about promptness, but lately he'd been in a perpet-
ually restless and tetchy mood . . . for no known
reason. Anything and everything seemed to set him
off. Perhaps it was as well that he'd been avoiding
Sam.

"In the library, my lord."

"In the library?"

"Shall I fetch her, my lord?"

"No," he said shortly, sweeping past the servant
girl and down the hall to the library. He opened the
door and found Sam sitting in a chair and, by the
light of a candelabra, reading a book. Several other
books were strewn at her feet. She was so absorbed
in whatever she was reading that she did not even
notice his intrusion.

She was a fetching sight, her pale curls pulled
into a sleek knot that showed off her delicate
features and the slim, elegant lines of her neck. The

blond satin gown she wore was a perfect color for her complexion, but he also noticed that the décolletage was rather daring. There was more than a glimpse to be had of her small, round breasts. And the fact that she was leaning forward did not help the matter. He could almost imagine that a nipple was about to make an appearance. . . .

"Oh!" Sam startled when she saw Julian at the door and leaped to her feet, causing the book she'd been reading to plunge to the floor. It landed in a heap of bent pages.

"That's certainly no way to treat fine literature, brat," Julian scolded, stepping forward and bending to retrieve the abused volume. But Sam bounded forward just as quickly, and she reached for the book at the same moment Julian did. Their hands grazed, their gazes locked. She held on, and so did he.

His gaze strayed to her décolletage. At such close range and at such an angle, he no longer had to imagine the appearance of a nipple; both of them were in full view. Feeling an instant warming in his loins, he hastily released the book and stood up, but not before he noticed a picture on one of the bent pages. It was a carefully detailed diagram of male genitalia, complete with arrows and labeling!

"What the *devil* are you reading?"

Sam held the book behind her and backed away, her eyes wide and frightened. "N-nothing, Julian," she stuttered.

"Nothing, my eye," he growled, bending to pick up several books from the floor. His eyebrows drew together in a frown as he read the titles out loud. *"The Fundamentals of Marital Coupling! A Guide for Training a Modest but Dutiful Wife! The Plea-*

sures of the Flesh, by Dr. Donald *Firmrod* . . . ! Good God, Sam, why are you reading this rubbish?" He stared at her, aghast.

She jutted out her chin. "Why do you call it rubbish? They are books I found right here in your library, Julian . . . although they *were* tucked away on the top shelf and I had to climb a ladder to reach them. But they were all written by scholarly gentleman who dealt with the subject scientifically." He watched a delicate blush bloom on her cheeks as her lashes lowered and she stared at the floor. "Well, perhaps Dr. Firmrod wasn't exactly scientific. His book had more pictures than anything else."

"I can well imagine," Julian muttered, barely able to keep his anger in check. "And what of the book you hold behind your back? Does it have mostly pictures, too?"

She licked her lips nervously, still looking at the floor. "Well . . . er . . . yes, it *is* mostly pictures."

"What is it titled, Sam?" he asked her with forced calmness.

One daintily slippered foot peeked out from under her gown and she slid her toe nervously over the carpet. "Er . . . it is called *The Anatomy of Man.*"

He nodded curtly. "I see. And did it never occur to you, Sam, that it is not appropriate for a young female to be reading about such subjects?"

Sam's tawny brows drew together and she lifted her head to meet his disapproving gaze with defiance. "How else was I to find out what I need to know?"

He controlled himself with an effort. "What makes you think you *need* to know about such things?"

"I assume I will be engaging in sexual activities

once I'm married, Julian. Shouldn't I know what to expect?"

"Good God, Sam," Julian expostulated, running a distracted hand through his hair. "It is for your husband to explain such things to you. Before marriage there's no earthly reason why you shouldn't remain completely—" He paused, searching for the right word.

"Ignorant?" she offered.

"Innocent," he returned firmly. "Men like their brides to be as ignorant . . . er . . . as *innocent* as possible."

"But that doesn't seem to keep them from running to their mistresses soon after the ceremony," Sam mumbled in a low voice, turning her eyes back to the floor.

Julian stepped forward and grabbed her arms, compelling her to look at him. He was beginning to feel more alarm than anger. "Who have you been talking to? What do you know of mistresses?"

Her blue eyes flashed. "My mother was one, wasn't she?"

She had a point. Julian didn't know what to think, how to feel. With Sam's background, it seemed almost ludicrous to imagine he could keep her as innocent of the world as other girls her age. But, as long as a young female was well chaperoned, a guardian could perhaps feel that there was a certain safety in ignorance. But Sam was not like most young females—in oh-so-many ways!

"Don't be angry with me, Julian," she said, suddenly contrite and pleading. She lifted a hand and stroked his lapel. "You know my nature. I can't help being curious. I want to know these things so I can be a good wife."

"As I said, your husband will explain everything

to you once you are married," he said with a weary sigh and finding himself, irrelevantly, admiring Sam's petal-shaped earlobes.

"But what if he's not a patient man . . . like you, Julian?" she said with a pout. "He might not like to explain and demonstrate . . . and such."

Any man would be thrilled with the opportunity to teach you the joys of lovemaking, Sam, Julian thought to himself, but said nothing. Suddenly he was imagining himself actually nibbling on those petal-shaped earlobes of hers. . . .

Luckily Sam spoke again, breaking his ill-directed concentration. "I think it best that I enter into marriage at least a *little* informed," she continued to argue with a tiny furrow between her brows. "Amanda isn't around to talk to, and as my aunts have never been married, I didn't think they'd be a good source of information. I felt my only recourse was to find out what I need to know from books."

Julian wondered why he was still holding on to Sam's arms, or why he'd even grabbed hold of her in the first place. He'd been angry, but now his anger seemed all but dissipated . . . or distracted. But there was a tension in the air that was still palpable. If it wasn't anger, what was it? His sudden fascination with her earlobes might lend a clue, but he really didn't want to overanalyze an idle thought and turn it into something it wasn't.

"I hope your curiosity has been satisfied," he murmured at last, hoping to bring an end to such an uncomfortable interview. "But I do not want you reading any more books about"—he swallowed against a suddenly dry throat—"sexual matters, Sam. Do you understand?"

She looked troubled and dissatisfied. "To be honest, I don't really care if I can't read any more of those stupid books. They left me with even more questions than I began with! I now understand the mechanics of the sexual act, but I'm sure there must be much more to lovemaking than what goes where!"

Julian's hands tightened on Sam's arms. "Sam—"

"For example, does one do the sexual act with one's clothes on, or without?" she asked earnestly.

"Sam, I don't think you should conjecture about—" Julian rasped.

"Does the man kiss the woman only on the lips, or does he kiss her other places, too? Is it considered proper for the woman to return the man's caresses . . . if he does, indeed, caress her? Or does he just perform the act and have done with it? Is the woman supposed to enjoy it? Do you think I shall have to hide my emotions from my husband, Julian? Because you know very well that I'm not the type of person that could engage in such an intimate activity with a man I was in love with and *not* enjoy it!"

Julian abruptly let go of Sam's arms and took a step back. An image of Sam, radiantly aroused and naked, had burst into his mind like a fireworks explosion. "I'm not the person to whom you should address these questions, Sam," he said in a beleaguered tone.

"But you've been my teacher in everything else, Julian," she protested. "Why not in this as well?"

"Now is not a good time to talk about this subject, Samantha," Julian said, feeling more desperate by the moment. "I've asked the Batsfords to sit in our box and have arranged to meet them at the theater. It would be most rude to keep Charlotte and her parents waiting."

Steeling himself against her hurt and bewildered expression, he turned to go, then turned back. "There's a hair loose . . . here," he muttered in a gentler tone, touching a tendril of hair that had fallen over her ear. "Go upstairs and tidy yourself, and I'll meet you in the hall in no more than five minutes. Do you understand?"

Then, without waiting for an answer, Julian resolutely left the room.

Five minutes later, with her nose in the air, Sam descended the stairs to the entry hall. After Julian had dismissed her and her questions as if she were a child—simply because he was afraid of keeping Charlotte waiting—Sam had been decidedly miffed. But her show of dignified affront was wasted. Julian wasn't watching her. When she reached the bottom of the stairs, she discovered him occupied in looking through a pile of calling cards and invitations that had been left in the course of the day.

"You look . . . er . . . lovely, Samantha," Nan said, glancing nervously at Sam's low décolletage. "But don't you think you ought to wear a little more lace just . . . er . . . *there?*" She pointed gingerly at Sam's chest.

"No, Aunt Nan, I don't," Sam said, her chin set defiantly, her gaze fixed intently on Julian . . . who continued to ignore her.

"It's no more than most of the girls show," Priss admitted, "but I'm surprised Julian approved it. Is it the same dress you were wearing when he found you in the library?"

"Of course it is," Sam replied, still staring at Julian's broad back in his elegant black evening jacket. He seemed totally absorbed in one particular unfolded sheet of parchment paper. He turned slightly and she noticed that his brows were lowered forbiddingly.

"Well, then, if Julian approves, I'll say nothing more about it," Nan said, but she didn't sound convinced.

Hedley came forward with Sam's matching satin cape, trimmed with ermine, but she felt a perverse urge to force Julian to comment on her dress before she left the house. He hadn't said a word about it in the library.

"Julian," Sam said in an imperative tone.

He lifted his head, his pale hair glinting in the light from the chandelier overhead. His eyes were intensely blue, but unfocused, as if his thoughts were elsewhere on some troubling point.

"What?" he said impatiently.

Sam's chin went higher and she puffed out her chest a little. "My gown," she said. "My aunts think it might be too provocative. What do you think?"

Julian blinked several times, then his eyes focused. Sam could swear she felt his gaze like a caressing hand as it trailed her person from top to bottom. A thrilling hope washed through her like a warm, spring rain. He had been too angry with her in the library to notice, but now he would see, now he would admit she was no child. . . .

"Well?" she prompted expectantly.

Julian's brow lifted sardonically. "As I am but a partial family friend—more of an uncle, as it were—I am perhaps a poor judge."

"A poor judge?" Nan said with a snort of disbelief. "You are *the* judge of taste and fashion in London."

Julian shrugged. "Although the décolletage is

low, if she minds her posture, she will safe enough in it. The gown is, indeed, beautiful. And Samantha is beautiful in it. She will have everyone staring at her."

Sam's heart soared.

"But I think, on the whole, the look is too sophisticated for her. To me she looks like a mere girl playing dress-up in her mother's clothes."

Sam's heart dropped like a rock.

In the carriage, on the way to the opera house, Julian looked determinedly out the window. Sam was sitting across from him, next to Priss, and it would be impossible not to notice that he'd hurt her feelings with his comment about the gown. He'd meant to hurt her . . . a little. He wanted her angry at him so she'd avoid him. He also wanted her to turn to the other men who would shower her with compliments tonight and hang about her like bees about the hive.

The conversation with her in the library had been taxing, and he did not want her to bring up the subject of sex again, particularly in a public place. At present he had another more pressing problem to deal with . . . a problem of monumental importance and urgency that made Sam's troublesome curiosity about sex, and her childish crush on him, seem a mere trifle in comparison.

Julian surreptitiously stuck his finger in the inside pocket of his jacket, touching the sharp edge of the paper he'd folded and slipped away. He needed reminding that the note had indeed come to the house. That it wasn't all a bad dream. It was hard to believe, but someone was threatening him. *Threatening Sam.* He remembered the few words that had been printed in a small hand on a single sheet of parchment.

Don't ask questions. Some secrets are best kept. I'm warning you. . . .

Chapter 6

❦❦❦

"The Royal Opera House at Covent Garden is the most beautiful theater in England, Samantha," said Priss, peering out the window as they drove at a snail's pace down Bow Street. It seemed that every carriage in town was headed in the same direction as they were. "You're going to be quite astonished when you see it. Isn't she, Julian?"

Sam glanced at Julian to see him turn slowly from his own vigil at the window on the opposite side of the carriage. In the light of the carriage lantern, he appeared very sober. Obviously he was not in a chatty mood, but she wasn't sure she wanted him to talk if he was going to be patronizing and hurtful and refer to her again as a "child." The memory of his comment about her looking as if she were playing "dress-up in her mother's clothes" still stung.

"Yes, the original theater was destroyed by fire in 1808, then rebuilt in 1809," Julian explained in the instructional tone he frequently used with Sam. But there was a weary edge to his voice and a bleak look in his eyes, as if he'd been reluctantly recalled to his sense of duty in preparing Sam for this latest foray into London society.

106

As well, he was probably still angry with her for attempting to satisfy her curiosity by reading books that were not appropriate for an "innocent" young girl's education. Sam still thought "ignorant" was a better term to describe what most men wanted in their brides.

"The new building was designed by Robert Smirke, who modeled it on the Temple of Minerva at Athens," he continued. "The facade boasts a Greek Doric portico and an ornamental frieze of literary figures by English sculptor John Flayman. But more importantly, along with the King Theatre, it is attended frequently by many luminaries of the *ton*. It's a good place to be seen. Even the Prince Regent has a box there."

"Did you hear that, Samantha?" Nan exclaimed bracingly, leaning over and giving Sam's hand a vigorously friendly pat. "Prinny has a box there!"

"I hear a box costs two thousand pounds per subscription," Priss interjected.

"Samantha, just yesterday you were saying that you hadn't yet seen the Prince Regent," Nan went on, at the same time throwing her sister an admonishing look for interrupting with such an unimportant detail. "Well, tonight you may!"

Sam realized then that her hurt feelings over Julian's comment were showing. She detested the very idea of appearing dispirited and sulky, so she stiffened her spine and rallied her spirits. She wasn't about to be defeated by a few discouraging words. Besides, she'd never been to the theater, and it was an event she'd looked forward to for a long time. She wouldn't let Julian spoil it for her. Moreover, the evening was still young, and she'd have plenty of opportunity to show him that she was much more than a green girl playing dress-up.

Tossing back her head and forcing a brilliant smile, she announced, "I'd like to see the Prince, but it doesn't matter if I don't. I'm very excited about seeing Genevieve DuBois perform in *Cleopatra, Queen of the Nile.* Jean-Luc tells me she's the shining star of London."

"I would have preferred to have introduced you to the theater by attending a Mozart opera or something similar," Julian answered coolly. "But it is my understanding that Madame DuBois was born to play the role of Cleopatra. Even though the music isn't as good as it should be, Madame DuBois's performance is said to be enthralling."

It was warm praise for the actress, but delivered in a distracted fashion. Clearly Julian had something on his mind, and Sam earnestly wished to know about it. She hoped he wasn't planning to make his courtship of Charlotte official and ask her to marry him that very night! Sam bit her lip, worried and feeling quite desperate that she might not have the time she needed to make her dreams come true.

When the carriage finally stopped at the theater entrance, and Julian escorted her inside, Sam's worries were forgotten for a while in the wonder of her surroundings. The outside facade of the building was magnificent, so she should have been prepared for the grandness and elegance of the vestibule and the staircase, which ascended between two rows of Ionic columns. Suspended between each of the columns was a beautiful Grecian lamp, and at the head of the staircase was a statue of Shakespeare on a pedestal of yellow marble. The play had not even begun and Sam was already enthralled!

Nodding and smiling at acquaintances, they walked down the lobby, which was divided with arched recesses filled with paintings from various scenes of Shakespeare. Finally they entered a box and sat down in comfortable seats covered with light blue cloth.

Sam hurriedly settled herself, then eagerly lifted her eyes and stared out over the five tiers of boxes and the horseshoe-shaped gallery, all filled to bursting with people. She was practically blinded by the shine and glitter of the chandeliers hanging from the ceiling and the diamonds and other jewels winking on the hands and necks of London's most fashionable females. Again Sam wondered if her mother was in the audience, but she quickly dismissed the painful thought and looked eagerly toward the large stage and crimson curtain.

"I think I'm going to like this," she murmured to Prissy, who was sitting on one side of her, with Nan on the other. Yes, she knew she was going to like it despite the irritating fact that Julian was standing outside the box in the lobby, waiting for the Batsfords.

"You ought to be enjoying yourself," Priss whispered behind her fan. "You've caught the eye of everyone in the house!"

"What?" Sam turned startled eyes to the semicircular tiers and was astonished to discover that she was indeed the object of many pairs of eyes. People were even using their opera glasses to stare at her. She felt herself blushing and wished her décolletage were not quite so low.

"You must expect a great many visitors at intermission," Nan warned her. "When a young man comes along that you want to sit beside you, just nudge me gently with your elbow, and I'll move to the chair on the other side of Priss . . . as if I wished to speak to her particularly, you know."

With this strategy settled between them, the orchestra finally quit tuning their instruments and began to play in earnest, a hush came over the audience, and the curtain lifted. Sam turned and glanced at the empty seats behind her. The opera was beginning and still Julian waited in the hall for Charlotte Batsford and her parents. How irritating!

But the minute Sam got her first glimpse of Genevieve DuBois lounging on a barge in the middle of the stage, with slaves rowing her down the wooden, blue-painted and curlicued waves of the Nile, she forgot about everything else.

Madame DuBois was wearing a jet-black wig and her large, eloquent eyes were lined with kohl. She was dressed in an ankle-length toga-style white gown of nearly transparent material, her bared arms were ornamented with golden snake bracelets, and her brow was crowned with a cobra coronet. She was stunningly beautiful and, as became increasingly obvious as the opera progressed, extremely talented. She had a fine voice, but the expressions on her face and the way her entire body vibrated with emotion were what made her truly the "star."

When the first intermission came, Sam was so wrapped up in the play, she had a hard time returning to reality. She felt dazed and was genuinely surprised to find that an hour had passed and Charlotte Batsford and her parents had joined them in the box without her being at all aware of their arrival. She bid them good evening and made polite chitchat, all the while wishing she were the one seated by Julian and not Charlotte. But then several young men entered the box to pay their respects, and Sam saw her opportunity to show Julian that she was not a child.

She flirted outrageously. She snapped open her fan and touched the edge of it to the curve of her cheek. She laughed and smiled, and she accepted compliments with a demure lowering of her lashes. Her admirers seemed to enjoy this new coquettish side of her, but she frequently felt they glanced too often at the low cut of her gown. Such ogling made Sam uncomfortable, but she reasoned that if Julian noticed that other men stared at her breasts, maybe he would finally acknowledge that she actually had some!

Whenever she surreptitiously turned to observe Julian's reaction to her popularity, he was usually immersed in serious conversation with Charlotte. Once or twice she caught him looking at her, but he wasn't glowering like a jealous man. In fact, his expression was carefully neutral, giving her no clue about what he was thinking or feeling. It was very frustrating.

As the first intermission bell chimed, signaling that the play was about to begin again, the men filed out till the only one left was Jean-Luc, who had apparently been hovering in the background. He stepped forward and bowed low, kissing her hand.

"Jean-Luc!" Sam exclaimed delightedly. "I didn't see you there!" She really was glad to see him, but since she was still hoping to stir Julian's jealousy, she injected her voice with extra warmth and enthusiasm. "My goodness, why didn't you come and say hello to me before now? The play is about to start."

Jean-Luc straightened and smiled. There was a conscious, rather amused twinkle in his dark eyes, as if he actually knew what she was up to, that he knew she was trying to make Julian jealous. But that was impossible . . . wasn't it?

"It is not my style to force my way through a throng of moonstruck men, Miss Darlington," he informed her wryly. "There is always the possibility of scuffing my shoes or mussing my cravat in the crush."

She chuckled appreciatively.

"But I cannot blame them for crowding about you," he continued suavely. "Miss Darlington, you are the loveliest woman in the house, your beauty as rare and brilliant as the finest diamond."

Sam glowed. She hoped Jean-Luc had been speaking loudly enough for Julian to hear him above Mrs. Batsford's continual chatter to her long-suffering husband. "So you like my gown? You don't think it's too sophisticated for me, do you?"

"It was made for you. It is perfect in every way," he assured her.

Satisfied, Sam smiled and slid a look toward Julian. It was still impossible to tell if he was paying any attention to their conversation. He certainly didn't appear to be listening to them or watching them. "Thank you, Mr. Bouvier."

"I know the play is going to start soon, but I do wish to visit with you, Miss Darlington. Perhaps your aunt—" He nodded at Nan. "Good evening, madam."

"Good evening," Nan replied with a smile.

"Perhaps your aunt," he continued, "will allow me to take the seat beside you. We can watch the next act together . . . if that's all right with you?"

"Of course it's all right," Sam replied, gently nudging Nan with her elbow . . . their agreed-upon signal to make room for a favored suitor. She had planned to offer the seat to Nathan so she could talk to him about Clara, but so far she hadn't seen him or Ninian at all that evening.

"What do you think of Madame DuBois?" Jean-Luc began, once Nan had moved and he'd settled in his seat and politely greeted everyone in the box.

"I think she's wonderful," Sam replied warmly, then her brows drew together in a slight frown. "But I don't detect the slightest French accent."

Jean-Luc laughed. "You don't detect an accent because she isn't French."

"She isn't? But her name—"

"Is a stage name, concocted to lend her a little glamour. It is the usual practice."

"Well, she deserves a glamorous name," Sam said decidedly. "I think her extremely beautiful and vastly talented."

A murmur of excitement suddenly rumbled through the room and they turned to see what was causing the to-do.

"Speaking of beautiful and vastly talented women," Jean-Luc murmured.

Sam looked to where he was looking, at a tier just below theirs on the other side of the gallery. Settling herself in a box, seated all by herself except for a lady's companion in the back, was the most stunning and exotic woman Sam had ever seen. She had black hair swept high on her head, white skin, and large, luminous dark eyes. She had a voluptuous figure and apparently no qualms about showing it off. She was dressed in an extremely low-cut, red gown trimmed in black braid. Sam noticed with chagrin that the woman had a great deal more to display above her décolletage than *she* did.

"She's very beautiful, indeed," Sam said. "But isn't her gown rather . . . er . . . daring?"

Jean-Luc leaned close to Sam's ear and whispered, "She's displaying her wares, Miss Darlington."

"Her wares?" Sam repeated.

"She's a courtesan," Jean-Luc clarified. "A very famous and expensive one, I might add."

"Goodness," Sam said, instantly interested. She stared at the woman. Perhaps Julian's mistress was a similar type of female. "She must be very wealthy if she can afford to buy a subscription box at the Royal Opera House."

"Rather, her protector is very wealthy," Jean-Luc corrected.

Sam turned to look at Jean-Luc. "So her protector purchased the subscription for her?"

Jean-Luc shrugged. "Of course."

Sam sighed. "You probably think I'm being vulgar, Jean-Luc. I know I shouldn't be speaking about such things, but I must confess I'm rather curious about gentlemen's mistresses."

Jean-Luc raised a brow, obviously amused. "Are you, indeed? And while I realize I shouldn't be talking with you about such things, either, Miss Darlington, I wonder why you find the subject of mistresses so interesting?"

Sam shifted uncomfortably in her seat and glanced over her shoulder at Julian, this time hoping that he *wasn't* listening. "I know very little about the subject, of course, but it sometimes seems that gentlemen treat their mistresses better than they treat their wives."

Jean-Luc nodded judiciously. "That is often true. But you must remember, Miss Darlington, it is very rare that a mistress has a single protector for her entire life. Her luxuries are never taken for granted. She must constantly struggle to please, and she feels the constant anxiety of knowing she could be tossed over for someone prettier or younger at any moment. On the other hand, a wife is secure for the rest of her life."

"You mean financially secure?"

"Yes. What else?"

"It would be nice for a wife to be secure in her husband's *love,* rather than his *money,* for the rest of her life," Sam said wistfully.

"You are a romantic," Jean-Luc suggested with a smile.

"Is that bad?"

"No, *chère,*" he assured her. "It is rather refreshing."

"Oh, look, Jean-Luc. That woman is staring directly into our box! She is even using her opera glasses. Why in heaven's name would she be interested in us?"

"You are a new face, are you not?"

"I don't think she's looking at *me.* . . ."

"Hush, *chère,* the curtain is rising."

But Sam had one more question. "What is her name?"

"Her name is Isabelle . . . Something-or-other. I don't remember."

"And who is her wealthy protector?"

But Jean-Luc must not have heard her above the beginning strains of the orchestra, because he did not reply. Sam was about to repeat her question, but the curtain rose, and she was instantly caught up again in the story.

Julian was not having a good time. Despite Charlotte's soothing presence and her sensible conversation, he was restless, irritable, and distracted. Not even the mesmerizing performance by Gene-

vieve DuBois could keep his thoughts from returning to the threatening note he'd received that day.

All he could think about was the fact that for
Sam's safety and security he needed to discover
who her mother was without delay. Now it appeared that her safety and security were also jeop-
ardized by the search itself. But the people who
knew about Sam's illegitimacy were all people he
trusted. He had even felt quite confident that
Humphries could be counted on to keep mum.

So, who was the traitorous tattler? And why did
someone feel so desperate about secrecy that they
would resort to sinister notes? The fact that
someone—a woman, perhaps?—was threatened
by his search for Sam's mother made Julian think it
even more likely that Clorinda had been telling the
truth in her diary about Sam's mother being a titled
lady of the *ton.* Had she seen Sam about town and
recognized her as her child?

Or, worse still, perhaps the letter was warning
Julian that the truth could hurt Sam in some way.
And there was nothing in the world he wouldn't do
to protect her.

The baggage, he muttered to himself. Why the
devil had she worn that dress? It was tasteful, and
truly not immodest. But she looked damned alluring in it, and half the male population of London
had crowded into their box during intermission to
ogle her. He hated a crowded box. . . .

Besides, the men had behaved so foolishly, the
lot of them practically drooling, their eyes nearly
popping out of their skulls as they stared down at
her. And as she'd remained seated the entire time,
what a view they must have had of her tender
cleavage!

Why was she flirting so outrageously? Could it be to try to make him jealous? The silly girl . . . didn't she know he was above such nonsense?

He hoped to God she hadn't been so enthralled with her reading that evening that she was thinking of experimenting with sex. She knew better than that . . . didn't she? But Sam was always so unpredictable. From moment to moment it was impossible to know what she'd be up to next.

Then Isabelle had to pick tonight of all nights to attend the theater! She generally did not enjoy watching plays or opera—she'd had enough of it as a performer for several years—but she'd wheedled for a box, and Julian had complied. But tonight she quite brazenly stared into their box, possibly making Charlotte notice the lady's interest in them and coming to the unfortunate and accurate conclusion that she was being scrutinized by his mistress. But Charlotte was a sensible girl, so sensible she might not even object to Julian keeping a mistress once they were married. Or, rather, she would outwardly pretend that she didn't know he had a mistress and act like she didn't care.

On the other hand, if he were married to Sam, she would probably take up arms and shoot him if he dared to keep a mistress. . . .

Julian found himself smiling at the picture he'd conjured in his mind. But then his smile slackened and quickly fell away completely. Actually he had no real idea what Sam thought and what she was feeling these days. Was she really infatuated with him, as Charlotte suggested, and trying to make him jealous? Or was she pragmatically pursuing a husband?

His eyes narrowed as he observed Sam's confiding manner toward Jean-Luc Bouvier. Hopefully she wouldn't decide that *he* was her man. Julian couldn't hear what the fellow was saying, but it was bound to be empty flattery and nonsense. No, he felt sure that there was no real possibility of a marriage proposal from that quarter. It was the American who would carry the day, then carry Sam off to the States—damn'im! What a shame. . . . Amanda and Sam had just been reunited, and now they would soon be separated by a huge ocean. They would miss each other a great deal.

Julian frowned. Yes, a very great deal, indeed.

During the next intermission, along with another influx of gentlemen, Sam was surprised to see a lady entering Julian's box. She was a tiny woman of late middle age, dressed in a long-sleeved, buttoned-to-the-neck, pistachio-green gown that was fussily trimmed with too many ruffles and bows and satin rosettes . . . and she was leaning heavily on the arm of Ninian Wentworth. Judging by the pained look on Ninian's face, the woman could be none other than his formidable mama. Julian stood and greeted her.

"Lord Serling," she began, peering peevishly up at him with pale blue eyes that looked too large for her thin face. "I can imagine how surprised and delighted you are to see me. Indeed, with my delicate health I do not often venture out these days. And our box is fully two stairs up and clear round on the other side of the gallery. I am fagged to death from the walk, I can assure you."

"I am fully aware of the honor you pay us by walking so far, Lady Wentworth," Julian replied politely. "Pray, sit down."

While continuing to carry on flirtatious conversation with the men surrounding her, Sam kept her ears tuned in to Julian's conversation with Lady Wentworth. She was certainly a fascinating woman to watch and listen to. She must have been a great beauty once, but now her hair had faded from shining blond to a pale, flat yellow. Her complexion was sallow, her small features were pinched, there was a deep furrow between her brows and long frown lines on either side of her mouth. But Sam suspected that except for eating too little to keep even a hummingbird alive, Lady Wentworth's state of health suffered most from acute disagreeableness.

"I don't like the theater, do you, Lord Serling?"

Before Julian could reply, Lady Wentworth continued, "No, of course you don't! Who could? It is nothing but a lot of noise. And that woman is nothing but a trollop. Her dress is quite vulgar. Quite vulgar, indeed!"

"Mama," Ninian ventured, his face flushed, "she's wearing a costume. You wouldn't recognize her as Cleopatra if she were buttoned up like a Quaker."

"I've come to meet your ward, Lord Serling," Lady Wentworth announced imperiously, ignoring Ninian. "And as I'm much too frail to force my way through that throng of young men, would you be so obliging as to call her over here?"

"Certainly, madam," Julian replied, his mouth showing a betraying twitch of amusement that probably only Sam noticed. "I'll fetch her for you immediately."

When Julian came, parting the crowd of men as ably as Moses parted the Red Sea, Sam was ready.

There was a subdued look of glee in Julian's eyes, as if to say, *I'm delighted to have you finally meet the greatest drawback to marrying Ninian Wentworth.* But Sam met his gaze with a challenging twinkle. She was going to prove that she was more than capable of gaining Lady Wentworth's approval.

As Jean-Luc and the other gentlemen watched— indeed, everyone in the box was watching—Julian took Sam's hand and led her to the chair where Lady Wentworth sat like a queen on her throne. Sam had the almost hysterical urge to curtsy deeply before her as if she were being presented in court to real royalty. Ninian stood just behind her—as squeamishly pale as his delicate mama—looking anxious and apologetic.

"Lady Wentworth, may I introduce my ward, Miss Samantha Darlington," Julian said, then stepped back.

"How do you do, madam?" Sam said, curtsying demurely.

"I do exceedingly *ill,* young lady," Lady Wentworth replied irritably, waving a handkerchief that was so heavily drenched in lavender water it could choke a horse. "The building is cold and the air is stale . . . not fit to breathe!"

"Indeed, I couldn't agree more," Sam immediately replied, her tone dripping with sympathy. "I wouldn't breathe at all if I could help it. But I can't help it, you see. Even if I hold my breath for an instant, I immediately fall into a swoon!"

Lady Wentworth's brows lifted with surprise and approval. "Do you indeed? Like myself, you must have a delicate constitution." Then her brows lowered as she eyed Sam's décolletage. "But if you have a delicate constitution and are apt to swoon easily, you are probably prone to inflammations of the lung, as well. I shouldn't wear my neckline so low if I were you, Missy. You'll catch your death."

Sam touched her fingers to her throat and tried to look alarmed, then grateful, for Lady Wentworth's dire predictions and advice. "Lady Wentworth, I can't thank you enough for pointing out what I should have seen all along. I was only trying to be fashionable, you know, but you're quite right that I ought to bundle up better when it's cold. I *do* tend to catch sore throats."

Lady Wentworth "hmphed" with satisfaction, her narrow chest puffing out a little. "You're very welcome to my advice, Missy, and if you'd like some more, perhaps Ninian could bring you to the house for tea one day. I have several recipes for medicinal poultices for the throat."

"That would be very pleasant, madam," Sam lied, so sweet and convincing in her manner she even drew a smile from the old hypochondriac.

"Then I'll expect you Thursday at four," Lady Wentworth said with a decided nod of her head.

Sam was a little taken aback by the quick invitation, but she managed to answer, "That would be quite . . . er . . . lovely, Lady Wentworth."

Lady Wentworth nodded some more, as if smugly acknowledging that Sam's expectation of enjoyment at the future tea were perfectly understandable. "Now that I've met you and I've ascertained for myself that Ninian isn't chasing after an unsuitable female—"

"Mama!" Ninian objected, turning red again.

"Well, I don't know your family, my dear," Lady Wentworth explained to Sam with a sniff. "I heard something about a clergyman in Cumbria, but before you moved in with your cousin, Amanda Darlington, you might have been raised on a de-

serted island for all I know! I'm sure you understand my desire to meet the young woman my son
seems so enamored of."

"Mama!" Ninian repeated, increasingly mortified.

Striving to keep a straight face, Sam murmured,
"Of course, madam."

"But now that I've met you, I can see by your
lovely manners and delicate sensibilities that you
were raised in the very *best* of homes."

"Sam had the finest education a young woman
could have," Julian assured Lady Wentworth, stepping forward and smiling down at Sam with avuncular pride. "But, madam, it seems to me that
you're sitting in a draft! Shouldn't you either sit
over there by the Batsfords or remove to your own
comfortable box?"

Julian was obviously trying to hurry Lady Wentworth away and save Sam from either dissolving in
giggles or saying something outrageous that would
shock the snobby old harridan. Lady Wentworth
immediately responded.

"Is there a draft?" she cried in alarm, pulling her
shawl more closely about her shoulders. "Why, yes,
I believe there is! But I won't stay; nor do I wish to
return to my box and endure any more of this
ridiculous play. That woman—! So vulgar! Come
along, Ninian, give me your arm, and we'll leave
before the caterwauling starts again. Send someone
ahead to get the carriage. I want it waiting at the
steps. I won't stand in the treacherous night air and
catch my death, you understand. It's much too
dangerous for me! Good-bye, Lord Serling. Good-
bye, Miss Darlington. Charmed, I'm sure."

Then she was gone, and the resulting quiet was
punctuated by stifled titters of amusement among

the young men remaining in the box. "It was a good thing you convinced her to leave," Sam whispered to Julian with a smile. "One minute more, and I would have told her what I thought of her taste. How could she possibly call Genevieve DuBois's divine singing caterwauling? Or refer to such a beautiful woman as vulgar?"

"Lady Wentworth's opinion of Madame DuBois is the least of your troubles in that quarter, Sam," Julian informed her with a mischievous glint in his eyes. "If you marry Ninian, you are doomed to a future filled with medicinal poultices and endless quackish advice. After tea on Thursday she will doubtless offer to *leech* you."

Sam laughed out loud, and for a single shining moment, the reserve that Julian had built up between them in the last few days, and particularly in the last few hours, dissolved like sugar in hot tea. His smile was warm and genuine and full of . . . affection? But then the sparkle dimmed in his eyes, his mouth conformed to its usual grim lines, and he returned to his seat by Charlotte.

Sighing to herself, Sam returned to her own seat, endured the attentions of her admirers for another couple of minutes till the bell chimed to alert them to the impending start of the play, then she lost herself again in the tempestuous life of Cleopatra, queen of the Nile.

Chapter 7

❝**I** didn't see you at the theater last night," Sam said to Nathan as they stood together in the foyer waiting for Clara to show up with Madison on a leash. It was a beautiful, sunny day, and they were going for another walk in Hyde Park, with plans to return to the house in plenty of time to avoid the fashionable crowds that converged daily on the park between the hours of four and six.

Hedley had just passed through the hall, throwing Nathan a sneering, suspicious look. Instead of answering her question, Nathan said, "Why does Hedley dislike me so much? Is it because I'm American?"

Sam shrugged. "Hedley's a snob. He doesn't like anyone that's not English. He doesn't like Jean-Luc either." Sam paused, then admitted, "But, for some reason, he especially dislikes Americans."

"Well, it's danged annoying the way he's always glaring at me," Nathan complained.

Sam raised her brows inquiringly as she gave the apple-green ribbon, tied into a large bow under her chin, a straightening tug. "I'm surprised you care so much about Hedley's good or bad opinion of you. Is it because of Clara?"

Nathan's startled gaze darted to hers. "What do you mean?" he asked cautiously.

"You needn't play the dolt with me," she advised him with a friendly smile. "I mentioned a minute ago that I didn't see you at the opera. You didn't answer, but I think I know the answer. You didn't come because you felt there was no chance of seeing Clara there."

"What's Clara got to do with anything?" Nathan muttered, averting his eyes. "I didn't go last night because I don't like opera."

"I'm sure you would have overcome your dislike of opera if there had been a chance of seeing Clara."

Nathan opened his mouth, about to deny Sam's assertions once more, when Clara's musical voice could be heard at the back of the house, headed their way. She was talking to Madison, telling him in lilting, playful tones what a fun walk he was going to have, what a good pup he was, what a handsome boy, etcetera.

Nathan closed his mouth, licked his upper lip, and stared down the hall like a hungry dog waiting for someone to throw him a fat, juicy bone.

Sam laughed. "I hope you're not trying to fool yourself, Nathan, because you're not fooling me. Look at you! The sound of her voice sends chills down your spine, doesn't it? Your mouth is dry, your hands are clammy, and it feels like your heart's going to explode in your chest from joy. Believe me, I understand the sensations you're feeling at the moment. You can't wait to see her. Come on, Nathan, admit it."

Nathan shook his head, then turned to her with equal portions of guilt and excitement reflected in his eyes. "I never meant it to happen, Sam. I truly liked you . . . in the beginning. No, I mean I *still* like you, but— The thing is, the same things I like about you, I like in Clara, too. Only . . . well . . . *more*. And with Clara I . . . I . . ."

Sam laughed understandingly and supplied the words for him. "You've fallen in love with Clara. And who could blame you? She's a delightful girl. I love her myself and will miss her sorely when you take her away to Virginia with you."

Nathan's jaw went slack and his eyes widened. "I never said I was going to—"

Sam's eyes narrowed. "You aren't going to dally with her, are you, Nathan?" she scolded teasingly.

Nathan looked horrified. "Of course not! It's just that I don't know how she feels about me yet. Marriage is quite . . . well . . . And as for her father, he appears to hate me. And what's more—"

But Sam wasn't destined to find out "what's more." Clara and Madison had arrived, and Nathan was obliged to keep the rest of his reservations to himself. But Sam thought it should be obvious to any idiot by the way Clara smiled and her eyes lit up when they rested on Nathan that she was as madly in love with him as he was with her. However, since the gentleman needed confirmation from the lady herself, Sam was going to arrange for the timid lovers to have a little time alone together that afternoon.

Once they arrived at the park, the going was slow as the consciousness of their feelings made Nathan and Clara too shy and uncomfortable to talk. Sam couldn't have been more relieved and happy when Jean-Luc finally showed up with her poodle, Louie, on a leading string, the dog sniffing his way through a cluster of tall daffodils.

"Well, well, well," Jean-Luc called cheerfully. "What a delightful surprise! Imagine running into you three this afternoon."

"They didn't tell you when you picked up your dog that we'd already picked up Madison?" Nathan drawled.

"They did, of course," Jean-Luc admitted ingenuously. "But they never told me where you were going. How could they? I daresay you didn't tell them."

But Sam *had* told Jean-Luc where they'd be, and at precisely what time, the night before at the opera, when she'd thought up this matchmaking plot to get Nathan and Clara together. Delighted to be part of something secretive and romantic, Jean-Luc had readily agreed to be a fellow conspirator.

"And besides," Jean-Luc continued, unfazed by Nathan's suspicious scowl, "it seems hardly fair that Madison gets walked all the time, and Louie not at all."

"I had imagined that Louie had rather eat and sleep than take a little exercise," Nathan remarked sourly.

"He seems to have plenty of energy today," Clara observed as Louie finally lifted his nose off the ground, noticed Madison, and strained at his leash to get to his stablemate. The dogs obviously didn't feel the same competitive rancor the three men felt toward one another. Judging by their furiously wagging tails, Louie and Madison couldn't have been happier to see each other.

"It seems a shame that George isn't here, too," Sam said with an exaggerated sigh. Then her crestfallen expression gave way to one of sudden happiness. "I know! Why don't Jean-Luc and I go back to the house to fetch George? Nathan, you and Clara can wait here with the dogs till we get back."

"But . . . but, miss," Clara stuttered, her eyes wide, her expression nervous. "I can't let you go back to the house unchaperoned with Mr. Bouvier. Lord Serling would have my head . . . and my job. Besides, it wouldn't look proper, and I won't have people talking about you, miss."

"Oh, posh, Clara," said Sam, dismissing her concerns with an airy wave of her hand. "We'll only be gone a few minutes, and I don't care a fig for the opinion of people who can find something to gossip about in an innocent carriage ride in broad daylight."

"But His Lordship will—"

"I can handle His Lordship," Sam insisted, already turning to go. She glanced at Nathan, who hadn't said a word, then kept on going. His expression was a mixture of consternation and nervous rapture. He knew Sam had arranged this time for him to be alone with Clara so he could find out how she felt about him. While he might not approve of Sam going off with Jean-Luc, he was too happy about the prospect of spilling his heart's desire into his beloved's pretty ears to have the strength of character to object to Sam's scheme.

Jean-Luc's high-perch phaeton was parked just a few yards away, his groom watching and tending the horses in his master's absence.

"Oh, my! Is this your carriage?" Sam exclaimed, eyeing with appreciation the shiny black equipage with silver detailing. "It's a high-flyer, isn't it? I've never ridden in one of these sporty vehicles."

"Well then, today is your lucky day, isn't it?" Jean-Luc lifted her easily onto the high seat over the tall front wheels. Then he took the ribbons from his tiger, who boarded behind them, and they were off.

"But this isn't the way to Queens Square," Sam said, as Jean-Luc turned in the opposite direction away from Julian's elite neighborhood.

"I thought you might like a little ride before we pick up the dog," Jean-Luc said with a smile as he urged the sleek black horses to a brisk trot. "Besides, this will give the lovers a little more time."

Sam knew her eyes must be shining like a child's at the circus. "That's true. And I would dearly love a ride, but do you think it wise? What if someone sees us together . . . as indeed they must . . . and starts a dreadful rumor?"

Jean-Luc threw her a devil-may-care grin. "I thought you didn't care about people's opinions. But if some nasty rumor does get started, I suppose I'll just have to marry you to preserve your reputation, Miss Darlington."

Sam must have looked aghast because Jean-Luc laughed out loud. "No, that wouldn't do at all, would it?"

"Wh-what do you mean?" Sam stuttered.

"You've put on a convincing show, but you've never had any intentions of marrying me, have you? Nor have you had serious designs on Ninian, or Nathan, or any of the men who have been trailing after you with their tongues dragging since the moment they clapped eyes on you."

"I don't know what you mean," Sam lied, biting her lip. "As you know, I left off thinking of Nathan when I realized he was in love with Clara. And it's only decent and natural to help their romance along."

"Even before Clara's interests and feelings were a matter of importance, you never gave Nathan a serious thought. You would no more leave England than cut off your pert little nose."

"I *like* America!" Sam declared.

"But you like England better . . . at least as long as a certain someone remains in residence here."

"I don't know what you're talking about, Jean-Luc," Sam insisted, turning her head away to stare, unseeing, at the passing buildings. Her heart was beating much too fast for comfort. Jean-Luc couldn't possibly know she was in love with Julian, could he?

"He's far too old for you, you know. And he's set in his ways, dictatorial, toplofty and arrogant into the bargain."

Sam's head snapped around again. She stared at Jean-Luc in horror. Who else could he be talking about but Julian?

Jean-Luc laughed, easily tooling his horse down a narrow alley in a part of town Sam had never seen before. "Yes, moppet. I know you're in love with your guardian . . . the stately and elegant marquess of Serling . . . and I pity you."

Sam's hackles were immediately raised and she couldn't help but burst out, "Pity me? Why? He's a wonderful man. You call him arrogant and toplofty, but under his reserved facade, Julian is full of tenderness and honor and passion!"

Jean-Luc slid a victorious look her way. "Aha. So I was right."

Sam realized that Jean-Luc's teasing trickery had made her betray herself. "Oh, you!" she huffed, crossing her arms and turning away.

"Don't worry, Sam," he said, reaching over with

one hand to pat her arm. "I don't think anyone else knows. But is this wise? Appearances have the whole of London—myself included—thinking that he means to marry Charlotte Batsford, a woman whose emotions are as carefully controlled as his. They'll make a cool pair," he added dryly.

"They won't make a pair at all, if I have anything to say about it," Sam muttered.

There was a rather lengthy silence as Jean-Luc continued to drive the phaeton up and down unfamiliar streets. She would have been enjoying the impromptu tour if she hadn't been so disturbed by the revelation that her love for Julian had been so obvious to a man she was supposed to be encouraging as a suitor.

"Did it never occur to you, Sam," Jean-Luc presently asked, "that you might be playing a bit fast and loose with Ninian's feelings . . . not to mention my own?"

Sam made a grimacing little face. "To be honest, though all three of you have been paying me a lot of attention, I never thought any of you were in danger of *really* falling in love with me."

Jean-Luc arched a brow. "And how did you come to that convenient conclusion?"

Sam's brows drew together in a thoughtful frown. "I always felt that Ninian only liked me as a friend. He seems comfortable around me, whereas I've observed that he's not as comfortable around other women. But I suppose I'm not your typical female, am I?"

"Indeed not. In fact, I would call that statement an *under*statement," Jean-Luc quipped good-humoredly.

"Yes, Ninian feels easy with me . . . which must

account for my charm where *he's* concerned. And, besides, everyone knows he doesn't want to marry. He wants to go into the military."

"But his mama won't let him. And now that Lady Wentworth has met you, and you took such pains to gain her approval—done, no doubt, to impress the marquess—she will badger Ninian constantly until he breaks down and proposes to you."

"Do you really think so?" Sam said worriedly. "I don't want to get him into trouble with his mama by refusing him, so I'd rather he didn't ask."

"Then you're planning to refuse Ninian?"

"Of course. I'm not in love with him."

"And you would use the same logic if *I* were to ask for your hand in marriage, I suppose? Pray, what excuse do you have for leading *me* on, Miss Darlington? Do you think I have no heart to break?"

Jean-Luc had a teasing smile on his lips, but Sam thought she detected a bit of tenderness, a vulnerability, behind the twinkle in his dark eyes. She tucked her hand in the crook of his elbow and leaned confidingly close, saying, "You are a shameless flirt, Jean-Luc, but women love you for it . . . among your other attractions. You could marry any one of a score of women just dying for you to glance their way. You would never hang your heart on the hope of marrying a hoyden like me!"

He smiled down at her. "Wouldn't I?"

"No, of course not! You and I are friends . . . the very *best* of friends."

"Friends make good spouses, Sam. Didn't you know?"

"Friends make good *friends,*" Sam disagreed.

"So, even though you've got your heart set on

marrying Julian Montgomery, you don't mind if I keep coming round, then?"

"I would miss you very much if you quit coming round."

"Besides which, you'd have to find another bloke to make Julian jealous."

"Well, *that's* true," Sam admitted with a rueful chuckle. "But you must know how much I enjoy your company, Jean-Luc. I'm not just using you, y'know!"

"Chère, use me all you want," Jean-Luc advised her. "You do it so charmingly."

Sam laughed and squeezed Jean-Luc's arm, but suddenly froze when she caught sight of a gentleman strolling down the walkway who looked just like Julian. No . . . it *was* Julian! She'd know that tall, athletic figure anywhere . . . not to mention the impeccable clothes, the commanding posture, and the confident stride. Even the woman hanging on his arm, gazing up at him, dressed in a red velvet walking cape with black trim, looked familiar.

Oh no! Could it be . . . ? Yes! It was the woman from the opera! The courtesan with the wealthy protector!

"Jean-Luc, look!" Sam cried, her grip on his arm going beyond a friendly squeeze to a viselike pressure.

"Lord, Sam, you're cutting off my circulation. What is it?"

"It's Julian!" she squeaked, pointing with a shaky finger. "And . . . and that *woman!* What did you say her name was? Isabelle Something-or-other! She's *Julian's* mistress, isn't she?"

Julian had been listening to something Isabelle was saying to him, or possibly simply gazing with dazzled affection into her face for no particular reason whatsoever, and he was not attending to oncoming traffic.

"We're in luck," Jean-Luc said, turning quickly onto another street to avoid driving right past them. "He didn't see us."

"He wouldn't have seen us if we'd pulled right up in front of him and blown a horn!" Sam said scornfully, looking back to observe Julian and Isabelle walking up the steps of a redbrick town house. Then, making an instant decision, she quickly scanned the wall of a corner building for an address and stored it away in her memory.

"Why didn't you tell me last night that Julian was her protector?" Sam demanded to know, crossing her arms again in an angry pose. "You knew, of course."

Jean-Luc sighed. "Yes, I knew. But I also suspected how besotted your were with the man, and I didn't want to ruin your evening by pointing out to you the woman he is presently——"

Jean-Luc paused and looked chagrined.

"Making love to?" Sam supplied grimly. "I already knew he had a mistress. I just didn't think she'd be that beautiful . . . or so different from *me* in every way! Her hair is as black as a raven's feathers, Jean-Luc! And her figure is very voluptuous." She groaned. "No wonder he thinks of me as a child. I'm too blond and too slender."

"Trust me, *chère,*" Jean-Luc said dryly. "It's not the way you look that keeps the marquess from acknowledging your womanhood. You are formed in a different style than his mistress, but you are just as beautiful, just as alluring. Or, in my opinion, you are decidedly more beautiful and alluring. As I said, trust me on this."

Although Jean-Luc was always liberal with compliments and couldn't be taken too seriously, Sam was a bit mollified by his reassuring comments. But still she knew there was something Isabelle had that Sam didn't have—secrets she knew, tricks she used that made Julian attracted to her—and Sam was determined to find out what those secrets were.

Later that day, after Jean-Luc and Nathan escorted Sam and Clara and the dogs back to the house, Sam hurried Clara up to her bedchamber to interrogate her. Then as soon as she'd closed the door behind them, she turned and demanded, "All right, Clara, tell me what happened. Ever since Jean-Luc and I returned to the park with George, you've been blushing like a bride!"

Clara sat down on the edge of the bed and pressed her palms to her pink cheeks. "Have I, miss?"

Sam sat down beside her and grasped Clara's hands. "Did Nathan tell you that he cared for you?"

"You planned all this, didn't you, miss?" Clara accused with a tremulous smile.

"Yes, and I'm glad I did, because obviously something good's come of it."

Clara shook her head, her smile fading. "I don't know if it's good or not."

Sam chuckled uncertainly. "What do you mean? How can it *not* be a good thing if the man you care about also cares for you?"

"Nathan's an American, miss, and you know how my father feels about Americans," Clara said glumly.

"But that's a lot of silliness," Sam said bracingly.

"He won't stand in the way of you marrying Nathan once he knows how much you care about each other." She leaned close and whispered teasingly, "And how very rich Nathan is!"

Clara shook her head again, pulling her hands free from Sam's grip and standing up to pace the floor. "You don't understand, miss."

Sam sobered as she watched a tear trickle down Clara's face. "Is there something I don't know, Clara?"

"Yes. It's not something that my father likes bandied about, mind you, but I know I can trust you, miss."

Sam sat forward on the edge of the bed. "What is it, Clara?"

Clara continued to pace as she spoke. "It's like this, miss. You know I've got lots of brothers and sisters and no mum, and you know how all we older ones work to help pay for the keeping and education of the younger ones?"

"Yes, I understand that. I think it's wonderful how you all work to stay together as a family. And I know it must be hard for your father to manage all he does—running Julian's house and keeping tabs on his own home and all his children. I assumed that's why he's sometimes a bit gruff with you and a bit sour-dispositioned."

Clara sighed and sat down on a chair by the window, gazing into the hazy afternoon sunshine. "That's not why he's such a grump, miss. He's been a grump since my mum left us."

Sam's eyes widened. "Left you? I thought your mother died."

"That's what most folks think, unless they know the facts."

"And the facts are?"

"That my mum left my pa for another man . . . a rich American."

"Oh. . . ." said Sam, nodding sagely. *"Now* I understand."

"Yes. And now you must see that my father would never allow me to marry Nathan. I'd have to run off with him. I'd have to elope . . . and that's not the kind of wedding I've always dreamed of, miss."

"Has he asked you to marry him, then, Clara?" Sam asked.

"He said he loved me," Clara admitted, blushing prettily. "And even though we've only known each other a few days, I love him, too. And, yes, he did bring up marriage . . . although we know it's probably too soon for a definite engagement. He hasn't formally asked me to marry him, you know."

"But he will," Sam said confidently. "So what are you going to do to prepare your father?"

Clara sighed. "Well, first I'm going to broach the subject with him and see what happens. If the news that his daughter's in love with an American makes him fly into the boughs in a rage, I suppose I'll have to make another very hard decision."

"Which is?"

"To disregard my father's feeling or not."

"Poppycock," Sam exclaimed. "That shouldn't be a hard decision at all. "I would do anything to be with the man *I* loved."

"Even elope, miss?" Clara asked timidly.

Sam smiled. *"Especially* elope."

Sam was supposed to be taking a nap in her room before dinner. After all, a big night was planned with several parties and routs at which they had to make appearances. But, unbeknownst to everyone—even Clara—Sam had waited to make sure Julian had returned to the house, then she'd slipped out, hailed a hackney coach, and hired the driver to transport her to the very same neighborhood Jean-Luc had given her a tour of earlier that day. And now, as dusk dimmed the sky to a rosy gray, she stood in front of the redbrick house she'd seen Julian enter with his mistress . . . Isabelle Something-or-other . . . rallying her courage to knock on the door.

"How long'll you be, miss?" said the hackney driver. "I'll be missin' lots o' fares if'n I wait fer ye."

"I'll pay you handsomely," Sam assured him. She reached inside her reticule, took out a shilling, and handed it to him. "I'll give you another of these if you're still here when I come out. Fair enough?"

"Fair enough," the driver agreed, eyeing the shiny coin avariciously. "Only don't be above an hour, or I'll get the fidgets and go. Understan', miss?"

Sam nodded her head to indicate she understood, but her mind was full of other thoughts. Her common sense told her that what she was about to do would be considered extremely improper by most people, but she was desperate to receive enlightenment on a subject that consumed her every waking hour . . . how to make Julian respond to her like a man responds to a woman. Knowing the mechanics of lovemaking just wasn't enough. If visiting and interviewing his mistress supplied her with the extra information she needed, then all the embarrassment and fear she was feeling at the moment would be well worth it. She climbed the steps and firmly made use of the door knocker.

A small-statured butler answered the door and

stared at her in some surprise. "Yes, miss?" he said. "What can I do for you?"

Sam forced a smile. "Good afternoon. I'm here to see your mistress."

The butler's eyebrows shot up. "Is she expecting you, miss?"

"No, but I only want a moment of her time."

"To do what, miss?" the butler persisted, looking puzzled, his quick gaze scrutinizing her appearance. He was undoubtedly wondering what business she could have with his mistress. She was too well dressed to be a beggar, too modest and understated to be a fellow courtesan, and too fashionable to be a religious missionary come to save his mistress's soul from eternal damnation. In short, the poor man had to be completely mystified.

"I only want to talk with her for a few minutes," Sam explained, knowing it was hardly an adequate explanation or likely to gain her admittance into the house. But how could she dare explain her true reasons for visiting this Isabelle Something-or-other? Obviously she should have come up with a credible excuse to demand a few minutes of the lady's time, but she had decided on this course quite suddenly and had had little time to think.

"What is your name, miss?" the butler inquired. "Perhaps if I send your card up, Mrs. Descartes will recognize your name and receive you. Otherwise, I'm afraid I can't help you."

"I don't think she'll recognize my name, but—"

"In that case—" The butler began to shut the door.

"No! Wait!" Sam cried. "Just tell her I'm the marquess of Serling's ward."

The butler stared through the opening between the half-shut door and the doorjamb. "Ward of the marquess of Serling, you say?" he repeated incredulously. "What can you want with Mrs. Descartes, then?"

Realizing that she was going to have to intimidate the man into letting her into the house, Sam raised her nose in the air and said, "My guardian owns this house and pays your salary, sir. Isn't that reason enough to admit me into the premises? Or would you rather send him a note and ask his permission first? In the meantime, I'll wait in the parlor!"

Sam slipped through the door and breezed past the butler into the hall. While he stood and watched, surprised and shaken by Sam's confidence, she took off her light redingote and gloves and handed them to him. "Well, what will it be?" she said. "Are you going to send a note while I kick my heels in the parlor? Or will you tell Mrs. Descartes that I'm here?" Then Sam held her breath. Offering to wait while he sent a note was very risky.

But the bluff worked. The butler apparently had no desire to send a note to his employer and possibly end up causing a ruckus. "I'll tell Mrs. Descartes that you're here," he said grimly, his sour expression testifying to his poor opinion of such goings-on. "Please wait in here for a moment." And he motioned to a small room just off the main hall, into which Sam retired.

Sitting down on a striped damask sofa, Sam looked about the room and let out the breath she was holding. The chamber was small and tastefully decorated. As she ran her hands along the cool, sleek cloth of the sofa cushion, Sam couldn't help but visualize Julian sitting there . . . or lying there. Did he like to make love in other rooms besides the bedchamber, she wondered? Had he pleasured his mistress in the very parlor she was sitting in? Or in the kitchen? Or . . . perhaps . . . in the stable?

Sam blushed as her thoughts ran amuck. If Mrs. Descartes was willing to talk, soon she'd know all about Julian, what he liked to do, and where he liked to do it.

Chapter 8

❦

"**Y**ou must be mistaken, Powell," said Isabelle, rising from her chair in front of the dressing table. She'd been powdering her nose, hiding the redness that was a result of the short spell of sniffles she'd indulged in that afternoon. She'd never cried over a man before, but losing Julian had been a blow. He had always been extremely generous and was a supreme lover.

And now her butler was telling her that his ward—the very same young woman Julian had used as an excuse to break things off with her that afternoon—was downstairs waiting to talk to her? Impossible!

"Madam, I know it seems strange," said Powell in an apologetic tone, "but that is who she says she is."

"What in the world could she want with *me?*" she exclaimed irritably. "Does Julian know she's here?"

But how could that be? Isabelle thought to herself. Julian had claimed to be extremely busy launching the girl into fashionable society and weeding out suitors. With so much at stake, he would never allow her to walk out alone, much less to visit his mistress! Or, as of today, his *ex*-mistress. It must be all the girl's idea.

"I don't know, madam," the butler replied. "But she said I could send a note to His Lordship to verify her identity and ask his permission to admit her into the house."

Isabelle raised a brow. "Indeed? As if you would! However, it was clever of the girl to suggest it. I suppose that's when you let her in?"

"Yes, madam," Powell admitted with a grimace. "I thought it the best way to handle the situation without a great fuss being made and getting His Lordship involved."

"Yes, we don't want to trouble His Lordship, do we?" Isabelle said with dry sarcasm. "However, you won't need to worry about troubling Lord Serling anymore after today."

Isabelle observed Powell's stricken expression with bitter amusement. "You don't mean, madam, that you and His Lordship have——?"

"Yes, Powell," she said, confirming the worst. "Lord Serling is no longer my protector. He gave me my *congé* this afternoon. But don't worry. He left me with a generous parting gift. Your salary is secure, and I'm sure there'll be another man of the house before we're quite destitute."

With an effort, Powell schooled his face into a passive mask, hiding his disappointment. Even the servants liked Julian better than all the others that had come before . . . better, no doubt, than anyone she would take as her lover and protector in the future, as well. *Damn the man.*

"Shall I tell the young lady that you'll be down presently, madam?" asked Powell, returning to the matters at hand in his usual professional manner.

Isabelle was about to automatically agree, when a sudden mischievous quirk came over her. "No, Powell. Bring her up here." Maybe she'd have a little fun with the girl. It was certainly no more than she deserved . . . coming between her and Julian like she had.

Powell's brows raised a notch. "Up *here,* madam?"

Isabelle sat down on her red silk divan and draped the diaphanous skirts of her lacy black dressing gown over the cushions. "Yes, Powell. Why not?"

The corner of Powell's left eye twitched as his gaze involuntarily flitted over Isabelle's suggestive attire, then round the room at all the seductive opulence of silk, satin, and gilded mirrors, finally returning to that middle distance he'd disciplined himself to stare into while in the presence of his usually scantily clad mistress.

"In twenty minutes, madam, so you'll have time to . . . er . . . dress, I suppose?"

"No, bring her up right now. She wasn't expected, so I don't see any reason why I should take the time and trouble to change for her."

Again Powell's eye twitched, but he only bowed and said, "Very well, madam," and marched decorously out.

Isabelle didn't have long to wait. Minutes later Powell showed the girl into her boudoir, then bowed himself out and shut the door behind him. Just to intimidate her, Isabelle did not immediately speak, but rather insolently looked the girl over quite thoroughly.

She stood just inside the room, her back ramrod straight, her hands clasped tightly at her waist. She was dressed in an ivory walking dress of embroidered muslin and wore a demure poke bonnet in a matching shade, with a large satin ribbon tied at an angle under her chin. Isabelle could see Julian's hand in the tasteful cut and understated elegance of the outfit. She was the image of privileged innocence.

As for the girl herself, Isabelle had to admit she was a beauty. Her style was what she'd always admired . . . probably because the girl was so diametrically different from herself. Short blond curls framed a small, heart-shaped face and large eyes. She was of medium height and as slender as a wraith, but she was not without curves. Her breasts were small and high, her hips as slim as a boy's but proportionately larger than her tiny waist.

"Er . . . thank you for seeing me, Mrs. Descartes," said the girl, breaking the silence by speaking first.

Isabelle looked haughtily into the girl's blue-gray eyes. Behind the wide, frightened stare she detected a sort of flinty determination. And the way the girl held her chin just so . . . She had spunk. Isabelle felt a reluctant admiration.

"Powell said you're Julian's ward, but he didn't mention a name. I assume you have a name?"

The girl took a tentative step forward, then stopped and stuttered, "My . . . my name is Samantha Darlington. But everyone—well almost everyone—calls me Sam for short."

"What does Julian call you?"

A ghost of a smile touched her lips. "He calls me 'brat.'"

"Because you are disobedient?" Isabelle suggested. "Because you gad about town without a chaperon? Because you think it's a lark to get a good look at your guardian's mistress?" Isabelle lifted one long leg onto the divan, the filmy fabric of her gown falling away to reveal a goodly expanse of creamy white flesh. "Well, take a good look, then be gone."

Sam's eyes got even wider . . . if that were possible. "Oh, but I'm not here to look at you. Well, actually I *am* here to look at you, but not in the way you're thinking. I want to *learn* from you."

Isabelle blinked. "Learn from me? Learn what? I'm not a bloody governess, you know."

"No, indeed," Sam agreed. "But you know things I want to learn. Things about— Things about *men*. About what pleases them, what arouses them." She blushed. *"You* know what I mean."

Isabelle's eyes narrowed. She put her leg down and sat up straight. "Did Lord Serling send you here?"

"No, he didn't. He'd skin me alive if he knew I were here," she admitted, and Isabelle believed her.

"But you'll be married soon, if Julian has anything to say about it. As a wife, there's no reason to learn about men. Only mistresses need to know about men . . . about what pleases them, arouses them, and such."

The girl stepped forward again, her hands falling to her side, her small fists clenched. "You spout the same silly logic that Julian does. But can't anyone understand that I don't want to be that kind of wife?" Her eyes flashed, and her mouth was set in a stubborn expression. "I don't want my husband going to a mistress to be pleasured! I want him to stay home with *me!"*

Isabelle couldn't help a small laugh. "You are an

odd one. Are you sure you don't want to change professions? Maybe you should try being a mistress instead of a wife. Sounds to me like you've got the right temperament."

Sam shook her head, her expression suddenly troubled. "I've thought about that, but I've decided that being a mistress isn't for me. I just want to be a wife that *acts* like a mistress."

"Poor darling," Isabelle clucked. "You're hopelessly, madly in love, aren't you?"

The pointed chin tilted upward. "Yes. Yes I am. And he's the most wonderful man in the world!"

Isabelle cocked a brow. "Do I know this paragon?"

The girl looked self-conscious. "I'd rather not name him . . . if you don't mind."

Isabelle shrugged. "I don't mind, I suppose. Is this . . . er . . . gentleman in love with you?"

The girl toed the carpet, her long lashes feathering against her hot cheeks as she looked at the floor. "Not exactly. I know he cares for me. He's very kind to me, and protective. But he still sees me as a child." Sam looked up, her expression earnest, fervent. "That's where you come in, Mrs. Descartes. I want you to teach me what to do to make . . . to make *this gentleman* see me as a woman."

Well, why not? thought Isabelle, chuckling gleefully to herself. It was patently clear that the gentleman Samantha Darlington was taking such pains not to name was Julian. The girl was obviously head over heels in love with him.

There was no denying she was a smart, determined chit, and brave, too, coming as she had straight to his mistress to find out what made the marquess purr. Isabelle couldn't help but admire such a pragmatic and unsqueamish approach to romance.

As Isabelle saw it, there were two possible outcomes of this little encounter, both of which she found vastly entertaining. The first was that once she imparted her worldly wisdom to the girl, Julian would have quite a difficult time trying to control such an innocent so well versed in the ways of seduction. Indeed, Sam might become very popular with the gentlemen. Too popular.

The second outcome might be that the chit would trap Julian into marriage. It would serve the old bachelor right to be married to that spirited sprite of a girl instead of sensible, serene, *boring* Charlotte Batsford. Indeed, Sam would lead him a merry chase. But then maybe it was more than he deserved. . . .

"Will you help me or not?" Sam prompted, glancing nervously toward the window. "I've a hackney coach waiting."

Isabelle nodded, stifling a smile. "I see. We don't want to keep the driver waiting, do we? How much time can you spare to learn valuable information it's taken me a lifetime to gather?"

"Less than an hour," Sam admitted. "Any longer, and I'll be late to dinner, and Julian hates it when I'm tardy."

"Does he? Well then we'd better talk fast."

Sam's face lit up. "You'll tell me what to do, then?"

"As long as you don't mind if I frequently use Julian as an example," Isabelle said with an innocent look. "After all, he's my most recent *amour.'*

Sam visibly swallowed. "No, I don't mind."

Isabelle smiled slyly. "Then come sit down, Sam." And she patted the red cushion beside her.

An hour later, Isabelle had sent away Julian's ward with a head swimming with erotic etiquette. She'd covered everything from coy flirtation to sexual positions. She'd shocked the girl, but Sam would get over it and someday—sooner or later—she'd put the knowledge she'd gained to good use.

Indeed, thought Isabelle, as she dabbed her pen in the inkwell and prepared to write a short missive to her old beau, all women about to embark on matrimony should have sessions with courtesans and given lessons on the arts of love. Perhaps then there would be fewer dissatisfied husbands.

Isabelle frowned. But then there would be less need for courtesans.

Never mind, she thought, her composure returning immediately. Passionate wives weren't likely to become the fashion in her lifetime, so she needn't worry.

She wrote the note quickly, read it with a smile on her face, folded it, sealed it, then pulled the rope to summon her lady's maid.

"Give this to Powell," she ordered when the woman came into the room. "Have him send our fastest lad to Queens Square to deliver it to the marquess of Serling. Make sure it is taken to him immediately upon arrival."

"Yes, ma'am," said the woman, curtsying, then quickly leaving the room.

Isabelle moved from her desk to her dressing table. She sat down and began to brush her long black hair, smiling at her reflection. "Julian should be just sitting down to dinner when he gets the note. Oh, if only I could be a fly on the wall and watch him lose his regal composure. . . ."

Sam was late. Again. First the fiasco before the opera last night, now this. Julian tapped his toe on the carpet beneath the table. He and the aunts were already seated in the dining room and the servants stood at attention, only waiting for Julian's command to ladle the soup. He just hoped she hadn't disobeyed him and was back in the library perusing his shelves for more books having to do with sex. God, he couldn't take another confrontation with her on that subject anytime soon!

"Would you like me to check on her, Julian?" Nan asked anxiously.

"No," Julian said gruffly, then added in a milder tone, "Thank you, Nan. No one should have to fetch the girl. She knows when we dine."

"Perhaps she slept late," Prissy suggested. "She was taking a nap earlier."

"Clara would have waked her in time to dress. She's probably just dawdling."

"As a rule, Sam is not a dawdler," Nan pointed out.

Julian did not reply, but he knew Nan was right. Sam did not routinely keep them waiting at the table or anywhere else. But he was in no mood to be fair or reasonable. He'd had a hell of a day, and waiting for his dinner did not improve his disposition.

He'd visited Humphries and been assured by the old man that he'd not let a word slip about Julian's search for Sam's mother. Julian believed him, largely because the fellow hardly got out anymore and had no one to tell. But his belief in Humphries's word left Julian no recourse but to suspect those closest to him, or to imagine some sinister stranger involved somehow. Furthermore, Humphries still had not remembered anything helpful in solving the mystery of exactly who Sam's mother was. It was a conundrum, and it made Julian decidedly blue-deviled.

And since he'd bid a permanent farewell to Isabelle that day—thinking to focus all his energies on Sam and Charlotte, the two most important women in his life—Julian no longer had a place where he could release his pent-up energies. But it was just as well. Isabelle was getting on his nerves lately. And, whereas he'd always thought her quite beautiful in the past, recently he had begun to think her too voluptuous for his tastes. And, strangely, he'd found himself wishing she were blond and blue-eyed. Ah, well. He supposed he was just bored and ready to move on. He wondered if Genevieve DuBois currently had a lover. . . .

"My lord?"

Julian looked up. His butler was standing at his elbow . . . had probably been standing there for a while as he daydreamed. "Yes, Hedley?"

Hedley lifted a silver salver on which reposed a folded sheet of parchment paper. "This note came for you just a moment ago with express orders from the lad that it was to be taken to you immediately."

Julian recognized the pink sealing wax and the rose seal. It was from Isabelle. He wasn't about to read a note from his mistress in front of two sweet old spinsters. And, since he'd just broken up with Isabelle, he had no great expectations of finding good news inside. The note was probably full of histrionics. "I'll read it later," Julian said, waving it away.

"Very well," said Hedley, turning to go.

But as Hedley walked away, Julian changed his mind. The aunts didn't need to know who the note was from, and, after all, he hadn't anything better to do as he waited for that brat, Sam, to show up. "Come back, Hedley. I'll take it after all."

"Very well, my lord," Hedley said, retracing his steps.

As Priss and Nan watched, trying not to appear nosy, Julian snatched up the note, popped it open and began to read. To both ladies, all the surreptitiously spying servants, and any fly that should happen by chance to be resting on the wall, it was quite obvious that Julian was not pleased by the contents of the note.

In quick succession, his expression went from irritably curious, to surprised, to appalled, to angry, to apoplectic. In the end, he crumpled the paper in his fist, stood so quickly he toppled his chair backwards, and headed toward the door at a furious stride, saying in a ragged underbreath, "Bloody Hell! May the saints help me keep my sanity . . . *and my temper!*"

"Should we follow, Priss?" asked Nan, staring after Julian with a horrified expression. "I'm sure he's gone to scold Sam about something . . . and it must be something quite dreadful!"

"He's not a violent man," said Priss, wringing her hands, "so I don't think we need fear that he'll beat her. I think we should just stay out of it, Nan."

"Well, if you think so, Priss," Nan agreed quaveringly, then turned to Hedley. "Better tell the cook to keep the soup on the fire till we hear from the marquess."

"Yes, Miss," said Hedley, with a long-suffering sigh.

* * *

Sam had just stepped into her gown, and Clara had pulled it up as far as her waist, when the door suddenly swung open and Julian entered the room. Clara gasped, let go of the dress so that it fell to the floor, then stumbled backward onto the bed with her hand at her throat.

Sam couldn't blame Clara for her reaction. Julian looked like an avenging angel sent by a wrathful God! She wouldn't have been surprised if the room had been filled with the sound of thunder, with bolts of lightning shooting above Julian's golden head. She'd never seen his chiseled features so sternly fixed, his mouth so grim and implacable, his eyes so bright with anger.

And he looked massive as he stood there . . . so tall, his arms crossed forbiddingly over his broad chest, his legs spread and braced like a soldier prepared to do battle. Sam quivered with fear.

"Leave us, Clara," he said, his voice deathly calm.

Clara got up and scurried across the room, sending a stricken look Sam's way as she slipped out the door. Just as she'd imagined many times, Sam was alone with Julian in her bedchamber wearing next to nothing. But instead of looking ardent and tender, as he had in her fantasy, he looked as though he would like nothing better than to wring her neck!

Clara had left the door ajar, but Julian reached back and, without taking his eyes off Sam, closed it. Then he approached, one slow step at a time, till they were separated by mere inches. Sam's heart thudded in her ears. He'd looked towering, intimidating, and stunningly masculine as he stood by the door. This close, he overwhelmed her with his presence. For a moment, she thought she was going to faint!

"This time, Sam, you've gone too far."

There was still that unnerving calmness to his voice. Sam swallowed hard. "I'm . . . I'm sorry, Julian," she whispered.

Julian's brows drew together. He cocked his head to the side. "What are you sorry for, brat? Do you know, or do you just say 'I'm sorry' without meaning it?"

"I . . . I assume you're angry with me for being late to dinner," she explained weakly. The candle-light flickered in his hair and made bright prisms in his icy blue eyes.

Julian's lips made a cynical curl. "You thought I burst into your bedchamber just now without knocking to chastise you for being late to dinner? Don't you think my reaction a trifle excessive for the crime?"

"I've never been late to dinner before, Julian. I didn't know what to expect you to do. And after yesterday. . . . Well, you *do* seem angry with me most of the time lately." She bit her lip and shrugged.

Julian's gaze fixed on Sam's lower lip, tucked as it was between her small white teeth. And, as she'd shrugged, her bare shoulders had looked so shapely, so round and pale and perfect. . . . His gaze wandered lower. Her small breasts were clearly outlined by the thin muslin of her chemise, the nipples erect.

His concentration wavered, and he forced himself to look away, then determinedly kept his gaze from wandering below Sam's neck. He focused on his anger, which he felt was more than justified.

"Of late you have given me plenty of reason to be

angry, my girl. But do you really think I would get so furious about something as trivial as your being late to dinner?" Julian demanded, his voice raising. "Am I such an ogre?"

Sam's brows drew together in a puzzled frown. "But what else have I done?"

Julian smiled mirthlessly. "What else, indeed? What an actress you are!" He lifted his right hand and opened his clenched fist. The wadded note from Isabelle slowly expanded in the cup of his palm. "Would you like to read some correspondence I received just a few moments ago?"

Sam stared at the crumpled paper. "Not really," she quavered.

"But I insist," Julian said with a brittle and menacing politeness. "It is from a woman whose acquaintance you only recently made." He held the wad of paper closer, compelling her to take it. She did take it, but with trembling fingers that revealed an awareness of her own guilt.

Julian watched as Sam pulled the note into a reasonably flat shape, then quickly read it. When next she looked at him, she seemed to be trying to control, to force away her fear. Her chin went up defiantly, and she returned his gaze with that pugnaciousness he knew only too well.

"I can explain," she declared.

"There's nothing to explain," Julian retorted. "Isabelle already did that. She said you came to her house and requested instruction in the ways of a courtesan."

"But not to *be* a courtesan! Only to—"

"Yes, I know," Julian said harshly. "To ensnare a man . . . one of your three favorite suitors, I assume. It's all there in the note."

"Then you understand why—"

"I understand nothing!" he said fiercely, making her jump. "You can't talk yourself out of this, Sam. There's no excuse for what you did. In one day you might have undone everything I've tried to do for you over the past several months! What if someone saw you entering or leaving Isabelle's house?"

"I was careful—"

He grabbed her wrist and pulled her close, holding her small fist in his much larger one and pressing it against his chest. He looked her square in the eye and spoke in measured, biting accents. "What if you weren't careful enough? It only takes one pair of eyes to see and one tongue to tattle. For all we know, your visit to my mistress could very well be the juiciest bit of gossip being devoured at dinner tables all over London at this hour."

Her chest heaved and her cheeks were flushed. "Julian, I never meant to—"

"You apparently have no regard for your own reputation," he continued relentlessly. "But did you for one minute consider how ridiculous you might make me appear as your guardian? People will see I have precious little control over my ward! And what of your aunts? Did you think of them? Young girls do not hobnob with their guardian's mistress! Not for *any* reason!"

"I had to see her, Julian," Sam said beseechingly. "No one else would tell me anything! Before the opera, you said it wasn't the right time to answer my questions about intimacies between men and women. But I *know* you. You would never find the right time to talk of such things!"

"Not with you, that's for certain," he agreed emphatically. "You already know too much from reading those damned books. More than is wise. . . . But even that wasn't enough for you. You had to visit Isabelle and . . . and . . ." Julian had finally run out of words. He shook his head and released her hand.

But Sam surprised him by grabbing his hand in both of hers and lifting it to her mouth. She grazed his knuckles with a kiss and said earnestly, "You worry so much about my social standing, my success in the *ton*. But there's more to life than that!"

"You feel my tutoring of you has been a waste of your time then?" he said stiffly.

"No! Of course not!" she said fervently. "You've been wonderful! I owe you so much. . . . You taught me how to be a lady, Julian." She turned his hand over and pressed the palm against her cheek. Her skin felt like silk. "But who will teach me how to be a woman?" she finished softly, her eyes full of sweet supplication.

Entranced by her artless allure, and startled by the damnable way his body responded to her despite his mind's reservations, Julian said nothing.

She moved closer and wrapped her arms around his neck. "Who will hold me . . . like this?" She pressed her body against him.

Julian found himself mindlessly circling the slim expanse of her waist with his hands. She seemed to fit perfectly against him.

She stood on tiptoes and drew his head down to hers till their lips were nearly touching. "Who will . . . kiss me, Julian?"

Julian's body had turned completely traitorous. His pulse was racing, his blood thrummed through his veins, and an ache had settled in his loins. And the only possible answer to her question seemed to be. . . .

To kiss her. The touch of his lips against hers was at first tentative and tender, but her eagerness, the way she pressed closer and sighed soft and low in her throat, inflamed his passion.

His hands slipped up her slim back and he pulled her firmly into his arms.

He deepened the kiss, parting her lips with his tongue and exploring the sleek borders of her mouth.

Every nerve in his body was on fire. After just one kiss, he wanted her. He wanted to make love to her.

Then it hit him. This was Sam's *first* kiss!

Julian was appalled. *What am I doing?* he asked himself. *I've been her tutor, her mentor. But it's not for me to teach Sam about love. That will be for her husband to do!*

He tore himself away from the sweet intoxication of her mouth, caught hold of her shoulders, and firmly put an arm's length of distance between them.

An apology hovered on his lips, but when he looked into her face, he hesitated, entranced by her appearance. Her cheeks were blooming with color. Her eyelids drooped languidly, but her eyes were unnaturally bright.

She smiled tremulously and Julian was filled with guilt. He had taken advantage of her vulnerability! He might even have frightened her. And he most certainly must have confused her. After all, she'd gone to Isabelle to learn about pleasing a man, and in the midst of scolding her for such improper conduct, he had given her her first hands-on lesson in love! What had possessed him? Where was his legendary control?

And who was the culprit who started this mischief? he wondered, wishing he had his hands around the fellow's neck at that very moment. What man was making her so eager to learn about love, to make her risk her reputation just to be well informed in seduction?

"Who is he, Sam?" he asked her, giving her a little shake. "Who is this man you think you must play the seductress to win?"

Sam stared at him. He didn't know, she thought incredulously. He truly didn't know that *he* was the man she wanted to seduce, the man she wanted to ensnare in a silken web of love and passion. She'd kissed him back with all her heart and soul, and still he didn't know!

When she didn't answer, he grasped her chin with one hand, his long fingers curving over her cheek. He looked into her eyes. His own expression was tender and troubled. She stared at his lips as he urged her, "Tell me, Sam." But all she wanted was for him to kiss her again. She trembled with longing.

"Did that damned American tell you that the only way to prove your affection was to allow him certain liberties?" he asked gruffly. "Or has that lout, Jean-Luc, been filling your head with nonsense about what young ladies do in France? It couldn't be Ninian. . . ."

Sam's heart ached with frustration. "Do I have to tell you who the man is, Julian?" she whispered plaintively, still held captive and close by his large, warm hand. "Don't you *know?*"

At that moment, Julian wasn't sure what he knew or didn't know. His feelings were a tumble, and his mind was chaos. He still wanted her, and it irked him to feel so little control over his desires. He was her guardian, not her lover. He was supposed to protect her from improper advances, not make them!

Julian continued to stare into Sam's eyes, over-whelmed by confusion. Charlotte had said that his young ward was in love with him, and Julian had at first believed her . . . at least to the point of conceding that Sam might have developed a schoolgirl infatuation for her tutor and friend. He'd even found it amusing, supposing her flirtatiousness and sudden eagerness to be married a naive ploy to gain his attention.

But lately he hadn't been so sure of that evaluation of Sam's behavior. She'd been spending a lot of time with Nathan and asking a lot of questions about America. Julian had begun to think she was leaning toward accepting Nathan's eventual proposal of marriage, and he was dreading the day when she'd sail off to America, thousands of ocean miles away. The very thought rankled him to the bone.

"Don't you know, Julian?" Sam prompted in a small voice. "Don't you know whom I care about?"

Julian gazed a little longer into those soft blue eyes, then gently pushed her away and took two steps back. He crossed his arms again and said, "It's Nathan, isn't it?"

Sam looked stunned. And when she didn't answer, he assumed he'd surmised correctly. "Well, you can expect a long engagement," he growled. "I won't let you shackle yourself to a man who intends to take you halfway across the world until you really know him. *I* will need to know him better, as well . . . not to mention your sister, Amanda, who will have a natural wish to meet her sister's fiancé before he whisks her away to the far corners of the earth. And since Amanda won't be back in England for several months yet, there will certainly be no undue haste in this matter. Do you understand, Sam?"

Sam still did not reply.

"And furthermore," he went on, compelled to fill the silence with words of admonition, "if you ever leave this house again without a chaperon, I will chain you to the bedpost. I've never heard of anything so harebrained and improper as paying a visit to a courtesan."

By her accusing look and the angry arch of an eyebrow, Julian could tell what Sam was thinking . . . that *he* paid visits to courtesans and didn't consider it harebrained and improper. But since that was an entirely different matter altogether—after all, he was a *man*—he didn't bother to argue the point but continued to bluster away like a fusty old schoolmaster.

"Your reputation may be ruined, and for what? Some perfectly useless so-called advice? Damnation, Sam, what do you need to know all that rot for? After all, your aim is to be a *wife!*"

But all the response he got was Sam's stony silence and a look of hurt defiance.

"Put some clothes on and be downstairs for dinner in fifteen minutes," he finally muttered, exhausted. "Do you understand, Sam?"

Up came Sam's chin and a brave, sweet, sad smile broke over her face as she said, "Better than you can ever imagine, Julian."

It was an enigmatic remark, and Julian had no idea what to make of it, but it unnerved him. To counter this strange and uncomfortable confusion—the confusion he'd felt ever since he'd tasted the sweetness of Sam's lips—he assumed his most upright posture and left the room with as much dignity as he could muster. But as he shut the door of Sam's bedchamber behind him, his nerves quivered and his body pulsed with pent-up energy.

Hell, he mused to himself, *maybe he'd served his mistress her walking papers just a tad too soon.* . . .

Chapter 9

When Julian returned to the dining room, he found Priss and Nan waiting anxiously. He sent all the servants out of the room, then quickly, succinctly informed the aunts what Sam had done. But instead of the news horrifying them, they hid giggles and smiles behind their hands.

Julian raised a brow. "I can't conceive why you ladies find this episode so amusing," he said dampeningly. "Indeed, it is dangerous for Sam to be so well versed in seduction. She needs to be admonished not to use the advice she gleaned from this woman, or else she shall find herself ruined and unable to secure a respectable husband."

Nan composed herself, but was still smiling when she answered, "You are quite right, Julian. We do not want Sam to make a mistake that will ruin her life, but it is hard not to appreciate the girl's resourcefulness and originality. Imagine . . . visiting a courtesan to learn about physical love! No ordinary girl would ever dream of doing such a thing."

Julian's mouth reluctantly curved in a rueful smile. "I never said she wasn't an original. But why didn't she come to you ladies for information? Isn't

163

that the usual way young ladies learn of the birds and bees . . . from their female relatives?"

"Posh! What could she learn from *us,* Julian?" cried Priss. "She was certainly smart enough to realize that she'd learn a great deal more from a courtesan than from two old spinsters. And you must admit that while she must be made to understand that none of what she learned can be . . . er . . . *employed* before she is married, she will undoubtedly have a happier union by enthusiastically utilizing what she has learned once she is legally wed. We could not, in good conscience, order her to *entirely* forget everything she heard today!"

"No indeed!" Nan concurred emphatically.

"Considering that neither of you are married, or ever have been," Julian commented wonderingly, "I am surprised that you have such strong opinions on the subject."

"We've been around long enough to know that a marriage with passion has a far better chance of being happy," Nan replied with a decided nod. "Although she is young and inexperienced, Sam seems to know that, too. And, as well, I don't think she has any intention of becoming a wanton. She knows firsthand how illegitimacy can ruin a child's life. She won't . . . er . . . dabble in the waters of passion, I daresay, except with the man she intends to spend the rest of her life with."

"However, to ease your mind, Julian, we will make sure she understands that sexual intimacy belongs within the bounds of matrimony," added Priss. "Are you satisfied?"

"Completely," Julian answered dryly. He had not expected Priss and Nan to be so unembarrassed and blunt. Apparently he need not worry that the aunts would handle the situation with aplomb. And to think he'd been hesitant to read Isabelle's letter in front of them.

Just then Sam came in, her expression one of studied indifference. Julian observed her subdued appearance, which was belied by the fiery flash in her blue eyes. And unexpectedly, for one brief moment of insanity, he envied Sam's future husband with all his might. What a handful she was . . . and what an *arm*ful she would be. And that kiss . . .

He forced the disturbingly erotic thoughts from his mind and rang the bell for the butler. *He* might be hot, but the soup was cooling. . . .

The next morning was overcast, cold and drizzly, spoiling Sam's plans for another walk in the park with Nathan and Clara. She tried to get the two lovers together as often as possible in this manner, but it appeared that today's rendezvous was not to be. And when Nathan came to the house, either the aunts or Julian chaperoned, rendering Clara's presence unnecessary. If Sam called her abigail into the room while Nathan was paying a visit, not only would it appear strange to the others, but it would serve no purpose to the lovers. Unless they were alone, or with Sam, Nathan and Clara could not act naturally with each other. Their romance was still a secret.

So Sam sent a note to Nathan expressing her disappointment in canceling the walk, and telling him she understood if he did not wish to come to the house. After all, although there was a chance of seeing Clara, there was no chance of spending private time with her.

A few gentlemen had braved the elements and called that morning, but none of her three favorites had made an appearance and Sam had had to force herself to be sparkling and flirtatious. It would never have done to behave as depressed as she felt, because Julian had been the chaperon sitting in the parlor that morning and Sam had no intention of letting him see how his behavior the night before had affected her.

Sam was discouraged. How was she ever going to work her newly learned wiles on Julian when, despite an ardent kiss and nothing but a chemise between his hands and her bare skin, all he could think of doing was lecture her? And today he was acting more like a watchdog than a man, sitting and glowering at her gentleman callers as if daring them to misbehave.

And the aunts. . . . It had been an amusing half hour that morning when Priss and Nan had invaded her bedchamber before breakfast and moralized ad nauseam about the perils of premarital sex. Then, having done their duty, they begged Sam to tell them exactly what she'd learned from the famous Isabelle Descartes. Sam imparted some of Isabelle's advice as the aunts avidly listened, then they fanned their faces with their hands, cleared their throats, and gave their opinion that if all married women took lessons from a courtesan, more marriages would be happy ones.

Sam couldn't agree more. But, sitting now, all alone in the library, with an open book in her lap and an ache in her heart, she wasn't sure whether or not she'd ever have the opportunity to try out her newfound knowledge. She would never marry if she couldn't marry Julian. And, at that very moment, Julian was with Charlotte Batsford. He'd announced his intention of visiting Charlotte directly after he'd taken lunch, which had been an extremely strained affair with the only conversation coming from Priss and Nan.

And now, since the aunts were doing needlework in the parlor for the Women's Shelter, Sam had the whole dreary afternoon to get through, with nothing but a book for company. But as she stared out of the rain-streaked window at the stable yard, she got an idea. She'd ring for Clara and have her bring one of the dogs inside for a romp. Also, it would be an excuse to get Clara away from some of the extra duties her father insisted on giving her, and the two of them could talk about Nathan and Julian.

But as soon as Clara walked into the library, she took one look at Sam and burst into tears.

"Clara, what's wrong?" Sam exclaimed, taking a wriggling Madison out of her arms and setting him on the carpet. "Tell me why you're crying!"

Sam led Clara, who had covered her face with her hands and was paying absolutely no attention to where she was going, to a wing chair by the fire. Once seated, Clara slumped forward and continued to sob quite disconsolately, so Sam simply perched on the chair arm, patted her friend's back, and murmured soothing words till the poor girl cried herself out. Sam knew she wouldn't get any coherent explanation out of Clara till the worst of the storm had passed anyway, so she kept her questions for later.

Eventually Clara blindly groped for a handkerchief in her apron pocket, which Sam found and handed to her, then wiped her eyes and blew her nose. She looked pathetically at Sam through red-rimmed eyes.

"It's hopeless, miss. I wished I'd never met

Nathan Ford, because now I'll spend the rest of my life wishing things had turned out differently. I'll never love anyone else, you know, so I reckon I'm destined to be a childless spinster."

"Have you seen Nathan today? Has something happened?" Sam demanded to know, standing up and looking down at Clara, her hackles raised. "Has that man done something to hurt you, Clara? Why, I'll . . . I'll—"

"Nathan's done nothing," Clara quickly clarified, her lip quivering. "The dear man's done nothing but be everything a girl could ever want. Only *this* girl can't have him."

"Why do you say that, Clara? If Nathan didn't do something to make you unhappy, who did?" Her voice lowered. "Was it your father?"

Clara's eyes welled up again. "Just now when I was leading Madison in through the back door, he scolded me for favoring 'that damned colonial's mutt.' He even kicked the poor pup in the hindquarters! He doesn't dislike dogs as a rule, miss . . . except when they soil the floor, or chew things up, or bark . . . but he hates Madison just because Nathan gave him to you." Clara swiped at her eyes with the back of her hand.

Sam shook her head disgustedly.

"It all goes back to the fact that my mother ran off with that rich American farmer," Clara continued. "That was years ago, so it's foolish of me to hope his attitude will ever change. I might as well face the fact that my father will never give his blessing or his permission for me to marry Nathan," she finished despairingly.

Sam crossed her arms and knitted her brows. "Does he know you're in love with Nathan?"

"Bless me, no!" Clara exclaimed. "I've no doubt

he'd take a strap to me if he knew! He's very calm most of the time, but he's got the devil of a temper when he loses control. By his angry reaction to my attachment to Nathan's dog, I'm quite sure he wouldn't take at all kindly to the fact that I'm a hundred times more attached to Nathan himself!"

"As I'm sure you know your father best," Sam said thoughtfully, pacing the floor and rubbing her chin, "I have no choice but to believe you. Therefore, there's only one thing left to do."

Clara's eyes widened as Sam stopped pacing and sat down again beside her. "What's that, miss?"

"You have to elope."

Clara pressed a hand flat against her chest. "La, miss. I couldn't! My father would never forgive me!"

Sam cocked her head to the side and gave Clara a sober look. "Is keeping your father's unreasonable rules more important to you than marrying the love of your life?"

"But my brothers and sisters. . . . I'll never see them again!"

"I don't believe that," was Sam's firmly spoken opinion. "They'll find a way to correspond with you, and maybe some of them will even follow you to America. In your new life, as the wife of a rich American horse breeder, you could do your brothers and sisters a world of good. Think about it, Clara. But in the end, don't base your decision on what your father's reaction might be, or on the fact that you could help out your siblings. You must decide if you love Nathan enough to leave everything behind and brave the future with him, and only him, by your side." Sam smiled slyly. "That is, until the little ones come along."

Clara blushed and chuckled nervously. "Aren't

we getting a little ahead of ourselves? He hasn't even officially asked me to marry him!" Bored with sniffing around the room, Madison rubbed up against her hand just then, and Clara reached down and stroked the dog's head.

"Oh, but he will, Clara," Sam said decisively, petting Madison, too. "He will! You know it, I know it, and Nathan knows it. And when he does, you'll have to tell him that a dash to Gretna Green is the only way you'll be able to tie the nuptial knot."

"But how's it to be done, miss?" Clara asked her. "How will I get away without my father knowing and following?"

"I'm sure Nathan will have some ideas," Sam assured her. She smiled broadly and added stoutly, "And I'm going to help!"

Just then there was a discreet knock on the door and Hedley entered. Clara quickly ducked her head over the pup to hide her red, watery eyes, but the sharp-sighted butler gave her a questioning look and a disapproving frown anyway.

"What is it, Hedley?" said Sam, standing up and hovering in front of Clara to try to divert the butler's attention away from his daughter.

Hedley fixed his gaze on Sam, but it was apparent that he was still wondering what the deuce was wrong with Clara.

"You have a visitor, miss. Mr. Wentworth is waiting to see you."

"Is he in the parlor with Nan and Priss?" Sam asked unnecessarily, trying to give Clara as much time as possible to compose herself before she was left to the ruthless interrogation of her father.

"Of course, miss."

"Good. Tell him I'll be there presently, Hedley."

Hedley had not expected to be sent back to relay a message, but he only gritted his teeth a little before saying, "Very well, miss," then turned on his heels and left the room.

"Now take Madison back to the stable and wash your face in cold water before he sees you again," Sam hurriedly instructed her abigail. "If he asks you if you were crying, tell him you got something in your eye. And when you're feeling more the thing, bring George to the small front parlor. I'm sure Ninian would love to see his pup!"

Clara nodded, snatched up Madison, and hurried out of the room before her father came back. And Sam headed for the parlor, eager to see Ninian after an unusual two-day absence.

When Sam entered the parlor, she was surprised to find Ninian alone. The two, well-padded chairs the aunts usually occupied by the fire were empty, but their scissors and thread and other sewing accoutrements were still scattered about as if they'd left in a rush. Ninian had his back turned to the door and was staring into the fire.

"Ninian?" Sam said, when he didn't immediately turn around. "Where are my aunts? It's not like them to abandon a visitor. Especially a gentleman caller!"

As Ninian turned slowly around, the forlorn expression on his face made her own welcoming smile disappear. "Good heavens, is something wrong? You look like you've just been told you need a tooth pulled!"

Ninian attempted a smile. "No, nothing's wrong, Sam. Nothing at all."

Sam frowned and shook her head. "I don't

believe you. Out with it, Ninian. 'Fess up. What's
bothering you?"

For the first time since she'd entered the room,
Sam noticed that Ninian was dressed even fancier
than usual. And for a dandy, that was saying
something, indeed. He wore a lavender morning
jacket, a daffodil-yellow waistcoat, and purple-
striped trousers. His cravat was intricately tied and
appeared so stiff, Sam marveled that he could even
turn his head.

"My, you look quite dashing, Ninian," she
couldn't help adding, hoping to bring a more natural smile to his lips. "What's the occasion?"

"Well, Sam, the occasion is . . ." He bit his lip,
stiffened his spine, and started over. "That is, your
aunts didn't desert me, I asked them to leave. You
see, I wanted to talk to you . . . er . . . *privately.*"

Now Sam was really growing alarmed. "Something *is* the matter, isn't it? Tell me what it is this
instant, Ninian!"

Ninian shifted uncomfortably, his arms stiff at
his sides and his hands—encased in lavender
gloves—curled into fists. "Truly, nothing is wrong,
Sam," he said, his tone a trifle irritable. "The
matter I came here to discuss with you today is not
of a distressing nature. Rather, it is a thing that
ought . . . nay, that *will* . . . bring a great deal of
joy into my life if only you will agree to—That is, I
wonder if you would be so good as to—Will
you—"

Sam laughed. "Will I what, Ninian? Goodness, if
I didn't know you better I'd think you were—"
Sam sobered as the truth dawned on her. Her eyes
grew wide with surprise. "Good heavens, you aren't
trying to propose to me, are you?"

Ninian whirled around, pounding his thigh with his fist. "I told my mother it was a bad idea!" he cried, striding away toward the window and staring out over the rain-drenched street.

"Oh, Ninian, you misunderstood me!" Sam exclaimed, hurrying over to touch his arm and peer up into his face. "It's not that I find the proposal disagreeable. It's just that I'm extremely surprised!"

Ninian frowned down at her. "Mother said you were expecting me to propose. And she said I had better do it before someone else beat me to the point. Mother likes you, and she thinks——"

"But, Ninian, what do *you* think?" Sam interrupted with an encouraging smile. "I can't suppose you were very keen on the idea of proposing to me. As I said when I first entered this room, you looked as though you were in need of a tooth drawn!"

Ninian blushed and chuckled, shaking his head with embarrassment. "Was I that transparent? I thought I probably looked nervous. I had not thought that I looked like I was in pain!"

"You looked like you were in pain of the most acute kind," Sam assured him, laughing.

Ninian laughed with her, then suddenly sobered. "You mustn't think my reluctance to propose any reflection on you, Sam," he eagerly told her. "In fact, if I were to marry, I'd as soon marry you as anyone else. I like you excessively. You're a real trump. But——"

"But you simply don't want to get married to anyone right now . . . right?" Sam suggested.

Ninian gave a relieved sigh. "Exactly. And so I've told my mother a million times. But she won't listen. She's tried before to get me to propose to a number of females with all the proper requirements of money, connections, et cetera, but . . ." He shrugged.

"But you've refused to do it before?" Sam inquired.

"Every single time," Ninian said proudly. "Despite her megrims and her swoons and her nervous palpitations."

"Then why did you give in this time?"

"Because, as I said, I *like* you, Sam. And because . . ." Ninian sighed again, but not with relief. It was a sad sigh. "Because I'm finally convinced she'll never put up the blunt to buy me a commission in the army. And I won't have a single groat of my own beyond my quarterly allowance till she's dead! And, though she can be the most colossal pain in the . . . *neck,* I don't wish her dead! But, in the meantime, I am reduced to frittering away my time doing nothing. I have no profession, no employment, no independence whatsoever! Lord, I might as well be the Prince Regent for all the use I am to anybody! In short, I reckoned that marrying you would be much more diverting than picking out yet another waistcoat and learning a new way to tie my cravat!"

Sam caught both Ninian's hands and turned him away from the dreary scene outside and toward her. She beamed up at him. "I'm so proud of you, Ninian. The majority of young men would be perfectly happy to do nothing but fritter away their time. You are better than the majority. You want to be about the business of something as useful and honorable as serving in the army. Your mother needs to be convinced that she's doing you a horrible injustice by limiting you in this way!"

Ninian was blushing crimson from Sam's praise.

"By Jupiter, Sam, if you keep flattering me so, I shall end up asking you to marry me in earnest!"

Sam giggled. "What? And deprive the army of such a fine officer?"

"I appreciate your confidence in me, Sam," Ninian answered dejectedly, "but I won't have a chance to prove myself a fine officer . . . at least, not for now. I suppose I shall have to continue to wait and hope, and fend off my mother's continued attempts to make me marry. She insists I haven't the *gumption* for the military!"

Sam looked coy. "What if someone—some occurrence, perhaps—convinces her otherwise?"

Ninian peered suspiciously down at Sam, his mouth curved in a faint smile. "Are you up to something, Sam?"

Sam nodded. "Indeed, I am. I have a plan. Would you like to hear it?"

Cautious, but hopeful, Ninian agreed to hear Sam's plan. Therefore, they were sitting close together and were deep in conversation when Clara showed up ten minutes later with George. As they were basically finished going over the fine points of Sam's plan, they happily greeted the pup and spent the next half hour romping with him on the rug. Their whoops of laughter could be heard clear down the hall in the library.

Julian had come home early from his visit with Charlotte. Since, owing to his run-in with Sam over the mistress business, he had not been in the best of spirits, Charlotte had suggested that he might benefit best from going home and having another talk with his ward. Charlotte reminded him that he was not used to being at odds with Sam; therefore, he was bound to be unhappy till they were on good terms again. After all, she was like a little sister to him . . . wasn't she? Naturally, Charlotte didn't know that Julian had kissed his "little sister." And he wasn't about to tell her. It had been a terrible mistake.

Then, as soon as he'd stepped across the threshold of Montgomery House, he was virtually attacked by Priss and Nan, the both of them telling him with a great deal of agitation that Ninian was at that very moment in the parlor proposing to Sam! As Ninian had not asked for permission to pay his addresses, Julian was a little surprised. But not for long. Certainly both Ninian *and* Nathan would propose to Sam. Julian had no desire to see her shackled to either man, but he very much feared that Ninian had no chance against Nathan, anyway. Nathan would doubtless win the day and cart her off to Virginia.

The aunts withdrew to hover in the hall to await the young people's emergence from the parlor, anxious to detect from the expressions on their faces whether or not to wish them joy or to give Ninian a sympathetic pat on the shoulder as he left in a state of abject misery. Showing, by the aunts' estimation, a strange lack of interest in the affair, Julian retired to the library for a glass of brandy and a warm seat by the fire. He did, however, leave instructions with Hedley to send Sam to him the minute she was no longer busy with her beau.

Julian had been sitting thusly for several minutes when the laughter in the parlor finally quieted, followed by the sound of the front door closing, followed by a commotion in the hall while the aunts demanded details and explanations of the would-be lover's interview with Sam, followed by Sam, herself, slipping through the library door and softly closing it behind her.

It was dusk, and the library was dark except for a single candle on the table at Julian's elbow and the soft circle of firelight that encompassed a small area that included his chair and a patch of rosy paneling behind him. The air smelled of hickory and cigar smoke, old leather-bound books, and the lemon oil the servants used on the furniture and walls.

To Julian, it was a comfortable, comforting room. Very male. A sanctuary. But now, the minute Sam had stepped inside his sanctuary, the air was fraught with a sort of titillating tension, and a new scent—that lilac fragrance he'd detected in her hair when he'd carried her up the stairs, and when he'd kissed her—mingled with the other scents in the room, and suddenly there was a feminine influence in the air. The effect was seductive and . . . disturbing.

Striving to overcome his initial reaction to Sam's appearance, Julian said in his usual sardonic manner, "So, brat, you have got your first proposal."

Sam, who had been silently standing in the dark near the door till Julian spoke, glided across the room and stood in front of the fire, facing out. She was dressed all in white, and the light of the small, embering fire behind her made her appear as though she were surrounded by a nimbus of soft, shimmering gold. She looked like an angel.

"It wasn't my first proposal, Julian," she answered softly, her face shadowed, and her expression, therefore, a mystery.

"It wasn't?" he said gruffly. "What other men have bypassed my authority in this matter and addressed you without asking permission?"

He wasn't sure, but he thought she shrugged. A slight, tantalizing roll of her shoulder. "It doesn't matter. I refused them, of course."

"And did you refuse Ninian, too?"

"Of course. I couldn't possibly marry a man I don't love with my whole heart."

"I thought you'd changed your mind about such romantic notions?"

"I wanted you to think so. I thought it was your wish." There was a pause. "And you do know how *very* much I try to please you."

Julian snorted. "And your visit to my ex-mistress was an example of this desire you have to please me?"

He'd meant it as a joke, but she didn't laugh. There was complete silence in the room except for the soft crackles and hisses of the fire.

"I'm only teasing you, Sam," Julian said in a conciliatory tone. "I don't want us to quarrel about that episode any longer. I trust you learned your lesson and—"

"She's your *ex*-mistress?" Sam interrupted.

Julian felt a moment's confusion. Why had he let that bit of information slip? "Er . . . yes. But that's not a material point in this discussion. As I was saying, I trust you've learned your—"

"As you know, I'm a good student, Julian," Sam said sweetly. "Certainly I learned everything I needed to know from my encounter with Mrs. Descartes."

Julian frowned, not sure exactly how she'd meant that last statement, despite her dulcet tone. Then, suddenly, Sam took a step forward, then another. Then, in a rush, she knelt on the carpet in front of his chair, folded her hands, one on top of the other, and placed them on his knee. Then she rested her chin on top of her hands and gazed up at him with a beaming expression.

Surprised, but touched and pleased, Julian

couldn't resist the urge to reach down and stroke her hair. It felt like silk. "Why this confiding pose, Sam?" he teased softly. "It's not your usual style, m'dear. Does this mean we're friends again?"

"Oh, yes, Julian," she said with a saucy smile. "The very best of friends."

He chuckled, but despite his amusement and pleasure, there was a strange, twisting sensation in the pit of his stomach and an ache in his chest. And gazing at Sam's glowing face and coy smile only made those uncomfortable sensations increase.

He found himself not only stroking her hair, but running his fingers slowly, gently, down her temple to her soft cheek, then to the curve of her jaw, the dip below her chin, and then going even farther, down her long, slender neck to the warm hollow at the base of her throat.

Her eyes had drifted shut and, through the pad of his thumb, he could feel her heart beating very quickly. Just as his was. . . .

At this point, Julian would have taken his hand away, if only she hadn't opened her eyes and looked at him . . . just so. At that moment Sam seemed much more a woman than a child. So, instead of taking away his hand, he slid it down the slope of her shoulder, splaying his fingers over the bare skin between her neck and the puffed sleeve of her gown. Her skin was warm and petal-soft.

She continued to gaze into his eyes, seeming to give tacit permission for him to touch her wherever and however long he pleased. But he must be mistaken; his own desires were making him see permission where it couldn't possibly be. She wanted Nathan, he reminded himself. Not her dictatorial guardian.

But his wandering hand apparently had a mind

of its own. He was running his fingers up her neck
again, tracing her jaw, then resting them lightly on
her lips. Like her skin, her lips were heaven to
touch. Yes, he remembered. . . .

He could feel her breath skimming over his
knuckles. With his index finger he traced the Cupid's bow shape of her upper and lower lip, mesmerized by the lush curves and blooming color. Her
eyes drifted shut again.

It was so pleasurable, so sensuous, so . . .
dangerous.

A pang of guilt struck Julian, and he was about to
pull back his hand, when Sam parted her lips and
drew the tip of his finger into her mouth.

Shocked and aroused, Julian stared down at
Sam's face. She looked up at him through her
slightly lowered lashes, a playful and provocative
gleam in her eyes. Her mouth was warm and moist,
and the edge of her tongue gently teased his finger.
He reasoned that she couldn't possibly know that
what she was doing was highly erotic.

Or could she?

"If only you weren't my ward . . ." he murmured.

As Sam sat up straight, Julian's finger slipped out
of her mouth. With her hands still propped on his
knee, she said, "What did you say?"

God God, did I say that out loud?

Julian cudgeled his brain for a believable reply.
In other words, he needed a good lie.

"I . . . I was just saying that you . . . you . . .
deserve an award, Sam," he blurted.

Her brows furrowed while her mouth turned up
in a smile. She was frankly disbelieving. "What?
Did you say I deserve an *award,* Julian?"

"Yes, for being the most beautiful debutante of

the Season," he extemporized. When she looked pleased, he congratulated himself for appealing to her vanity. Lies were always more easily believed when they were flattering, and no one was immune to flattery.

"Do you really think so, Julian?" she asked him, her eyes aglow with pleasure.

"Yes, I do," he answered truthfully. *Too beautiful,* he added to himself. Then, desperate to bring an end to their little tête-à-tête, he said in a bracing, jocular tone, "Hadn't you better dress for dinner, brat? You were late last night. Perhaps tonight you'll do better, eh?"

Still glowing from his compliment, Sam used his knee to push herself to her feet, then rose gracefully from the floor. But—was it his imagination?—did her hand linger on his knee a tad longer than necessary?

"See you at dinner, Julian," she said with another sweet, melting smile. Then she slipped out the door and was gone.

Julian stood abruptly and poured himself a hefty shot of brandy, then downed it in two swallows. "Bloody Hell," he grumbled under his breath.

Chapter 10

"**B**ut I don't want you involved, Sam," Nathan said. "Lord Serling'll tan your hide once he finds out you helped Clara run away with me!"

While Madison sniffed the grass behind them and barked at every passerby, Nathan, Sam, and Clara sat on a stone bench in Hyde Park, their heads close together as they conspired to plan a successful elopement. Peering around Clara, who had been clutching Nathan's hand and looking slightly dazed ever since accepting an *official* marriage proposal from him only moments before, Sam laughed and said, "Tan my hide? What a delightful expression! It must be American."

"It's not a joke, Sam," Nathan insisted with a frown. "I don't want you getting into trouble on our account. We'll find another way."

"There is no other way. Or, at least, there is no *better* way. Besides, I'm always in some kind of trouble with Julian. He'll deliver me a thundering scold, refuse to talk to me for a few hours, then forgive me . . . as he always forgives me."

Sam realized she sounded rather smug and sure of herself, but after last night she couldn't help but be convinced she had Julian wound round her little finger. His touch as he'd caressed her had been so tender and loving. And the look in his eyes . . . Just the memory of it made her feel warm and trembling inside. In short, she had reason to hope that Julian was finally beginning to see her as a woman.

"You're going to need plenty of time to get well away from London before Clara's father discovers she's missing," she continued, pushing to the back of her mind her own concerns for the moment. "With so many miles between you, there's no way he could follow and catch up with you before you've reached Gretna Green. And, I daresay, seeing the futility of it, he won't even try. So, as I was saying—"

"I'm still not convinced that I can't just snatch 'er away in the dead of night," Nathan grumped, wrapping his arm around Clara's waist and giving her a squeeze. "That's the usual way it's done."

"Oh, and it sounds *so* romantic," Clara agreed with a sigh and a blush as she gazed adoringly at Nathan.

"Indeed," Sam murmured drily. "Quite romantic, I'm sure. But quite idiotish, too . . . as well you know, Clara. Your father's got the ears of a cat. None of the servants can sneak in or out of the premises without Hedley quoting them the exact hour and minute over breakfast the next morning in the servants' hall. It's become something of a game with him, and he takes great pride in it. Therefore, do you suppose he'd sleep through his own daughter's elopement? And can you imagine his reaction should he catch you in the act?"

Clara shivered. "Vividly, miss." She turned to Nathan. "She's right, love. We'd best listen to her."

Nathan sighed and smiled at his bride-to-be, then turned to Sam. "You were saying?"

Sam nodded approvingly. "I'll tell Julian that Clara and I will be spending all day tomorrow at the Women's Shelter. Then—"

"But what about your aunts?" Nathan interrupted. "The shelter is their pet project. Won't they want to accompany you?"

"My aunts won't be home tomorrow," said Sam, "which is why I fixed on tomorrow in the first place as the perfect time for you two to elope. The fact that Priss and Nan are driving down to Darlington Hall to spend the day, and staying overnight, in order to take care of some household business while Amanda is absent, fits perfectly into our plan. There will be two fewer people to maneuver around, and, since the aunts will be using Julian's carriage for the trip, we'll have the perfect excuse for hiring a hackney coach to drive us to the shelter. That means there will be no servants watching what we do, either, and questioning why we don't actually go to the shelter."

"But doesn't Lord Serling insist that some male servant accompany you to that quarter of town?" Nathan asked.

"He used to," Sam admitted. "But the aunts and I have gone so often to the shelter, we are now quite well known in the area and have many friends . . . some of whom are great, burly fellows who make sure we come to no harm whilst doing charity work in Spitalfields. Julian has become quite sanguine about our visits to the Women's Shelter."

"How convenient it all seems," Nathan murmured.

"Yes, it's all falling into place, isn't it?" Sam enthused. "Just as if it were meant to be!"

"And no one will suspect a thing when I carry a bag into the coach containing a few of my belongings," Clara added eagerly. "They'll assume we're taking clothes and blankets to the women at the shelter."

Nathan's brows knitted. "So far, so good. But once I meet you at the King's Arms on the outskirts of town, Sam, I don't like the idea of Clara and me hightailing it off to Scotland, leaving you to kick your heels at the inn till dusk."

"If I go right home, everyone will wonder where Clara is. And what am I to tell them? If I tell them the truth, Hedley will come after you. And since I must tell the truth as soon as I'm asked, the later they find it out the better. Besides, I will be perfectly safe at the inn, shut up in a room. I promise I won't venture out all day and will even have my food sent in. Are you satisfied?"

Nathan sat up straighter, his chest swelling. "No, I'm not satisfied. It seems a shabby business depending on you to bring me my bride, then bear the brunt of your guardian's displeasure. The manly thing to do would be to go straight to Clara's father and tell 'im I'm in love with his daughter, then demand her hand in marriage!"

Clara gave a worshipful sigh as she gazed at her beloved.

"I daresay it would be manly," Sam agreed matter-of-factly. "And very stupid."

Nathan's chest deflated. "But why?"

"Because we can depend on a disastrous outcome of such a display of manliness. Hedley would rant and rave and lock Clara in her bedchamber, and Clara would cry her eyes out and try to starve herself by refusing meals. Hedley might even take a strap to his disobedient daughter to teach her a lesson, which would infuriate you and cause you to punch your would-be father-in-law in the nose. Verla, the housekeeper, would fall into hysterics at this juncture and send a stable lad for the police. Once the police came upon the scene—"

"No need to go on, Sam," Nathan growled. "I see your point. Only, one might hope for reason and judgment to prevail in such a case, especially when one is trying to do the right and honorable thing."

"Not in *this* case." Sam looked at Clara. "Do you agree with my prediction of the course of events should Nathan insist on being manly and honorable, Clara? Or am I being overly pessimistic?"

Clara bit her lip and turned to Nathan. "I love you for trying to do the right thing, Nathan. But Sam's right again. While we might get my father to come about eventually to our way of thinking, it wouldn't be till after much suffering on all sides. By going away and marrying, then writing later to reconcile with him, he might be philosophical about it and eventually accept and forgive. Either way, he's going to be angry for a while. Isn't it better that we're far away from such anger . . . at least till it cools off? In the meantime, we can be honeymooning in bonny Scotland."

Nathan was convinced, and the tender looks exchanged between him and Clara prompted Sam to take Madison on a short walk to grant the lovers a few moments' privacy. While she walked, she allowed her thoughts to return to her favorite subject . . . Julian. She thoroughly enjoyed helping Clara and Nathan, and she hoped to be able to help Ninian, too, when she met with his mother the day after tomorrow for tea. She hoped that both plans would go off without a hitch. Then she could concentrate on her own plan to become Julian's brat . . . that is, Julian's *bride* . . . and live happily ever after.

Julian had made a point of staying away from the house all day. He'd even sent his excuses to the aunts and eaten dinner at Whites. Ever since those highly charged moments in the library with Sam, he'd been more restless and edgy than ever and, for some reason, he felt more comfortable away from home. He didn't know what had come over him lately, but whatever it was, he didn't like it. He could only suppose that he was feeling rather at loose ends since breaking things off with Isabelle.

Certainly he was worried about Sam and the mystery surrounding her mother, and was concerned about the threatening note that had warned him to cease looking into the matter, but he suspected that his restlessness and edginess had sexual origins. In short, he was probably just randy.

He was beginning to seriously consider making inquiries about Genevieve DuBois's current romantic status to ascertain whether or not she was available. Although he had met her on more than one occasion and had acknowledged her beauty and wit before, he had never felt the slightest urge to initiate a more intimate relationship . . . until recently. Yes, it had been only very recently that he'd felt a strong attraction to the lady.

Leaving Whites after dinner, Julian was glad he'd taken his carriage because the light shower that had begun to fall around teatime had developed into a heavy downpour. When he entered Montgomery House, he headed directly to his library, but as he walked past the front parlor the aunts liked to occupy, Priss stuck out her head and smiled warmly.

"Julian? So it *is* you! Samantha said she was sure she heard your step in the hall, and why didn't I pop out and entreat you to join us for a few moments? None of us are going out, of course. We were invited to several parties, but the rain is quite dreadful. Do come in and get warm by the fire. We've got hot chocolate and biscuits. Are your stockings wet?"

Julian hesitated for a moment, but he couldn't very well refuse such a barrage of kindness. Besides, he hadn't seen the aunts or Sam since breakfast, and the enticement of a cozy sort of family group around the fire was too much to resist. He ruefully acknowledged to himself that, for an old bachelor, he was getting rather fond of having a bevy of females around all the time.

"Certainly, Priss," he said at last. "I'll sit with you ladies for a while. But don't fret about my stockings. I'm wearing boots, and my feet are quite dry."

When Julian entered the room, his gaze was instantly drawn to Sam. She was sitting on the rug by the fire at the foot of Nan's chair, her feet tucked under her skirt, and with all three puppies sleeping and snuggled against her. She looked up as he approached, her expression happy and glowing. His heart felt a tender pang as he helplessly smiled back at her. But his common sense cautioned him not to get too attached to such domestic scenes and such welcoming smiles. Sam would soon be bestowing her smiles on a husband.

"Please don't scold, Julian," Sam said, her voice barely above a whisper as she tried not to disturb her slumbering pets. "I know I'm only supposed to have one pup at a time in the house with me, but on such a cold, wet night, how could I possibly rescue only one from the stable? Their faces, their expressions, their wagging tails, were too much to resist!"

Julian knew all about irresistible faces, expressions, and . . . er . . . wagging tails.

"Never mind, brat," he said as he pulled a third chair near the fire and positioned it between Priss's and Nan's, then sat down with a sigh. "I suppose I can make an exception this once. But don't make a habit of it."

"I won't," Sam promised, but her coy smile was utterly unconvincing. As always, she'd try to get away with as much as possible.

"How was your day, Julian?" Nan inquired, peering over her spectacles, her knitting needles clicking away without a pause.

"It was exceedingly wet," was all the reply Julian gave. After all, he couldn't very well tell Nan he'd been worried, restless, and randy all day, now could he?

"Indeed, it was far too wet for anyone that isn't a duck," Nan concurred. "And I'm beginning to think we might have to put off our trip to Darlington Hall on the morrow. If this keeps up, the roads will be ghastly."

Sam sat up straight, abruptly waking up Madison, who had been lying on his back in her lap. "Oh, no, Aunt Nan. Don't do that!"

At everyone's surprised and curious glance, Sam seemed to recollect herself and stuttered, "I . . . I was looking forward to hearing how Zeus and Neptune are doing."

"I'm sure you don't wish to hear news of those disorderly curs at the risk of putting your aunts in peril, do you, Sam?" Julian admonished her. Somehow, by taking on the role of the stern taskmaster again, he felt measurably better. Things were as they should be. Sam was the child and he was the guardian.

"No, Julian, of course not," Sam said, lowering her head. "I wasn't thinking."

"Never mind, dear," Priss said, handing Julian a steaming cup of hot chocolate. "We know how much you miss your dogs. Which is why I'm so surprised that you don't wish to go to Darlington Hall with us . . . if the weather permits. There are no important engagements tomorrow. And we'll be back in plenty of time on Thursday for you to keep your date to have tea with Lady Wentworth."

"Yes," said Julian, taking an experimental sip of the frothy chocolate and watching Sam's downcast face with suspicion. "Why don't you go to Darlington Hall, Sam? Have you something better to do?"

"She's going to the Women's Shelter, Julian," said Nan, looking up briefly to smile with affection on Sam. "She's such a good girl to put off her own pleasures to help the needy and afflicted."

Sam still did not raise her head, but seemed quite intent on scratching George behind the ears. Then, before Julian's fascinated eyes, she blushed as pink as a full-blown rose. Such a charming reaction could be the result of modesty caused by Nan's remark, certainly, or . . . Sam might be feeling guilty about something. But what?

"So, you're intending to do good deeds tomorrow, eh, Sam?" Julian said.

"Yes, Julian," Sam replied, still looking down.

"Only *good* deeds, brat?" Julian pressed, eyeing her keenly.

Finally Sam looked up. And, though her face was rosy, her voice was steady and her tone sincere as she said, "Yes, Julian. Only good deeds."

Julian was satisfied. He had to be. He trusted

Sam, and he knew she was no liar. And, as he sipped his hot chocolate and gazed at the fire, he felt the most contented he'd felt all day. Except, of course, that he was still damned randy. It was odd, too. One would think that sitting by the fire with two sweet old ladies, a childish ward, and a passel of sleepy puppies would obliterate every carnal thought in a man's head. Especially a man, like himself, who had always been able to firmly control his thoughts and emotions.

At length, as they all sat in companionable silence, Julian's thoughts turned again to Genevieve DuBois. What was it about her that he suddenly found so appealing? Those blue eyes, that blond hair, that determined, pointed little chin . . .

Then it hit him like a horse's hoof between the eyes. Genevieve DuBois reminded him of . . . *Sam.* The realization was too much, too sudden. It implied an idea quite unwelcome to his fastidious sensibilities. His hand jerked and he spilled a large splash of very hot chocolate on his trousers, high on his left thigh, not two inches away from a certain . . . er . . . vital part of his body.

"Bloody Hell," he growled, grabbing for a doily to scrub at the scalding spot.

But Sam had already jumped to her feet, doused a napkin in a flowerpot filled with water, and stood over him, her rag at the ready. "Here, Julian, let me dab it for you," she said, bending near.

"Like hell you will," he rasped, rising to his feet so rapidly that Sam backed onto Louie's paw and made him yelp.

By now the aunts were fussing and tsk-tsking and advising him to remove his trousers immediately, Madison was barking furiously, Louie was whining pitiably and much more than his injury warranted,

and George—though stoically refusing to bark—
was pacing and panting like an expectant father.
Sam simply held Louie in her arms and soothed
him, her startled blue eyes fixed questioningly on
Julian's crimson face. He knew it was crimson
because he felt as though he'd just dunked his head
in a bucket of burning coals.

"Bloody Hell," he growled again, then turned
and strode out of the room, guiltily aware that he'd
turned their calm and cozy fireside gathering into a
chaotic ruckus.

"Oh, miss, I'm going to miss you so much,"
Clara said, weeping against Sam's neck as they
hugged in the stable yard of the King's Arms.

"I'll miss you, too, Clara," said Sam, hoping
she'd be able to keep her own tears at bay till Clara
and Nathan were gone. She certainly didn't want
them to think she ever cried, for goodness sake. She
caught Clara by the shoulders and looked into her
reddened eyes. "You must quit calling me 'miss'!
We're friends, and my friends call me Sam. Besides,
you'll be married in a few hours, and you'll be a
great lady with servants of your own. Though,
knowing you, you probably won't let them lift a
finger to do anything for you. Now, quit crying or
you'll have a swollen nose for your wedding."

Clara laughed and wiped at her teary cheeks with
shaky hands. "It's just that everything will be so
new, Sam . . . and I'm scared. I love Nathan so
much"—she glanced at Nathan, who was talking
with his coachman—"and I don't want to disappoint him."

"You aren't going to disappoint him. I'm quite
convinced of that," Sam assured her. "And as for

being scared, anything worthwhile comes with a certain amount of risk. I never wanted to leave Thorney Island, you know. But look at all the good things that have happened to me since I did."

Clara grabbed Sam's hands and squeezed them tightly. "And I hope with all my heart that more good's coming your way. I want you to be as happy with Julian as I am with Nathan. You will write me, Sam?"

"As soon as you let me know where you are."

"It will be weeks."

Sam smiled impishly. "You'll write to tell me you're with child."

Clara blushed. "La!"

"And hopefully I'll at least be married by then."

"It's time to be off, Clara," said Nathan, coming up behind his intended and draping his arm over her shoulder. He smiled at Sam. "I can't thank you enough, Sam, for all your help. You'll stay in your room till time to go, won't you? I'll be worried sick unless you promise me you won't get into any mischief today."

Sam grinned. "I think I can promise to stay out of mischief for at least one day."

"Do it, then," Nathan said, bending down and surprising Sam by kissing her on the cheek. Then, undoubtedly hoping to avoid another farewell scene between the females, he hurriedly hoisted Clara into the coach, climbed in behind her, and yelled to the coachman to "be off!" In three shakes of a lamb's tail, they were hurtling down the north road away from London, with only Clara's handkerchief trailing out the window as a final good-bye.

Sam watched wistfully and allowed a tear or two to fall, till a roll of thunder and a drop of rain on her nose alerted her to the fact that she had better go inside. Luckily the early morning had been fair and the aunts had left for Darlington Hall on schedule, but now, at midmorning, the sky had clouded up again rather ominously. However, she trusted that when it was time to head home at six o'clock, the weather would not be too inclement to impede her short journey across town to Montgomery House.

As Sam passed by the taproom to the stairs, she saw the tall, balding innkeeper sweeping the floor. He looked up and returned her smile with a suspicious frown. She was sure he thought she was involved in some sort of havey-cavey business, because Nathan had procured and paid for her room—to which she and Clara and Nathan had all retired for a half hour to talk and drink tea—then he'd gone off in a coach with what was obviously Sam's maidservant. Sam chuckled as she reached the landing and turned toward her room at the end of the hall. Such goings-on would appear rather odd to anyone.

Inside the room, Sam sat by the window overlooking the street and peered through a glass that was already streaming with raindrops. It was pouring outside. Still optimistic about the weather not complicating her return home, however, she calmly opened a workbasket of sewing she was doing for the Women's Shelter.

Sam had determined that she would spend the day in such a worthwhile employment to partially make up for lying to Julian about going to the Women's Shelter. But she did not consider the part about doing only "good deeds" today a lie. After all, wasn't it a good deed to help two people get together for a lifetime of love and happiness?

Of course it was, Sam thought complacently, threading her needle. And once she had a chance to explain, certainly Julian would agree with her.

"My hat and cane, please, Benson," said Julian, addressing the butler at Whites. "Then send for a hack, will you? I don't fancy walking home in this deluge."

"Yes, my lord," Benson intoned, immediately turning to do as he'd been bid.

Julian walked to the bow window that overlooked St. James Street and looked out on the sodden scene below. It was only five o'clock but, because of the heavy clouds and persistent rain, it was already growing dark outside, and few people were braving the elements. He, however, would be braving them at least three more times that night.

Nan and Priss wouldn't be home for dinner that evening, and to avoid a tête-à-tête with his ward, Julian intended to return to Whites later for a bite to eat. As for Sam's dinner, he had instructed Cook to send a meal to her room as soon as she returned from the Women's Shelter. This had all been arranged and talked over that morning, but Julian still felt a need to return to Montgomery House for a few minutes just to make sure Sam and Clara had had no trouble getting back safely from the shelter in such a downpour.

He wasn't terribly worried, of course, since London hack drivers were certainly used to driving in the rain. But he would feel infinitely better to see his ward snug and safe at home before he left for an evening at his club.

He supposed he was feeling a protective "older-brother" solicitude toward Sam. Such familial concern sounded harmless enough, but who would have thought that having the feelings of an older brother could be complicated and confused by a little sister growing up to be so innocently alluring? It made a fellow . . . uncomfortable. A perfect example of such discomfort was the way he'd overreacted when Sam wanted to dab at the spill of hot chocolate on his trousers last night. She hadn't meant anything by it, but he'd been skittish about her touching him. Although perhaps "skittish" wasn't a strong enough word.

Then there had been the kiss. . . . He'd never gotten over that. He'd never apologized to Sam for it, either. But since she never brought it up, he felt it was best not to mention it at all. Perhaps for her it was as good as forgotten. He wished *he* could forget as easily.

"Here are your cane and hat, my lord," said Benson, handing Julian the items. "And a note came for you just now, as well." Benson indicated a folded sheet of parchment paper on a silver salver being held forward by a liveried footman.

Frowning, Julian picked up the parchment paper and unfolded it. At a glance, he immediately perceived that it was from the same person who had sent him the threatening note about Sam. A chill crept into his heart as he read, *"Despite my warning, you paid another visit to Sir Humphries. Why do you persist in delving into the past when it will serve no good purpose to your young ward? There is danger in the truth. Please spare Samantha the pain she will surely endure if her mother's identity is revealed. Heed my warning this time, or beware. . . .*

Revealing no outward reaction to the note, Julian refolded the paper and put it in his coat pocket. Still waiting for the hack, he returned to the bow window and stared, unseeing, into the darkening gloam.

Julian had been expecting another note, but it was still quite unnerving to feel that someone was always watching what you were doing, and that that same someone knew a secret which she claimed could destroy Sam's happiness. Going over in his mind the contents and tone of the note, Julian couldn't decide if the person who wrote the note was more concerned with saving herself from scandal, or of saving Sam.

Suddenly Julian realized that, without consciously meaning to, he had been thinking of the note writer as a woman. The message conveyed in the missive sounded much like a mother trying to shield her child from the slings and arrows of an unforgiving society. As well, the handwriting appeared more feminine than masculine.

Could the note be from Sam's mother? If not, what other female would care so much for concealment? A concerned mother wouldn't be expected to issue threats and ultimatums, certainly, as the note writer did, but perhaps the threats were meaningless and were included simply with the hope of frightening Julian into abandoning his pursuit of the truth.

Well, whoever wrote the note didn't know him very well, Julian concluded grimly, because he had no intention of giving up the search for Sam's natural mother. For his ward's sake and safety, he was more determined than ever to discover the truth.

Perceiving a hack pulling up in front of the club, and assuming it was his, Julian left the room more eager than ever to be at home. However, as he was about to dash out the door and into the hired coach, a man, who had just arrived, stopped him by grasping his arm.

Irritated, Julian turned to see who dared delay him in such a manner. It was Sir Jeffrey Percival, a man with whom he was superficially acquainted. They occasionally played cards together at the club, and while Julian deemed him a bit of a rattle, he also thought him basically harmless and good-hearted. He wasn't a personal friend, certainly, but he was not someone he could shrug off, either.

"Sir Jeffrey," Julian said, nodding and smiling tightly. "How do you do?"

"I do very well, Serling," said the jowly, red-faced gentleman, returning the nod perfunctorily. "However, there is something I wish to tell you in private, sir, before I ask how *you* do. You're in for a bit of an alarm, I'm afraid."

Despite his impatience to be gone, Julian couldn't help but be affected by Sir Jeffrey's grave countenance and serious tone. The old fellow was usually quite jolly. Feeling a dread that was impossible to describe, but remaining outwardly calm, he inquired, "What could possibly alarm me at this stage in my jaded life, Jeffrey?"

Sir Jeffrey looked about him, eyeing everyone even remotely nearby with exaggerated suspicion. Julian had no tolerance for such an unnecessary display of drama—which rather drew more attention to them than otherwise—but he had a sinking feeling that Jeffrey's news was important . . . and that is was about Sam.

Jeffrey led Julian into an empty window embrasure off the main hall and drew near. "I sent a note to Montgomery House earlier. Did you not get it?"

"I did not. I haven't been home all day."

"Damn! A pity." Jeffrey rubbed his chin and looked dour. "Perhaps it's too late, then."

"What the deuce are you talking about?" Julian prompted, hating the way his heart had begun to hammer against his ribs.

"It's about your ward, Miss Darlington," he whispered.

"So I suspected," Julian drawled, affecting unconcern. "What social *faux pas* has she committed to put you in such a pucker?"

Jeffrey's eyes widened. "Oh, this is much more serious than a social *faux pas,* Serling. Oh, yes indeed!"

"Cut line, Jeffrey, and tell me what my ward has been up to."

"I'm not sure what she's been up to, but it can't be anything good at the King's Arms."

"The King's Arms?"

"Yes, I saw her there this morning. I was passing by and I noticed her standing in the courtyard with—"

"That's impossible," Julian cut him off. "She went to the Women's Shelter in Spitalfields this morning to do charity work, which is in the other direction altogether. What would my ward be doing at the King's Arms?"

Sir Jeffrey nodded sagely. "Indeed, that is a reasonable question." He leaned closer. "She was with . . . a *man.*"

"Nonsense! What man?"

"I don't know him well, Serling, but I believe you do. It's that American chap from Virginia. Ford, I think he's called. Tall, sandy-haired, rather well built, speaks with a colonial twang—"

"Yes, I know him," Julian snapped. "But you must have mistaken the girl. I'm sure it wasn't *my* ward you saw with Ford."

There was a pause as Sir Jeffrey seemed to be deciding whether or not he should say more. Julian was trying very hard to keep his emotions from showing, but perhaps he was losing his touch. Perhaps Sir Jeffrey could tell how angry and shocked he really was. Finally Julian could stand the silence no longer.

"What was Ford doing with this girl?" he asked with forced calmness. "Did they go inside the inn?"

Obviously relieved to resume the conversation, Jeffrey said, "As I told you, I was only passing by, so I don't know what happened after I had gone round the corner, but it appeared to me that they were preparing to go on a . . . well . . . on a *journey.*"

"The devil you say," Julian growled. "Why would you suppose so?"

"There were boxes strapped on the top of the coach, and four horses pulling the coach instead of two. I saw Ford consulting with his coachman, then, looking back again as we sped past, I saw him bend down and *kiss* your ward on the cheek! After that, I don't know what happened because we'd gone round the bend. What do you make of it, Serling?"

Julian could only make of it one thing. The evidence seemed irrefutable that Sam had run off with her American suitor. She had eloped. Apparently she was not willing to endure a long engagement—such as Julian had told her would be necessary—nor was she willing to wait for her sister's return to England before shackling herself to Nathan Ford.

Controlling himself with an effort, holding back strong feelings of betrayal, confusion, anger, and panic, Julian coolly replied, "I thank you, sir, for taking the trouble to send the note to Montgomery House, and stopping me just now to convey your concerns. But I'm quite certain there's a reasonable explanation for my ward to be at the King's Arms today with Nathan Ford . . . if, indeed, the girl in question truly was my ward. Mistakes can be made. But I'd better not waste another moment finding out the truth of the matter. In the meantime, I'm sure I can trust you to stifle any rumors that might arise."

Then Julian gave Sir Jeffrey a measured look, tipped his hat, and hurried out the door to the waiting hackney coach.

"To the King's Arms!" he shouted at the driver. "And be quick about it!"

Chapter 11

Julian wasn't sure why he was racing across town to the King's Arms. If Sam had eloped, she'd be long gone by now. And if he was only going to the inn to obtain information, it would be smarter to go home first and see if Sam had left him a note. But a visceral feeling compelled him to go to the King's Arms before doing anything else to unravel this mystery.

If he were being honest with himself, however, he'd have to admit to entertaining a remote . . . and most unwelcome . . . possibility that there was another explanation for Sam being seen at a public inn with Nathan Ford. This other explanation might allow for her still being at the inn . . . in Nathan's arms, trying out some of the "tricks" of the trade that had been explained to her during that infamous visit she'd paid to his mistress!

Julian ground his teeth together till his jaw ached. His hands, resting on his knees, clenched and unclenched in impotent rage. He couldn't bear the thought of Sam—in a misguided attempt to prove her affection—giving herself to that man! He didn't deserve her. He wouldn't do right by her, and Sam deserved all the respect and love a decent man could give.

And even if they did elope and Nathan did mean to marry her before bedding her, it was still a shabby business carrying her away to Scotland to exchange vows over an anvil when she could have stayed home and had a lovely ceremony in a church, surrounded by her family.

Julian was not happy with either explanation, though he would, of course, prefer that she were married than compromised.

Or . . . would he?

If she married Nathan Ford, she'd be lost to him forever, stranded in distant Virginia on a horse farm. If she were only compromised . . .

Julian shook his head and rubbed his temples distractedly. *Only* compromised? What was he thinking? If Nathan had compromised her, Julian would demand that he either marry her or face him in a duel. And if he and Nathan pointed pistols at each other at twenty paces, Julian would be hard put not to blast a hole through the blackguard's heart. Such a violent act against her supposed "beloved" would probably turn Sam against him forever.

Either way she was lost to him. Either way things would never be the same.

Julian looked grimly out the window. If only there were another explanation for this latest bumblebroth Sam had gotten herself into. . . .

Sam put her sewing back into the basket and went to look into the mirror over the dressing table. Except for her eyes being a little strained from sewing all day, her appearance hadn't changed a bit since the moment she'd arrived at the inn several hours ago. But, since she hadn't stirred from the room all day, there was no reason why every hair shouldn't still be in place.

Therefore, there was nothing left to do but fetch her bonnet and pelisse, and go downstairs to ask the innkeeper to send for a hackney coach to take her home. Hedley would immediately inquire after Clara, and a confession would have to be made, but, as Julian was spending the evening at Whites, there was still plenty of time before Sam would have to face her guardian's particular brand of frosty anger.

The thing was, Sam was actually looking forward to her confrontation with Julian. Remembering how angry he'd been the other night when he'd found out that she'd visited his mistress, she shivered with delicious anticipation. Underneath that chilling hauteur, he'd been sizzling. She knew there was passion beneath his carefully controlled facade, and she was more than willing to make him angry with her again to bring that passion to the surface.

Her smile broadened. Maybe tonight that passion would result in something much more interesting than a mere scolding. . . .

"Wait for me," Julian tersely instructed the hackney driver as he stepped out of the coach and into the muddy courtyard of the King's Arms.

"Aye, m'lord," the driver muttered, hunching his caped shoulders against the onslaught of the pouring rain.

Despite his preoccupation with Sam's dilemma, Julian couldn't ignore the miserable and wet condition of the hackney driver. "Wait inside," he amended, his own hat already dripping rain from the brim. "Order a drink that'll warm you. I'll stand the ready. Cold, hot, spiked or not, I don't care. Then stand by the fire till I'm ready to go. Understood?"

"Aye, m'lord," said the driver with some surprise.

Then, as the driver called for the ostler to tend his horse while he was occupied much more agreeably inside, Julian entered the building, took off his hat and set it by the fire to dry out, then looked about for the innkeeper.

The innkeeper soon appeared, his face instantly brightening at the sight of such a swell on his humble premises. "What can I do for ye, sir?" he inquired obsequiously.

"You can give me some information," Julian said.

"If I can, sir," the innkeeper replied, hiding his disappointment that that was all the well-heeled gent wanted.

"I'm here to inquire after a lady who was seen in your courtyard earlier today."

"There've been a lot of o' ladies comin' and goin' today, sir," the innkeeper cautioned respectfully. "It's rare if'n one of 'em sticks in my mind."

"This one is hard to forget," Julian said dryly. "She is quite beautiful, about yea high"—he indicated a height a few inches below his chin—"has blond hair and blue eyes, and was in the company of an American man with sandy hair and—"

"Oh, *that* one," said the innkeeper, nodding sagely. "I always remember the colonials. Though it's supposed t' be the King's English, *their* manner o' speakin' is hard t' understand."

"Yes, quite right," Julian interrupted impatiently. "Now, about this American—"

"He paid fer the room," the innkeeper went on, his brows knitted with puzzled irritation, "but he only used it fer a half hour. Seemed a waste o' good blunt t' me."

Julian felt his temples throb as his heart pounded hard and fast. "He . . . er . . . *used* it for a *half hour?*" he choked out. "I don't suppose he went to the room . . . alone?"

The innkeeper sniffed. "I'll say not. He and the lady you asked about and—"

"And then they left together, shortly thereafter?"

"He left, but the lady you was askin' about, she's still upstairs," the innkeeper finished with another sniff. "Don't know why. Don't claim t' understand those colonials and their lady friends."

Julian couldn't believe it! Not only had Nathan compromised Samantha—accomplishing the task in a mere half hour!—but he'd abandoned her, too! He could feel the color rising up his neck, flooding his head with heat, making his eyes burn. "The bloody bastard," he rasped. "I'll kill 'im."

"Beggin' yer pardon, sir?" said the innkeeper, backing up a step.

"What room is she in?" Julian demanded in a voice of repressed violence that brooked no opposition.

"She's . . . she's in the farthest room on the right, at the first landing, sir," the innkeeper stammered. "But, if'n ye please, sir, don't make no trouble," he pleaded, as Julian strode purposely toward the stairs. "Don't smash no furniture. And please don't break the basin and water pitcher . . . they're new!"

Except for the directions to Sam's room, Julian

hardly registered a word the innkeeper said. He was so angry at Nathan, if the fellow had been nearby there would have been a murder . . . and the biggest scandal the *ton* had seen since Lord Byron and Caro Lamb brawled at Carlton House right under the nose of the Prince Regent.

Julian could just imagine the article in the *Times* telling the lurid tale of how the cool, controlled, oh-so-civilized marquess of Serling ruthlessly, single-handedly choked the life out of a wealthy American. And all to avenge the sexual ruination of his young ward . . . the sweet, innocent Miss Samantha Darlington.

The sweet, innocent Miss Samantha Darlington. The words reverberated in Julian's tortured conscience as he took the stairs two at a time and moved hurriedly down the hall to her room. Dear, spirited Sam! He'd failed her. *He'd failed her.*

But as he reached her room, Julian forced himself to at least seem outwardly calm. He did not want to draw attention to himself or to Sam's predicament. Somehow he had to get her out of the King's Arms and across town without the entire world finding out what had happened. He'd take her home and repair the damage of this dreadful day if it was the last thing he ever did!

The poor girl—*the disobedient baggage!* He was torn between wanting to comfort her and wanting to blister her backside with a willow switch!

But surely she was in a desperate, miserable state, and heartily sorry for being so foolish, he reminded himself. After being abandoned so cruelly, she had probably cried herself sick. He prepared himself for the pathetic sight of a frightened, bedraggled Sam, weeping and weary.

* * *

Humming to herself, Sam had just picked up her pelisse and bonnet and was about to leave the room to summon a hackney coach, when a knocking on the door startled her considerably. No one had bothered her all day, except when she'd expressly ordered food and drink to be brought to her room. Pressing her hand to her fluttering heart, she called in a low voice, "Yes? Who is it?"

"Sam, open the door."

The voice was just above a whisper, the tone urgent and imperative and undeniably Julian's. Now Sam's heart was beating harder than ever and she could barely catch her breath. How did he know where she was? How did he find out so soon about Clara's elopement?

"Sam? Can't you hear me?" he hissed impatiently. "It's Julian. Open the door this instant!"

Although she had thought earlier that she was prepared for, and would even welcome, Julian's anger, now Sam wasn't so sure. She hadn't expected to have to face Julian before that evening, and as he'd actually tracked her down, there was no doubt that he was looking forward to wringing her neck. All kinds of excuses ran through her mind as she walked slowly to the door, but she knew she'd have to tell the truth.

She took the doorknob in both hands, leaning close to the paneled wood. "Julian? Is that really you?" she stalled.

"Of course it's me. Didn't I say so?" Then, more gently, "Don't be afraid. Just open the door and let me in, and we'll soon put all to rights."

Sam was perplexed. Although he'd started off sounding terse, he moderated his tone to one of gentle solicitude, as if he were worried about her. But why?

Pondering this strange behavior, Sam decided that maybe he was trying to trick her into thinking he would be understanding about her part in Clara's elopement. Naturally his tone would instantly change the minute she undid the lock and allowed him entrance.

But there was only one way to find out. Turning the key in the lock, she opened the door, and Julian slipped through and into the room. Then, no sooner had he closed the door behind him than he grabbed Sam by the shoulders, gave her a quick hard shake, then pulled her roughly into his arms.

"Sam! Are you all right? No, that's a stupid question. Of course you're not all right. That bloody bastard is going to pay with his—"

Crushed against Julian's hard chest, Sam was too stunned to say a word. He was caressing her, almost *mauling* her in the most delightful way! He held her head against his heart, kissing her hair. His hands roamed her back.

But then he grabbed her shoulders again and held her at arm's length, looking her over with a mix of anguish and anger in his eyes. Sam felt like a rag doll at the mercy of his strong hands. "Why did you do it, Sam? How could you be so deceived by that blackguard? I could shake you till your teeth rattle!"

Blinking confusedly, Sam was about to ask him what he was talking about, when he suddenly bent and kissed her on the forehead, then, in fast succession, her temples and both cheeks. He was showering her face with earnest, urgent kisses.

Julian felt dazed. He was in a fever of feelings. As soon as he'd stepped inside the room, he'd taken Sam into his arms, and a fierce protectiveness had made him hold her as tightly as a lover would. He knew an overwhelming sense of relief, mixed with grief and frustration. He felt compelled to kiss her and caress her, as if she were somehow slipping away from him forever.

But as the first rush of emotions settled to the point that Julian could see and assess the situation more clearly, he found several matters to be surprised and perplexed about. To begin with, he noticed that the bed was still made.

Not a pillow was dented.

Not a blanket was stirred.

It didn't look like it had even been sat on.

Then Julian looked, for the first time with discernment, at Sam. She was just opening her eyes. As the thick lashes lifted, he could see that she did appear as though she could have been crying—her eyes were slightly pink and glistened with moisture—but not as if she'd been crying all day. Her nose wasn't the least bit red and swollen, and her face wasn't mottled and streaked with tears.

This led, of course, to a more thorough scrutiny of the rest of her person. He'd seen Sam leaving that morning; he'd watched from the top of the stairs as she'd slipped on her pelisse in the entrance hall. The dress she wore now, which was the same dress she'd had on that morning—a white muslin sprigged with blue cornflowers—appeared just as crisp and neat as it had then. There did not appear to be any signs of the dress having been removed at some point, or of having been rumpled or pulled at or even amorously pawed.

And her hair . . . Except for the damage *he'd* done to it, the demure knot and escaping tendrils that were the style among females of Sam's age, were still in place.

In short, unless Nathan Ford was the hastiest,

neatest lover in the world—mysteriously doing the deed without contact of any kind—Sam had *not* been compromised! But when profound relief and happiness should have overpowered him, a bad feeling still nagged at him like a pebble in his shoe.

"Sam?"

Sam looked slightly dazed. "Yes, Julian?"

"What is going on here? Where *is* he?"

Sam blinked. "Where is whom, Julian?"

"You mean where is *who*," he automatically corrected her.

A slight frown creased her brow. "Where is *who*, then?"

Julian's hands slipped to Sam's waist and he firmly set her back a few inches so that their bodies were no longer pressed against each other. "Whom do you think, brat? Where is that scoundrel, Nathan Ford? Did he abandon you, as the innkeeper said?"

Suddenly the dazed expression in Sam's eyes cleared away, like morning mist lifting from a blue, blue lake. She began to look guilty, and Julian's suspicions took root. She might not have been compromised, but perhaps she'd wanted to be.

He let go of her waist and removed himself to a spot across the room near the fireplace. He crossed his arms and spread his legs in the usual pose he assumed for interrogation of underlings and troublesome wards.

"Are you going to answer my question, Sam?" he prompted her, his tone dripping with cool hauteur.

She, too, crossed her arms and spread her legs. She was mocking him, the disrespectful little baggage! "Why would you suppose I have any idea where Nathan is? And how did you even know where to find *me*?"

"I'm asking the questions here," he informed her frostily. "Not you."

"Don't I have any rights?" she shot back.

"You forfeited your rights, brat, when you lied to me." He opened his arms and indicated the room with a sweeping flourish. "This doesn't look like the Women's Shelter to me. That is, not unless they're harboring the homeless in public inns these days."

Sam blushed hotly. At least she still had enough scruples left to be embarrassed when she was caught in a lie.

"Well?" he prompted. "Tell me what's going on. You can't imagine what I've been thinking, fearing—" He stopped suddenly, unwilling to lose his leverage by showing his concern.

Too late. Sam's chin was already lifting defiantly. Her blush had quickly disappeared, replaced by two determined spots of color high on her cheeks. "I told you I was going to the Women's Shelter because it was the only way I could think of to get away from the house without a chaperon."

"That much I figured out for myself," he answered with dry sarcasm. "Yes, a chaperon would definitely put a damper on a secret liaison with a lover at a public inn." He paused to gather his composure, then proceeded with steely calm. "How could you be so foolish, Sam? What were you thinking? You had nothing to prove to Nathan Ford. Men do not routinely sample the wares before tying the knot. Like as not, once the wares are sampled, they're on to the next 'shop,' so to speak."

Sam's eyes widened and her mouth fell open in an appearance of patent disbelief. "Is that what you think happened here? Is that why you were so emotional at first, so . . . so *sweet* to me? You thought I'd met Nathan here for an amorous tryst, and that he'd then left me to fend for myself?"

Julian glowered. "Do you dare to deny it? When I spoke with a gentleman I know at Whites, informing me that he saw you and Nathan kissing in the courtyard of the King's Arms this morning, what else was I to conclude?"

"Indeed, I suppose it was impossible for you to even consider that there might be another explanation," she retorted. "I'm not a . . . a . . . 'shop,' Julian!"

Julian tapped his toe on the floor. "You have been visiting courtesans, Sam," he reminded her tartly. "You have been reading books about sex. It seemed likely to me that you were putting your newly acquired knowledge to the test."

Sam did not reply. She simply glowered back at him.

"That you meant to allow the gentleman liberties I still believe to be true," Julian continued. "And though you have acted a bit miffed by my assertions, you have not outright denied them."

Thinking this a perfect moment for denials, Julian waited for some response from Sam, but she remained stubbornly silent. Julian sighed and gave his waistcoat a straightening tug. "Thank goodness nothing came of this so-called tryst, a circumstance for which I am profoundly grateful. I only hope that *you* were the one to put a stop to this immoral debacle . . . that it was you who searched your mind and heart and finally decided not to employ the tactics you learned from Isabelle and, instead, sent the fellow packing!"

Sam covered her mouth and shook her head, her eyes suddenly brimming with . . . not tears of shame . . . but of *amusement*.

"What's so funny?" Julian demanded.

"You, Julian," she informed him with a laugh that bordered on the hysterical. "You are a brilliant man. But today, for some reason, you are acting like an absolute *nick-ninny!"*

Doubt and foreboding flooded Julian's heart. "You're not telling me that you *did* dally with Nathan Ford, are you?"

Sam shrugged. "Why do you suppose we didn't? Isabelle certainly told me everything I need to know to be quite good at 'dallying.' And to be quite *diverse,* too! I'll certainly never be a *boring* lover."

"The bed's still made," Julian growled.

"What makes you think we used the bed?" Sam taunted him. "Perhaps he took me against the wall, or maybe we got down on the rug and—"

"Stop it, Sam," Julian rasped. The visions she was conjuring up were torture.

"Or perhaps we indulged in a *ménage à trois,"* Sam persisted, pacing the rug and gesturing wildly. "After all, what else were we to do with *Clara?* We figured we might as well put her to good use!"

"Sam, I said to stop talking like a—"

Julian stopped short. Clara. *Clara.* He had not thought of her all day! No, even though he'd seen her leave with Sam that morning, not once had he wondered where Clara was!

"Good God, Sam, where *is* Clara?" Julian inquired in a wondering voice.

Sam crossed her arms and smirked. "I should say she's halfway to Scotland by now."

"To Scotland?"

"Aye, to our wee, bonny neighboring country to the north," Sam confirmed in a fair imitation of a Scottish burr and with a cheeky grin.

Julian frowned. "How did she get there?"

"She didn't walk. And since no one has invented a method for humans to fly from place to place, you must certainly realize, Julian, that she went in a horsedrawn carriage."

"You incorrigible brat," Julian grated out. "Don't mock me, or I shall be tempted to . . . to . . ."

Sam raised her brows in a look of saucy interest. "To do what, Julian?"

"Never mind! Just tell me with whom she was traveling and why. Her father will be in a tizzy. I gather she eloped with someone . . . but who? I had no idea Clara was keeping company with anyone."

With her arms still crossed, Sam simply shook her head at Julian and smiled. "Your friend at Whites saw the very man whose name you press for . . . in the courtyard, kissing *me!*"

Julian's frown deepened. "Nathan? You're not telling me that Clara ran off with Nathan, are you? I don't believe it! He's in love with you! And *you're* in love with *him!*"

"So you seem determined to believe," Sam said. "But there is absolutely nothing going on between Nathan and me. There never was. Not love, or lust."

Julian's eyes narrowed. "If there was nothing going on, why was he kissing you?"

"He was kissing me good-bye. And he merely gave me a peck on the cheek. People—your friend at Whites, too, no doubt—love to exaggerate, you know."

Julian seemed finally to be putting all the facts together and attempting to fathom what must seem to him unfathomable. He walked slowly to a reed-backed chair by the fireplace and sat down, his arms hanging limply at his sides. He looked at the oval braided rug at his feet for a few moments, seemingly deep in thought, then lifted his troubled, reflective gaze to Sam.

"You told me you loved him," Julian accused.

"I never said so," Sam disclaimed.

"You implied it. In fact, I thought I understood that your visit to Isabelle was for the sole purpose of learning how to please Nathan in bed."

Sam took a tentative step closer. "I never named Nathan as the man I wished to please . . . in . . . in that way."

Julian eyed her warily, his gaze flitting over her from tip to toe. "I distinctly remember his name being mentioned."

"His name was brought up by *you*." She took another step.

"You didn't correct my mistake." He looked her over again, this time his gaze lingering on her lips. She saw him swallow hard.

"I wanted you to figure it out for yourself," she said, taking one more step toward what she hoped would be an embrace. "But it appears that I must make explanations." Now it was her turn to swallow hard. "I know I've given you reason to believe otherwise, but the only man for me, the only man I could ever want and love and employ my newly acquired knowledge in behalf of, is . . . is . . . *you*, Julian Montgomery."

Chapter 12

Julian stared at Sam. Then it was true, he thought numbly. Charlotte had been right when she'd told him that Sam fancied herself in love with him. He'd thought it amusing at first, even a little touching, because surely all Sam felt for him was an immature infatuation . . . a sort of confused gratitude.

Then, when she'd appeared so smitten with Nathan Ford, had spent so much time with him recently, and had asked so many questions about America, he'd naturally concluded that Sam had found another object for her affections.

But, apparently, Julian had been completely wrong. The questions had been for Clara's benefit. And all those walks in Hyde Park with just the three of them and that undisciplined pup, Madison, had been to further the romance between Clara and Nathan!

Julian still believed Sam's feelings for him were not the sort that made for a mature and lasting attachment, but her infatuation was obviously more firmly entrenched in her youthful and unworldly imagination than he could have ever imagined.

"Bloody Hell," Julian muttered. "How could I have been so blind and stupid? I've always prided myself on my wit, but it appears I haven't enough to fill a thimble."

"Nonsense, Julian," Sam assured him softly, taking another step closer. She stood directly in front of him now, with only an arm's length separating them. "Everyone in London names you as the cleverest man in town."

He frowned. "Then why didn't I see how you were . . . er . . . feeling about me? Why didn't I see what was right in front of my nose?"

She shrugged, that subtle, sensuous movement of her slim, round shoulder that Julian found so unnerving. He looked away. "Perhaps, as now, you didn't *want* to see what was right in front of your nose," she suggested coyly.

Goaded, Julian locked eyes with her again, but did not allow his gaze to stray below her neck. He had no business lusting after her. And she must never know. . . .

He raised his brows and drawled, "That's unlikely. Why wouldn't I?"

"Maybe because if you confronted the notion of me being in love with you, you'd have to admit that . . ." Her voice trailed off. She blushed and looked timid.

"Admit what, brat?" he prompted her with assumed boredom.

She took a breath, seeming to gather courage. "That you're in love with me, too."

Alarmed, Julian immediately stood up, nearly toppling Sam backwards. He caught her by the arms, just below the shoulders, her eyes large and startled as she stared up at him.

"There is something we must get straight right now, Sam," Julian said gruffly, more than a little distracted by how nice her small, firm breasts felt against his chest, how sweet and clean her hair smelled. "I am *not* in love with you, child. Nor, even if I were so inclined, would I be free to indulge in such a . . . a . . . foolish fancy. I'm as good as engaged to Charlotte Batsford."

Sam's eyes flashed rebelliously. "As good as engaged, but *not* engaged. And, pray, why not? You could have asked her any number of times."

She was right, but he'd no intention of analyzing his reluctance to pop the question to Charlotte. He countered with, "I'm old enough to be your father."

"That could be said of several of the men who have pursued me recently, Julian," Sam retorted. "You never raised objections to any of them because of a discrepancy in age. Besides, age means nothing in a relationship. Two people being *alike* is what matters."

Julian gave a harsh laugh. "You call us 'alike'? Don't be absurd, Sam. *Charlotte* and I are alike. Calm, cool, collected."

She wrinkled her nose. "Boring, stodgy, and *far* too controlled."

"Hmph! If I'm so stiff-rumped, I'm surprised you find me at all attractive."

While Julian still held fast to her forearms, Sam reached up and began to lightly stroke the lapels of his jacket. "You're not stiff-rumped. Not really," she said in a lilting tone, as if reassuring him. "Underneath that steely control you exert over your emotions, there's so much passion, Julian."

While Julian allowed it for reasons he did not

completely understand, her hands wandered to the gap in his jacket. She slipped her hands into that gap and laid her palms flat against his chest. He could feel the warmth of her skin through the thin material of his shirt.

"You have so much heart hidden under this meticulously laundered muslin shirt," she whispered, gazing earnestly into his eyes. "If you married Charlotte, so much would stay hidden. So much would be held inside—"

"Where it belongs," Julian muttered.

"—and you'd never feel the freedom and the joy of truly letting go. Truly allowing yourself to *feel.*"

"I feel all I need to feel. A maudlin excess of sentimentality is not my style."

"You're afraid, Julian."

Julian laughed again, but not as convincingly. "Afraid of what?"

"You're afraid of losing control. You're afraid of loving too much. And you know that you could never love *me* by halves. Charlotte would demand so little, but *I* would demand every fiber of your being and soul!"

"Every fiber?" he said dryly, hiding his desperation behind mockery. "You were always too greedy, Sam."

"You tease and make fun of me because what I've just said frightens the very devil out of you, Julian Fitzwilliam Montgomery," Sam accused.

"Not much frightens me," he returned laconically. "Least of all a scrap of a girl like you who doesn't know the difference between a man's fatherly affection for his ward and true love."

"Then kiss me, Julian," Sam dared him, tilting her chin, her lips hovering an inch from his. "You kissed me once before, and you can't deny you felt something, that I aroused you. Kiss me again, if you're not afraid to, and show me by your lack of response that all you feel for me is the platonic affection of a guardian for his ward."

Despite recent suggestion to the contrary, Julian was not a complete dolt. He knew the temptation of a dare had frequently led rational men down dangerous paths they would otherwise have assiduously avoided. And Charlotte had warned him against Sam's innocent wiles and what they could accomplish.

But in this case, Julian reasoned that backing away from Sam's dare would be a mistake. She would never be satisfied, she would never give up till he'd proved to her that their romantic destinies were not intertwined.

It was simple. All he had to do was kiss her and control his response. Despite the automatic urges that plagued all men when they held beautiful women in their arms, Julian was sure he could execute the kiss without losing his famous, and well-honed, control. He'd walked away from the last kiss, hadn't he? He could do it again. And if he did feel something, he'd hide it.

Supremely confident that he was about to nip his ward's ardor in its tender bud, he bent his head and kissed her.

The first shock of lips touching lips was a bit more startling than Julian remembered. As any young girl's would be, Sam's lips were soft and full and warm. But beyond the pleasant physical sensation he registered, there was something more. . . . Something immediate and urgent. Something that welled in his chest and made him light-headed and shaky and dazed. Something that made him want to deepen the kiss and prolong it for as long as possible.

Be careful, old boy, whispered his celebrated self-control. But, for some strange reason, Julian found it quite easy to ignore that inner voice of caution. Especially when Sam parted her lips. . . .

On a gasp of surprise and pleasure, Julian opened his eyes briefly and looked down at Sam's flushed face. She appeared as absorbed in their kiss as he was. He closed his eyes again and released his hold on her arms, then slipped his hands around her slim waist, pulling her close. She fit perfectly against him, her soft curves nestling against his hard body as if she'd been created solely for his embrace. She must have thought so, too, because she twined her arms around his neck and pressed even closer.

The kiss deepened. Without a conscious decision to do so, Julian slipped his tongue inside Sam's mouth and explored the silky textures within. And, just as she had the first time he'd kissed her, Sam eagerly accepted Julian's advances and imitated everything he did.

She had always proved herself a fast learner, but Julian had never imagined himself sharing this particular educational experience with his pupil. Nor had he ever imagined himself enjoying a kiss with his ward like he was enjoying this one. They seemed so attuned to each other, as if they'd kissed many times before . . . not just once. But there was still so much excitement, so much thrill in the discovery of each other.

Sam was in heaven. She had been wanting Julian to kiss her again for days. That first kiss had been a hurried one, but this time there was no one to interrupt them. Every night, she had been dreaming about being held in his arms again. Usually when your expectations are sky-high you are bound to be disappointed, but Sam was not disappointed in the least. Julian's kiss was everything she remembered and more. It was certainly not platonic or fatherly. It was a scorcher.

Then there was the feel of him against her. So hard and strong and warm. Her body instantly responded. Her breasts tingled. Her heart raced. Her skin yearned to feel his touch on every part of her body.

She had clasped him about the neck, but now, as his mouth left hers and he began to trail kisses down her jaw, under her chin, and behind her ear, she slipped her arms around his taut waist and caressed his back and shoulders, which were fluid with muscle.

It was such a joy, such a luxury to touch where it had been so long forbidden! And her heart brimmed with happiness to know that he hadn't stopped with one kiss. He was still kissing her, returning again and again to her eager mouth for more.

Julian tried hard to think clearly. But everything was a fog. He was so overpowered by the longings of his heart and body, the rational functioning of his brain was rendered useless. All he could do was "feel." In fact, he felt so much it hurt. He thought his heart would burst with yearning.

Emotionally, he was confused and aching and longing for fulfillment. Physically, there was no confusion, but there was plenty of aching and longing for fulfillment. He wanted Sam more than he'd ever wanted another woman. He'd always been able to exert control over his body's reaction and pace himself as a lover, but with Sam he'd become instantly aroused. Blood coursed through his veins and pooled in his loins. He hadn't even touched her intimately and yet he was "ready."

He couldn't resist. He had to explore the curves that teased him so relentlessly as she pressed against him. His hands wended their way from her waist and around to the dip in her slim back. Then, in one slow, sensuous move, he slipped his hands over her small derriere and cupped the firm mounds of flesh.

She moaned against his mouth and he couldn't stop himself from lifting her and rubbing her against his erection. The shock of pleasure that coursed through him, and the way her head lolled against his shoulder as if she, too, were overwhelmed with pleasure, made him want her more than ever.

He caught her jaw and kissed her . . . deeper, harder. In a dim corner of his brain, he knew that if he could think clearly, he'd be horrified by the fierceness of his passion. But for now, all that mattered was Sam. Sam. . . .

With his free hand, Julian traced the uncorseted edge of Sam's ribs, then moved up to cup one small breast. *Just enough to fill a champagne glass,* he thought hungrily, and his mouth watered and his tongue ached to suckle there.

He was just calculating how best to bare her breasts without letting go of her for even an instant, when Sam breathed in his ear, "Julian. . . . I can't get this off. Please help me."

Julian concentrated. He fought through the fog of desire and focused on what Sam was saying and doing. She had reached behind her and was attempting to undo the ties of her gown. Her face, as she beseeched him to help her, was flushed, her lips kiss-swollen, her hair tumbled by his caresses. Her eyes were bright with innocent, eager desire and . . . trust.

Reality hit Julian like a mule kick between the eyes. There he stood in a public inn, about to toss on the bed and make unbridled love to the young female with whose care he'd been intrusted. She was Amanda's sister, Jack's sister-in-law. She was family! Yet, after having primed and protected her for a respectable match, even rushed gallantly to save her from the nefarious designs of another, he was on the verge of squandering her innocence for his own selfish pleasure.

Lord! Her dare had proved just as dangerous as he'd feared. The little vixen had done what no one else had ever come close to accomplishing before! She had made him completely lose control!

But, no . . . there was still time to save himself from that fate worse than death. There was time to gather his usual cloak of dignity and reserve about him and put a stop to all this ridiculous excess of "feelings."

"I will not help you undo your ties, Sam," Julian informed her succinctly, taking hold of her shoulders and firmly putting distance between them. "You are not going to take off that dress. In fact, you are going to put *on* your pelisse and we're getting out of here . . . right now!"

"But . . . but . . . Julian!" Sam stuttered, blinking confusedly. "You were kissing me. We were about to—"

Julian ran a shaky hand through his hair. "We were not about to do anything. I could never make love to you. You're my ward!"

Sam gave a huff of exasperation, tossed a strand

of hair out of her eyes, and crossed her arms over her heaving chest. "You impossible man! How can you ignore what happened between us just now? I dared you to kiss me, and when you did, exactly what I expected to happen, happened! Admit it, Julian. You wanted to make love to me. You still do!"

"For the love of God, Sam, don't you understand? I'm responsible for you. You're under my care!"

Her chin jutted out. "I'd rather just be *under* you!"

Julian felt his face suffuse with heat. "Don't talk like a common tart," he snapped. "I taught you better than that!" He grabbed her pelisse off a nearby chair and held it up for her. "Now, cease all these ridiculous theatrics and put on your wrap."

Sam stamped her foot and crossed her arms tighter than ever. Her eyes gleamed with anger and stubbornness. "I'm not going anywhere until you admit that you wanted to make love to me."

Their gazes locked. It was a standoff. Gritting his teeth with frustration, Julian finally said, "All right, you mulish girl. I admit it. I wanted to make love to you. I wanted to strip you bare and kiss every inch of your body."

Sam's face softened. Her eyes widened, her lips parted, and she bit her bottom lip.

"But I would have felt the same way about any female of similar physical charms who made herself as available to me as you did," he added with calculated coldness. "There were no feelings involved whatsoever, Sam. I *don't* love you."

Julian hardened his heart as he watched Sam's eyes brim with tears. He had to be cruel. He had to cure the girl of her silly infatuation . . . for both their sakes.

Suddenly she turned and marched toward the door.

"Where are you going?" he demanded.

"I'm going home," she said, her voice indignant and choked with emotion.

"Without your pelisse? The hackney coach isn't as warm as my carriage."

Sam caught hold of the doorknob, then turned to look scathingly at Julian. "I'm not going home with *you,*" she announced haughtily. "'Tis but a short distance. I'm walking to Montgomery House." She opened the door and stepped into the outer hall.

"In this rain?" he growled, slinging her pelisse over his arm and following her into the hall. "And in the dark, too? You're behaving like a sulky child, Sam!"

"You treat me like a child," she tossed over her shoulder as she tripped lightly down the stairs, "so I might as well act like one."

Standing at the top of the stairs, Julian tried to decide how best to handle this sticky situation. By now he and Sam had attracted the attention of everyone sitting in the tavern . . . the innkeeper, the hackney driver, and two gentlemen enjoying a pigeon pie and a tankard of ale.

Not wishing to make a scene that might somehow be described to the wrong person, then repeated for the amusement of some influential member of the *ton,* Julian hesitated longer than he should. While he stood and racked his brain indecisively, Sam opened the door leading outside, leveled him one last smoldering look, then ran out into the dark, wet night.

"Bloody Hell!" Julian expostulated, no longer caring what the others thought. Once again, he had to rescue Sam from her own foolishness. While his audience watched with slack jaws, he descended the stairs quickly, tossed Sam's pelisse on a nearby chair, and ran out the door after her.

Looking left and right, he spied her hurrying away in the direction leading *away* from Montgomery House. He cursed vehemently under his breath, then ran after her.

It was raining buckets outside, the deluge rivaling what Noah must have endured when the earth flooded. Mud puddles were everywhere and Julian couldn't avoid them. In fact, in the dark, and with rain streaming down his face and into his eyes, he couldn't even see them. But he knew they were there when he felt the icy water splash against his trouser legs.

Julian caught up with Sam just thirty feet from the inn, but he was already soaked through. So was Sam.

"Let go of me, you . . . you . . . *bastard!"* Sam shouted, twisting and writhing in Julian's grasp.

"This is hardly mature, ladylike behavior, Sam," Julian hissed between gritted teeth as he wrestled with his wayward ward. "I taught you better than this. And I thought I'd cured you of cursing."

"I refuse to go with you," Sam gasped, kicking and thrashing as he dragged her through the mud toward the King's Arms. "I hate you!" she screamed. "You're nothing but a bloody sod!"

"Tsk, tsk," he said, bending to scoop her into his arms. "I thought we were friends."

As Julian carried Sam toward the courtyard where the hackney coach was parked under a sheltering eave at the side of the building, she continued to curse and to struggle, making it extremely difficult for Julian to keep his footing on the slick ground. He had almost made it to the coach when a particularly slippery patch of mud sent them both flying. Julian fell hard on his rump in the middle of a puddle with Sam sprawled on top of him.

The sudden baptism was a shock. Sam quit cursing immediately and looked about her, a bit dazed. She'd left the inn in an angry huff, not caring about the rain or the darkness or anything else. Since Julian had continued to deny his feelings for her, Sam had been unable to bear remaining under the same roof with him another minute. She'd needed a little fresh air to cool her anger and clear her brain.

But this was ridiculous.

In fact, the sight of the elegant marquess of Serling sitting in a mud puddle, looking fit to spit nails, was so ridiculous Sam couldn't help but laugh out loud.

"I'm so glad I could afford you some amusement at my expense, brat," Julian growled, struggling to his feet, his trousers plastered to his muscular thighs, his coat dripping brown water. "But, if you don't mind, I think it's time we went home and got out of these wet clothes before we both catch our deaths."

"Oh, Julian," gasped Sam between spasms of laughter. "You can't imagine how *un-Julian* you look!"

"I daresay you would be surprised at your own reflection in the mirror, as well," Julian retorted, pulling her to her feet, then scooping her into his arms again. "We're ten feet from the coach. I trust you've had enough amusement for the night and you'll not thrash about and topple us into another puddle?"

Sam nodded, her anger gone, even her laughter dying away as she felt the full impact of the cold air on her wet body.

"You're chilled to the bone," Julian said accusingly as he opened the door of the hackney coach and lifted her inside.

Sam merely nodded, her teeth chattering too hard for speech.

Frowning, he said, "Stay put. I'll get the driver and be right back."

Sam nodded again, quite meekly, and he shut the door. Though he was probably not gone above three minutes, it felt like an age before the door to the coach opened again and Julian climbed in with a bundle of something in his arms. Sam was shivering convulsively, her arms wrapped around her updrawn knees as she tried to conserve what was left of her body's warmth.

As the coach immediately rocked into motion, Julian said, "Take off your clothes, Sam."

Sam stared. "Wh . . . what?"

"I said, take off your clothes. I've brought blankets, but they won't do you any good unless you first take off those wet clothes."

If her blood hadn't been so sluggish, Sam was sure she would have blushed.

"What's this?" Julian drawled. "Displaying a bit of modesty, are we? You were so eager to take your clothes off a few minutes ago, and now you shy away like a shrinking violet?"

"Th-that w-was different," Sam explained quiveringly.

"Yes, earlier it would have been complete foolishness to take off your clothes. Now it will be complete foolishness if you leave them on. Come on, Sam. It's dark in here. I won't see a thing."

Sam looked longingly at the blankets piled beside Julian on the carriage seat. She wanted more than anything to be warm again, but she'd never imagined disrobing for the first time in front of Julian under such wretched circumstances. It was hardly romantic.

It was, however, quite necessary. She took a shaky breath and reached back to undo the ties of her dress, but her fingers were so numb, she couldn't even feel what she was doing. She fumbled for a while, reluctant to ask Julian to do now what he'd refused to do before, when he said, "Here, brat. Let me do it. Turn around."

Sam turned her back to Julian and he swiftly undid her dress and slipped the sleeves off her shoulders. As his fingers brushed her bare back, they felt warm against her skin. She dared a peek at him and, from the occasional light from a street-lamp flashing into the coach, she observed that his chiseled features seemed set in stone. He looked downright grim. Apparently undressing her bothered him more than he was ever likely to admit. And if she hadn't been so darn cold, she'd have made it even harder for him. . . .

Julian removed Sam's clothes as expeditiously as possible. It was imperative to get the wet, icy garments away from her skin so that she didn't catch a dreadful cold. And, for more than one reason, he was anxious to see her bundled up in a blanket from head to toe as soon as it could be managed.

As he quickly worked, he tried to see as little as possible of his ward by immediately covering each bared part of her with a section of the blanket, but even in the dark coach he caught tantalizing glimpses of creamy, almost luminescent, white skin.

And just the process of disrobing her was arousing, particularly taking off her stockings. Her legs, which he had never before seen so much of, were long and shapely, her ankles small, the arch of her foot graceful and supple. He loved a good arch on a woman. . . .

A brief, erotic fantasy flashed through his mind of kissing that delectable dip in her foot, then working his way up, kissing and licking every inch of her, till—

With some difficulty, Julian forced away his erotic thoughts, then finally . . . *finally* . . . he had Sam wrapped up in a blanket with another one thrown over her for good measure.

"Aren't you cold, too, Julian?" Sam asked him, peering over the bunching of blanket at her chin where she held it tightly together.

Julian considered the question. He supposed he did feel a bit chilled externally, but he was so heated up internally by his unwilling attraction to Sam, he didn't seem to feel the cold as he ought.

"I'm not cold," he finally replied. "Don't worry about me."

"But I can't help worrying about you, Julian," she protested. She lifted the edge of her blanket. "Would you like to share the blankets?"

Julian caught a glimpse of slim, white thigh and said, emphatically, "No, thank you. Now tuck that blanket snugly around you or you'll feel a draft." Then he determinedly looked out the window the rest of the way home and replied in cool monosyllables to all Sam's attempts at conversation, or, more times than not, he outright ignored her. All he wanted was to get home, get Sam tucked in bed . . . *by herself* . . . and make himself comfortable with a hot bath and a bottle of brandy in front of a roaring fire, whereupon he was greatly tempted to get roaring drunk.

Julian's efforts to repress Sam had worked. By the time they reached Montgomery House, she had sunk into a defeated silence.

Julian got out and paid the driver well for his service and patience, gave him another shilling to forget that he'd ever seen them before, then carried Sam up the front steps to the door. Hedley heard their approach and opened the door to admit them. As Julian carried Sam into the hall, still dripping from his mud bath, Hedley's eyes nearly popped out of his head.

"My lord! What happened?" he exclaimed, forgetting his usual decorous manners in his surprise. He looked back at the hackney coach still waiting at the street, and, seeing no one else alight, added, "Where is Clara?"

"I'll tell you everything as soon as I take Miss Darlington upstairs," Julian answered. "Do not fear. Clara is safe. Now I want you to send someone outside to fetch Miss Darlington's wet clothes, shoes, and pelisse from the coach, if you please."

And with that meager explanation, Hedley was forced to be satisfied. Perplexed, he stood in a daze for a moment watching his employer carry Miss Darlington up the stairs, tracking mud on every step, before he ordered the footman out into the rain to bring inside the young lady's clothes.

As Julian carried her up the stairs, Sam made a resolution. She built up her courage for one last, colossal effort to make Julian see her as a woman and to admit his feelings for her. It was a desperate move, but if it failed, she felt as though she had nothing to lose. If she didn't try, she'd lose Julian anyway.

So, as curious servants scattered and hid behind potted plants and curtains to gape, Julian strode grimly past them all to Sam's bedchamber. He managed to turn the knob, kick open the door, and carry Sam inside without assistance. Then he set her on her feet on the Delft tile by the fireplace and turned instantly to go.

"Ring for a bath, Sam," he said tersely, tossing the words over his shoulder. "You can choose whichever of the maids you want to stand in for Clara till we can get a more suitable replacement. Afterward, I suggest you go immediately to bed."

His hand was on the doorknob when Sam cried out, "Wait, Julian! Don't go yet. There's something I wish to . . . That is, I . . ."

Sam watched as Julian's broad shoulders drooped a little, as if reluctant to turn around. She had obviously tried his patience to the breaking point. But finally, slowly, he turned.

"What is it, Sam?" he muttered in a beleaguered tone.

For a moment, Sam just stared at him. In the candlelight from a sconce on the wall behind him, and in the glow of the firelight, she could see the damage that had been done to his usually fastidious, elegant appearance.

His clothes were wet and mud-splattered from top to toe. His cravat was sodden and limp. His shiny boots were caked with mud and . . . if her nose did not mistake . . . horse manure from the courtyard at the King's Arms. Yes, his clothes had definitely been ruined by their little adventure.

But as for the man himself . . . Julian's wet hair

clung close to his well-shaped head, the fringe that hung over his collar curling against his neck. His complexion glowed from the exercise of carrying her up the stairs, and the sheen of rain on his face gave him an earthy, basic sort of appeal . . . even surpassing the appeal he typically exuded when he was groomed to his usual perfection. His features were implacable, his mouth a thin, grim line. Oh, if only she could kiss away that stern expression. . . .

"What is it, Sam?" he prompted her impatiently. "I haven't got all night. I have to tell Hedley his daughter's eloped before I can even take a bath."

Sam took a deep breath, then, lifting her arms, she let the blanket that hid her nakedness fall to her feet.

Julian couldn't help himself; he had to look. His gaze traveled the length of her, from head to toe. Sam was beautiful. She was like a goddess, slim and white and perfectly formed. But he was transfixed by more than her beauty. The look in her eyes, the longing, the vulnerability, the love . . . was hard to resist.

"Can't you tell Hedley the news later?" she whispered. "Perhaps you and I could . . . could bathe together? The servants needn't know."

Julian tried to ignore the hard ache in his loins, the rush of blood to all his nerve endings, and forced himself to look her straight in the eye. But that was a mistake. Her eyes beseeched him, beguiled him. Her desire, so simple and honest, was obvious in her expression. And he wanted her as much, or more, than she wanted him.

Despite his sure conviction that it would be wrong, he knew that if he stayed another moment he would go to her. He knew, too, that Sam saw his hesitancy. He saw her face light up with hope and joy. She reached out a hand with the palm up-turned. "Please come to me, Julian," she said. "It's all right, you know. Because . . . because I love you."

That stopped him.

He dropped his gaze to the floor and turned away. As he slipped through the door and into the hall, he murmured, "Good night, brat."

Chapter 13

❧ ~~∽ஓ∽~~ ❧

Julian was out of sorts. He'd had the devil of a
night. He'd got roaring drunk and was suffering
for it now with a lion-sized headache. As well, he'd
barely slept a wink and had dreamed nonstop of
Sam during the rare, fitful moments of actual
slumber.

Drifting in and out of his disjointed dreams,
sometimes Julian was with Sam at home, sometimes at Hyde Park, sometimes at the theater or an
elegant dinner party. But in every setting he conjured up, Sam was always . . . naked.

Oh, she had her accessories . . . her fan, her pearl
necklace and earrings, her reticule, even her shoes.
And he'd have to say he'd never seen her hair more
fetchingly coiffed. But between the neck and the
ankles, Sam wasn't wearing a stitch.

As well, no one else in these oh-so-vivid dreams
seemed to notice anything amiss . . . least of all
Sam. She chatted and laughed, batted her lashes
and fluttered her fan in her usual playful fashion,
and none of the men that swarmed about her in
admiration showed any signs of noticing that she
was without clothes.

237

But Julian noticed. And he always woke up sweating and aroused. Damn.

But what else could he expect? he asked himself, sitting at the breakfast table alone the following morning. Last night when she'd dropped her towel and invited him to bathe with her, it had taken every ounce of self-control to refuse her.

Standing there with her arm outstretched, her skin so smooth and white, she had looked like a Greek statue. She was even more beautiful than he had imagined. Her breasts were small, creamy, rose-tipped globes. Her hips were boyishly slim, her waist was tiny, and those long, long legs of hers . . . Bloody Hell!

Julian rubbed his eyes and took another sip of black coffee. He wondered if Sam was going to join him for breakfast. But he had a feeling she wouldn't even be speaking to him for a while. He knew he must have hurt her terribly when he left her bedchamber last night without a word, but what else could he have done? If he'd stayed to argue with her, he'd have found her nakedness a daunting distraction and would have ended up ravaging her within an inch of her life.

Just then the door to the breakfast room opened and Julian hoped and feared that it would be Sam. It wasn't. It was Hedley, Friday-faced and going about his work in as bad a mood, or worse, than Julian's. Last night, when Julian broke the news to him about Clara's elopement, he'd displayed the stiff upper lip he was famous for, but underneath his stoic calm, Julian could tell he was angry and hurt.

"This just arrived, my lord," Hedley said, wincing as if he had a headache, too. "The lad said it was urgent."

"I've been getting far too many urgent messages lately," Julian muttered. He picked up the note, relieved to see it was not from Isabelle. He turned the envelope over and recognized Sir Humphries's seal and blue wax. He immediately opened it and read a single line of correspondence.

I have remembered.

Julian finished his coffee in a couple of hasty gulps, then stood up and strode toward the door. Sir Humphries's memory breakthrough was an unexpected and most welcome surprise. Perhaps if he could settle this issue of who Sam's mother was, he'd be less restless and edgy and better able to cope with life in general . . . and Sam in particular.

Julian had been surprised at what little interest Sam had shown in the outcome of his search for her mother. It was not at all what he'd expected of her. In fact, she appeared to have put it out of her mind entirely. But maybe that was her way of coping with the situation, he reasoned. Perhaps she was only pretending not to care.

"You won't be eating breakfast, my lord?" Hedley inquired as Julian grabbed hold of the doorknob.

Julian did not wonder at Hedley's question. Typically, he never missed breakfast and got excessively tetchy if it should happen to be delayed. "Not this morning, Hedley. But be sure to send up a tray to Miss Darlington if she doesn't come down shortly."

Hedley's nostrils flared. "Of course, my lord," he intoned haughtily, apparently unable to hide the fact that he largely blamed Sam for Clara's elopement. He realized now, as Julian had also belatedly realized, that all those walks in Hyde Park were for the forwarding of Clara's romance with Nathan Ford.

"I trust no arsenic will be stirred into her tea?" Julian drawled, hoping to lighten Hedley's mood.

But Hedley's nose only lifted another notch in the air as he sniffed and replied, "Certainly not, my lord."

Julian sighed and opened the door leading into the hall. But as he stepped through the passage, he bumped into Sam. Fortunately, she was fully clothed.

"Excuse me," he said, stepping hastily back and eagerly searching her face for some sign of how she was feeling. To a casual observer, to someone who didn't know everything Sam had been through the night before, nothing would seem amiss about her appearance this morning. In fact, they would think she looked especially beautiful, dressed in a blue-and-white-striped spencer and a blue walking dress, with her curls loose and arranged in artistic disarray. She was loveliness incarnate.

But Julian instantly recognized a difference in her, in the rigid way she held herself, in the formal tilt of her head, in the evasiveness of her gaze.

"Good morning, Julian," she said coolly, walking past him into the breakfast room. "I trust you slept well last night?"

Julian raised his brows. Was that remark a deliberate stab? he wondered, or was she just being painfully polite?

"I . . . uh . . . slept very—" He found he could neither lie nor tell the truth without creating an awkward situation, so he resorted to the weather.

"It is a beautiful day, Sam. Do you have plans?"

Hedley, looking as sour as curdled milk, pulled

out Sam's chair, then scooted her in. "Yes, I do have plans," Sam said composedly, never quite meeting Julian's eyes as she unfolded her napkin and laid it on her lap. "Jean-Luc is coming over, then later I'll be going to Lady Wentworth's for tea."

"How . . . er . . . nice," Julian offered, then fell silent. He realized with consternation that not even in his salad days had a woman made him feel so helpless and ham-handed.

Damn.

"Yes," Sam agreed, lifting her cup so Hedley could pour her tea. Then, for the first time that morning, she met Julian's gaze squarely. "I'm quite looking forward to a lovely day. And, you?"

She took a sip of tea, raising her brows and peering at him over the rim of her cup. Her entire manner was artificial and insincerely polite. Julian hated it.

"I have plans, too," he answered obliquely, determining then and there not to tell her about Sir Humphries's note until he knew what information the old tattle-tongue possessed about Sam's mother. Her mood was so odd, he didn't know how she would react to news that could possibly be quite disturbing. While she assumed a hard-as-granite facade, nonetheless he knew that right now Sam was particularly fragile.

Sam was sure Julian's "plans" included Charlotte Batsford. She didn't know why he didn't just say so instead of acting so mysterious. He'd made it perfectly clear last night that he wanted nothing to do with her, even after she'd bared her soul . . . *and* her body . . . to him.

Sam blushed with mortification as she remembered the way he'd walked out on her. It had been humiliating and painful to be so summarily rejected, and she'd spent half the night crying over the cruelty of fate and the stupidity of men. But this morning she awoke with new resolve. She was going to forget Julian! Once and for all, she was going to quit beating her head against a stone wall. If he didn't want her, she wouldn't moon after him any longer.

In fact, she had resolved never to marry at all. She would live happily as a spinster for the rest of her life. She would be quite comfortable at Darlington Hall with Nan and Priss and her collection of dogs . . . thank you very much.

"Well, I'm glad you have 'plans.' Give my regards to *Charlotte,* won't you? And do have a lovely day, Julian," Sam said dismissively, putting all her attention to the task of buttering her toast. "Good-bye."

There was a long pause as Sam waited for Julian to return her cool farewell salutation, and after a while she was forced to look up to see if he still stood at the door. He did. And he was looking at her with an expression that was half exasperation, half sympathy. But, in Sam's mind, sympathy was too much like pity, and she wanted no such sentiment bestowed on her by Julian. She glared back at him with haughty disdain.

Finally he sighed, said, "Good-bye, Sam," in a beleaguered tone, and left.

To relieve her feelings of frustration, Sam attacked her slice of ham and poached eggs with energy, cutting them into minuscule pieces. Then she simply sat and looked at her yoke-smeared plate with absolutely no appetite or intention of eating the mess she'd made.

Sam was nudged out of her stupor by Hedley, standing at her elbow and noisily clearing his throat. She looked up into his proud, almost sneering countenance and remembered that she had much more important things to do and think about than feel sorry for herself. Her first order of business had to do with Hedley, but before she could speak, he said stiffly, "If you don't like your breakfast, Miss Darlington, I should be happy to fetch you something different."

"Thank you, Hedley," Sam replied, trying to get him to look at her, but failing, "but I'm not hungry this morning."

"Is there nothing I can get for you, then?" he inquired, punctiliously respectful, but chillingly cold.

Sam reached into the deep pocket of her gown and pulled out an envelope. "No, but I can give *you* something," she informed him, holding out the letter.

Hedley's nose stayed in the air, but his eyes slid down to observe the item being offered. "If I might ask, Miss . . . what is it?" he inquired, his manner still as icy as an arctic breeze.

"It is a letter from Clara," she told him in a whisper, not wishing to draw the attention of the two footmen standing by the door. "She asked me to give it to you this morning."

At first Hedley did not budge. He simply stared at the letter, his features immobile except for a slight twitch in his left eye. Then he slowly held out his hand and took the note, stashed it immediately away in his jacket pocket, and remained standing at attention.

"Hedley," said Sam, amused and touched by his forced self-control, "you can go away and read it, you know. I'm certain you must be dying to. But before you go, I want to tell you something."

He flicked a cold glance her way. "Yes, miss?"

"Clara has explained everything in the letter," Sam continued, still whispering, "but I do want to add *my* little bit. I know you're very angry with Clara and with me, and I don't mind if you never forgive *me*. But Clara loves you very much, and I know she would be devastated if you stayed angry with her. And Hedley, she's so happy! I know you must want that for Clara, because she's so deserving and such a good girl."

Hedley's brows had lowered during Sam's little recital, but, otherwise, he'd shown no reaction. Finally, after a long pause, he said, "Thank you, miss," and walked out of the room, his back as straight as a broomstick.

Sam sighed, hoping Hedley's attitude would change over time. Clara wouldn't be completely happy until she'd received her father's blessing on the marriage.

As she finished her tea, and as her thoughts drifted persistently to Julian, Sam resolutely forced them away. Just as she had done with that whole business about her mother, she found it much easier to put the entire painful affair out of her mind.

She thought instead of Hedley, and wondered how he would react to Clara's note. At Clara's insistence, she'd read the note before it had been sealed up, and Sam had been impressed with its honesty, as well as Clara's sincerely expressed respect and affection for her father. He'd have to have a hard heart to resist such honest emotion.

And maybe if he forgives Clara, Sam thought ruefully, *someday he'll forgive me, too. And poor*

Madison. But just to be sure the pup Nathan gave her didn't bear the brunt of Hedley's unhappiness over the elopement, she would frequently keep Madison with her. Maybe she would even take him with her to the Wentworths that afternoon.

Sam pursed her lips and furrowed her brows as a sudden inspiring thought came to her. Maybe she would take all *three* of the pups to the Wentworths! They would work quite well into her plot to forward Ninian's interests with his mother.

Sam was just working out in her head the details of this new idea, when a footman entered the room, bowed, and said, "You've a caller, miss. Shall I tell 'im you're still at breakfast?"

Sam set down her cup. "Who is the caller, Bob?"

The lesser servants always seemed surprised and pleased when Sam remembered their names. Bob was no exception. "It's . . . it's Mr. Bouvier, miss," he said with a shy smile.

Sam smiled back, making the youthful footman blush to his roots. "I'm expecting Mr. Bouvier. Please take him to the small parlor, Bob, and I'll join him momentarily."

The footman bowed and backed himself out the door, nearly overturning an expensive Grecian-style urn in the process. He blushed deeply and left in a fluster.

Sam smiled with sad ruefulness, wishing she had a similar effect on Julian. Then she shook off her melancholy, dabbed her mouth with a napkin, stood up, and walked toward the door. Despite her distress over Julian's rejection, she still stopped at the mirror over the sideboard to inspect her appearance and tweak at a curl or two.

As she entered the small parlor, Jean-Luc turned from looking out the window and smiled warmly.

"*Mon Dieu,* you get more beautiful every day, Sam." He winked. "It must be love."

Sam "hmphed," then sat down on a green velvet sofa and smiled wanly. "Is unrequited love supposed to make a girl more beautiful, Jean-Luc? I thought it was supposed to make me pale and thin."

Jean-Luc sat down beside her and gave her a considering look. "Unrequited love, eh? I gather things are not progressing as you would wish with the marquess?"

"Things couldn't be going worse. He's probably proposing to Charlotte Batsford even as we speak," Sam said dejectedly. "But I am resolved not to think of it anymore. I've given up on Julian Montgomery for good, Jean-Luc."

"This is not like you, *chère,* to surrender so easily. You always come up with wonderful, daring plans to help your friends, and you are fearless in executing those plans. I was delighted to read in your note about the success of Nathan and Clara's elopement! Why can't you do as much for yourself?"

"Believe me," Sam said wryly, "I've been far more daring and fearless than you think in endeavoring to help myself. In fact, I believe I've done everything in my power to convince Julian to seriously consider me in a romantic light. Nothing has worked."

Jean-Luc's expressive brows raised with interest. "What have you done, *chère?*"

Beginning with a sigh, then in a rush of words, Sam told Jean-Luc about her enlightening visit to Isabelle Descartes and the resulting confrontation with Julian over it, her earnest confession of love to him at the King's Arms, the argument and the mud bath, and, finally, her attempt at seduction by removing her towel.

"I mean, really, Jean-Luc, what would *you* have done if I stood naked before you and invited you to bathe with me?" Sam entreated him.

For a moment, Jean-Luc said nothing. He merely swallowed hard . . . several times. Finally, he said, "I'm beginning to think the marquess of Serling is made of stone or marble, or something similarly cold and unyielding. *I* would have succumbed to your charms long ago, Sam. That is . . . I mean . . . did you really visit Isabelle Descartes just to learn how to . . . to . . . pleasure the marquess? Not many respectable females would even think of doing such a thing."

"I want respectability, Jean-Luc," Sam said thoughtfully. "I want to be a wife, not a mistress. But I don't want to be *boring*. I mean, who wants to be married to a woman who only knows one sexual position?"

"Er . . . yes," Jean-Luc said faintly, inserting a finger between his collar and his neck. "You do have a point."

"Of course I do. And it stands to reason that no healthy man wants to be married to a woman who is only willing to make love in the dark, or only in the bedchamber. And it would be quite mundane if she were unwilling to learn something new and . . . and, you know, *different,* every once in a while."

"Yes, different," Jean-Luc murmured, taking out his handkerchief and wiping his brow. "But . . . that is . . . in what way do you mean . . . *different?*"

"But Julian doesn't appreciate anything I've tried to do to make him a good wife," Sam continued to lament, barely attending to Jean-Luc, who seemed to be suddenly rather flushed and sweaty. "It's very frustrating."

"Yes," Jean-Luc concurred, nodding pensively. "Very . . . er . . . frustrating, indeed. Er . . . is it hot in here?"

"Goodness, it must be," Sam said, standing up. "Although *I* feel quite comfortable, *you* look rather pink." She moved to a window, undid the latch, and swung it open about an inch. Then she sat down beside Jean-Luc again, put her hand over his where it rested on his knee, and smiled gratefully. "Thank you so much for listening to me ramble on. But I promise I won't bother you any more with my troubles. After all, you're here to go over the details of our plan to help Ninian. And I must thank you again for agreeing to help. You're such a wonderful friend!"

Jean-Luc nodded distractedly and slid his hand out from under Sam's, stood up and walked to the window. Throwing the sash open several inches, he breathed deeply of the cool morning air.

Sam was concerned. "You're not coming down with something, are you, Jean-Luc?"

"I'm afraid I might be," he admitted in a strange, rueful tone.

" 'Tis nothing serious, I hope," Sam said.

" 'Tis quite serious, but not deadly," Jean-Luc answered, finally turning to smile at her, but still not looking quite his old, suave self. "It is an affliction I've managed to avoid my entire life, but it seems I'm finally about to succumb."

Sam frowned. "You're not making sense. What affliction? Or perhaps you're teasing me."

Jean-Luc nodded. "Indeed, yes. I'm teasing you," he agreed. "Now we had better go over those details before the morning is quite gone."

"Isn't it fortunate that Priss and Nan won't be back till this afternoon and Julian's gone off to visit fusty old Charlotte," Sam said, smiling determinedly. "In his rush to see his beloved, my *guardian* quite forgot that I'm completely *un*-guarded this morning! No chaperons! We can talk as long as we want and do anything we please." She patted the cushion next to her. "Now, come sit down, Jean-Luc, and let's make our plans to help Ninian."

To Sam's surprise, Jean-Luc eyed the cushion next to her with what appeared to be misgiving, then settled himself in a chair opposite the sofa.

When she gave him an amused and questioning look, he explained, "It's nearer the window here. If I sit over here, I'm sure I'll be much more able to resist succumbing to that . . . er . . . *affliction* I mentioned."

Sam shrugged and let it go, perfectly willing to allow Jean-Luc to sit wherever he pleased. Besides, they had lots to talk about, and a long explanatory note to write and send to Ninian, before Sam left that afternoon for the Wentworths and tea.

When Julian left Sir Humphries's town house, he walked slowly down the street without a thought about where he was headed. He certainly did not want to return to Montgomery House just yet. He wasn't ready to face Sam and calmly tell her of her mother's identity. He didn't know how she'd feel about it. He wasn't even sure how *he* felt about it yet.

One thing he knew for sure, however. Diaries could not be trusted to contain the truth . . . and certainly not if the writer of the diary was married to a liar. Poor Clorinda Darlington. . . . Simon

Darlington was proving to be the biggest and bes liar Julian had ever had the misfortune to meet.

Well, he hadn't actually met the hypocritical sod but he felt as though he had. He just wished ol Lucifer could somehow relieve Darlington from th dreadful duties he was undoubtedly performing i Hell, and let him return to cool and lovely Englan for an hour or two so Julian could land him a fev vicious jabs to the nose . . . and sundry other vita organs.

Darlington had lied to Clorinda, to Amanda, t Sam, and to Sam's mother. He'd made up whateve was convenient and appropriate for eacl victim . . . and they'd all suffered. Julian onl hoped the suffering would not continue on with thi latest revelation. But the only way to know for sur was to pay a visit to Sam's mother.

Taking a left at the next corner, grateful for th fact that it was a sunny day for a change, Julia walked purposely toward an unfashionable addres on Upper Wimpole Street.

A few moments later, Julian was standing i front of a small but respectable, redbrick tow house. He had originally expected the residence o Sam's mother to be rather grand. And now that h knew who she was, he was still surprised to discov er her living so modestly. She certainly had th "means" to command a more affluent lifestyle. H wondered why she did not.

Presently Julian walked up the steps to the doo and knocked. A butler opened the door and gav Julian a look of mild surprise. "Yes, sir. May I hel you?"

"I hope you may," Julian answered. "I would lik to see your mistress. Is she in?"

"The mistress is in," replied the butler, "but I don't think she'll see you. She sees no one at this hour. She's abed."

Julian reached inside his vest pocket and took out a card. "Give this to her, if you please. I think when she observes my name on the card, she'll agree to see me."

The butler looked at Julian's calling card and allowed his eyebrows to lift ever so slightly. His gaze shifted to Julian, and there was a spark of interest, of new respect in his expression. Julian often thought that the best thing about being a marquess was the unmerited impression it made on certain people. It was perfectly silly to be treated better simply because of a title one doesn't earn but simply inherits. However, it was sometimes quite useful.

"Please come in, my lord," the butler said, bowing low. "You may wait in the drawing room while I tell the mistress of your arrival."

Julian followed the butler inside, settled himself on the couch in the tastefully appointed drawing room, and waited. However, he did not have to wait long. When the door opened, he stood up and watched a slender, delicate-featured woman enter the room in an elegant, sapphire-blue dressing gown. Her golden blond hair was down, as if she'd been sleeping or resting. Julian felt a strange stirring at the sight of her. There was no strong physical resemblance between Sam and this woman, but there was a gracefulness, a certain spirit they both shared.

"Lord Serling," she said, extending her fine-boned hand.

"Madame DuBois," Julian returned, taking her

hand and bowing over it. "How kind of you to see me. I beg your pardon for disturbing your rest. Do you have a play tonight?"

"Yes, I'm still performing in *Cleopatra, Queen of the Nile.*" Genevieve DuBois eyed him keenly. "But then I expect you know that. You seem to know everything about me." She motioned for him to sit down, then sat opposite him in a chair.

Julian sat down. "I'm surprised at your civility toward me . . . considering how uncivil your notes were."

She smiled tightly, her gaze skittering away to other objects in the room. "You must understand that I was trying to divert you from the truth. I'm not a violent person, or given to threats and such, but I wanted to alarm you and frighten you away from Sir Humphries before he remembered my affair with Simon Darlington nearly twenty years ago. The old gossip remembers everything eventually, even such a minor affair as mine when I was first making a name for myself in the theater. He was part of the Drury Lane group I ran with back then . . . one of the men who panted after opera dancers and such." Her gaze rested on him again and he could see in her expression how difficult this interview was for her. She might speak calmly, but she was feeling a lot of pain.

"How did you know I was seeing Sir Humphries?" Julian asked. "He assured me that he wouldn't breathe a word about the substance of my visits to anyone, and I believed him."

Her forced smile had a bitter edge as she replied, "A man does not consider his mistress as 'anyone.' Sharing a bed with someone loosens the tongue considerably."

Julian shifted uncomfortably. "You're not—"

"No, I'm not Sir Humphries's mistress," she said drily. "In fact, it might interest you to know that I've never been anyone's kept woman."

That answered Julian's question about why she was living so modestly.

"I've taken lovers, of course," Genevieve went on, "who have given me gifts and such . . . jewelry, clothes . . . but I've never depended on them for my living expenses."

"Although I have made your *past* personal life my business," Julian said with careful politeness, "your *present* personal life is none of my business."

She gave him a candid look. "Nevertheless, it is important for you to know that I am not a . . . a . . . *whore.*"

Julian nodded gravely.

Genevieve heaved a small, tired sigh, then continued. "I am well acquainted with the woman who is presently under Sir Humphries's protection . . . Sally McQueen."

"And it was she who told you about my visits and what I discussed with Sir Humphries?"

"Yes. Sally and I are very close friends. In fact, she's the only person I've ever talked to about . . . about the baby. Everyone . . . except for Sir Humphries, of course . . . has long forgotten that I had to quit for several months early in my career to give birth to a child." She turned and looked wistfully at a robin hopping on a windowsill outside. "Only she's not a child anymore, is she? I've caught glimpses of her here and there about town. She's very lovely . . . even though she *does* resemble her scoundrel of a father. I was never so shocked in my life to find out she was alive."

Julian furrowed his brows. "Why did you think she was dead?"

Genevieve sighed deeply, appearing much older at that moment than she'd ever looked on the stage. "At Simon's insistence, I retired to the country for the last months of my breeding period. It was only by doing exactly as he stipulated that he was willing to assist me financially at the time. And as I could not work . . ."

"Go on," Julian prompted her.

"I gave birth to Samantha in a small cottage in West Sussex. It was a difficult delivery and I was given laudanum for the pain. Hours later, when I woke up, the midwife was gone and there was no sign of a baby." She paused for a moment and ran a hand over her eyes, as if finding the memory quite distressing. "Simon told me the child had died," she continued in a quavering voice. "He said he'd buried it already, so I wouldn't suffer at the sight of its poor deformed body."

Apparently too agitated to remain seated, Genevieve stood up and began pacing the carpet. "I suppose I must be grateful that he didn't actually murder her on the spot!" she said grimly.

Julian waited while Genevieve grappled with the painful past. Presently she seemed more composed and sat down.

"After returning me to London, I never saw him again," she continued. "But since his behavior during my pregnancy had been cold and cruel, revealing his true nature, I had already grown disgusted with him and was glad he was out of my life for good."

"How did you meet Samantha's father?" Julian asked her.

The bitter smile came back. "When I met Simon Darlington, I had just arrived in London from Yorkshire. I was little more than a child, a fledgling actress . . . and very naive. Simon was a respectable country gentleman in town on business. We had an affair for two years. Whenever he came to town, we spent all our nights together. He taught me how to speak properly, you know, so it would be easier for me to get roles. I thought he was wonderful."

She sighed. "I never knew he was married. In fact, I really believed that eventually he and I would wed. So, when I found out I was with child, I was horrified when he told me he had a wife in Surrey, that he had been lying to me all along."

"He lied to everyone," Julian assured her. "He did eventually tell his wife about you, you know, but he said you were a titled lady of the *ton.*"

"He would," Genevieve said disgustedly.

"Sam . . . that is, Samantha . . . thought her mother was dead, that she'd died giving birth. But Mrs. Darlington's diary, which we just recently found, stated that Sam's mother was highborn and did not die during childbirth. Naturally, I was concerned because I did not wish to accidentally marry Sam off to her brother. It was imperative that I find you. Fortunately, after Sir Humphries had searched his memory in vain for a titled lady who might have consorted with a man named Simon Darlington at the time of Sam's birth, he finally connected the name . . . with you."

Genevieve nodded, then tilted her head to the side. Her eyes narrowed. "How did you come to be so involved in Samantha's life? I didn't learn everything I wanted to know from Sir Humphries's confidences to Sally, and I'm sure you will understand my curiosity."

And your protective instincts as a mother, Julian thought to himself. She probably was suspicious that his motives weren't completely pure. Sometimes he wondered himself. . . .

In as short and concise a manner as he could manage, and without dwelling on the neglect and suffering Sam experienced while being virtually imprisoned on Thorney Island, Julian related the whole story to Genevieve. She listened in silence, but her beautiful, expressive face reflected all the emotions she was feeling of sympathy for Sam, anger toward Simon, incredulity and regret.

Afterward, Genevieve got up and began pacing again. "I know it is useless to agonize over what Simon did. I won't put myself through such torment, and it can't help Samantha now. 'Tis enough to know that she is presently well and with friends and people who love her. I can't tell you my feelings when I found out she was alive. . . ."

Genevieve's voice broke and Julian was sorely tempted to comfort her with an arm around her shoulders. But he feared it would not be taken in the spirit in which it was offered. Genevieve probably had ample reason not to trust men.

Presently she got command of her emotions, sat down again, lifted her chin, and looked Julian square in the eye. It was a gesture, a look, that reminded him oh so much of Sam. "I don't want her to know."

"I can't *not* tell her," Julian replied.

"Yes, you can. Why does she need to know? You said yourself that the only reason you searched for me was for fear of marrying Samantha to a sibling. Now you know that's not possible. I never had another child. Not even when I tried. . . . If word got out that I'm Samantha's mother, she'd be ruined. No respectable man would want her. I can't bear to think of her ending up alone or . . . or . . . desperate."

"Sam will never be alone or desperate," Julian said with steely determination. "Not as long as she has *me* to take care of her."

Genevieve raised her brows in a look of interested surprise.

"And her sister, of course," Julian amended in some confusion. "Sam has a lot of people who care about her."

"Evidently," Genevieve murmured.

"And any man who wouldn't want Sam because of the unfortunate circumstances of her birth, isn't worthy of her," he continued harshly. "Any blockhead can see that Sam is everything that is pure, unspoiled, good, and gracious. She has spirit and compassion and intelligence."

"Your praise is warm," Genevieve commented.

"But not excessive or undeserved," Julian emphasized. "Sam has a right finally to be happy, and it is my aim that she be happy *and* secure. Therefore I want her to make a respectable match. But I promised her that I would not promote a marriage for her with a man who does not love her, or whom she doesn't love. I promised her that she would marry the *right* man . . . the one and only man for her . . . the man who will make her the happiest woman on earth."

Julian was surprised and embarrassed to hear himself repeating, verbatim, such sentimental claptrap, but it had all come out in a passionate rush. And he was equally surprised to discover that he'd meant every word. He dreaded Genevieve's reaction.

But her reaction was much different than he

expected. "Then am I to conclude, Lord Serling," she queried with a faint smile, "that *you* are intending to marry my daughter?"

Chapter 14

At first Julian wasn't sure he'd heard her correctly. "I beg your pardon . . . ?"

Genevieve DuBois twined her slender fingers together and rested her clasped hands on her knees. "I *said,* Lord Serling—as I'm sure you heard quite clearly—I conclude that you intend to marry my daughter."

Julian shifted uncomfortably. Attempting to appear just as composed as she did, he answered, "Indeed, Madame DuBois, marrying Sam has never been my intention. I can't imagine what gave you such an idea."

"Your manner of speaking of her just now gave me the idea."

"My manner of speaking?"

"Yes. It was very warm. In fact—might I presume to say?—it was quite possessive and loverlike."

Affecting nonchalance, Julian took out his snuffbox, deftly opened it with one finger, and took a sniff. "Now I see where Sam gets her romantical notions," he drawled. "Like your daughter, you see loverlike inclinations where there is only friendship."

Genevieve's eyebrows rose. "So, Sam has found you out, too? Good girl!"

"Nonsense," Julian continued repressively. "Sam has merely nurtured an infatuation for me of late, and fooled herself into believing that I returned her feelings. That I have a great deal of affection for Sam, I will not deny. That I intend to settle her in a happy and respectable home as someone's wife is also quite true. But it shall not be *my* home, nor shall she be *my* wife. I do not love her."

"The gentleman 'doth protest too much,'" Genevieve suggested soberly, but with the glimmer of a smile in her eyes.

"I do no such thing," Julian protested stiffly. "I merely state the facts."

"And the fact is, you *are* in love with my daughter," Genevieve insisted, "whether you choose to believe it or not."

Julian got up and moved to the window. He gazed at the quiet scene outside, feeling anything but quiet *inside*. First Sam, now her mother, was trying to tell him that he was in love with his ward. The idea was ludicrous. He could never be in love with a young woman so different from his ideal of a wife.

Instead of decorous and circumspect, Sam was playful and impetuous. And instead of encouraging his reserve and control, she flouted it, broke it down. An attachment to such a woman would be unwise; therefore, it was unthinkable. Judging by his behavior the other night at the King's Arms, if he was foolish enough to fall in love with Sam, he would be doomed to live a goodly portion of his life spinning out of control.

No, that would never do.

Besides, he was honor-bound to Charlotte Batsford. His particular attentions to her could not be construed in any other light than as a positive . . . er . . . *pre*-engagement.

Mentally reinforced, Julian turned around and looked at Genevieve. "I repeat . . . I will make sure Samantha is well and happily married, but not to me."

Genevieve shook her head, a rueful, regretful smile on her lips. "Then you will not be keeping your promise to her."

"I refuse to discuss this any longer, Madame DuBois," Julian stately firmly, assuming his most toplofty pose . . . back rigid, chin up, lips compressed, eyes narrowed. "Before the conversation wandered quite off the subject, we were debating whether or not to tell Sam that you are her mother. You did not think it a good idea. Do you still hold firm to that opinion?"

"No, I've changed my mind completely," Genevieve said, surprising Julian considerably. "My main objection to telling Sam about me was the fear . . . indeed, the *hope* . . . that she and I might become friends and that such a friendship would be unacceptable to a respectable man who might seek her hand in marriage. I didn't want to ruin her chances for happiness. But now I am convinced that I needn't fear for Sam's happiness in the least. After all, as you said yourself, she has *you*, hasn't she?"

Julian was completely exasperated. *Like mother, like daughter,* he thought to himself. Genevieve DuBois seemed determined to believe him besotted with Sam. But he had not the time or the patience at the moment to convince her otherwise. It was enough that she did not object to his telling Sam that she was her long-lost mother.

"Thank you, Madame DuBois, for your cooperation," Julian said with a deep, formal bow. "I will let you know how my interview goes with Samantha."

But when Julian would have quitted the room and gone away in stiff civility, Genevieve hastily rose from the chair and moved to stand in front of him. She caught his hand and squeezed it tightly. She looked up at him with tear-filled eyes and said with a great deal of feeling in her voice, "No, I must thank *you,* Lord Serling, for demolishing a terrible memory, for restoring a horrible loss that I've felt every day of my life since I woke up and was told my child . . . my little girl . . . was gone forever. Perhaps I don't deserve it . . . but I'm very, *very* happy."

Julian was no proof against such sincere and open emotion. His icy facade melted like snow in April. He returned her squeeze and answered gruffly, "I'm glad. Good day, Madame DuBois. I'm sure we'll meet again very soon."

As Sam followed Lady Wentworth's butler, Pigeon, to the parlor, she tugged Madison, Louie, and George by their leading strings behind her. She hoped that the pups would play their part well and support her confidence in them by behaving abominably. Certainly Madison could be depended on to be noisy and disruptive, but George seemed always to be on his good behavior. And Louie was too lazy to be very naughty.

Case in point, Madison had barked at the butler and was busily sniffing every corner and every piece of furniture en route to the parlor. Pigeon eyed the pup nervously, undoubtedly fearful that the animal would lift his leg on a priceless antique. George was looking curiously at everything, but briskly kept up with his mistress, and Louie, as usual, lagged behind and acted blasé.

But even if Madison was the only truly disobedient of her canine entourage, Sam reasoned that the sheer number of dogs would accomplish her purpose for bringing them in the first place.

Pigeon opened the parlor door and stepped inside, announcing as he made way for Sam and her furry companions to move past him, "Your tea guest, my lady. Miss Darlington and . . . er . . . *company!*"

Lady Wentworth, who was stretched out on a peach-colored chaise longue by the fire, turned with a smile on her face. But the smile instantly fell away and was replaced by a look of utter dismay when she observed Sam's "company." Ninian was standing behind his mother's chaise longue, barely succeeding in suppressing a laugh.

"How do you do, Lady Wentworth?" Sam said cheerfully, approaching her hostess with a bright smile. "I hope you don't mind that I brought my pets along. I'm sure you've longed for an age to see the pup Ninian gave me, and I couldn't very well leave the others behind, now could I?"

"Well . . . I . . . I . . ." Lady Wentworth stuttered.

"With all the rain recently," Sam continued gaily, "they've had so little exercise, and they enjoyed the walk from Montgomery House excessively. We go past the park, you know, and there's so many trees!"

"I . . . I suppose I don't mind," Lady Wentworth

conceded doubtfully, "as long as they're house-broken and well behaved. They *have* been taught not to chase cats, haven't they?"

Not until that moment had Sam observed that Lady Wentworth held a large, white, very fat cat in her lap. She had not reckoned on Lady Wentworth having a pet cat, but, although she would never have planned to inflict such a traumatic experience on an innocent animal, Sam knew the cat's presence would do a great deal toward exciting the dogs and causing a desirable amount of instant mayhem.

Sam assumed a look of chagrin and alarm and said, "Well, actually, Lady Wentworth, my dogs have *not*—" But, just as she expected, her words were interrupted by a barrage of barking. The cat had been spotted. Madison howled as if he were baying at the moon, and even lazy Louie and obedient George were yapping their heads off.

To no one's surprise, the cat reared up its head in terror and exited its mistress's lap immediately, racing across the room toward the closed door of the parlor. Lady Wentworth turned white and exclaimed, "Oh, no! My precious Snowflake! They'll eat her alive!"

Intending no such outcome, Sam held tight to the leading strings of all three pups and sent a speaking look across the room to Ninian. Stifling a stronger-than-ever urge to break out in the giggles, Ninian hurried to open the parlor door, allowing the terrified cat to escape.

The cat was gone and the parlor door closed, but the agitated dogs still strained at their leashes and continued to bark. "I *do* apologize, Lady Wentworth," Sam shouted over the din, finding herself twined in the dogs' leashes and struggling to unravel herself. "I did not know you had a cat, or I shouldn't have brought the dogs along. Truth to tell, they're much happier outside than in, but I daren't give them over to your servants as they are too often tempted to snap at strangers. Oh, if only we could have tea in the park!"

Clutching her throat, her face still ghostly pale, Lady Wentworth simply stared and said nothing.

"By Jupiter, that's a capital idea, Sam," Ninian said with enthusiasm, placing himself halfway between his mother and Sam and turning this way and that as the conversation warranted. "Let's have our tea *al fresco,* Mama. Pigeon can have the necessaries packed up in no time. While we lounge and dine on a blanket thrown on the grass, the pups can romp to their hearts' content."

Lady Wentworth finally recollected herself and threw Sam a thin, nervous smile. Then she turned to Ninian to say through gritted teeth, "But, Ninian, the tea will be cold. You must recollect, *dearest,* that there's nothing worse for my digestion than tepid tea!"

Ninian shrugged. "Pigeon can swaddle the pot in towels. I daresay it will stay positively toasty."

"But I wasn't planning on going out today," she persisted, trying to preserve a veneer of politeness while still stubbornly pushing to get her own way. "The weather has been so unpredictable of late."

"The day is fair," Ninian replied with an affable but steely smile.

Lady Wentworth raised an imperious brow. "But *my darling boy,* the grass will surely still be wet from yesterday's storm."

Ninian, no doubt bolstered by Sam's supporting presence and his earnest desire for her plan to work, stood firm. "The sun has been shining so strongly all morning, as long as we do not put up camp under a tree, I'm certain there will be large patches of dry grass to be found."

Lady Wentworth looked a bit nonplussed by Ninian's uncharacteristic firmness. She decided to change tactics. In a peevish, pathetic tone, she said, "But you know how my skin breaks out in spots if I sit in the sun, and how decidedly swoonish I get when overly warm."

He sniffed. "You have a parasol."

She pouted. "My arm gets tired holding it up."

"Then I will hold it for you, Mama."

"But I don't *want* to drink my tea outside!"

Ninian clasped his hands behind his back, struck a pose with his nose in the air, and rocked diplomatically on his heels. "Very well, madam," he clipped out. "I see I must explain the dilemma so that you perfectly understand. We either drink tea *inside,* sharing close quarters with Miss Darlington's pups, or we drink tea *outside* where the pups might . . . er . . . sniff each other, drool, wrangle over scraps, and . . . er . . . relieve themselves at will. It is *your* house, after all, so I leave the final decision up to you."

As Lady Wentworth's dismayed gaze shifted to her, Sam attempted to look embarrassed and apologetic. Then, luckily, Madison chose just that moment to vigorously sniff a sofa leg, his hindquarters wriggling suspiciously. While Sam had no fears of the pups making puddles in the house—Hedley had done an excellent job of terrifying them into being house-broken—Lady Wentworth had no such knowledge to reassure her.

"Oh, but of course we can take our tea *al fresco* today," she exclaimed suddenly, rising quickly to her feet and rushing over to gingerly nudge Madison away from her Egyptian-style sofa. "It is a charming idea! A *delightful* idea! Now why don't you order the curricle brought round, Ninian, and you and Miss Darlington and the pups can wait for me *outside.* I'll instruct Pigeon to pack us a basket, then I'll run upstairs to put on something warmer. I'll just be a moment. Now, hurry along, my dears. Hurry along!"

Lady Wentworth, showing a great deal of stamina for a female of purportedly delicate constitution, corralled them all into the hall and out the front door in a matter of seconds.

Standing outside on the front steps of the Wentworth town house, situated on a modest but genteel square, Sam and Ninian exchanged glances, then burst into laughter.

"Why didn't you tell me your mother had a cat?" Sam presently demanded, her voice thick from laughing, her eyes watery.

"There wasn't any time," Ninian replied with an answering smile. "As it was, I had only a half hour to read and thoroughly commit to memory that hideously long note of instructions you sent over! I hope we shall be able to pull off this little charade without Mama getting suspicious."

"Well, we have done all right so far. Thanks to the cat's effect on the pups, we managed to lure her out of the house much sooner than I anticipated."

"But the hard part is yet to come," said Ninian, sobering.

Sam squeezed Ninian's arm. "You can do it. I know you can!"

Ninian put his hand over Sam's and smiled weakly. "Lord, Sam, she must really be determined to make you her daughter-in-law, because I'd have never made her back down like that on my own."

"Nonsense, Ninian," Sam replied bracingly.

"You don't know your own abilities. Mark my words, before the night is over your mother will consent to any scheme you propose. Soon I'll be calling you 'Captain' Wentworth."

A few minutes later, Ninian tooled the curricle down a northerly country road, flanked on either side by Sam and his mother. Madison hung over Sam's arm, his ears flapping in the light breeze created by the movement of the curricle, his tongue lolling happily. Louie lounged on the floorboards, fast asleep at Sam's feet. And George sat quietly, his ears submissively flat, on Lady Wentworth's lap.

"I thought we were only going to the park," Lady Wentworth complained, drawing her shawl more closely about her while George glanced up nervously to make sure he wasn't the source of the lady's irritation.

"You saw yourself, Mama, that the park was far too crowded for comfort," Ninian replied, turning down a narrow, rutted road through a grove of tall, overhanging oak trees.

"But why are we turning here? The road is muddy," Mrs. Wentworth observed peevishly. "The grass will be wet."

"I know this area, Lady Wentworth. There is a large open field just ahead. The ground will be quite dry, I promise you," Sam assured her.

But, as planned, they never made it to the open field. Whether or not the grass was dry would remain forever a moot point, because while they were still in the cool, dark shadows of the grove, a figure jumped out from behind a bush and aimed a pistol at them.

"Whoa!" cried Ninian, pulling on the reins and stopping the horses in their tracks. "What the deuce . . . ?"

Lady Wentworth's eyes grew enormous at the sight of a tall, masked man, dressed entirely in black, with a handkerchief tied round his head, brandishing a firearm.

All three dogs started barking, and it was all Sam could do to keep them from jumping over the sides and charging to the attack. She looped the leading strings around her wrists till their length was quite short, then held tight with all the strength she could muster.

"Don't worry, Lady Wentworth," Sam whispered fervently. "Ninian will protect us!"

"Ninian? *Protect* us? Oh, *no!* I knew we should have brought a servant along . . . and a pistol, too," she choked out in a strangled voice. "But *I* thought we were only going to the *park!*"

At this point, Ninian shocked Lady Wentworth within an inch of her life by standing up in the carriage, puffing out his chest, and bellowing, as bold as brass, "What the devil do *you* want? Put down that gun and let us through!"

Horrified, Lady Wentworth tugged on Ninian's coattail and quavered, "Sit down, you foolish boy! He'll *shoot* you!"

"Better listen to yer mum," snarled the man. "If'n ye don't hand over all yer valuables, I'm blastin' a hole through yer bloody heart."

Sam buried her face in Madison's furry neck to hide her smile. Jean-Luc had the most ridiculous accent! He sounded like a gravel-voiced pirate!

"We're not giving over our valuables, you-you blackguard!" Ninian blustered.

"Then prepare t' meet yer maker, laddy," threatened the robber, leveling his gun at Ninian.

"Only a craven coward would point a gun at defenseless females and an unarmed gentleman,"

Ninian declared in a superior tone. "A *real* man would engage in hand-to-hand battle."

"Hand-to-hand battle?" growled the highwayman, squinting menacingly through the eyeholes of his black mask.

"Yes," Ninian affirmed. "Fisticuffs! That's the ticket! Put down your pistol and fight me with your bare fists . . . if you dare! Only if you knock me unconscious shall I submit to your outrageous demands. Come on, put up your dukes! Or are you afraid?"

"Ninian, oh, *do* consider to whom you are speaking!" Lady Wentworth begged. "He's a brute, and he looks prodigiously strong!"

"Trust me, Mama," Ninian said in heroic accents. *"I'll* win this fight. You wait and see!"

"Ye're a fancy talker," snarled the robber. He threw down his pistol and lifted his fists in the classic pugilistic pose. "Let's see if'n ye fight as well as ye jabber!"

His challenge accepted, Ninian leaped majestically from the carriage. Unfortunately, he wobbled on impact and stumbled to his knees, but he got up immediately and . . . with only a brief embarrassed glance over his shoulder at Sam . . . faced the robber with his fists at the ready. The two men circled each other, sneering viciously, but just as the robber pulled back his fist for the first punch, Lady Wentworth gave a loud gasp and fainted dead away.

"Stop! Stop, Ninian!" Sam cried, letting go of the pups and allowing them to jump out of the carriage. "Your mother has fainted! There's no need to finish the charade."

The pups charged Jean-Luc as he headed for the carriage, but as he completely ignored them, and since they soon ascertained by his familiar scent that he was no threat to their mistress, they turned their attention to the numerous surrounding trees.

Ninian hurried to the carriage, as well, and they all stared down at Lady Wentworth's pale, unconscious face as she slumped against the cushions of the seat.

"It was too much for the old gal," Jean-Luc suggested in his normal voice, peeling off his handkerchief and allowing his thick, dark hair to spring free.

"Seeing a large bug is too much for her," Ninian observed mildly, laying the back of his hand against her parchment-thin cheek. "She'll be all right. She faints two or three times a week. I should have expected her to swoon today of all days."

"Aren't you going to revive her, Sam?" Jean-Luc inquired.

"Not with *you* standing about," Sam retorted. "If she had any suspicion that this was all an act to convince her that Ninian's got gumption, she'd tan our hides!"

"Good lord," Jean-Luc drawled. "Isn't that one of Nathan's crude American expressions? *Tan our hides . . . ?* Conjures up a ghastly picture."

"Never mind," Sam said, exasperated. "It is too bad that Lady Wentworth fainted, but we can count ourselves lucky that you two didn't have to fight. When she wakes up, I'll just tell her how heroic Ninian was and how he beat the robber to a pulp. I must confess, I was a bit worried about *that* part of the plan! I knew it would be hard for you two to pretend to fight convincingly without hurting each other!"

"*I* wish she'd stayed conscious long enough to

watch the fight," Ninian declared, straightening his shoulders and swelling his chest. *"I* thought I was doing rather well."

"Only because it was a farce," Jean-Luc said dampeningly. "I'd have popped your cork if this had been a real mill!"

"Well, what makes you so sure of that, you braggart?" Ninian demanded to know, thrusting his face to within inches of Jean-Luc's.

"You're being ridiculous, Wentworth," Jean-Luc said with a patronizing sniff. "You know I'm the better boxer."

"Well, why don't we just see about that!" Ninian challenged, thumbing his nose and rotating his fists in the air.

"You're both being ridiculous!" Sam hissed, glancing nervously at Lady Wentworth as that lady's eyelids began to flutter. "Go away, Jean-Luc! *Now!* And, Ninian, you go and fetch the dogs before they get lost or snag their leashes on a bush and strangle themselves!"

With a chagrined nod from Ninian, and a wink and a roguish smile from Jean-Luc—and a promise that he would see her that night at the Wilmots' ball—the gentlemen obeyed. Once Jean-Luc was completely out of sight, Sam took out her smelling salts and waved them under Lady Wentworth's nose.

As she revived, Sam regaled her with a glowing account of Ninian's incredible skill and bravery during the fight, and how the villain had scrambled away like a dog with a tail between his legs. Lady Wentworth listened and marveled and glanced frequently toward her son with a look of astonished pride.

* * *

Julian had only been waiting a couple of minutes in Charlotte's parlor when the door opened and she entered the room. Although Charlotte was not exactly a green girl anymore—she was going on five-and-twenty—her lady's companion usually attended her whenever Julian came calling. Today she was alone, and Julian couldn't help but wonder if Charlotte was giving him the privacy he might require in order to propose to her.

Julian felt a trifle guilty about it, but proposing marriage was the last thing on his mind. He wasn't ready for Charlotte's hand; he rather needed her advice. He needed her calm, clear headed, rational conversation. Even as she approached him, her appearance soothed his mind and heart. Charlotte was like a tranquil island in a stormy sea. She would speak sense to him and soon he'd be able to dismiss all the nagging doubts that had besieged him since Sam and her mother had both accused him of being in love with his eighteen-year-old ward.

By noting that Charlotte was without a chaperon, Julian was reminded that he had left Sam alone all day without supplying her with a substitute for Clara . . . not that Clara had been much of a check on Sam's behavior! But Julian couldn't help wondering, with grave misgiving, what his unchaperoned charge had been up to all day!

"By that beleaguered look on your face," Charlotte began, smiling faintly as she held out her hand to Julian, "I can guess that your ward is giving you trouble again."

Julian gave a grimacing smile in return and kissed her fingers in a perfunctory and distracted fashion. Charlotte raised her brow a notch and took a seat, motioning for Julian to do the same. Julian sat down on a settee opposite her, resting an elbow on the overstuffed arm, and rubbed his forehead.

"Tell me what's happened, Julian," Charlotte prompted him.

"I don't know where to begin," Julian admitted ruefully. He paused, then hurriedly added, "But it's very bad manners of me to launch directly into a list of my grievances without first inquiring after you, Charlotte. How are you?"

Charlotte gave a gentle laugh. "I'm very well, thank you. Now you may proceed without feeling a qualm of conscience."

"You're very kind," Julian murmured.

Charlotte reached across the short distance that separated them and laid her hand over his. Her usually smooth brow was furrowed with concern. "I can tell you're very much disturbed. Much more so than I've ever observed in you before. Please, Julian, feel free to confide in me."

Julian did confide in her. Beginning with Clara's elopement and ending with his discovery that Genevieve DuBois was Sam's mother, Julian told Charlotte everything. Everything, that is, but about the passionate kissing between him and Sam at the King's Arms and Sam's removal of her blanket later that same evening. He didn't think Charlotte would . . . er . . . understand. He only hoped she did not wonder about "holes" in the story where he'd left things out.

After this censored recital of events was concluded, Julian leaned back in his chair and observed Charlotte's face. The furrow in her brow remained, and there was a puzzled expression in her eyes.

"Julian," she began musingly, "I don't precisely

understand why you and Sam quarreled at the King's Arms, and why she ran out into the rain. I know you better than to believe you'd ring a peal over her head simply for assisting in Clara's elopement, no matter how much you—"

"She lied to me," Julian interposed.

Charlotte leveled him a keen gaze. "But there's more to this story, isn't there?"

Julian stood up and agitatedly paced the rug. "Yes. There's more, all right! But it's utter nonsense! Sam, *and* her newly discovered mother—who, by the bye, has a natural and most inconvenient turn for the dramatic—have somehow got it in their heads that I'm . . . I'm . . . in love with . . ." He gave a strangled laugh. ". . . with *Sam,* of all people! Can you believe it, Charlotte? And to prove it, Sam dared me to kiss her at the King's Arms!"

"Did you?" she quietly asked.

"Yes, I kissed her. But it meant nothing! It was like kissing my little sister. It certainly didn't *prove* I was heel over ears in love with the chit."

Suddenly Charlotte stood up and stood in front of Julian, forcing him to stop pacing. He stared down at her, a harried question in his eyes.

"I dare you to kiss *me,* Julian Montgomery," Charlotte said in a perfectly grave voice, tilting her head and lifting her lovely face invitingly close to his.

Julian automatically grasped Charlotte's arms. He frowned. "What are you doing, Charlotte?"

She linked her hands behind his neck and snuggled close till Julian could feel her soft, full breasts against his chest. "I'm conducting an experiment," she answered, a tentative smile curving her lips.

Julian was completely bewildered. And finding

himself in such an intimate embrace with Charlotte seemed somehow . . . wrong. "So now *you* have something to prove, too, eh? We've kissed before, Charlotte."

"But not *ardently,* Julian," Charlotte pointed out. "We've never been alone much, and you've always been polite and respectful. This time I want you to be . . . *passionate."*

"What *are* you trying to prove?" Julian asked nervously.

"Just kiss me," she ordered softly, closing her eyes and offering her lips in a tantalizing pucker.

Julian stared at those luscious lips, feeling like a man with his neck in a noose. He had a sinking notion that he knew exactly what Charlotte needed proof of . . . his desire for her. But why should that worry him? he reasoned desperately. Of course, he desired her! He would give her the proof she required, and then some!

Julian bent his head and captured Charlotte's eager mouth in a long, deep, slow kiss that definitely eclipsed any kiss they'd shared before and was definitely beyond the bounds of propriety . . . even the more liberal bounds of an "almost engaged" couple. He didn't end the kiss till he was absolutely in need of air. Then he lifted his head and surveyed her face to gauge her reaction.

Her face was flushed. Her eyes were glazed. Her breath was quick. He could feel her heart pounding against his chest.

"Don't tell me you didn't enjoy that?" he challenged gruffly.

Charlotte swallowed and licked her lips. "I enjoyed it very much, Julian," she said faintly.

"Do you have your 'proof' now?" he demanded.

"Not yet," she answered, gently easing out of his

arms and putting several inches distance between them.

He frowned. "What the deuce do you mean, Charlotte?"

"I have a single question for you, Julian."

"Yes?"

She took a deep breath, as if mustering her courage. "How did kissing *me* compare to kissing *Samantha?*"

Julian had been so intent in practicing his amorous expertise on Charlotte and eliciting a satisfactory response from her, he had paid no attention to his own response to the kiss. But then, perhaps that was because there *was* no response.

Kissing Sam had been extraordinary. Time had passed without his knowing or caring. All his senses had been inflamed. He had been utterly out of control. With Charlotte, he'd been fully anchored in reality, *completely . . . in . . . control.*

Julian stared at Charlotte, his glib tongue tied. He cudgeled his brain for something to say that would please her, appease her. But an alarming idea continued to swirl through his brain like the rhythmic rotations of a taffy-maker's stick. . . .

Perhaps losing control was part of "falling in love." Perhaps there was no avoiding a few cracks in his composure if he wanted what his brother, Jack, had with Sam's sister, Amanda. Perhaps he was in love with Sam. . . .

Pushing aside these shocking, revelatory thoughts, Julian forced himself to focus on Charlotte's face. She appeared sober, resigned, sad. Apparently she already knew the answer to her question. The way he felt about Sam when he kissed her . . . and the way he *didn't* feel about Charlotte when he kissed her . . . told the tale.

"You *are* in love with her, Julian, aren't you?" she whispered.

"Bloody Hell," Julian muttered under his breath.

Chapter 15

Julian returned to Montgomery House in a daze. There was no longer any use in denying it . . . he was in love with Sam. He'd probably been a little in love with her from the moment he'd first clapped eyes on her, dressed as a ragamuffin boy on Thorney Island. But self-deception and pride had kept him from admitting to himself that he could have fallen hard for such a . . . well, such a *brat!*

If this was love, he grumbled to himself as he climbed the stairs to his front door, he wasn't sure he liked it. He had always thought it would be a soothing experience to fall in love . . . a serene, orderly state of bliss. But perhaps that was why he hadn't recognized his recent miserable condition as the combined symptoms of what the French called *amour*. He had not supposed that being irritable, edgy, confused, and out of control meant he had been hit by Cupid's arrow! But then perhaps he was experiencing those unpleasant sensations because he had been suppressing his feelings.

Julian paused at the top of the steps and frowned. Now did not seem the appropriate time to give vent to those feelings, or even to explore them a little.

279

After all, he still had to tell Sam who her mother was and deal with the repercussions of such a revelation.

In fact, he mused, opening the door and stepping out of the gloomy dusk and into a bright, candlelit entryway, it would take a great deal of time and thought to decide whether or not he should *ever* give vent to his feelings. After all, he understood *his* feelings at last. But did Sam really understand *her* feelings? What she felt for him could still be nothing but gratitude and infatuation. Then, once he began to wear flannel waistcoats to fend off rheumatism, she might wish she'd married someone considerably younger!

"Good evening, my lord," said Hedley, magically appearing to take his hat, gloves, and cane. "Did you have a pleasant day?"

Julian gave Hedley a pained look and said, "It was about as good as yours, I'll wager."

Hedley nodded understandingly. Then, after a slight hesitation, he said, "My day improved somewhat after I read a letter from Clara."

Julian raised an interested brow. "She left you a letter? Where did you find it?"

"Er . . . Miss Darlington gave it to me," Hedley admitted sheepishly.

"I see. Well, I hope you found the contents to your liking."

"I don't blame her anymore, sir." He cleared his throat. "And I don't blame Miss Darlington for what happened, either. I just hope she . . . my daughter, Clara . . . will be happy with that"—he sniffed—*"colonial."*

Julian chuckled. "I hope so, too. One never knows, Hedley, how, where, and with whom one will fall fatally in love. Nor does one, I suppose,

have the least control over the process," he added
with a sigh.

Hedley sighed, too, and both men stood in silent,
companionable contemplation of the tricks of fate.
Presently, Hedley roused himself and said, "Miss
Priscilla and Miss Nancy are back from Darlington
Hall."

"Excellent," Julian replied, sifting distractedly
through the cards that had been left for him in his
absence. He was glad the aunts would be around to
lend support when he told Sam about Genevieve
DuBois. "Are they fatigued?"

"They seem anything but, my lord," Hedley
observed with the merest semblance of a smirk.
"They have been in the little parlor with Miss
Darlington for the last few minutes, talking and
laughing quite gaily."

Julian looked down the hall toward the closed
door of the parlor. "Indeed?" he said, ashamed to
admit he felt a bit piqued at Sam for recovering so
quickly from her despondency over his rejection.
And was it just a couple of days ago that she had
recognized his step in the hall and sent Priss to
fetch him? Today no one popped her head out and
invited him in. No one at all.

"One thing more, my lord," Hedley said, interrupting Julian's jealous thoughts. "Do you wish for
dinner at the usual time?"

Julian considered the question. Should he tell
Sam about her mother before or after dinner?
There was that damned ball at the Wilmots' to-
night, too. . . .

Suddenly he heard a peal of laughter filter
through the thick-paneled door of the parlor and
drift down the hall. It was Sam's laugh. Julian
decided then and there that since Sam was in such a

good mood, he had better tell her immediately what he'd found out.

"Put dinner back a half hour, Hedley," Julian ordered.

"As you wish, my lord," Hedley said, then bowed and retreated, no doubt headed for the kitchen to inform Cook of the change.

Again Julian debated what to do. Should he go upstairs, freshen up, and dress for dinner before talking to Sam, or should he simply enter the parlor now? Then he chided himself for deliberating over such a trivial point. Could it be that he was suddenly concerned that Sam saw him at his best?

Impatient with such nonsense, Julian threw down the calling cards he hadn't been able to read with any understanding anyway, and strode purposely toward the parlor door. However, he could not resist stopping at a mirror en route to ascertain if his hair had been mussed by the breeze, and to give his cuffs and waistcoat a straightening tug. Put to rights, he opened the parlor door and entered the room, feeling as silly and nervous as an unlicked cub paying his first courting call.

All three pairs of eyes turned in his direction . . . but he saw only Sam. Sitting on a footstool near the fire, she was dressed in a simple silvery blue gown he'd chosen for her himself because the fabric complemented her eyes. The skirts of the gown swirled at her feet in a pool of shimmering silk. But as he gazed at her, the laughing expression on her face changed to one of forced composure. And in the depths of her eyes there was the look of a wounded animal. Suddenly, he wanted to go to her then and there and, right in front of her aunts, take her in his arms and make the hurt go away.

But since that would hardly be seemly or wise, he forced himself to resist such an urge. *Yes,* he thought grimly to himself, *I will still exercise some control in my life!*

"Julian!" cried Priss. "How are you, dear boy?"

Julian wrenched his gaze away from Sam and stepped to the sofa where Nan and Priss were seated and, smiling, bowed over both of their outstretched hands. "Dear ladies," he said warmly. "I'm glad you are home."

" 'Home' he calls it," Nan exclaimed delightedly. "I declare, sister, we have more homes than we know what to do with! I thought we just left home behind at Darlington Hall!"

"You will always be welcome in any of *my* residences," Julian assured them.

"I dare swear, Nan," Priss began with a sly look, "that Julian is happy to see us because Sam has been such a naughty puss in our absence. She's a hard one to keep down, isn't she, Julian? But no harm done, I say. I'm glad Clara's gone off to America with Nathan. And I'm sure no mischief was done at the Wentworths today that wasn't done for the good of that young man." Priss's brow furrowed. "Although I must admit to sympathizing with Lady Wentworth a little. If a pistol had been pointed at *me,* I'd have done more than faint. I probably would have turned up my toes for good!"

Julian was filled with dread. Recalling that Sam had been unchaperoned all day, he supposed he ought not to be surprised that she'd made mischief. But a *pistol?*

Julian's consternation must have shown on his face because Sam immediately began to defend herself with a detailed and hastily spoken explanation. As he listened to her unfold the events of the day, Julian couldn't help but admire her resourcefulness, her spirit, her . . . *cheek!* And while he wanted to smile and was tempted to laugh out loud a time or two at the humorous scenes Sam described, Julian forced himself to appear grave and disapproving. But the idea of Ninian grandly playing the foolhardy hero, Jean-Luc masquerading as a horseless highwayman, and all those pups barking their heads off . . . ! He'd have given a pretty penny to see the entire farce firsthand!

"I can't help it, Julian," Sam finally concluded, pouting a little, her blue eyes flashing rebelliously. "I just want my friends to be happy."

"It's the way you go about it, Sam, that has me worried," Julian said with a half smile and only half-teasing.

She shrugged. "Sometimes it takes drastic measures to bring about the desired objectives. If I had been circumspect and cautious and stuck to the rules in Ninian's case—and in Nathan and Clara's, too—I daresay I wouldn't have been able to accomplish anything to promote their happiness!" She thrust out her small chin in that pugnacious way she had. "There's usually a certain amount of risk in obtaining anything worthwhile, you know."

Julian could not doubt that the lecture was meant for him. Ever since he'd withstood her advances, even going so far as to turn away when she stood naked before him, she had probably concluded that he was a milquetoast. While the idea irritated him considerably, he wasn't prepared at this point in time to reverse her limp opinion of him. And, anyway, it was time to tell her about her mother . . . the actress.

"I'm glad Lady Wentworth decided that Ninian

has enough gumption for the army and plans to purchase him a commission," Julian conceded, sitting down in a wing chair near Sam. "And I'm equally happy for Nathan and Clara. I wish them very happy. But now that you've managed the affairs of your friends so admirably, it's time to apply yourself to your own concerns."

Sam's eyes widened. "What do you mean?"

"I mean that I have discovered who your mother is, Samantha."

She heard the aunts gasp and exclaim with surprise, but Sam found herself unable to react at all. For weeks she'd forced thoughts of her mother quite out of her head. She found it much too painful to think about the woman who had abandoned her to a life of cruelty and neglect and then returned to her own life of pleasure and plenty. *A titled lady of the* ton, Clorinda's diary had described her. But Sam wanted nothing do with her.

"Don't you want to know who she is, dearest?" prompted Nan, leaning forward and patting Sam's arm solicitously.

"No, I don't believe I do," Sam said coolly. "For a so-called 'lady of quality' she behaved very badly."

"She's not a lady of quality . . . or, at least, not in the way you mean it. And she didn't behave badly at all," Julian said. "Like everyone else your father had anything to do with, she was tricked."

Sam turned to Julian, sudden hope making her heart beat fast and her throat go dry. "Wh-what do you mean, Julian?" she stammered.

"Your mother is an actress, Sam. An actress you have seen and admired. She is Genevieve DuBois."

Sam's mouth dropped open in astonishment. "Genevieve DuBois?" she repeated faintly.

"Genevieve DuBois?" the aunts chorused together.

"Now you know how you got your penchant for drama, Sam," he said dryly.

"But how . . . ? Why . . . ?" Sam was full of questions, but was too shocked to be able to form the necessary words and string them together in a coherent sentence. But Julian understood. It was amazing, Sam thought, how he could be so smart about some things and so stupid about others! He was too stupid to believe in and return her affection, but he knew exactly what she needed to hear about her mother; *everything!* Everything from *before* Sam was born, and everything *since* she was born.

Sam paid rapt attention as Julian told the sad and shocking story that painted an even uglier picture of her father than before. But as difficult as it was to hear the sordid details and to believe her own flesh and blood capable of such cold and cruel duplicity, at least now she knew the truth . . . the whole truth. And the truth absolved her mother of all guilt!

When Julian was done talking, Sam noticed that he sat very still and studied her face, waiting for her reaction. But, from the smile that was tugging at the corners of her mouth and the tears of joy that filled her eyes, it wouldn't take him long to figure out that she was deliriously happy. Too happy to keep it to herself!

"Oh, Julian, I'm so glad!" she exclaimed, jumping up from the footstool and throwing her arms around his neck as he still sat in the chair.

Shocked, and a little too pleased to find Sam sprawled across his lap with her arms twined around his neck, Julian pushed himself to a standing position while Sam held on, clinging to him like a barnacle to a ship's hull. Once he managed to get in a vertical position, Julian gave the aunts a sheepish grin over Sam's shoulder while he tried to limit his caresses to a few brotherly pats on the back. But the embrace continued, and Julian was beginning to fear that he would become visibly aroused while the aunts watched with unabashed interest. Then, just as Julian was growing desperate enough to forcibly pry Sam's arms from around his neck, she abruptly let go.

"This is wonderful!" Sam exclaimed, pacing the floor in feverish excitement. "I can't believe it! I have a mother, a *real* mother. She didn't abandon me! She wanted to keep me! Oh when can I see her, Julian? Tonight?"

Julian had not been prepared for Sam's excited and joyful response because he had not perfectly understood her seeming indifference over the past few weeks about finding her mother. He had suspected that she was only pretending not to care, but it wasn't till this moment that he realized why. Apparently she had been afraid of being hurt and rejected again.

Sam had been stunned and hurt to discover that her mother was still alive and, presumably, prosperous, while she had been abandoned by both her parents to a life of severe emotional and physical deprivation. She was afraid that by finding her mother, her worst suspicions would be confirmed.

Julian could well imagine how relieved and overjoyed Sam felt to find out that her mother had had no part in contributing to her suffering. That Genevieve DuBois had, in fact, wanted to keep Sam and was devastated to wake up from a drug-induced sleep to be told her child was stillborn.

"Well, Julian?" Sam prompted, standing with her hands clasped eagerly before her and bouncing restively on her heels. "Can we go to meet my . . . my *mother* tonight!"

"Sam . . ." Julian began, placing his hands on her shoulders. She was so excited, he could feel her trembling. He fought the urge to pull her into his arms again. "Perhaps visiting Madame DuBois tonight would . . . well . . . not be a good idea."

"Why not?" Sam asked, her eyes shining, her face aglow as she gazed up at him. "I know there's the Wilmots' ball tonight, but *that* isn't important! We'll send them a note tomorrow morning telling them I was sick or something." Her face suddenly clouded. "Or do you mean my mother might not *want* to see me tonight? Should I send her a note first, asking her when it would be convenient? Only I *do* think she'll be just as eager to see me as I am to see her, Julian!"

"I daresay you are quite right about that, Sam," Julian agreed cautiously.

"Then what are we waiting for?" Sam demanded happily.

Julian lightly ran his hands up and down Sam's shivering arms, praying that he would find the right words to say without hurting or offending her. "You have an impulsive nature, my dear. Don't you think you should take some time to think about this before committing yourself to a . . . er . . . relationship with your mother?"

Sam's brows drew together. Her smile vanished. "What do you mean? Why wouldn't I want a relationship with her?"

Sam's look and question were so endearing, so naive, Julian wasn't sure he had the heart to go on. He glanced over Sam's head at Priss and Nan, both their faces etched with empathy and concern. He telegraphed a question and they both nodded. *Yes, of course,* he thought to himself. *I must speak plainly to her. She must understand every repercussion.*

"Sam, please sit down," Julian suggested, gently turning her and seating her in the chair he'd just vacated. Then, just as he had on the night he first broke the news that her mother was presumably still living, he knelt down beside her and caught hold of her hands.

By now, Sam's face reflected suspicion and dread. "I don't like the tender way you're treating me, Julian. I have a feeling I'm not going to like what you're about to say."

"I'm sure you won't," Julian agreed. "But it must be said."

She straightened her shoulders. "Then say it."

"My dear . . . have you considered what will happen if it becomes public knowledge that you are the illegitimate daughter of a stage actress?"

He felt her immediately stiffen. A look of surprise flitted over her face to be quickly replaced by one of angry pride. "No, I had not considered what people would think. I was too happy to find out that I have a mother to give the idle reflections of shallow, hypocritical people a single moment's thought!" She turned away, but she still gripped his hands tightly.

"That the majority of people are shallow and hypocritical is not an opinion that I could successfully argue against," Julian began. "Nor would I even try, because I completely agree with you. However, the facts are as plain as a pikestaff, my dear! If word got out that Genevieve DuBois is your natural mother, you would be shunned by polite society. Very possibly, you would not be able to make a respectable marriage. Most men shy away from scandal when looking for a bride."

Sam's head jerked around as she flung at him, "Oh, but I'm sure I'd still be quite popular with the gentlemen! Only instead of marriage proposals I would receive propositions of a decidedly different nature, wouldn't I, Julian? Men don't give a fig who your mother is if they only want to *bed* you. But perhaps I was never meant to make a respectable marriage. Maybe, all things considered, I'm destined to be someone's mistress after all!"

"Don't talk that way, child!" Nan exclaimed, jumping up from her seat on the sofa and scurrying over.

"You have as much right to a respectable marriage as anyone," Priss corroborated, fast on her sister's heels. "You're as good as anyone. Better than most!"

"But only as long as I don't let them know the truth about me. Only if I hide the fact that Genevieve DuBois is my mother," Sam angrily retorted. "But she *is* my mother, and I don't care who knows!"

Julian had been silent since Sam made the remark about being destined to be a mistress, because he had had to take a moment to compose himself before speaking. Now he caught Sam's chin and forced her to look at him. "Firstly, my dear girl," he said in a voice that vibrated with suppressed fury, "if I ever hear you malign yourself in such a manner again, I shall be tempted to take a strap to you."

"Bah! Don't talk so, Julian!" Priss exclaimed, wringing her hands.

"He wouldn't do it, Priss," Nan interposed scornfully. "He'd just be *tempted!*"

"And secondly," he continued in the same chilly tone, "how do you even know that Madame DuBois *wants* it known that you're her flesh and blood? Did it never occur to you, brat, that she has a reputation to preserve as well? That *she* has a right to privacy, too?"

Julian watched to see what effect his words would have on Sam. He was pleased to see her features alter as she obviously considered what he'd said.

"I never thought of that," she finally whispered, glancing uncertainly at him.

"Well, I don't suppose you can think of everything," he conceded, his manner immediately softening. "I know that Madame DuBois is eager to make your acquaintance, Sam, but I'm not so sure she wants your relationship to become public."

Sam looked stricken. "Do you think she's ashamed of me?"

"No, my dear," Julian assured her, releasing his hold on her chin and running his fingers down her soft, smooth cheek. "She is prodigiously proud of you. She told me so herself. I talked of her wanting to protect her privacy, but I'm very sure that it's *you* she wishes to protect. She doesn't want you to ruin your chance to be respectably married just because your mother happens to be an actress!"

Sam shook her head, looking perturbed. "But don't you understand, Julian? If my mother wished it, I would gladly keep my past and my parentage a secret from the whole world. However, there would have to be *one* exception."

Julian raised a brow. "And who might that exception be?"

"I could never lie to my husband. And he's the very person I'm supposed to keep this information away from in order to snag him in the first place! Do you see how ridiculous this situation is?" She sighed deeply and gave him an accusing look from under her thick lashes. "Therefore, I suppose there's no doubt now that I shall die a *spinster!*"

The aunts immediately began arguing against such a harebrained idea, and Julian was spared the necessity of replying. However, had the aunts not been available to reason away Sam's dismal predictions, Julian might have been tempted to offer himself as a willing bridegroom on the spot. After all, he knew everything there was to know about Sam, her past and her parents . . . and he still loved her. Hell, maybe he loved her even more because of everything she'd been through.

But, thank God, the aunts *had* been available and he had not made the mistake of proposing. The realization that he was in love with Sam was too new. It was too soon to make decisions, especially impulsive decisions based on raw emotions. He must be cautious. After all, there was time. It wasn't as if Sam were going to engage herself immediately to some other man if Julian didn't pop the question that very night.

Besides, even though Sam was insisting that she must be completely honest with any man who wanted to marry her, perhaps she would eventually change her mind. So, instead of charging in on his white horse to rescue her from spinsterhood, Julian thought it prudent to bide his time and give Sam the opportunity really to know her own mind and heart. It was the wise and cautious thing to do.

Once the aunts had finished their loving lecture, Julian convinced Sam that it would be best if they kept their original plans for the evening and went to the Wilmots' ball. Genevieve DuBois would be performing that night at the theater, anyway, and they could send her a note in the morning and then visit her later the following afternoon.

Sam agreed to this plan, although she was obviously very sorry to put off a meeting she had been wishing for her entire life.

Julian, however, was only too happy to postpone the meeting and all the other crises that were presently brewing in his formerly smooth-as-silk life. Damn . . . when had he so completely lost control?

The Wilmots' ball was a rather grand affair, but Sam was in no mood for the glitter and gaiety of the elite social world she had strived so hard to fit into. As her usual admirers flocked around her, all she could think about was that if they knew the truth about her, they'd make themselves scarce in an instant. For the sake of appearances, Sam tried to appear her usual vivacious self, but it was a struggle.

As for Julian, he had kept his distance all evening, mingling with friends and acquaintances, but not dancing. The aunts were playing cards in the next room, leaving Julian to guard his charge alone.

So far, Sam had not seen Charlotte there, but she frequently came late to parties and might still appear. Then maybe Julian would shake off his melancholy, Sam thought wistfully. He looked very grave tonight and was probably looking forward to unburdening himself to Charlotte about all his problems. And the biggest problem facing him at the moment was what to do with his troublesome ward!

Sam could well imagine that Julian was worried that he'd never get rid of his charge now that she was insisting on total honesty with any man who aspired to be her husband. As Julian had said himself, most men shy away from scandal when looking for a bride. But Sam had never wanted to marry anyone but Julian, anyway, so the idea of spinsterhood was preferable to being married to someone she didn't love. She'd only thrown the "doomed to die a spinster" complaint in Julian's face to remind him that he had the power to change her destiny . . . if only he would admit he was in love with her!

Having just finished dancing a cotillion with a talkative pink of the *ton,* Sam was delighted to find Jean-Luc walking toward her. She held her hands out to him with a relieved and welcoming smile. "Jean-Luc," she exclaimed. "How glad I am at the sight of you!"

Jean-Luc took her hands and immediately drew her away from the crowd toward the less populated end of the ballroom. Then he bent near her ear and whispered, "And how glad I am to see you smile, *chère.* I was watching you dance, and, though you tried to look happy, I could tell that something was bothering you very much. I would like to flatter myself into believing that you were simply missing *me,* but, alas, I know that can't be the *only* reason for your gloomy disposition," he teased. Then he sobered and squeezed her hands affectionately. "What is the matter, Sam?"

Jean-Luc was looking at her with such kindness and seemed so sincerely interested in her concerns, Sam was very touched. "Oh, Jean-Luc, how I wish I could tell you everything. It would be such a relief."

"Then tell me. You trust me, don't you? Perhaps I can help." He smiled crookedly. "I proved myself useful today when I masqueraded as a robber, didn't I?"

Sam laughed. "Yes, indeed. But my problem can't be fixed so easily as Ninian's was." She sighed and smiled resignedly. "And this is far too public a place for a conversation that must be private."

Jean-Luc raised a sly brow, his eyes suddenly gleaming with mischief. "Ah, but I am familiar with the Wilmots' house, having spent an entire spring holiday here when I was going to Eton with the Wilmots' eldest son, Sebastian. It would be easy for me to find us a private chamber."

"I don't think so, Jean-Luc," Sam demurred. "If anyone should see us leave and then remark on our absence . . . Everyone always enjoys thinking the worst, you know."

"I will take you to the supper room, then we can escape down the hall."

"But it's not time for supper. Won't people wonder why we're going there?"

"As the next set for dancing forms, there will be enough confusion to hide our escape."

Sam bit her lip. She was tempted. "I don't know. . . ."

"I promise not to keep you away above ten minutes. No one will miss us in so short a time. But will that be long enough for you to tell me what's troubling you?"

"With time to spare," Sam acknowledged, warming to the idea. She couldn't help but think that getting a friend's view of her situation might be helpful.

"Then perhaps there will be time to talk to you

about something that troubles *me,* as well," he suggested, his handsome dark eyes peering inquiringly into hers.

Sam was surprised—she had not supposed that anything troubled devil-may-care Jean-Luc—but she readily agreed. Certainly if Jean-Luc was willing to listen to her talk about her problems, she was willing to listen to him talk about his.

"Let's go, then," Jean-Luc said in a conspiratorial whisper.

Sam nodded, glancing toward the crowd to make sure no one—especially not Julian—was watching them suspiciously. But she shouldn't have worried. She saw Charlotte enter the ballroom on her father's arm, and then observed Julian immediately approach them. There could be no doubt of it, Sam thought with a sigh, Charlotte was still Julian's first object. She turned and left with Jean-Luc, sadly certain that she would never be missed even if she were gone an hour!

Chapter 16

❧✦❧

Like truant children, Jean-Luc and Sam held hands and sneaked down a dimly lit hall to a back section of the large house. At one point, Jean-Luc snatched a branch of candles off a table so that when they entered a certain dark chamber, Sam was soon able to see that they were in what appeared to be a small parlor.

Having set the candelabra on the mantel, Jean-Luc turned and rubbed his hands together like a villain in a play, saying with a devilish smile, "Alone at last!"

Sam laughed, not afraid of him in the least. She sat down on a forest-green satin sofa and patted the cushion next to her. "To show you how much I trust you, Jean-Luc, I am inviting you to sit beside me."

Jean-Luc took the seat she offered and said ruefully, "I think I would rather you were at least a little bit afraid of me. Think of my reputation, Miss Darlington!"

Sam laughed again, already feeling less encumbered by her troubles. "You are good for me, Jean-Luc," she told him, impulsively grabbing his hand and squeezing it. "You make me laugh."

But when Sam would have released his hand, Jean-Luc held fast. She looked at him inquiringly and was a little shaken by the soft glow in his dark eyes. Then she remembered that there was something troubling him and allowed him to keep hold of her hand for comfort, prompting him gently, "Would you like to tell me now what's troubling you, Jean-Luc?"

"Are you sure you don't wish to go first, *chère?*" he asked politely, but with a hopeful air. Obviously he was anxious to get something off his chest.

"No," she assured him. "Just being with you has made me feel worlds better already." She knew she was exaggerating, but the smile that broke over Jean-Luc's handsome face was worth it.

"Good. I am encouraged," he murmured.

"Speak!" Sam commanded him playfully.

His expression became deadly serious. "Sam, do . . . do you remember yesterday when I told you that I was suffering from an affliction?"

Sam was instantly concerned. "Do you mean when we were talking at Montgomery House and you became rather overheated? But I thought you were only teasing me!" They were still holding hands, so she gave him another squeeze. "Oh, don't tell me you're really sick, Jean-Luc!"

He smiled crookedly. "Oh, but I am, *chère,*" he whispered hoarsely.

Alarmed, she asked, "But it's not serious, is it?"

"It is very serious, indeed," he answered soberly.

"But you aren't going to . . . to—"

"Die?" he supplied for her in what Sam could only think was a very cavalier manner of speaking of one's own mortality. He smiled again, his eyes glinting strangely. "That depends entirely on you, Sam."

"Me?" Sam was beginning to think he was on some sort of medicinal drug. "How can it have anything at all to do with me?"

"I will die, Sam, if you don't marry me," he told her with a straight face.

"Marry you?" she exclaimed. "How can that save you from your affliction?"

He laughed. "It will save me from dying of lovesickness. I never thought it would happen to me, Sam, and to be perfectly truthful I fought it for a long time. But I've fallen head over heels in love with you. And if you don't agree to be my wife this instant, I am sure I will die. But you are stunned, *chère*. Had you no idea I was languishing for you, sweetheart?"

"Truly I *am* stunned," Sam admitted faintly. "Everyone told me I mustn't take you seriously, Jean-Luc, so I never did."

Jean-Luc lifted her hands and kissed them. "But you must take me seriously now, *chère*. I have meant every compliment I've ever paid you. You are beautiful. You are brave. You are full of wit and life and spirit. I love you, Sam. I *adore* you. Will you marry me?"

Sam didn't know what to say. Jean-Luc's passionate words rang with sincerity. If only Julian would say those same words to her and look at her with the same melting adoration in his eyes. If only . . .

"You are not thinking of your guardian, are you, Sam?" Jean-Luc beseeched her, frowning. "I was never more glad when you told me you'd finally given up on him. I must confess I was extremely surprised when he did not succumb to your charms. I was aware of your infatuation for the marquess nearly from the moment we first met, and I always

felt it was a shame you were wasting your time
mooning over such a cold man."

"You don't know him, Jean-Luc," Sam couldn't
help herself from inserting. "He's a good man."

"In a remote, philanthropic sort of way, I suppose," Jean-Luc coolly conceded. "But he doesn't
deserve you. Even if he returned your feelings—
which I am convinced he never could—he would
never make you happy. He belongs with Charlotte
Batsford. You are too full of joy and fire to be
shackled to the likes of Lord Serling. You need a
man who will share that joy and fire with you. Let
me be that man, Sam."

Sam knew that Jean-Luc was not intending to
hurt her, but nevertheless his words did hurt. She
was afraid he was right. She didn't believe for a
minute that Julian was cold, but it was possible that
he might never let anyone tap into his inner
warmth, his deep passions. And she was afraid
Jean-Luc was also right when he said that Julian
could never feel for her what she felt for him.
Possibly Julian could be reached by someone,
someday, but perhaps the sad fact was that *she* was
not that person.

"Say something, Sam," Jean-Luc entreated her,
his eyes gazing eagerly into hers.

Sam's first instinct was to thank him for the very
great compliment he'd paid her by proposing marriage, then gently decline the offer. But she decided
that before serving him such a hard blow, she
would tell him about her past and who her parents
really were. Then he could politely retract his
proposal, saving her the difficult task of refusing
him. Even if she really wanted to marry Jean-Luc,
she was honor-bound to be completely honest and

had intended to confide in him about the matter, anyway.

So, she took a deep breath and said, "There is something you must know, Jean-Luc, which might make a very great difference in your way of thinking about me."

"I can only love you more, *chère,*" he insisted. "But if you must clear your conscience of some trifling schoolgirl indiscretion, I am all ears."

Sam could tell that Jean-Luc was not expecting to hear anything more awful than that she'd kissed some callow youth behind the church. And she knew he was going to be very shocked, indeed, when she told him her fantastic life story. But tell him she must.

She started at the beginning, explaining the circumstances of her birth, her rescue by Amanda and Jack, Julian's kind mentorship and tutelage, the deception under which she was introduced and had won over the *haut ton,* and lastly her discovery that she was none other than the offspring of London's brightest star, Genevieve DuBois.

Sam was not surprised to find when she was through that Jean-Luc was staring at her in some considerable amazement.

To spare him the awkwardness of searching for something to say, Sam spoke first. "I know. You are very much shocked. I imagine anyone would be. But I hope we may still . . . still be friends, Jean-Luc."

Jean-Luc seemed to shake himself out of a reverie, then exclaimed, *"Mon Dieu!* I knew you were not an ordinary girl, and now I know why! You have been pitted against the worst luck in the world and have come out the victor! Sam, you are truly amazing!"

Sam blinked. "You aren't shocked?"

"Of course, I'm shocked, *chère*," he admitted. "But do not think that I blame you, or esteem you less, for all that has happened to you in your short life. None of it was your fault. And you have overcome it all and are sitting before me a beautiful, intelligent, accomplished young woman."

"Well, I don't know about accomplished," Sam demurred modestly. "I can't sing or play the pianoforte worth a penny . . . or so says Julian."

"Sam," said Jean-Luc, grasping both her hands and sinking to his knees before her. "I don't care a fig about your past or who your mother is. I still want to marry you. In fact, I want to marry you more than ever. Tell me, darling . . . will you?"

Now Sam was forced to make a decision. Jean-Luc had amazed and impressed her by proving himself to be above the littleness of most of London society. He didn't care about her antecedents. He didn't care about her past. He wanted her and all the scandalous details of her life that came with her. He was just the sort of man she needed for a husband.

There was only one problem. She didn't love him. And he wasn't Julian.

And until Julian officially belonged to someone else, there was a part of Sam that, despite all her ranting to the contrary, simply could not give up on him.

"Jean-Luc, I can't—" she began, but he interrupted her.

"Don't say no, Sam," he said, seeming to anticipate her refusal and hoping to delay it. "Don't make up your mind this minute. Take some time to think about it."

"But I really don't need—"

"Just one night? Can't you sleep on it, darling?"

"Jean-Luc—"

"Please, Sam?"

Sam couldn't resist the supplication in his dark, soulful eyes. She sighed and smiled. "Very well, Jean-Luc. I will sleep on it and tell you my answer on the morrow. Are you satisfied?"

"I won't be satisfied till you say 'yes,' *chère*," he told her, standing up and pulling her to her feet. "Now we must return to the ball. Even as we speak your guardian could be ransacking the house in search of you."

Sam only wished he were.

"Why don't you go after her, Julian?"

"I will if she's gone above fifteen minutes. I don't wish to make a scene unless it's absolutely necessary."

Charlotte gave Julian a sympathetic look. "But you're dying to go after her, aren't you?"

Julian did not reply. He was standing with Charlotte in a window embrasure in the supper room, into which Sam and Jean-Luc had disappeared ten minutes earlier. When he and Charlotte likewise entered the room and did not see the pair anywhere, Julian concluded that Jean-Luc had stolen Sam away to some private chamber for the purpose of either proposing to her or making advances.

Neither of these probable explanations for their removal from the crowded ballroom pleased Julian. In fact, he was exercising the strictest control over his temper to keep himself from searching the house for the miscreant couple, then dragging that Frenchman outside by his heels and landing him a facer. But such behavior would cause a scene and a scandal. He was forced to trust Sam to take care of herself in this situation . . . at least for another five minutes.

"She will not allow Jean-Luc liberties, even if he is so unwise as to press them on her," Julian said calmly, even though he felt anything but. "However, I hope no one else saw them leave together. Sam is not considering her reputation . . . the foolish chit!"

"If she insists on publicly acknowledging Madame DuBois as her mother, a ten-minute tryst with Jean-Luc will be the least of your problems as far as guarding her reputation." Charlotte sighed. "Poor Julian!"

Julian turned to Charlotte with a wry and tender smile. "You are a good friend, Charlotte! I am amazed you are still speaking to me."

"Yes, so am I," Charlotte agreed ruefully.

"I have behaved abominably," Julian continued contritely, taking hold of both her hands.

"Yes, you have!"

"Yet you have forgiven me."

"*I* have forgiven you. However, my father and mother are another story."

"Yes, your father's curt nod at the door set me down a notch or two."

"And my mother wouldn't even come tonight for fear of seeing you," Charlotte admitted with a chuckle. "When I told her there was no chance of our becoming engaged, she indulged in a fine fit of hysterics."

Julian squeezed her hands and said in a low, gentle voice, "You speak lightly, Charlotte, but I know I've hurt you." Charlotte blushed and looked down. "My attentions to you were very marked. I had every intention of asking you to marry me. You knew it. Everyone knew it."

"But you cannot help how you feel," Charlotte murmured. "You were not aware that your heart was elsewhere engaged. I suspected it, but I chose not to believe it, just as you fought against it yourself."

Julian grimaced. "Yes. But in the end I lost the battle."

Charlotte peeked up at him. "But if you finally allow yourself to follow your heart, Julian, you will win something very special indeed. I hope you and Sam will be very happy together."

Julian sighed. "As to that, I don't know——"

"As your friend, Julian, may I ask two favors of you?" Charlotte interposed.

"You may ask me anything," Julian gallantly replied.

"First, I want you to resolve to take risks in your personal life. Otherwise, you will never find happiness. You will be comfortable, but you will be lonely."

Julian nodded soberly. "And the other favor?"

Charlotte smiled demurely. "Please do not introduce me to any other of your male relatives. I believe I've had quite enough to do with Montgomery men!"

Julian laughed and impulsively bent down and kissed her on the cheek. "I promise, Charlotte."

When Sam and Jean-Luc entered the supper room from the hallway, it was impossible not to observe the tender scene going on between Julian and Charlotte in the window embrasure. Protected somewhat from the view of others, they were nonetheless being openly affectionate in a public place.

Shocked, dismayed, and rooted to the spot, Sam

watched Julian kiss Charlotte on the cheek. Then, as he straightened up, he looked down at her with the tenderest of smiles. Charlotte was blushing prettily, and Sam thought she detected the sheen of a tear on her face.

Sam's heart felt as though it had been ripped apart. The facts were before her, as clear as crystal. She could come to no other conclusion than that Julian had just proposed to Charlotte and been accepted. What else would induce him to behave so . . . well, so much like she wished he would behave toward *her*?

"Well, well, well," Jean-Luc whispered in Sam's ear. "So he has finally popped the question. It's about time, I should say," he added with a satisfied air.

"Yes," Sam said faintly. "It appears he has finally done it."

"He's bound to be in a benevolent mood for the next few hours," Jean-Luc mused. "I hope you make up your mind soon about my proposal, *chère*. Apparently this would be an excellent time to approach your guardian for permission to become betrothed . . . what with love in the air and all."

"Yes," Sam agreed absentmindedly, unable to wrench her eyes away from the touching tableau in the window embrasure. "It would be a perfect time to approach him, wouldn't it?"

Jean-Luc stared at her, then he caught her hands and turned her to face him. "Sam? Are you saying that you *will* marry me? You don't need to sleep on it, *chère?*"

Sam looked at Jean-Luc's eager face and at his eyes, shining with hope and excitement and . . . love. Love for her.

Giving in to a sudden impulse to soothe the pain

inside her, to enjoy being loved even if it wasn't by the man you adored, and maybe, too, to salve her wounded pride, Sam summoned up a smile and said, "Yes, Jean-Luc, I will marry you. Please, feel free to address my guardian on the matter first thing tomorrow morning."

"Oh, Sam! You have made me the happiest of men!" Jean-Luc exclaimed, then he drew her hands to his lips and showered her fingers with fervent kisses.

Sam stared at Jean-Luc's bent head, at the dark curls and handsome brow, feeling curiously detached. Then, while her betrothed continue to reverently kiss her hands, she turned to look toward the window embrasure.

Charlotte had mysteriously and suddenly disappeared and Julian now stood alone. Their gazes locked across the narrow room. His eyes glinted like silver sapphires, and his brows were contracted in a suspicious and disapproving frown.

Sam raised her chin and stared haughtily back, her mouth tilted in a faint, contemptuous smile of triumph. But her victory was hollow, like her heart . . . for it had been shattered into a thousand pieces.

Julian was lost to her forever.

Sam spent a sleepless night. She rose in the morning feeling weary and depressed. But it was imperative that she behave as though she were happy, so she wore a bright yellow gown, had her curls arranged in a carefree style, and pinched her pale cheeks till they were pink.

Last night Jean-Luc had requested an audience with Julian for ten that morning, and as they routinely ate breakfast at nine, she was dreading sitting through a meal with her guardian with the impending betrothal hanging between them and nothing yet settled. Julian had not questioned her about Jean-Luc's intentions, but he couldn't possibly doubt what they were after seeing him fervently kissing her hands last night.

The drive home from the Wilmots' ball had been filled with chatter between the aunts, who had had a marvelous evening playing whist and piquet. Julian replied briefly and civilly to questions directed to him, and Sam had pretended to be attentive and interested in the aunts' cheerful gossip.

Julian never said a word about his own good news. And since there was no one to apply to for Charlotte's hand—her father having smiled his approval on the match for months now—there was no reason that Sam could think of why Julian kept his betrothal a secret.

As for sharing her own impending nuptials with the aunts, Sam didn't have the courage. She wasn't sure she could bear up under the onslaught of felicitations and immediate plans for the wedding. Priss and Nan liked Jean-Luc and could have no suspicion that Sam had been pining for Julian all these months, so she supposed they would be well pleased with the news.

As luck would have it, Julian did not come down to breakfast.

"Oh, dear," said Nan, addressing Hedley. "His Lordship isn't feeling unwell, I hope?"

Hedley continued to pour tea as he answered, "Not that I'm aware of, Miss Nancy."

"How did he look?" she pressed.

"He looked his usual self," the butler replied coolly.

"But he never misses breakfast," Priss observed worriedly. "I hope he's not out of sorts about something. Did he order a tray?"

Hedley's lips thinned. Obviously he did not approve of discussing his master's looks and orders, or speculating on his health and disposition. "I daresay, madames, if you are concerned about His Lordship, perhaps you should send written inquiries up with the footman," he said dampeningly. "Lord Serling can best speak for himself."

Undaunted by the butler's set-down, the aunts continued to discuss Julian's strange absence from the breakfast table and asked Sam if she had a theory to put forth in explanation.

"I'm sure I don't know why he isn't here," Sam said, forcing a smile. "But I don't think we need worry about him going hungry. You should know him better than that, my dear aunts."

The aunts agreed and eventually the conversation turned to other matters. Sam ate a very small breakfast, then retired to her bedchamber. She did not want to be nearby when Jean-Luc came to call. In fact, she didn't even want to catch a glimpse of him leaving the house. She could hardly bear to imagine the look of satisfaction on his face after receiving permission from Julian to seek her hand in marriage. And since he'd already procured her own acquiescence, it was only a matter of time before the betrothal would be puffed up in the papers and her own matrimonial fate sealed for good.

Sam was only too aware this morning that she'd made a terrible mistake. If she couldn't marry Julian, she had no business marrying anyone. But the die had been cast, and there was no turning back. By and by she hoped she'd become reconciled

to the marriage and make Jean-Luc as happy as he
deserved to be.

At exactly ten o'clock, there was a knock on
Julian's library door. *The eager bridegroom-to-be is
exactly on time,* Julian thought bitterly, rising from
his chair behind the desk and coming round to the
front to greet his visitor. "Come," he called, and
the footman entered, announced Jean-Luc, then
bowed himself out.

Julian braced himself for the interview he'd been
dreading ever since he saw Jean-Luc kissing Sam's
fingers last night at the Wilmots' ball. And when
Jean-Luc later asked to meet with him this morning, Julian's worst fears were confirmed. It had
taken him too long to understand his own heart,
and meanwhile Sam had made other plans. He had
pushed her away one too many times. But was it
entirely hopeless? he wondered. He would soon
know.

Jean-Luc strode in, fashionably dressed and im-
peccably groomed as usual, but the sparkle in his
eyes and the broad smile on his lips made him a
different man today. He obviously felt himself the
luckiest man on earth.

He bowed, and Julian returned the courtesy with
a slight nod of his head. Jean-Luc's cheerfulness
and confidence was like a knife in Julian's heart. It
reduced his own hopes considerably. He would be
civil, but he could barely tolerate Jean-Luc's happiness.

As if sensing Julian's irritation with him, Jean-
Luc seemed to try to smile less, to appear less
joyful. But it didn't work. His eyes still glowed, his
mouth still persisted in turning up at the corners.

"Good morning, Lord Serling," Jean-Luc began.

"Is it?" Julian drawled with a faint smile.

Jean-Luc's expressive eyebrows lifted. "Haven't you noticed what a beautiful day it is outside?"

"No, I haven't," Julian replied, indicating a chair for Jean-Luc to sit in, then sitting down himself. "But, in your present mood, I imagine you would think it a fine day even if it were pouring rain. However, you did not come here to talk of the weather." Julian wanted to get this ordeal over with as soon as possible.

Jean-Luc sat down on the edge of the chair, leaning forward, as if he were too excited to relax. "Of course you know why I'm here. I'm quite sure I'm not the first to ask for Sam's hand in marriage, but I flatter myself that I'm the first she has encouraged."

"You have already asked her to marry you?"

"Yes."

"At the Wilmots' ball last night?"

"Yes."

"And she said . . . yes?"

"*Yes!* And I'm the happiest of men."

Julian turned away. "Obviously," he muttered. Then it was settled, Julian thought morosely. As he had feared, Sam had already told Jean-Luc that she would marry him. So what choice did he have but to give Jean-Luc his consent and blessing to the betrothal?

There was certainly nothing he could reasonably object to in the fellow. He was rich and well-connected. He had been a bit of a philanderer over the years, but he now seemed quite ready to settle down. And if Sam wanted him, how could he refuse her? But *did* Sam want him more than any other man? Did she *love* him more than any other man? Was he truly the right man for her?

"You must know I am well able to give your ward a very comfortable lifestyle, Lord Serling," Jean-Luc continued when Julian did not speak. "I've an estate in Derbyshire and—"

"I am well aware of your ability to provide for my ward," Julian cut him off. "I am more concerned that you are . . . er . . . compatible as a couple."

As well he might, Jean-Luc looked surprised. Compatibility between a man and a woman was probably hardly ever discussed in these sorts of interviews. Money and connections were all that mattered to most guardians.

"We are extremely compatible," Jean-Luc assured him. "We are the best of friends. She confides in me, and I in her. We have a great deal of fun together, and—"

"Do you love her?"

Jean-Luc's handsome face beamed with tenderness and sincerity. "Very much," he said with quiet conviction.

Jealous beyond bearing, Julian wanted to strangle Jean-Luc. But how could he dislike—much less strangle—a man that had such exquisite taste in women? If he didn't desperately want Sam for himself, he would be overjoyed at the prospect of giving her away to such a fellow.

But there was one more point that had to be covered. The most important point of all.

"And does Sam love you?"

Jean-Luc hesitated. Some sort of emotion— doubt?—flashed in his eyes for an instant. But soon he was smiling as broad as ever. "I believe she does. But if she doesn't, I will *make* her love me! I will make her the center of my life. If you consent to our marriage, Lord Serling, I promise to devote myself to her happiness. What is your answer, sir? May I have Sam's hand in marriage?"

Julian observed Jean-Luc for a long, considering moment. Then he said, "It appears that I have no choice in the matter. There's only one possible answer to your request."

Jean-Luc leaned eagerly forward, his face reflecting his joy and triumph.

Twenty minutes past the hour of ten, Sam was startled by a knock at her bedchamber door. She'd been thinking of her mother and wondering how that lovely lady would have advised her to handle her present problems. And she had been trying very hard *not* to think about what was going forth in the library during Jean-Luc's interview with Julian. But it appeared that now she was going to find out whether she wanted to or not.

She opened the door, half-expecting to see Julian himself, but it was Hedley.

"Lord Serling wishes you to come to him in the library, miss," he said. "Immediately," he added with emphasis.

Sam followed Hedley down the stairs to the library. He opened the door for her, she went in, and much sooner than seemed possible she was facing her guardian across the narrow width of the room.

Julian was leaning in a negligent pose against his massive mahogany desk, his shapely, lean-muscled thigh hiked over the edge. He was wearing buff-colored pantaloons and tall Hessian boots, a Devonshire-brown jacket and an oyster-shell brocade waistcoat. As usual, he looked magnificent and, despite his casual attitude, he exuded strength and virility. He took her breath away.

"So, Samantha," he began in a measured voice, the expression in his silvery blue eyes intense and aloof at the same time, "Jean-Luc is the man you have chosen for your bridegroom."

Samantha's gaze dropped to the Axminster carpet at her feet. She felt a constriction in her throat and the pressure of beginning tears behind her eyes.

"Is there anything wrong, Sam?" The question was quietly and coolly spoken.

Sam swallowed the lump in her throat and forced back the tears. If there was one thing she was determined to hold on to at this point, it was her pride. She threw back her head and smiled brightly. "No, there's nothing wrong, Julian," she lied, her voice remarkably steady considering how wretched she truly felt. "It's just that it felt odd to hear you speak of my marriage as a . . . a . . . positive thing. There was a fluttering in my chest. I'm so very happy, you see."

Julian pursed his lips and nodded thoughtfully. "So, Jean-Luc was not just indulging a bit of wishful thinking when he told me that you had already consented to an engagement?"

"He was not," Sam agreed, still forcing a tremulous smile.

"Then you . . . care for him?"

Sam gave a short, artificial laugh. "How could you doubt my feelings for Jean-Luc after what you witnessed last night at the Wilmots' ball? I do not allow just any man to . . . to kiss me."

"Indeed, I should hope not," Julian returned, still quite sober. "Kisses should not be strewn about like rose petals. Not even kisses on the hand."

"Or on the cheek," Sam couldn't resist adding,

conjuring up a painful memory of Julian and Charlotte at the Wilmots' ball last night.

He stared hard at her, seeming to try to read her thoughts. But Sam didn't so much as flinch. She had resolved to get through this ordeal without losing her composure. After all, Julian was engaged to Charlotte now and honor-bound to keep his promise to spend the rest of his life with her. Sam would keep her promise, too. She would marry Jean-Luc.

Thinking the interview nearly at an end, Sam was surprised and unnerved when Julian slowly slid his thigh off the desk top and stood. He paused, simply looked at her, then deliberately advanced.

Immediately Sam's heart began to beat faster. It was one thing affecting unconcern with Julian far across the room. But the closer he approached, the harder it was for Sam to pretend that her heart wasn't breaking, that she wasn't yearning to throw herself into his arms, that she didn't love him more than life itself.

He stopped just in front of her and looked down, gazing steadfastly into her face. She bravely stood her ground, her eyes locked with his. Still he said nothing.

Sam felt gooseflesh erupt on her arms, her back, her breasts. He was so close she could feel the heat of his body. She could smell his unique scent of soap and linen and clean masculinity, taking her back to that night at the inn when they'd kissed and he'd held her close against him. Her body responded to the memory . . . quickening, warming, aching.

He lifted his arms and cupped her shoulders with his large, strong, beautiful hands. Sam gasped, then hoped Julian had not noticed her involuntary response.

"Sam, may I ask you a question?" he said at last, his eyes searching hers.

"Y . . . yes, of course."

"You and I have kissed . . ." His gaze strayed to her lips.

"That . . . that was not a question, Julian," Sam quavered. "That was a statement."

"If you are so particular about whom you kiss, Sam, why did you allow me to kiss you? Nay, why did you *dare* me to kiss you?"

Sam did not understand why Julian was asking such a question, especially now that neither of them were free. Was he doubting her affection for Jean-Luc . . . or testing it? Her pride would not allow him to suspect that she'd decided to marry Jean-Luc on the spur of the moment, and that she had only succumbed to such a whim because she couldn't have the one man she truly loved . . . him.

Reminding herself that she was the daughter of an actress, Sam forced herself to answer lightly. "I had an infatuation for you . . . remember?" she said, somehow managing a sheepish smile. "I would have tried anything to get you to see me as a woman."

"Well, guess what?" he said softly, lifting his hand and lightly stroking her cheek with his thumb. "It worked. I do see you as a woman now."

"You . . . you do?" she said wonderingly.

"Yes, a young woman quite grown-up and ready for a relationship with a man." He cupped her cheek in his hand and looked into her eyes. "Only I wonder if you've chosen the right man. Have you, Sam?"

Sam wanted to tell him the truth. She wanted to tell him that he was the only man for her. But to what purpose? To admit that her feelings for him had not changed since she'd confessed them to him at the King's Arms, then been rebuffed, would only make her look foolish and pathetic. After all, even though he had not told her of it yet, he'd made his choice. He was engaged to someone else, and he was far too honorable to cry off from an engagement even if she was able to somehow get through to him this time . . . which seemed extremely unlikely. If her bare body had been so easily ignored by him, why should she bare her soul? No, there was no point in doing so. No point at all.

Again Sam forced a smile and told a lie. "But of course I've chosen the right man, Julian! It has just taken me a while to . . . to understand my true feelings. I am sure Jean-Luc will make an excellent husband. He loves me very much."

"But do *you* love *him?*" Julian persisted, his eyes intensely bright.

It was time for another lie, but Sam couldn't get it out. She felt dazed, disoriented by Julian's closeness. Why was he torturing her? Why didn't he just leave her alone and let her be miserable in her own way!

"If you're not sure, there's one way to find out," he advised her in a soft-as-silk voice. "When he's this close to you, do you want him to put his arms around you . . . like this?" He slid his arms around her waist.

"Do you want him to hold you close . . . like this?" He pulled her flush against him. His hard body against hers awakened a thousand pulse points that throbbed throughout her.

He bent his head till his lips were inches from hers. "Do you want him to kiss you . . . like this?" he breathed.

Julian stared into Sam's wide, questioning gaze. Tension pulsated in the air between them. Then, throwing caution aside for once in his life, he claimed her mouth in a passionate, possessive kiss that made rational thought impossible. He was wonderfully out of control!

She, too, seemed to welcome the recklessness of their embrace. She clung to him and wrapped her arms around his neck, fervently returning his kisses.

"Sam," he rasped, his mouth gliding down her throat to the frantic pulse at its base. Thrilled by her eager trembling and gasps of pleasure, his hand moved to her small, round breast and caught the taut nipple between thumb and forefinger. She moaned, and he was drunk with joy. She wanted him as much as he wanted her.

He picked her up and carried her to the sofa, sitting down and cradling her in his lap. Still holding her, he pressed her back against a pile of throw pillows, kissing her mouth, her neck, the fragile ridge of her collarbone.

She sighed and arched her back in invitation. He took the invitation, burying his face in the dip between her breasts, gently but urgently pushing down the bodice of her gown as he kissed and lathed her soft skin. Soon he had exposed a creamy breast and could not resist the urge to suckle there. He swirled his tongue around the rosy nipple, teasing and tugging. She clutched at his hair, drawing him closer and closer.

His hand wandered down to caress her rib cage, her slim waist, and the swell of her hips. She curled against him, her own hands roaming his chest and shoulders. He caught the edge of her skirt and pulled it up and up . . .

There was a knock at the door. Julian cursed eloquently under his breath, then immediately struggled to a standing position, pulling Sam up with him. "Just a moment, please," he called in a hoarse voice. As Sam wobbled on her feet in a seeming stupor, Julian straightened her gown, then pushed her into a chair. Ordering his own slightly disheveled clothing, he then walked quickly to the door and opened it a crack. Hedley was on the other side, looking frankly perplexed by the delay.

"What is it, Hedley?" Julian inquired in as cool a voice as he could manage. "I'm talking with Miss Darlington and do not wish to be disturbed."

"I beg your pardon, my lord," Hedley said in a mortified voice. "I was not aware that you did not . . . er . . . wish to be disturbed."

"Never mind. What is it?"

"Miss Nancy and Miss Priscilla sent me to fetch Miss Darlington. A note has arrived from her mother, and they will not be easy till she has opened it and divulged its contents to them. Or so they say, my lord."

Julian sighed. "Tell them we'll be down momentarily."

"Of course, my lord," Hedley said, then marched away down the hall. He had been easy to get rid of, with no questions asked, but such would not be the case with the aunts.

Julian closed the door and turned around. Sam was still sitting where he'd placed her, looking a bit shocked and considerably confused. Though it had not seemed so at the time, Julian conceded to himself that a note from Sam's mother couldn't have come at a more propitious time. He had been at the point of actually making love to Sam in the middle of the afternoon with the possibility of interruption almost a certainty. She obviously made him careless and crazy.

"Julian . . . what just happened here?" she asked him in a faint voice.

Dragging a trembling hand through his hair, he said ruefully, "I went slightly mad."

Her brows furrowed in a troubled frown. "That's no explanation."

"There's no time for explanations, Sam. We'll talk later."

"You always say that and we never do! I want to talk *now!*"

"Sam, the aunts are waiting for us with a letter from your mother."

Sam seemed to be momentarily distracted by the news that her mother's note had arrived, but she immediately returned to the original subject, saying fretfully, "You must *promise* me you'll explain later, Julian!"

"I promise," he said, and it was a promise he fully intended to keep . . . but in his own time.

Chapter 17

~~~⌒⌒⌒~~~

Madame DuBois's note to Sam was brief and polite, requesting that Sam visit her that evening at eight o'clock. She further explained that she would have been delighted to see "her daughter" at an earlier hour, but after performing to a crowded theater most nights, she wasn't fit for company till she'd had her beauty sleep. She signed the note *M. DuBois*. Sam held the note to her heart and hoped fervently that she and her mother would have something to say to one another when they finally met.

Because Priss and Nan did not think Sam would especially care for an audience when she and her mother first clapped eyes on each other, the aunts did not accompany Julian and Sam to Madame DuBois's house that evening, but arranged to meet them later at an elegant gathering for a musical soiree at the McAdamses'.

To ensure their comfort and safety, the aunts were conveyed to the McAdamses' on Cavendish Square in Julian's crested carriage, while Julian and Sam hired a hackney coach to transport them to the much less fashionable Upper Wimpole Street.

Sam was not perfectly satisfied with such an

arrangement. She thought she and her mother would require several hours at least to become acquainted with each other. She wanted more time, and she didn't like the feeling of sneaking around to visit her own flesh and blood. In her mind, the whole affair smacked of a sort of unsavory furtiveness. But it had been Madame DuBois who requested the short first meeting, thinking it wise that they proceed cautiously and not draw attention to themselves.

Much to Sam's dismay, it seemed that Julian had probably been right in supposing that Madame DuBois wanted to protect her by keeping their relationship to each other a secret from the general public. But Sam was in no mood to be discreet. She was losing Julian, and she had no desire to lose a mother she had just found, and for no other reason than to keep the London tattle-tongues from wagging.

However, it would all be settled according to her mother's wishes. While she was feeling rather reckless about her reputation at the moment, Sam did not want her mother to be uncomfortable about it. No doubt, Madame DuBois would blame herself if her daughter suddenly became a social pariah.

Sam had dressed carefully for the meeting. Keeping in mind that she was having to attend a dressy affair afterward but still more concerned about the first impression she'd make on her mother, Sam had worn a simple gown of white crepe. Her new abigail, Dorcas, had arranged her hair in a classic Greek style with tendrils of curling hair wisping about her face. She wore a three-string pearl choker about her neck, and pearl pendants in her ears.

Long white gloves and plain white satin slippers finished the ensemble.

Despite her nervousness about meeting her mother, Sam was still extremely aware of Julian's presence in the coach. How could it be otherwise when they'd shared such a passionate interlude earlier that day? But since he flatly refused to discuss what had happened, saying that "this was definitely not the time for such a discussion," and that "she should be thinking only of her mother," Sam gave up and sat as silent as he did for the duration of the drive to Upper Wimpole Street.

But Sam felt Julian had another reason for not wishing to discuss what had happened. As he had explained when Hedley interrupted them, he'd simply gone slightly mad for a short period of time, and now he was heartily regretting it! While he obviously finally saw Sam as a woman, he didn't see her as a wife! He'd probably wanted to kiss Hedley for stopping him before he compromised her!

It was too cruel to be in love with such a man, Sam thought sadly, gazing at him in the dim glow of the carriage lantern. As always, he looked wonderful. He was wearing pale gray breeches, a burgundy waistcoat, and a dark gray jacket. His clothes, as usual, fit precise to a pin, showing every sinewy muscle in his legs and accentuating the broad strength of his shoulders.

Sam always marveled that he could look so civilized, so elegant . . . yet still exude such virility and power. She found herself drifting back and forth between concerns about her first meeting with her mother . . . and wonderful erotic fantasies about Julian that went far beyond what they did together in the library that afternoon. Despite the fact that she'd had no real opportunity to put them to the test, Isabelle Descartes's lessons of love had not been forgotten.

Besides the torture of being closely confined with a man you lusted for and didn't dare touch, Sam was still very much devastated by his engagement to Charlotte, and in shock about her own engagement to Jean-Luc. At least, she *assumed* it was a positive engagement between herself and Jean-Luc! That was what Julian had implied, but, strangely, Jean-Luc had not called on her at all that day after his interview with Julian. However, she knew he was going to be at the McAdamses' soiree, so she was sure they'd have plenty of opportunity to talk there.

Finally they drew to a stop in front of a respectable-looking, redbrick town house. Sam glanced out and nervously patted her hair and smoothed her gown.

Julian stepped out of the coach first, then turned and held out his hand to Sam. She took his hand, gathered her skirts, and was about to alight when he leaned near her and whispered, "Don't be nervous. You look beautiful. She'll love you instantly."

The kind words nearly brought tears to Sam's eyes. It was precisely what she needed to hear, and meant even more to her because it had been Julian to offer the comfort. He was an exasperating man, but his praise, his support were so important to her.

"Thank you, Julian," she whispered with heartfelt gratitude, then she smiled. He smiled back and squeezed her hand as he assisted her from the coach. They entered Madame DuBois's house together, but the joy Sam felt walking arm in arm with the man she loved most in the world was a bittersweet happiness. She knew it would end someday very soon.

Julian watched Sam as they sat in the drawing room waiting for her mother to appear. He marveled at her outward composure, because he knew that inside she was quaking. Finding her mother was so important to Sam, Julian prayed that nothing would happen to disappoint or disenchant her when the two of them finally met.

However, since he—a person wholly objective— had been favorably impressed with Madame DuBois, there was no doubt in his mind that Sam—who wanted desperately to like her—would find just as much to be pleased with.

Dressed all in white, Sam looked like an angel. He imagined she would look just as angelic on her wedding day.

On her wedding day. Yes, eventually that day would come. But whom would she marry? When questioned, she still claimed to be in love with Jean-Luc, but her eager response to him in the library that day had given Julian reason to hope otherwise. But why would she lie? Had she accepted Jean-Luc's proposal of marriage because she'd finally realized that the so-called "love" she'd felt for *him* had been only a girlish infatuation . . . a passing fancy?

Yet, could she respond to him so passionately and be in love with another man? Julian had decided that he was going to find out. It was foolish to go on this way, not really knowing each other's hearts and minds. But he felt it would be too much to expect Sam to deal with meeting her mother for the first time, and choosing between two men, all in one night. Although the wait was torture, Julian had decided that tomorrow would have to be the soonest he declared his love to Sam.

The door to the salon opened, interrupting Julian's thoughts. Genevieve DuBois appeared at the threshold and stood there, poised like a lovely statue. She was dressed in a pale lavender gown, with lots of jewelry on her slender neck and arms. But her gown and her jewelry paled in comparison to the expression on her face and the light shining in her fine eyes.

Sam stood up, wobbled a little, and put her hand to her throat. Both women seemed incapable of speech, but their delight in seeing each other, in finding each other, was obvious.

Finally Genevieve took a step forward and held out her arms. Sam went to her and they embraced. There were no dramatic exclamations, no noisy sobbing, and no swooning. But the emotion in the room was palpable, and the scene between mother and daughter very touching to observe. Perhaps too touching to observe. . . . Julian stood up and left the room, leaving the two women to their reunion.

After pacing the hall for twenty minutes, Julian reentered the room. He found Sam and her mother seated cozily on the sofa together, talking like long-lost friends. They looked up when he cleared his throat.

He smiled. "I gather the reunion has been a success?"

"She is already calling me 'Mother'! I asked her to, and she agreed. Isn't it delightful?" Genevieve effused. "Lord Serling, I'm so glad you disregarded my threatening notes. Meeting Samantha has been the highlight of my life!"

"What threatening notes?" Sam asked, looking with surprise at Julian, then at her mother.

Genevieve appeared to wish the words back, and turned questioning eyes to Julian.

"I never told her about the notes," Julian confirmed. "I didn't want to alarm her."

"I sent a couple of . . . shall we say . . . *cautionary* notes to Lord Serling, my dear," Genevieve hurriedly explained, taking hold of both Sam's hands and speaking earnestly. "I didn't want him to find me."

"Why not?" Sam asked with an anxious expression. "I thought you wanted to know me."

"Oh, I did!" Genevieve assured her, squeezing her hands. "But it would have been selfish of me to think only of myself. Samantha, my dear, I did not think it would be in your best interests to have it known about town that your mother is an actress." She looked over her shoulder at Julian. "In fact, I was even afraid that Lord Serling's attitude toward you might change. But I needn't have feared. It seems he has been your stoutest ally from the very beginning."

Sam lifted her eyes to Julian's face and smiled faintly. "Yes. Julian has been the best of friends."

Genevieve looked back and forth between the two of them, then said rather archly, "Yes, it's hard to find a good man with a broad mind these days. I hope you are wise enough, my dear, to marry him before your sister returns in the summer. Why waste precious time waiting to get the whole family together for a church wedding when you could be happily honeymooning?"

Julian could tell that Sam was just as stunned as he was by her mother's comment. He was rendered momentarily speechless, but Sam darted him an embarrassed glance and blushed hotly, saying, "Mother, what makes you think Julian and I have the least idea of getting married?"

"But he is the perfect man for you, my dear," she stated with some surprise, as if the fact were self-evident. "He knows everything about you. In fact, he probably knows you better than your sister, Amanda, does. I daresay he even likes *me* . . . his future mother-in-law! What better recommendation could you have for a husband?"

"He doesn't want to marry me, Mother," Sam said in a low, stiff voice, growing rosier by the minute. "He doesn't love me. And *I* don't love *him.*"

Julian felt Sam's words like a dagger to the heart. She was wrong on at least one point. *He* certainly loved *her*.

"Nonsense!" Genevieve scoffed. She turned to Julian. "For heaven's sake, Lord Serling, set this girl straight. She thinks you don't love her!"

Julian crossed his arms over his chest and frowningly observed Sam's mother. He was trying to decide what she was up to. From their conversation the day before, he knew she had guessed that he was in love with Sam . . . and had come to that correct conclusion even before he'd admitted the truth to himself! And now it seemed she had decided to play matchmaker.

Trouble was, Genevieve didn't realize that Sam had possibly gotten over whatever feelings she'd had for him, and had promised herself to someone else.

"Madame DuBois—"

"Call me Genevieve," she countered. "After all, we'll soon be family!"

"Madame DuBois," Julian repeated firmly, "you are laboring under a mistaken idea. You see, Sam plans to wed Mr. Jean-Luc Bouvier."

Genevieve's eyes widened and she blinked several times. Julian couldn't decide if she was acting or if she was truly surprised. "Jean-Luc Bouvier? Why, how on earth did this come about, Samantha? You know you aren't in love with the fellow. He's handsome and rich and quite amusing, I daresay, but he's not the man for you. And what about Julian? If you don't marry him, who will?"

"I'm not quite without prospects," Julian murmured dryly.

"No indeed, Mother," Sam assured her, appearing very flustered by the whole conversation. "In fact, I have it on good authority that Julian intends to . . . to marry Charlotte Batsford. Don't you, Julian?"

"No doubt it's the prevailing opinion," Julian hedged, a sudden and most interesting suspicion coming into his head.

"The prevailing opinion?" Genevieve repeated. "Pray, what does *that* mean? Speak plainly, Lord Serling. Are you betrothed to Miss Batsford or not?"

"Mother! You are hardly acquainted with Julian. Do you think you should be demanding information from him in such a high-handed manner?" Sam scolded in an agitated whisper.

"I daresay it is the only way I'll find out what I want to know," she retorted. "Indeed, Samantha, if the two of you were more honest and plain-speaking with each other, matters wouldn't have come to such a pass and you wouldn't need my assistance to straighten out the muddle you've made of your lives!"

"I *have* been plain-speaking with Julian," Sam insisted defensively, glancing self-consciously at Julian. "And he has been just as blunt with me. *Brutally* blunt, at times. I assure you, Mother, Julian does not want to marry me. And even if he did, he could not. Not after last night."

"What happened last night?" Genevieve demanded.

"Yes, brat," Julian agreed, raising his brows, finding Sam's behavior and the things she said more and more enlightening. "What *did* happen last night?"

Sam stood up and paced the floor, fidgeting nervously with her rings. "Oh, don't play the fool, Julian!" she snapped, flashing him an accusing look. "You know very well what happened last night. You proposed to Charlotte! I *saw* you do it! I don't know why you haven't announced it, or even told me and the aunts about it, but I suppose you have your reasons. You have reasons for everything you do, don't you? You're so *excessively* practical and logical." She paused in front of the fireplace and frowned down at the flames.

Julian unfolded his arms and followed, then stood beside her. "You, on the other hand, are excessively *im*practical, *il*logical, and much too impulsive for your own good," he informed her acidly.

She turned to face him. He loved the way her eyes lit up like sapphires when she was angry.

"Am I indeed?" she shot back. "At least I'm not predictable and boring!"

"I'd rather be boring and predictable than forever getting into scrapes because I jump to conclusions, then make foolish, life-altering decisions based on false assumptions."

Sam looked incredulous. "And just what does *that* mean? Mother's right. You must speak more plainly, Julian!"

Julian eyed her complacently. He felt that, suddenly and miraculously, all his troubles could be very close to an end . . . if he played his cards right. He felt he knew exactly what had happened last night to make Sam enter into a hasty betrothal with Jean-Luc Bouvier. She must have seen him with Charlotte in the supper room and misconstrued their tender conversation as a marriage proposal being offered and accepted. She then must have turned impulsively to Jean-Luc and accepted the marriage proposal *he* had undoubtedly made just moments before in some back chamber of the Wilmots' town house!

Yes, incredible as it seemed, it all made sense! Julian was thrilled, exhilarated! This meant that Sam still loved *him!*

Of course the thing to do now would be to sit Sam down immediately and explain to her that there had been a ridiculous misunderstanding, then beseech her—as her mother had also urged—to speak plainly about her feelings. And to express his true feelings to her.

Julian coughed gently behind his hand to hide his smile. Yes, that would be the logical and practical thing to do. But it would also be predictable and boring. He could think of another way of bringing out Sam's true feelings that was much more fun. . . . But what to do about Madame DuBois?

"I would like to explain what I mean, Sam," Julian began, "but I'd rather do it at some other time and place."

"Naturally," Sam said with weary sarcasm.

"Besides, I daresay your mother would not appreciate—" He stopped suddenly as he turned to defer to Genevieve and discovered her missing. They were quite alone in the room. "Where the deuce has your mother gone off to, I wonder?" he muttered.

Sam turned and also looked toward the sofa where her mother had been seated just moments before. "Oh, dear! She's gone!"

"She certainly slipped out quietly," Julian observed, not displeased.

"The way we were screaming at each other, we wouldn't have heard her even if she'd stomped out and slammed the door behind her!" Sam lamented.

"Speak for yourself, brat. *I* never scream," Julian informed her haughtily.

"We've probably offended her, Julian. We've behaved like a couple of children!"

"A *couple* of children?"

Sam propped her fists on her hips and glowered. "If you're going to say that *I'm* the only child in this room, I'll . . . I'll . . ."

Julian smiled a dare. "You'll do what, brat?"

They were at a standoff. She was simmering mad, and he was thoroughly amused.

And aroused. Hell, he'd never seen her look more lovely. Her eyes were brilliant blue. Her skin was rosy. And with her chin jutting out and her lips in a pout, she looked damned kissable.

He was about to throw all caution to the wind and take the baggage into his arms right then and there, when there was a discreet knock at the door. Julian and Sam both startled—like guilty children indeed!—and turned, expecting to see Sam's mother enter the room. But, instead, it was the butler, Smead.

Smead was not robust like Hedley. Rather he was

small and thin and his bald pate was as smooth and shiny as a billiard ball. And he had a perpetual look of puckered disapproval around his thin lips and gaunt cheeks. Balancing a silver tray aloft on the tips of his fingers—on which reposed a bottle of wine—he positioned himself just inside the door and fixed his gaze on a point just to the right of Julian's left ear.

"Lord Serling, Miss Darlington," he announced in formal accents. "I have a message from the mistress."

"A message?" Sam exclaimed, alarmed. "But where is she?"

"The mistress has left for the theater, miss. She—"

"Without saying good-bye?" Sam interrupted.

"If you will but allow me to continue, miss," Smead intoned gloomily.

"Please go on, Smead," Julian prompted him, fascinated by the turn of events. It seemed that Madame DuBois was as unpredictable as her daughter.

Smead cleared his throat and stood a little straighter, as if about to spout a lengthy recital of some sort. "Madame DuBois instructed me to inform you that she has gone to the theater."

"You already said that!" Sam complained impatiently.

Smead gave her a dampening look and continued, "As I said, Madame DuBois has gone to the theater, but she begs you to stay and enjoy the hospitality of her home for as long as you like."

"What?" Sam exclaimed.

"Furthermore," Smead went on with a pained look, "Madame DuBois has instructed me to tell you that you will be entirely alone in the house since I, and the other members of the staff, have been given the night off."

"Good for you, Smead!" Julian said heartily.

Smead sniffed ungratefully. "None of the staff will be permitted . . . that is, none of us will be returning from our er . . . *holiday* till Madame DuBois returns herself, tomorrow morning at seven o'clock."

Sam darted an embarrassed look at Julian, her eyes wide with astonishment. "What can she be thinking, Julian? Surely this is a mistake!"

Julian shrugged and tried to look as perplexed as Sam. But he knew exactly what her mother was up to, and it suited his purposes exactly.

"Madame DuBois said that you would probably wonder what her reasoning is in offering you an empty house for the evening," Smead continued in a weary voice. "Therefore she instructed me to tell you that she was doing it because, and I quote, 'You are both too proud and stubborn for your own good. It is obvious that a long, frank talk between you, conducted in complete privacy with no interruptions, will clear the air and reveal your true feelings. And if you still cannot be happy, I daresay there's nothing more a loving mother can do.' Unquote."

Julian laughed out loud! He couldn't help it; Smead had recited Genevieve's heartfelt words with absolutely no expression on his face or in his voice. He sounded quite put out and bored to tears.

On the other hand, Sam was looking more and more confused and distressed. She stared at Julian as if he'd lost his mind.

"Was there anything else, Smead?" Julian said at last, feeling quite mellow after such a good laugh and anxious to be rid of the Friday-faced butler so he could apply himself to the task of helping Sam relax, too.

"This champagne is for you and Miss Darlington, my lord," Smead said, lowering the tray and placing the bottle of wine on a rosewood console by the door.

Julian stepped forward and picked up the bottle, examining the label. "An excellent sort, and a good year," he murmured approvingly.

"It is the best of Madame DuBois's stock," Smead informed him with a slight puffing of the chest. "The mistress also begs you to eat whatever you choose out of the pantry and highly recommends a basket of fresh-picked and washed strawberries that have been left on the table in the kitchen, along with a bowl of heavy cream that has been whipped to a superior thickness."

"Your mistress thinks of everything," Julian observed dryly.

Smead nodded smugly and moved to the door, but just before he left, he turned and said, "Oh, and one thing more, my lord."

"Yes, Smead?"

"Madame DuBois gives you leave to use any chamber in the house to do your . . . er . . . talking."

"Thank you, Smead," Julian said gravely, and finally the butler bowed himself out the door and was gone.

Sam was thoroughly perplexed. Didn't her mother realize that by leaving her and Julian alone in the house that she was setting the scene for disaster? Perhaps her mother wasn't aware of it, but in the society Julian had introduced her to, such a situation would give rise to speculation that a compromise had occurred—even if it hadn't! And knowing Julian's notions of honor, there was no way he was going to compromise his ward, then turn around and marry Charlotte Batsford without batting an eyelash.

Sam sighed. No, he wouldn't compromise her . . . more's the pity. He'd make quite sure the "madness" he'd fallen victim to in the library that afternoon would not be repeated. As a rule, the man had inhuman self-control. Perhaps if he loved her, he'd be less able to resist her, but he had demonstrated his lack of love for her when he proposed to Charlotte.

But then Sam had another thought. Maybe her mother *perfectly* understood the repercussions of putting two members of the opposite sex together in an empty house! After all, why else would she supply them with champagne, strawberries, and whipped cream? Mrs. Descartes had been very enthusiastic about the aphrodisiac effects of that sparkling wine, luscious fruit, and rich cream.

Then the most disturbing thought of all burst upon Sam with the impact of a lightning bolt. *Maybe her mother was trying to trap Julian into marrying her!*

Sam's own sense of honor recoiled at such an idea. As well, she had no desire to be wife to a man who only married her because he'd *had* to. That would not fit her ideas of marital bliss at all. No indeed. She would be deliriously happy to be married to Julian, but only if he loved her to distraction.

"Sam?"

Julian's voice recalled Sam from her reverie. He was standing by the door, holding the champagne bottle under his arm.

"I can't imagine how he forgot them, but it seems

that Smead did not bring us any glasses for the champagne," he said. "But then perhaps he assumed we'd fetch them ourselves when we went in search of those lovely strawberries. Shall we go to the kitchen?"

Sam eyed Julian warily. His expression was bland, his words were innocuous, and he appeared to be perfectly at his ease. But there was something about her guardian at that moment that made Sam's skin tingle. He exuded a sort of latent power behind his calm, almost languid, facade . . . like a tiger crouched for the pounce. And behind his slightly drooping eyelids, his eyes shone brilliant blue.

"Why . . . why must we go to the kitchen?" she finally stuttered, stalling for time.

"I thought I just explained that, Sam," he said smoothly. "Unless we do like the bohemians and drink the champagne straight out of the bottle, we need glasses."

"Must we drink the champagne?"

Julian cocked a finely arched brow. "Oh, don't you want to? Champagne goes wonderfully with strawberries and whipped cream. Have you never before had them together?"

"No. Never." Though she hadn't meant it to be, her tone was wistful.

"It is a highly sensual experience," he assured her with a faint but devastating smile. "The flavors fairly burst on the tongue." His gaze drifted to her lips, paused there a breathless moment, then returned to her eyes. "As your tutor, I feel it my duty to introduce you to another 'first experience.'" He reached forth his hand. "Come to the kitchen with me, my dear. I have no doubt you will enjoy yourself excessively."

Why did she get the impression he was inviting her to do something more than eat strawberries? Even if his intention *was* only to eat fruit, a few days ago Sam would have given anything for such an opportunity. But now that they were both promised to others. . . .

Sam looked at Julian's outstretched hand. She had always been fascinated by his hands . . . the long, elegant fingers and neatly clipped, short nails. They were beautiful, but strong and manly, too. That afternoon she had felt them on her body, caressing her, loving her. . . .

Sam put her own hands behind her back and stood a little straighter. "Julian, I think it is time we were off to the McAdamses' soiree," she announced primly. *"Jean-Luc* will wonder where I am. And *Charlotte* will probably be there, too."

Mentioning the names of their intendeds did not seem to faze Julian in the least. He shrugged carelessly. "It is not even nine o'clock yet. Surely, Sam, we have time to talk a little over a glass of champagne. It was your mother's wish, you know."

"But she thinks that by giving us all this . . . this privacy to *talk,* that we'll . . . we'll—"

"Come to the conclusion that we are meant for each other? That you are the only woman for me, and I'm the only man for you?"

His tone was so matter-of-fact that Sam felt a little foolish. But she stood her ground and said, "Yes. I'm afraid that's exactly what she thinks."

"But, my dear, I would never break a positive engagement to another, and neither would you."

"No, not if it is a *positive* engagement," Sam admitted miserably.

"Then what are you worried about? Come, Sam,

don't tell me you're afraid to eat strawberries with me? What could possibly happen?"

Full of doubt, but tempted and . . . yes . . . even a little hungry, Sam frowningly studied Julian's expression. His smile was lazy and mocking. Amusement twinkled in his eyes. His whole manner seemed to dare her.

And Sam never could resist a dare. . . .

Chapter 18

❧

Sam walked beside Julian down the candlelit hall. The short journey between the parlor and the kitchen had a sort of processional feel about it, as if she were being formally escorted to an important event, like an ordination or, perhaps, a *beheading*. There was a definite feeling of anticipation—fearful, ominous, and exciting all at once.

The events of the last hour seemed like a dream to Sam, and everything still felt strange and unreal. Indeed, the situation in which she presently found herself was certainly unusual and unexpected. She never would have believed she'd be alone in a strange house with Julian, and given full leave by her mother to go into any chamber they chose in which to talk, drink their champagne, and eat their strawberries and whipped cream.

Sam's hand was tucked snugly in Julian's arm. She could feel his muscles flexing beneath her fingertips. She looked shyly up at him. He gazed down at him and smiled. The candlelight flickered in his eyes and glinted off his white teeth. Sam shivered like a lamb in the clutches of a wolf . . . and liked it rather too much.

There was a fire burning in the kitchen hearth,

and a three-tapered candelabra stood on a long, narrow wooden table in the middle of the large room. The walls were lined with copper pots that reflected back the light from the fireplace and candles. It was very warm and cozy and homey. Sam allowed herself to breathe a tentative sigh of relief; certainly the kitchen was no place for a seduction.

As promised, there was a large china bowl full of strawberries on the table, and a smaller bowl of glossy whipped cream with peaks that towered two inches above its rim.

"We must be grateful to some poor maid with a sore arm," Julian commented. "I'm sure it took an hour of beating to get that cream so stiff and lustrous."

"It certainly looks very delicious," Sam agreed carefully, gently pulling her hand free of Julian's arm and moving to the opposite side of the table. To avoid the confusion and blushes that came so easily to her that evening, Sam did not look at Julian. Instead she fixed her gaze on the whipped cream. She decided that the frothy confection looked innocent enough, but had a suspicion that it hid some quality in its pure white folds that was latently dangerous to a young girl's willpower.

"Why don't we see how it tastes?" Julian suggested. "But first I'll get the champagne glasses."

He set the bottle on the table and turned away to open a glass-fronted cupboard full of crystal and plateware. Estimating that she could now safely look at him without his looking back, Sam lifted her gaze from the whipped cream to Julian.

Even from the back, he was beautiful. His broad shoulders and narrow hips were the perfect shape that all men should aspire to, she decided. But then she didn't suppose that most men could attain Julian's elegant and athletic form. She suspected that even though he was extremely active, honing his skills in the boxing ring with Gentleman Jackson and riding hell-bent-for-leather with the best of them on the hunting field, he had simply been born beautiful and would always be beautiful.

He turned, holding two fluted wineglasses. "We shall sample the champagne first," he announced, "then the strawberries."

Sam could do nothing but nod, then watch silently as he expertly poured the champagne into the glasses. He handed her a glass across the table and lifted his own in a salute.

"What shall we toast to, Sam?" Julian asked her, his eyes snapping devilishly in the firelight.

"To King and Country?" she suggested, for want of a better idea.

Julian's brow furrowed and his lips curved in a smiling scowl. "How boring, Sam," he teased. "And how terribly . . . predictable."

To have her own words thrown back at her so effectively made her want to smile, but Sam was so nervous she knew she'd end up giggling like a schoolgirl instead, so she bit her lip and remained silent.

"Instead, I propose that we toast to 'first experiences,'" he said. "After all, that's what tonight is all about, isn't it?"

"You mean . . . you mean because I'll be eating strawberries and whipped cream with champagne?" she stammered.

"Of course," he said with a faint smile. "What else? To first experiences." He stretched his long arm across the table and tapped his glass of champagne against hers.

"To first experiences," she repeated uncertainly, then took a sip of the effervescent wine. She liked champagne very much, but if she drank too much of it, she always got a little giddy. Deciding that caution ought to be the order of the day, she set the glass down on the table.

Julian raised his brows. "You must be ready for strawberries," he observed, setting down his own glass. "But you will have to come round to my side of the table, Sam, because you cannot eat strawberries with white gloves on, and I daresay you need someone to help you remove them."

Sam had not thought of that, but, indeed, her gloves would be stained with red berry juice if she kept them on, and she couldn't get them off without help. Each glove had a dozen tiny pearl buttons that started at her wrist and continued to just above her elbows. She had only managed to get them on earlier that evening with the assistance of her abigail.

Sam knew she would feel more comfortable if she could stay where she was, but she also knew she would appear extremely foolish if she made Julian unbutton her gloves across the table. So she bravely went round to his side, turned her wrists to reveal the underside of her gloves, and offered Julian both her arms.

Again he raised his brows. "Just one arm will do," he said. "Relax, my dear. In fact, why don't we sit down?"

Sam couldn't imagine feeling relaxed with Julian unbuttoning any part of clothing she might be wearing . . . even gloves. But she obediently sat down in a chair he pulled out from the table, lowered her left arm to her side, and propped her other arm on her knee. Julian smiled approvingly, a gleam of something like amusement in his eyes. Goaded by that gleam, she lifted her chin and tried to act completely unfazed by the whole business.

Still looking amused, Julian pulled out another chair and sat down directly in front of her, so close their knees were brushing. Unnerved by this closeness, Sam sat ramrod straight, her bottom pressed against the back of the chair. He took hold of her right wrist and said, "Bend a little, Sam."

"What do you mean?" she asked stiffly.

"I mean . . . lean closer," he clarified, smiling crookedly. "I want you to lay your arm on my leg."

She swallowed hard as he pulled on her wrist till she bent forward, and till her arm, from the elbow down, rested flat on his thigh. "This way I can use both hands to work at the buttons and you won't have to hold your arm up and get tired."

Sam couldn't dispute the sense of resting her arm on something, but a fuzzy part of her brain told her that the table would be a more logical surface to use for the purpose. However, Julian had already started on the first button at the very top of her glove and she felt she would appear prudish and silly if she objected to the present arrangement.

Besides, she liked the present arrangement. . . . Julian's head was bent over his task, the shiny blond hair so close to Sam's face she could smell the soap he used to wash it. She could hardly resist the urge to bury her nose in the golden waves and breathe deeply. She desperately wanted to run her fingers through his hair, too. He didn't use pomade, and she knew it would be clean and silky-soft to the touch.

His fingers worked dexterously on the buttons, revealing a bit more of flesh as each one was undone. Feeling the cool air kiss her freshly exposed skin was an exquisite torture. His mere proximity made her body temperature soar to an uncomfortable degree, and the feel of his hard thigh next to her arm was very disconcerting.

Finally he finished with the buttons of the first glove and slipped it off her hand with slow deliberation. "There," he said, his voice a deep purr, "how's that feel?"

It felt wonderful. Everything felt wonderful. *Too* wonderful.

"It feels much better," was all she dared admit. "The buttons were pinching me a little."

He hadn't met her gaze since beginning his task. He still held her hand and appeared to be examining her arm, the white skin showing tiny spots of pink where the buttons had pressed into her skin.

"I see what you mean," he murmured, lightly trailing his fingers up and down her arm. She shivered.

He lifted his gaze to her face. The gleam of amusement was gone from his eyes, to be replaced by an expression that took Sam's breath away. "Those damned buttons," he said softly, seductively. "How dare they hurt you?" Then he bent his head and pressed his lips to her wrist.

Sam gasped. The delicious shock of Julian's lips against her bared flesh sent a thrill up her arm and into her heart. And he didn't stop with one kiss. It seemed that he intended to kiss every small pink circle the buttons had made, working his way up from her wrist. Sam could only close her eyes and allow her head to loll to the side, every nerve quivering and focused on the feel of his mouth against her skin.

When he came to the tender hollow of her elbow, he lingered. Her fingers convulsed around his, gripping them tightly. The sensation of pleasure was so intense, she wanted to moan. But before she could utterly make a fool of herself, he lifted his head.

Sam blinked her eyes open and focused on Julian's face. A smile curved his lips, and his eyes were warm as they gazed into hers. "I believe it's time for those strawberries now," he said softly, touching the tip of her nose with his finger.

"Oh, but what about my other glove?" she whispered, desperate for him to repeat such a wonderful performance on her other arm.

His eyes glimmered with tender amusement. "You only need one hand to eat strawberries, my dear. But if you decide later that you want the other glove off, I'll be happy to oblige you."

Sam wasn't sure what to make of this comment. In fact, she wasn't sure what to make of anything that was happening. She had tried to seduce Julian before, but he'd always drawn back at the crucial moment. And now, when there was no honorable way they could be together, *he* seemed to be seducing *her!*

But Sam told herself that perhaps Julian was just a little carried away by the circumstances and was only flirting with her. And when that crucial moment came, if he didn't draw back, *she* would. For now, she was simply eager to see what he'd do next.

He stood up and pulled the bowl of strawberries and the bowl of cream to an easy reaching distance, then sat down again. Giving her a sly look out of the corner of his eye, he picked up a strawberry and dunked it in the cream, swirling it around till it was coated in white.

Thinking it appropriate to follow suit, Sam reached for a strawberry, too.

"No, not yet, my dear," Julian admonished her, catching her hand and holding it tight.

"Why not?" Sam said, her playful nature beginning to counteract her shyness. "Am I just to sit here and watch you eat that lovely strawberry, my mouth watering and my taste buds screaming for satisfaction?"

"Actually, brat," he said dryly, "this luscious berry is for you."

"Oh," she said, feeling stupid. But how could she have known that? she thought to herself. Mrs. Descartes had told her that eating strawberries and whipped cream was excellent foreplay, but she had not told her that your partner prepared your berries. Nor had she told her that your partner fed them to you. But that's apparently what Julian intended, because he was holding the strawberry by its stem, right in front of her nose.

"Open your mouth, brat," he ordered, and she happily obeyed.

It was awkward for Sam at first, not knowing exactly how far to open her mouth or how big a bite she was supposed to take, but Julian proved to be as excellent a teacher in the art of eating strawberries as in every other area of a girl's education.

"Don't be prissy," he urged. "Open wider and take the whole thing in your mouth at once."

Sam did as she was bid and bit the strawberry off just below the stem. The taste of tart juice and sweet cream exploded on her tongue. She closed her eyes and chewed, but was horrified when she felt a dribble of juice run down her chin.

She opened her eyes and reached up to catch it with a finger before it dropped on her white dress, prepared to mumble an apology for being such a sloven, but Julian was quicker than she. He cupped her chin, caught the dribble of juice with a deft stroke of his thumb, then inserted his thumb in his mouth and slowly sucked it clean.

Sam watched Julian's method of tidying things up with a strange quivering in her stomach. Fascinated and aroused, she couldn't wait till he fed her another strawberry.

"Well?" she prompted impatiently when he did not immediately oblige her.

He chuckled throatily. "You were always too greedy," he teased, repeating an opinion he'd first uttered in the room at the King's Arms. "It's your turn to feed me."

Sam liked that idea even better. She eagerly chose a plump, red berry from the bowl and dipped it in the cream. But when it was time to actually feed it to Julian, she found herself feeling unaccountably shy.

"Do you need some help, brat?"

She nodded mutely.

"All right. Here, let me guide you." Julian lightly took hold of Sam's wrist and drew her hand to his mouth. He took the strawberry and slowly chewed it, all the while looking into her eyes and keeping hold of her hand. Then, he drew her hand to his mouth again and sucked the juice off the tips of her fingers.

Sam felt a jolt of electricity pulse from her fingers to her toes. Julian's warm, wet mouth around her fingertips was the most titillating thing she'd ever felt. But she had a feeling that with Julian the potential for titillation was limitless. However, it was not something she should be thinking at the moment!

Nor should she be thinking how wonderful it would be to kiss him. . . . Lost in a fantasy, she parted her lips and swiped them quickly with her tongue.

Julian's gaze darted to Sam's mouth and that provocative lick of her lips. To him it meant only one thing; that she wanted to kiss him as much as he wanted to kiss her. He reached out and put his hands on Sam's waist, then lifted her onto his lap.

Surprised, she clung to his shoulders, but she didn't resist. "Julian," she whispered. "What are you doing?"

"It's much easier to kiss you this way," he answered, then he slipped his arms around her and pulled her close, pressing his lips to hers.

Julian was no longer fighting a useless battle against his desires, against his emotions. He knew that he wanted Sam, and he knew that he loved her more than his soul's salvation. He would bet everything he owned that she loved him just as much, and tonight he was going to make her finally and irrevocably his.

No matter what Isabelle had taught Sam about lovemaking, her response to him was the pure, sweet desire of an innocent. And her arousal was expressed in eager, open ways. She kissed him with abandon, parting her lips to welcome his tongue, and slipping her tongue into his mouth, too . . . tentative at first, then with ardent and skillful enthusiasm. She always was a quick learner.

Julian couldn't hold her close enough. His hands roamed her back and shoulders, then slowly came around to caress her breasts. She gasped as he cupped the small, firm shape of her, rubbing the pad of his thumb over her taut nipple. She grasped his shoulders and arched her neck, gazing at him through drooping eyelids.

"Julian, you . . . you make me feel so . . . so *good*. Like a woman."

"Just as I told you this afternoon in the library, you *are* a woman, sweetheart," he murmured, nuzzling her neck and the swell of her breasts above the décolletage of her gown. "A beautiful, desirable woman." He flicked his tongue into her cleavage.

"Oh, Julian!" she moaned. "It's so wonderful to hear you say that!" Then, much to Julian's surprise, Sam shifted sideways, hiked her skirts to her knees, drew her right leg up and over his lap—grazing his abdomen in the most damnably stimulating way!— and straddled him.

His hands slipped to her waist. "Sam," he said with a nervous chuckle, his voice hoarse with passion, his groin aching and so suffused with heat that he was tempted to make love to her on the spot. "What are you doing, sweetheart?"

Sam's cheeks were flushed, her eyes were aglow, her lips with berry-red and swollen from his kisses, her hair was a tumble of curls, half-up, half-down. "It's something I learned from Mrs. Descartes," she said ingenuously. "She . . . she said it is called 'postilion.' " She rocked forward, the swell of her womanhood rubbing against his hard erection.

"Don't do that, Sam," Julian hissed through gritted teeth.

Her eyes grew wide. "Didn't you like it?" she asked him with a little pant. *"I* liked it."

He smiled grimly. "I liked it prodigiously well, brat. But I don't intend to take your virginity 'postilion'! It is rather an advanced position, my dear. Besides, I have plenty of other delicious things in mind for you before we're quite to that point!"

"Oh," she said wonderingly. "I see!"

"However, if you don't quit being so delightfully teasing, I'll disgrace myself by ravaging you like a madman."

Her eyes grew even wider. "Oh, but *that* sounds rather fun, too!"

He laughed, clasping her to his chest. "Oh, you wicked little charmer. You dreadful, delightful, beautiful, terrible *brat!*"

Sam laughed, too, her arms around his neck and her fingers buried in his hair. Then she caught his face between her hands and smiled impishly. "Mother said we could use any chamber in the house to *talk.* Perhaps we could *talk* better somewhere else? I'm absolutely dying for you to *talk* to me, Julian!"

Julian smiled back and stood up, swinging her into his arms. "Pick up the candelabra, Sam. We'll come back later for the champagne and strawberries. After all, we've got all night."

By the sudden guilty expression on her face, Julian could tell Sam was thinking about Jean-Luc and Charlotte again and wondering if they were waiting for them at the McAdamses'. He pressed a finger to her lips, saying, "Don't mention them again, Sam. This night is for us and us alone. For the next several hours, I want to hear only *my* name on your sweet lips. Tomorrow the names of others might intrude into our conversation . . . but, please, *not* tonight."

Her anxious expression faded away and she looked peaceful and happy again. "I'm quite willing to forget there's another human being on the earth besides you and me," she said softly. "I won't let a single person's name—except yours, Julian— pass my lips tonight."

He cocked a brow. "Not even the name of Isabelle Descartes?" he queried archly.

She laughed. "Not even hers. Besides, I'm quite sure you'll be able to teach me everything I need to know about lovemaking. I'm a very apt pupil and willing to try anything, you know."

He swallowed hard and headed for the door. "I only wish there were more hours between now and tomorrow morning at seven o'clock."

Sam nestled her head against Julian's neck as he carried her up the stairs. She couldn't believe that all her dreams had finally come true! Julian had held her, kissed her. And soon he'd be making love to her.

But Sam's bliss was tempered by the fact that he had not yet said he loved her. And his words just now, implying that he wished seven o'clock wouldn't come so soon, seemed to indicate that he intended to spend this night, and *only* this night, making love to her.

But was that possible? Sam wondered, frowning to herself. Julian was an honorable man, the most honorable man she'd ever met. Surely he did not intend to deflower his ward and then go his merry way.

Was it possible that Julian had *not* proposed to Charlotte at the Wilmots' ball last night? she speculated. But when she'd asked him about it earlier, speaking of the engagement as if it were a fact, he had not denied it.

However . . . Sam suddenly remembered Julian's enigmatic statement about "getting into scrapes because you jump to conclusions, then make foolish, life-altering decisions based on false assumptions."

Sam felt as though a huge burden had been lifted from her heart. She wanted to laugh out loud! Obviously Julian had *not* proposed to Charlotte last night! But, for some reason, he had decided to allow her to keep believing he was spoken for . . . the wretch! No doubt he thought it made things more interesting.

Smiling against Julian's neck, Sam felt immense relief. Then she remembered Jean-Luc and sobered. What was she going to do about Jean-Luc? But Julian had asked that no name other than his would pass her lips the rest of the night, and she determined that she wouldn't think about anyone else, either. The night was hers and Julian's . . . and it had just begun.

At the top of the stairs they were presented with four doors from which to choose. They opened the first door on the left, saw that it must be the master bedroom and therefore belonged to Sam's mother, and quickly closed it.

The next room appeared to be a handsomely appointed guest chamber, boasting amongst its furnishings a burgundy red chaise longue. Julian and Sam exchanged looks and knew their minds to be of one accord. Sam set down the candelabra on a table just inside the door, then Julian carried her into the room and set her down on the chaise longue.

Sam nestled against the pile of exotically patterned pillows with Turkish tassels and smiled up at Julian. She extended her gloved hand and said playfully, "Oh, Julian, *dahling*. I've decided that I want to take off my other glove now. If you could but *assist* me?"

Julian's eyes gleamed with appreciation. He shrugged out of his jacket and threw it on the bed. "You minx! How have I managed to resist you all this time?"

"I haven't the slightest idea," she retorted, loving the look of him in his shirtsleeves and vest. "I've always found *you* irresistible."

"Have you?" he quizzed her, expertly undoing the intricate folds of his neckcloth as he stood over her. "I'm very flattered." She loved watching his hands move. They were so strong, so skillful. She shivered as she thought that they'd soon be touching her body with the same strength and skill.

"You *should* be flattered," she sniffed, assuming the air of a pampered, spoiled miss, trying to hide the fact that she was mesmerized by him. "There have been a great many gentleman trying to gain my fickle favor, you know."

"I know," he grumbled fiercely. "I have been watching with a great deal of interest and frustration." He threw the neckcloth on the bed next to his coat, unbuttoned his waistcoat, slipped it off, and threw it on the pile with his other discarded clothes. Sam feared . . . *hoped* . . . that he'd strip off every stitch while she watched.

But apparently that wasn't the way Julian had things planned. And that he had a plan she was quite certain. But, in this case, Sam had a feeling that she'd greatly benefit from Julian's characteristic careful planning.

He came down on one knee on the chaise longue, propped his hands on either side of her head, and hovered over her, smiling . . . and not touching her. Sam took it as long as she could, then reached up and grabbed him by the collar, pulled him down on top of her, and claimed his mouth in a passionate kiss.

Bracing on his forearms as they kissed and caressed, Julian allowed only a certain amount of his weight to press against her, and there was a particular part of him that Sam felt more than others. His manhood felt hard and hot and . . . er . . . rather large as he gradually parted her legs and nudged himself against her. There was a stirring in her stomach and a pulsing ache in her woman's core. Suddenly she was dying to lie naked beneath him.

Sam lifted her left arm, which was still sheathed in a long glove and said, "Julian. Look! You still haven't taken off my glove. Don't you think it's about time?"

He stared laughingly into her eyes. "Do you think so? But I could go on kissing you *forever.*"

She cocked a disbelieving brow. "Liar. You know you could not do it forever. Surely there's something else you want to do to me . . . ?"

"There are many things I want to do to you, brat," he assured her with a devilish smile. "But the first thing I want to do to you is take off all your clothes."

Sam shivered with anticipation. "I thought you would never get around to it."

"Baggage!" he said gruffly, rising to his feet. "Stand up, if you please, and turn around so that I can get at those ribbons and hooks holding your gown together in the back. There's a good girl."

Sam obediently struggled to a sitting, then a

standing, position, pushing a tumble of curls out of her eyes. "But what about my glove, Julian? Shouldn't you take that off first?"

"Actually, my love," he told her with a mischievous gleam in his eyes, "I believe we'll leave that on till the very last."

"What was I thinking when I called you boring and predictable?" she murmured wryly.

He laughed, turned her about, then set to work on the various devices holding her dress together in the back. He was quick about it, and soon he was slipping her puffed sleeves down and bending to kiss and nuzzle her shoulders. Her gown fell to the floor in a rustle of crepe.

"Ummmm. . . . You're so beautiful, Sam. So smooth and pale and perfect."

"I'm glad you find me beautiful, Julian," she whispered, her eyes drifting shut with pleasure. "I want you to desire me. I always have."

"And I suspect I have *always* desired you," he confessed, his breath warming her skin and making it tingle. But his words thrilled her even more than his kisses.

While she remained facing away from him, he removed the rest of her clothing in as swift and gentle a manner as he had her gown. Lastly—with a great deal of fun and fanfare—he removed her glove. When she was completely naked, he turned her around and looked at her.

Sam felt a little shy as his gaze lovingly roamed her body, but the pleasure she gave and received more than made up for a little momentary embarrassment.

"You're just as beautiful as I remember," he whispered reverently. "The image of you, that night when I brought you home from the King's

Arms and you shed your blanket for me, has haunted my dreams . . . sleeping *and* waking."

"I'm glad," she said unrepentantly. "And though I've had no image of your naked body to haunt and taunt me, Julian, my imagination has been torture enough."

His hands cupped her shoulders and stroked her arms. "You imagined me in the buff, eh, brat?" he inquired with a pleased grin.

"Yes, and I was always quite impressed by what I imagined," she returned with a corresponding saucy smile. "Why don't we see if reality measures up to my imagination?"

Her suggestion sounded very much like a dare, and Julian reacted accordingly. With a glint in his eye and a smug smile that indicated he wasn't too worried about "measuring up" to Sam's imagination, Julian began to unbutton his shirt.

"May I?" said Sam, catching hold of his hands, kissing them, then firmly pushing them aside. "I want to undress you, Julian."

Julian drew a steadying breath and nodded. "Go ahead, brat. Tonight I can refuse you nothing."

Sam smiled and set herself to the task of undoing buttons. When she had finished, she drew the tail of his shirt out of his breeches, pushed the material aside, and slid her splayed hands over his chest.

He had a smooth, beautiful chest. Except for a very fine dusting of blond curls just in the center, there was no other hair, and the color of his skin was a pale golden brown. He was muscular, but not at all bulky. He was taut and lean and beautifully sculpted.

"Julian," she whispered in awe, her hands stroking, exploring. "You're so beautiful."

"A man does not usually care to be called 'beau-

tiful,' brat," he said with wry gruffness, "but if it
pleases you to say so, I will endure the adulation."

"It doesn't just please me to say so, it's very
true," she assured him. She slipped the shirt off his
shoulders and down his arms, and tossed it on the
bed. Then she braced her hands at his waist and
bent to cover his chest with kisses. He cupped her
shoulders, his fingers pressing into his skin as she
traced each rib with her mouth and tongue, then
nuzzled, nipped, and suckled at each of his small,
wine-colored nipples.

"I can stand this no longer, you imp!" he said on
a moan, pulling her against him and claiming her
mouth in a passionate kiss.

Every nerve in Sam's body caught fire. Her bare
breasts against Julian's hard chest created sensations she'd never imagined. It was so intimate, so
thrilling, so *right*. And when Julian's hands reached
up and cupped her breasts, caressing and stroking
her hard nipples with gentle, erotic deliberation,
she thought she would swoon from the pleasure.

Several kisses later, breathless and dizzy, Sam
pulled free and gasped, "Maybe I'd . . . I'd better
finish undressing you."

"I thought you would never get around to it,"
Julian teased.

But when Sam reached down to unbutton Julian's breeches, her hands were shaking. "I'm positively cow-handed!" she complained with a
chagrined smile. "Perhaps you'll have to do it after
all, Julian."

Julian smiled understandingly and Sam watched
as he undid the buttons of his breeches and pulled
them off, carelessly and most uncharacteristically
kicking them to the side when he was through.

With his hands negligently propped on his hips, Sam got her first hard look at Julian "in the buff."

With his broad chest, narrow hips and long, leanly muscled legs, Julian looked like a flesh-and-blood Michelangelo statue. He was perfect. He was glorious. He was everything she'd imagined . . . and more. Helplessly, she stared at his manhood, large and hard and nestled in a triangle of tawny-colored hair. Yes, *much* more.

Chapter 19

❦

"**H**ave I frightened you, sweetheart?" Julian inquired with tender amusement.

Sam tore her eyes away from that most impressive part of his anatomy and looked her guardian in the eye. "I'm . . . I'm not exactly frightened," she said. "Rather I think I'm a bit awed!"

He laughed and reached for her, saying, "I assure you, the feeling is entirely reciprocated." Then they tumbled onto the chaise longue in each other's arms and lay side by side, kissing and caressing.

Sam couldn't get close enough. She couldn't touch him enough. She stroked his chest, his flat, taut stomach, and finally she wrapped her curious fingers around the velvety hard length of his manhood.

He gave a moan of pleasure and slipped his leg between her two, pressing his erection against the rise of her mons. Honeyed heat surged through Sam's bloodstream.

Their kisses grew deep and greedy, their breathing sharp and labored. He shifted atop her, his weight supported by an arm on either side of her, his manhood heavy and tumid against her stomach.

He lowered his head to her breast to suckle there, to tease and tantalize with his clever tongue.

Sam felt a rising tension in her stomach, a tremulous languor in her legs. Her woman's core was suffused with heat and pleasure. She wanted him to fill her, to assuage the need that seemed to be taking her at breakneck speed toward a state of blissful madness.

She instinctively rocked her hips against Julian, and he whispered in her ear, "Are you ready, Sam?"

"Yes. I . . . I think so," she whispered back, trembling with both fear and excitement.

"Then I will prepare you," he murmured. She felt his hand slip between her thighs, his fingers tangling in the curls there. As he slid one long finger into her weeping center, she gasped with astonished pleasure, grasped his shoulders, and arched against him.

"What . . . what are you doing, Julian?"

"I told you, brat. I'm getting you ready to receive me," he explained in a hoarse whisper as he moved his finger inside her, probing, stretching, preparing her for their joining.

"But I want you . . . *all* of you, Julian," she begged, consumed by a need she didn't understand and felt powerless against. "Please, Julian, love me *now!*"

Julian heaved a ragged sigh and eased himself between her thighs, then slowly entered her. He watched her face and saw the tiny furrow of pain appear between her brows. She was trying to be brave, and he loved her even more for pretending it didn't hurt. He waited with each slight forward thrust for the tight channel of her womanhood to adapt to him, but he wanted consummation as much as Sam did, and it was hard to hold back. For Sam, though, he could and would do anything.

"I know it hurts, sweetheart, but soon the pain will go away and there will be nothing left but pleasure."

"I know," Sam said, smiling weakly. "I trust you, Julian."

Presently he asked, "Does it still hurt?"

She lifted her hips and took him deeper inside her. Oh, so deep. . . . For a panicked moment, Julian thought he was going to lose control, but he held on, taking delight in the sight of her as her eyes fluttered shut and a gasp of utter enjoyment broke from her lips.

"No, it doesn't hurt anymore," she finally said, gazing up at him wonderingly. "In fact, it feels very, very good."

Julian couldn't agree more. He began to move, setting a slow, gentle pace to their lovemaking, but she was as needful as he, as eager to satisfy the yearning that had been part of their lives since almost the moment they met . . . a yearning they had denied and ignored. Or, at least *he* had denied and ignored it! And he always fancied himself so wise. . . .

Sam's hips rose eagerly to meet his thrusts, her innocent desire setting a much faster, much harder rhythm than Julian had intended.

He was losing control. Yes, Julian Fitzwilliam Montgomery, the marquess of Serling, was losing control . . . and loving it. He was filled with joy . . . filled with the wonder of loving Sam.

Sam had wanted this from the moment she'd first clapped eyes on Julian, that day he'd shown up on

Thorney Island with Jack and Amanda. She didn't understand then about making love, but she'd instinctively known that she needed to belong to him, to be as close to him as two human beings could be. She'd wanted to take the starch out of his reserve, to ignite the passion she knew he'd tidily buried beneath his cynical and ultra-elegant exterior.

And she had succeeded. She saw that success now in his face, in the ardent flush spread over his beautiful, patrician features, and in the love that shone from his eyes.

He hadn't said so, but she knew he loved her. And that was enough. For now. . . .

A tear trickled down Sam's cheek, and Julian kissed it away. She was losing control, being swept away by emotions that were stronger than she'd ever imagined or wished for.

Then, suddenly, there were fireworks . . . bright sparks against the black backdrop of her spinning consciousness.

Julian cried her name and strained against her, and she against him, as ripple after ripple of debilitating pleasure seized them in its velvet grip.

Later, wrapped in each other's embrace, they slept.

Julian awoke to the disconcerting aspect of Madame Genevieve DuBois, still wearing her dramatic theater makeup and black wig, staring down at him. Knowing himself to be have been completely naked when he fell asleep after making love to Sam a third time, he fumbled about, hoping to assure himself that he was not exposed. He was quite relieved to discover a quilt covering him from the waist down.

Holding it securely in place, he pushed himself to a sitting position in the chaise longue and sleepily inquired, "Where's Sam?"

"That's what I was just wondering," Genevieve admitted, chewing her lip. "She's nowhere in the house. None of her clothes are about . . . only yours. You didn't quarrel, did you?"

"Hardly," Julian drawled, raking a hand through his disheveled hair.

"I see you enjoyed the strawberries and the champagne," Genevieve added, gesturing toward the nearly empty bowl and the absolutely empty bottle.

"Yes, thank you," Julian murmured, rubbing his eyes. "Your plan was very clever, and very effective."

"But did it work? Did you talk?"

He peered at her out of one bleary eye. "Did you really intend us to talk?" he inquired laconically.

"Yes, of course . . . among other things," she answered impatiently. "I knew you wouldn't be able to resist each other if left alone, but I counted on you coming to some understanding of each other's feelings. You *did* propose, didn't you?"

"Not exactly," Julian hedged, starting to worry about Sam's absence, too. He wasn't especially concerned about her safety; she was quite resourceful, and he assumed she'd hailed a hackney coach and had gone back to Montgomery House that morning before he was awake. He was, however, becoming just as worried as Genevieve that perhaps they hadn't communicated sufficiently last night. In fact he knew Sam was laboring under some profound misunderstandings. Misunderstandings, moreover, that he had intended to clear up, but had not got around to.

"You did, at least, tell her that you loved her, didn't you?" Genevieve demanded.

Julian sighed. "No."

"Good God! Why not?"

"I thought she understood that."

"Oh, you men are all alike! You have to *tell* a woman that she's loved, Serling! We can't read your minds, you know!"

"Yes, I do know," he snapped, his guilt making him testy. "But I thought I had plenty of time to talk to her this morning about . . . all that. I was more concerned with other things last night."

She raised a fantastically arched, kohl-black brow. "Indeed, I'm *quite* sure you were."

"You misunderstand me, madame," he growled. "I was not even sure till last night that Sam truly loved me. Everything happened so suddenly, and my head's in a spin."

"Well, screw it on tight and go after my daughter," Genevieve exhorted him. "She probably thinks of herself this morning as a loose woman, a *femme fatale*. You must tell her at once that you're going to marry her!"

"And what made you so sure I would?" Julian inquired. "How did you dare leave us alone last night? Did it never occur to you that I might be a libertine and intended to have my way with your daughter, then abandon her?"

"No, of course not!" she scoffed. "The thought never entered my head. If I hadn't thought you completely honorable, I'd have never left her alone with you. I knew you'd never compromise her unless you meant to marry her. Now, *do* get up, Serling! Haul your aristocratic arse out of bed and go after my daughter!"

"I might be persuaded to haul my aristocratic

arse out of bed if only you will be so kind as to leave
the room," he advised her acidly.

She "tsked." "Oh, very well, but I daresay I
shan't see anything I haven't seen before."

Julian gave a bark of laughter. "But since you are
destined to be my mother-in-law, Madame DuBois,
I think the more decorum we practice, the better."

She smiled brightly. "You're quite right, of
course. I'll send Smead up with some hot water so
that you can wash up a bit before you go." Then she
abruptly left the room, shutting the door behind
her.

Julian stared at the closed door and acknowledged with some considerable amusement that he
was going to have his hands full with *that* one for a
mother-in-law. Like Sam, she seemed to be completely unimpressed by the dignity that was due a
marquess.

Julian looked ruefully at his crumpled clothes
scattered on the floor and the bed, at the strawberry
and whipped cream bowls, and at the empty champagne bottle. Then, he dwelled briefly and painfully
on the fact that he had been awakened that morning by the mother of a young woman—his ward, no
less—with whom he had spent the better part of
the night cavorting. He was naked, unshaved,
unbathed, and, no doubt, smelled of sex. What
dignity could he be thinking of?

But he was too in love to consider his loss of any
consequence. There was plenty of time to reclaim
his dignity, he decided, throwing off the guilt and
reaching for his pants. First, he had to find Sam.

It bothered him more than he'd admitted to her
mother that, after a night of tender lovemaking,
Sam had not been there when he woke up. As far as
he knew, she still believed that he and Charlotte

were engaged. In view of this, what must she be thinking, doing? He had to tell her that he loved her . . . and the sooner the better.

"We thought we heard you come in, dearest. But who are you writing to so early in the morning?"

Still dressed in her white gown from the night before—though considerably worse for the wear—Sam peered over her shoulder at Nan and Priss, who were standing at her open bedchamber door. Garbed in nightcaps and gowns, they looked like they'd just crawled out of bed.

Sam chuckled. "My dear aunts! My darling *chaperons!* I never made it to the McAdamses' soiree last evening, and I've been out all night, but all you want to know is who I'm writing to?"

Nan and Priss looked at each other and shrugged. "We weren't worried about you, Samantha," Nan said. "We knew you were with Julian."

Sam shook her head and smiled affectionately at her aunts, then returned to her task without answering their question. She needed to get the note written and sent as quickly as possible.

Nan and Priss ventured into the room and stood just behind her as she scribbled away at her desk. "You seem in rather a cheerful mood this morning, Samantha," Priss said. Sam looked up just in time to see Priss slide a coy glance at her sister, as if hinting at some secret understanding.

"I *am* cheerful," Sam admitted with a contented sigh . . . then followed it with a frown. "But I have no right to be! I'm just about to break someone's heart."

Again the aunts exchanged glances, but this time they looked concerned. "Oh dear," said Nan. "Whose?"

Sam folded her note and sealed it with wax. "Jean-Luc's," she said soberly. "But since I don't want him to be publicly humiliated, as well, I'm writing to tell him not to send an announcement of our engagement to the papers. Despite my promise to him, and Julian's given permission, I *cannot* marry him."

The aunts had been listening with identical expressions of patent disbelief.

"You are incredulous," Sam said, chagrined. "Is it so very bad to break off an engagement when you find your heart is not . . . not committed to that person? Do you think me awful, aunts?"

"My dear girl," Nan exclaimed, "I assure you, Priss and I are not the least surprised to hear you do not wish to marry Jean-Luc. How could you do so when you are so obviously in love with someone else?"

Now it was Sam's turn to be dumbfounded. Could they possibly know . . . ? But before she was able to ask Nan what she was talking about, Priss forestalled her, saying, "Indeed, what surprises us, Samantha dear, is that Julian gave his permission to Jean-Luc in the first place. Are you quite sure you heard him correctly? Perhaps you misunderstood?"

"How could I possibly misunderstand him on so important a point? Although I don't *exactly* recall him saying outright that he had given Jean-Luc permission, I'm sure it was implied." She stood up and hurried to the bell pull by the fireplace and gave it a tug. "Now I must get this note to Jean-Luc as soon as possible."

While Nan and Priss watched with fretful faces, Sam handed the note to the footman, who had almost instantly appeared at the bedchamber door. She directed him to take the note to Jean-Luc's address immediately. He bowed and left, and Sam sank onto her bed with a relieved sigh.

"I don't think that was really necessary, Samantha," Priss said, wringing her hands. "I daresay the poor man will be quite confused when he receives your note."

"But why, Priss? I had to tell him right away that our engagement was off, so he wouldn't advertise it."

"But I'm sure there never was a positive engagement, Samantha," Nan said. "I'm *sure* Julian wouldn't have agreed to a betrothal."

"Why not? He knew I wanted to marry Jean-Luc," Sam said. *Or, at least, he thought I wanted to marry Jean-Luc.* The only reason Sam could think of for Julian to refuse to consent to an engagement between her and Jean-Luc was that he was in love with her himself. And while she had great hopes that he would fall deeply in love with her eventually, she was not at all convinced that he already loved her. After all, even though he'd made passionate, tender love to her last night, he had not once said that he loved her.

The aunts raised their brows at each other and pursed their lips. "Is it possible she doesn't know?" Nan whispered out of the side of her mouth.

"Sometimes the woman *is* the last to know," Priss said consideringly.

"In this case, however, I believe *he* was the one entirely in the dark . . . up till the day of the Wilmots' ball, at least. It was then that I noticed the difference in him. But men—especially brilliant ones—tend to be quite stupid about knowing their own feelings. But surely, when they did not show up at the McAdamses' soiree last night, I assumed they had come to *some* understanding!"

"Come, my dear aunts, you must realize that I can hear everything you're saying," Sam informed them with amusement. "And since you are discussing my affairs, I demand that you speak directly to *me*. What is it, pray tell, that I don't know?"

The aunts again communicated with a look and seemed to come to an immediate mutual agreement.

"We had better get dressed, Nan," Priss said briskly.

"Yes, we had," Nan concurred. "And so had you, Samantha. I'll send Dorcas in and have Sally bring up water for a bath. Make haste, my love. I daresay you're going to want to be presentable when your visitor arrives."

"What visitor?" Sam asked. But Priss and Nan had already swept past her and were out the door. She shrugged and began to undress for her bath. She wasn't expecting any visitors, but she had no doubt that Julian would be home soon, and she wanted to be fresh and beautiful for him. Wrapping herself in a dressing gown as she waited for the bathwater, Sam stared at her reflection in the mirror above the dressing table. Her complexion glowed and her eyes shone like stars. That's what being made love to by the man of your dreams did for you, Sam thought bemusedly.

But she knew things were by no means settled between her and Julian. She had broken off her engagement with Jean-Luc, and since Julian had had no engagement to break off in the first place, both of them were free to marry whom they pleased. But Julian had compromised her—what a cool word "compromised" was for such a warm and wonderful thing as making love, she marveled—and he would probably propose marriage. But Sam wanted more than that from Julian. Until he said he loved her, and meant it, she wouldn't marry him . . . no matter how many times they made love! And she knew they'd make love again. It was just meant to be.

Dorcus assisted her in dressing after a quick bath and, though the hour was still quite early, Sam headed downstairs to the breakfast room. She'd drink tea and nibble on toast till Julian showed up. *The poor dear,* she thought with a self-satisfied smile. *I must have exhausted him.* But Sam had no sooner sat down and took her first sip of tea when there was a knock at the front door. A moment later, Hedley entered the room and, with a disapproving expression, told her that Mr. Bouvier awaited her in the parlor.

"I mentioned the early hour and also informed him that you had just sat down to breakfast, but he would not be refused," Hedley said dourly.

"It's all right," Sam said with a smile. "I'll see him." But she did not feel anywhere near as calm as she tried to appear. Though she had not told him specifically why, she had been very clear in the note that their engagement was off. Surely Jean-Luc, who was so very sensitive and sweet, did not mean to make a scene. However, he *was* half-French. . . .

"Chère!" exclaimed Jean-Luc as Sam hesitantly entered the parlor. He had been standing by the window, but he hurried over as soon as Sam set foot in the door, grabbed hold of her hands and stared earnestly into her eyes. "I came as soon as I received your note. Sam, I don't understand what's going on."

Sam averted her eyes, embarrassed and sorry for the pain she was causing such a dear friend. "But Jean-Luc, I thought I explained in my note."

"It was the explanation that confused me," he admitted. "When you warned me not to send the announcement of our engagement to the papers, I didn't know what to think. What right would I have to do such a thing when Lord Serling refused his permission? He said I might still spend time with you, but that he didn't think you were ready for a positive engagement, so I—"

Sam's head reared up. "He *refused* his permission?"

Jean-Luc looked surprised. "Didn't he tell you?"

Sam shook her head incredulously. "No, he did not. In fact, he allowed me to believe that he'd *given* you his persmission. I think the wretch was *testing* me!"

Sam pulled away and began to pace the floor. After a moment's reflection, while Jean-Luc watched in confusion, Sam laughed out loud. "Ours has been the most impossible courtship in the history of man!" she exclaimed. "There has been one misconception after the other . . . several of which were deliberately planned! And not just by him, but by me, as well. I am just as much to blame. Hah! I do believe we deserve each other!"

When Sam had finally calmed down, she stopped pacing and noticed that Jean-Luc looked very sober. His beautiful, soulful eyes were clouded with sadness. "Your courtship?" he inquired softly. "Then the marquess has finally won the day, I gather?" He came to Sam and gently tilted her chin, his gaze wandering over her face. "I should have known immediately. You are radiant today, *chère*.

Last night, instead of coming to the McAdamses' soiree, you were . . . with him, I suppose?"

Sam blushed and nodded shyly. "Yes. I'm sorry, Jean-Luc, if I've hurt you. But I love him so much."

Jean-Luc cupped her face in his hands and shook his head, a smile of regret on his lips. "Then he is the luckiest man on the face of the earth. I just hope he deserves you. Tell me, Sam, that he's not the cold man he appears to be. At least, not with you. He couldn't possibly be cold with *you.*"

Sam blushed even deeper. She shook her head. "No, Jean-Luc. Just as I've always known, beneath Julian's cool and elegant exterior lies the soul of a very passionate man."

Jean-Luc's smile grew grim. "Damn him. And he loves you?"

"I wasn't sure till just now. You helped me to realize it, Jean-Luc."

"How sporting of me," he said, wincing.

Sam placed her hands over Jean-Luc's. "I will always love you as a friend, Jean-Luc."

"I will always love *you,* Sam. May I kiss you good-bye?"

She nodded and he bent and kissed her gently on the cheek. They drew apart and smiled at each other. His smile was one of wistfulness. Hers was of genuine friendship.

"How cozy," drawled a deep voice from behind them.

Sam and Jean-Luc startled and turned toward the open door. Julian stood there . . . looking very *un*-Julian. In fact, Sam had never seen him look less himself. His hair was an unruly tumble of waves. His cravat was tied in a crude, haphazard knot, and every stitch of clothing he wore looked as though it had been lying in a crumpled heap on the floor all night . . . which, of course, it had. At that moment Julian looked anything but cool and elegant, but to Sam he was irresistible.

"Julian, you've finally come," she said with a tremulous smile, feeling suddenly shy after their passionate night together.

"And not a moment too soon," he growled, darting her an accusing look and sauntering into the room. Then his hot gaze bored into Jean-Luc. "What's the meaning of this, Bouvier? What are you doing here at this damnably early hour? I refused your petition for Sam's hand in marriage yesterday, but then I come home to find you kissing her! Sam can't marry without *my* consent, Bouvier. No amount of wooing *her* is going to make a difference."

"Julian, you don't understand—" Sam began, appalled that they were having yet another misunderstanding, but Jean-Luc interrupted her.

"I've had time to think since our interview yesterday, Serling," Jean-Luc said in a voice of bravado. "And I've decided that I totally disagree with you about Sam's readiness to get married." Jean-Luc turned to Sam and surreptitiously winked at her. "Aren't I right, Sam? You *are* ready to get married, aren't you?"

Understanding that Jean-Luc meant to have a little fun, Sam played along. After all, didn't Julian deserve some teasing after keeping certain things a secret from her? "I've never been readier," Sam agreed.

"So, unless there's some other reason why you won't permit Sam to become engaged to me—"

"There's a reason," Julian snarled, towering over

Jean-Luc like an angry bear. "She can't marry you because she's going to marry *me*. Is that clear?"

Jean-Luc shrugged as only a Frenchman could shrug and said with a satisfied smile, "Perfectly." Then he bowed to Julian, and he bowed to Sam and, with one last wistful smile for Sam, strolled out of the room.

Julian turned to face Sam. He was scowling. "Sam, why did you leave before we had time to talk?" he gruffly asked her, but she could tell that he was hurt and puzzled by her disappearance without a word that morning, and by what he thought he saw just now between her and Jean-Luc. Sam was tired of misunderstandings. She wanted only truth between them from then on.

"I came home so I could write a note to Jean-Luc," she answered.

"Why?"

"Because I wanted to stop him before he sent an announcement of our engagement to the papers." She arched a brow. "You see, I was under the mistaken idea that he and I were positively engaged. That you had given your consent. You allowed me to believe I was promised to Jean-Luc, Julian."

He looked a little shamefaced. But *only* a little. "I wasn't sure what your true feelings were. I had to find out if there was still hope for me before I could allow Jean-Luc to claim you as his prize."

"And you let me believe you and Charlotte were engaged as well."

"You came to that erroneous conclusion on your own, brat. I didn't know till last night that that's what you thought had happened between Charlotte and me at the Wilmots' ball."

"But still you let me go on believing it . . . you wretch!"

"I'd never have made love to you if I was engaged to Charlotte."

"I know," she admitted.

"I was going to explain everything to you this morning, Sam, but you ran out on me."

"Well, now you know why."

They stared at each other, her heart aching for him to take her into his arms, to tell her that he loved her. But he held back, looking troubled and still angry, and Sam thought she knew why.

"Jean-Luc was only kissing me good-bye, Julian," she explained in a small voice. "Can I possibly make it more clear that you're the only man in the world I love?"

Julian's brow gradually cleared. A rueful smile even began to relax the corners of his stern mouth. "I'm a jealous fool."

"Yes," she agreed, smiling broadly and holding out her arms to him.

He advanced. "And it's time I made it very clear who *I'm* in love with, too." He slipped his arms around her waist and gazed down at her beaming face. "It's you, Sam. It's been you from the first moment I clapped eyes on you. I love you, Sam," he murmured. "I love you more than my soul's salvation." Then he pulled her roughly against him and kissed her thoroughly.

Sam was in heaven. Her dearest dream was realized in those three small words. *He loved her.*

Several moments later, Julian finally released her. She'd been thoroughly kissed, thoroughly caressed, and now she was thoroughly aroused.

"There's one thing more I want to do, Sam," he

breathed, kissing her nose, her chin, then the line of her jaw.

"Only *one* thing, Julian?" she inquired breathlessly.

"And I'm going to do it right now."

"Here?" she squeaked.

"Here and now," he assured her. In a daze, she allowed him to lead her to the sofa. He assisted her in sitting down, then he got down on one knee in front of her and took both her hands in his.

"You see, brat, I'm bound and determined to do this properly," he said with a grin.

"You're sure you're not just 'bound'?" she inquired with a responding smile, but she wasn't entirely teasing.

"I'd be down on my knees in front of you, Sam, even if we hadn't made love last night," he assured her. "Can I possibly make it clearer that you're the woman I love more than anyone in the world?" he asked, using her own words to make his point. "Dearest brat, will you marry me?"

Sam's heart felt as though it was going to burst with happiness. Her eyes welled with tears. She was so choked up, she couldn't speak.

"Don't keep the poor man in suspense. Say yes, Sam!" exclaimed Priss from the doorway.

"He put it so charmingly," Nan quipped, peeking over Priss's shoulder. "How can you refuse?"

Sam laughed. "Yes, Julian. Yes, I'll marry you. And do you want to know why?"

"Why, my love?" he asked, indulging her.

"Because you're the right man for me, the one and *only* man I could ever love. And I know you'll make me the happiest woman on earth!"

"But of course, Sam," Julian drawled. "I couldn't

allow you to marry anyone else, now could I? After all . . . I promised."

She fell into his arms and he kissed her again, even more thoroughly than before. Satisfied, the aunts softly closed the parlor door behind them and tiptoed away, their rosy faces wreathed in smiles.

Epilogue

Montgomery Manor
Hampshire, England
October 15, 1817

"What do you read, my love, to bring such a smile to your lips?"

Sam looked up from her letter and saw her husband standing just inside the door of her sitting room, drawing off his gloves. Julian had just returned from riding, and his cheeks were ruddy from the exercise, his eyes aglow. Dressed in buckskin breeches, tall boots, and a forester's green jacket, he looked like an especially dashing country squire. Even after almost four months of marriage, the mere sight of him still made Sam's heart flutter with excitement.

In the mood to tease him, she refolded the letter and slipped it into a pocket of her gown, saying demurely, "I received a letter from America today. Can you guess who it is who writes to me from the United States, my darling?"

With a faint smile and an arched brow, Julian threw his gloves on a piecrust table by the door and sauntered slowly toward her.

"Perhaps it is the president, finally writing to thank you—or abuse you—for naming that disreputable mongrel of yours after him."

Sam shook her head, looking coy. "No, it is not from President Madison."

He paused and leaned his hip against the back of the pale yellow satin sofa, his arms crossed over his broad chest, his gleaming eyes fixed intently on Sam's face. "Then it must be from that Ford fellow, begging you to come to Virginia. Perhaps he's already divorced Clara—or shut her up in the barn with his horses—and wants another wife."

Sam chuckled. "How very far off the mark you are, my dear husband! As well you know, Nathan was, and still is, quite daft about his wife. The letter, in fact, is from Clara. She writes to tell me that she is finally with child!"

"Indeed?" said Julian, raising his brows in mild interest. "I'm sure they are both quite pleased."

"Clara is more than pleased," Sam assured him. "She is deliriously happy. She has been wishing for a child since the moment they said their vows over the anvil in Gretna Green." She frowned. "Why do you suppose it took Nathan so long to get her pregnant?"

Julian looked amused. "My dear love, they've only been married since April."

"But Amanda got with child on her honeymoon, and *I* got with child that first night we made love in my mother's house on Upper Wimpole Street!"

"It must be the natural superiority of the English over the Americans," Julian suggested wryly.

"No, I daresay it is the natural superiority of the Montgomery men over all of mankind," Sam countered grandly.

"My dear girl, you make me blush," Julian demurred.

"And you make me wonder why you haven't kissed me yet," Sam retorted. "Am I already grown too fat for your tastes, my lord?"

Julian let loose a bark of laughter. "Too fat? My dear wife, you're not even showing yet!"

Sam rose from the chair in which she had been sitting by the sunny window, and laid her hand on her stomach. "But I *am* showing, Julian," she protested. "At least . . . a *little!* Come . . . *feel.*"

"How can I refuse such an invitation?" he drawled, strolling over. "But first things first." He took her into his arms and thoroughly kissed her, his hands wandering over her body with that familiar expertise that Sam had come to cherish. When he caressed her breasts—which were indeed larger and more sensitive than before—Sam wished they were in a more private chamber of the house.

"Goodness," Sam said, moments later, flushed and tingling. "Now you are making *me* blush. What if my mother came in while you were so delightfully mauling me?"

"Knowing your mother, she wouldn't blink an eye," he answered.

Sam laughed. "You're right. But you must stop kissing me—for now—and feel my stomach. I assure you, Julian, I have grown quite large since—"

"Since this morning?" he quizzed her, obligingly allowing her to place his large hand on her stomach, with her smaller hand pressed on top. "If you remember correctly, we made love this morning and I believe I . . . noticed every inch of your body."

"But you can't have noticed that the—" Sam was interrupted by a movement, a fluttering like a goldfish swimming inside her stomach. Wide-eyed, she looked up at Julian. "Did you feel that?"

But Sam could tell by the look on his face that Julian had indeed felt their baby's kick. "Yes," he said wonderingly. "How long has he being doing that?"

"He?" Sam teased.

"But of course," he replied.

"For the last month. But I never expected him to do it on cue! He must have heard his father's voice and immediately stood at attention."

"Clever little fellow," Julian observed, a bemused smile tilting his lips. "But do you suppose he'll be as obedient when he's twelve?"

Sam was about to reply when the sitting-room door was suddenly flung open and her mother sailed into the room with Zeus and Neptune close behind, their tongues hanging by several inches from their parted jaws. Julian and Sam drew apart, but stood holding hands as they watched Madame Genevieve DuBois make her entrance.

"Julian," she began in a scolding voice, the sheer skirts of her rose-pink gown flaring around her small, satin-shod feet as she hurried over to them. "What can you be thinking taking these dogs riding with you? They are run ragged, the poor dears! They must have each drank a bucket of water in the stable yard just now!"

"They were not invited to go with me," Julian informed her dryly. "I beseeched, then ordered them to go back to the house several times. I raised my voice and was quite stern, but they paid me no heed whatsoever. They are very willful animals, Genevieve."

"They are devoted to you, Julian," Sam said with a laugh, bending to pet the large dogs on the head. They wagged their tails and gazed adoringly at both Sam and Julian, then made their way across the floor to the briskly burning fire, where they collapsed onto the braided rug in front of it for a restorative nap.

"You poor dears," clucked Genevieve, gazing with eloquent and sympathetic eyes on the well-exercised and perfectly content animals. "What will become of you when I return to London next week?"

"But, Mother, I thought you were staying for another two weeks?" Sam expostulated. "You can't go yet!"

"But I must, dear," Genevieve assured her. "My new play, *Joan of Arc,* begins in a month, and even *I* need *some* time to rehearse. Besides, your sister and Julian's brother are expected any moment and will stay till Christmas. You're going to have a very crowded house."

"There are four-and-thirty bedchambers in Montgomery Manor," Julian reminded her.

"Don't brag," Genevieve sniffed. *"That's* not the point. You two are barely home from your honeymoon. Wouldn't you rather be alone?"

"If a man can't find a place to be alone with his wife in a house like this, then he is not very motivated," Julian observed. He turned to Sam and slid an arm around her waist. "I assure you, my dear mother-in-law, I am always quite motivated."

Genevieve tried to look offended by this provocative comment, but she smiled instead. "That is undeniably true, I daresay, but I still must return to London in a very few days. Since word got about that you are my daughter, Samantha, the theaters are packed fuller than ever for my performances. The notoriety certainly has done *me* no harm."

"Nor me, either, Mother," Sam reminded her. "At least none that I care about. Julian has intimidated the *ton* into viewing the whole matter as a nine days' wonder and of trifling consequence . . . or, at least, so they say to his face. And our real friends—of which we can count some of London's best society—understand that what happened to me was no fault of mine, nor do they think it shocking that my mother is the famous Genevieve DuBois. In fact, I think they are rather jealous!"

"Posh, my dear, don't flatter me," Genevieve said modestly, but was obviously quite pleased.

"Samantha! Julian! Genevieve!" came Nan's voice as she rushed into the room. "Amanda and Jack are here!"

This breathless announcement was followed by the entrance of Priss, energetically wringing her hands, and the three pups . . . who were no longer pups . . . prancing about and yapping in response to the excitement of their various human companions.

Madison had grown to be a large and clumsy animal with a sunny disposition and a playful temper. George was loyal, obedient, and devoted to Sam. And Louie, as lazy as ever but very charming with his large brown eyes and toad-eating ways, had ingratiated himself into the French cook's good graces and spent most of his time in the kitchen being pampered and fed.

Now the entire room, including the five barking dogs, emptied into the hall and headed *en masse* toward the front door, where Amanda and Jack had just stepped over the threshold.

The pandemonium was considerable. The two

sisters embraced first, then arms were hugging everywhere and fluttering handkerchiefs were dabbing away lots of female tears. Even Genevieve, who did not know the new arrivals except by report, was misty-eyed.

Julian and Jack, always glad to see each other, shook hands firmly and thumped each other hard on the backs, smiling like Bedlamites.

In the midst of this chaos, a young woman, looking a bit alarmed by all the noise and fuss, timidly slipped in the door and inquired of Amanda, "What shall I do with the babe, my lady?"

Amanda turned and peered lovingly into the sleeping infant's face. "Why, you must give him to Lord Durham, Betty, for I'm sure his father will want to show him off."

Jack, looking as handsome as ever with his glossy dark hair and snapping brown eyes, seemed to puff up with fatherly pride. He took the child from the nurse and gently cradled him in his manly arms, tilting him so that his shock of black hair and his round cheeks could be seen and appreciated by all.

Among the females, there was a general gush of admiration.

"He looks just like you, Jack," Sam exclaimed, touching her nephew's fat little cheek with her finger.

"But I daresay he'll still fare well enough in the world if he has inherited his mother's brains," Julian replied with the expected brutal wit of an older brother.

Jack laughed heartily and, in so doing, woke up his son. The babe blinked a few times, looked up into a half dozen strange faces, and immediately began to exercise his lungs.

This indignant outburst from his offspring seemed to delight Jack, who smiled wide and shouted above the din, "This noisy fellow is my son . . . Jonathan Jackson Montgomery. Isn't he a strapper?"

Everyone enthusiastically agreed.

Dashing away the last of their tears, Priss and Nan suddenly recollected their duties as great-aunts, shooed the dogs outside, and bade everyone to retire to the parlor where the weary travelers and little Jonathan could be made more comfortable.

Remembering her duties as lady of the house—a marchioness, no less—Sam ordered refreshments and made sure the housekeeper was busily directing Jack and Amanda's servants and belongings to the proper chambers.

Finally everyone was settled in the parlor, Jonathan had been whisked away by his nurse for a nappy change, and Genevieve was introduced and warmly welcomed into the family by Jack and Amanda.

General conversation ensued for a half hour, while the details of Jack and Amanda's travels and trials while returning home from a villa in Italy with an infant in tow were discussed with humor and liveliness.

Presently, Genevieve excused herself and the aunts followed suit, with Priss saying on her way out, "We old folks are fagged to death by all this excitement. We'll see you all later at dinner."

"Sam, your mother is charming," Amanda said when they were gone. Betty had brought back the baby—changed and fed—and Amanda sat on the sofa, holding him.

"Thank you," Sam said, very gratified, standing

over them and gazing down at the Madonna-like scene.

"I remember seeing her on the stage last autumn," Amanda further remarked. "I always thought her vastly talented, but I never imagined she was your mother!"

"Nor did I," Jack whispered in an aside to Julian as they stood together near the fire. "I'm very glad she rebuffed me that time I tried to kiss her. It would be devilish awkward now if I had succeeded."

"You never would have," Julian said with ruthless candor. "As it happens, the lady is very particular."

"Rebuffed you, too, eh, big brother?"

"I never tried," Julian murmured. "Although, I must admit, it did cross my mind a time or two. But, thank God, fate intervened. Think how awkward it would have been for *me!*"

Jack nodded soberly, and both gentlemen looked toward their wives.

"We're much luckier than we deserve, Julian," Jack mused.

"That's the truest thing you've ever said, little brother."

Just then, Amanda caught Jack's eye and called, "Come, dear. Why don't you sit down?" Readily compliant, Jack sat next to Amanda on the sofa and gazed fondly down at little Jonathan, who was sleeping peacefully.

Julian sat down in a wing chair opposite the sofa, and Sam perched on his knee, her arm slung around his neck and his arm about her waist.

Sam thought her sister looked more beautiful than ever, her pale blond hair shining, her skin glowing, her eyes sparkling with happiness. Presently, when Amanda was able to tear her eyes away from her sleeping son, Sam smiled and said with heartfelt sincerity, "I am glad you are home. I've worried about you."

"It was rather hard staying in bed for so many weeks, but it was worth it," Amanda said with a contented smile. "And Jack kept me very well entertained." She slid a sly look toward her husband. "He brought me flowers and candy and read me racy novels. He even made up some stories of his own. I must confess that they were the best of them all. Believe me, Julian, marriage has not subdued your brother's lively spirits in the least."

"Heaven help us," drawled Julian with a faint smile, and Jack smiled back, wholly unrepentant.

"But I was very sorry I missed your coming-out, Sam," Amanda said. "However, I thought of you constantly, and I knew Julian would take very good care of you."

"He certainly did *that,*" Jack agreed, cocking a suggestive brow at his older brother.

Wisely ignoring her husband's naughty inferences, Amanda continued, "And you've turned into such a lovely, accomplished woman, Sam. I am not at all surprised to hear you had admirers in abundance. But whatever happened to your French suitor? I must confess that although I hoped all along that Julian would finally realize the two of you were meant to be together and declare himself—"

"God God, was I the only one in the dark?" Julian interposed.

"—from your description of him I became rather attached to Jean-Luc!"

"How careless of you, my dear," Jack murmured playfully. "You should have kept such a confession to yourself. Now I'll have to call the fellow out!"

"That won't be possible, Jack," Julian assured him. "He's left the country."

"Left the country?" Amanda cried, alarmed. "He's not gone off with a broken heart, has he?"

"Hardly," said Sam with a chuckle. "He regretted me for a month or so, I'm told. But then he met an exotic heiress whose father is a wealthy plantation owner in the West Indies. They married in August and have gone to live in Jamaica for a year or two. I truly believe he's in love."

"I'm very glad of that," Amanda replied, her soft heart soothed by such good news. But then she got a stricken look in her eyes, lifting them first to Jack, then to Julian. "But what about poor Charlotte?"

The mention of Charlotte's name threw a gloomy pall over everyone in the room . . . except, of course, for Jonathan, who couldn't care less. But everyone else felt a particular interest in the happiness of Charlotte Batsford and wished they could somehow promote it.

"Dashed bad luck she ever met the two of us, eh, Julian?" Jack muttered.

"I just wish she'd liked any one of the several men who asked for her hand over the years. You and I were the only two she's ever favored." Julian sighed. "But she's a Trojan. She's forgiven us both."

"If only there was someone we could introduce her to, Julian," Sam said. "Someone who reminds her of *both* of you."

"Now there's a frightening thought," Julian murmured. "Besides, she's expressly asked me to never introduce her to any male relatives. In fact, I promised. She's through with Montgomery men forever!"

"But *I* didn't promise," Jack said, stroking his chin thoughtfully. "Which gives me leave to—"

Everyone looked toward Jack and waited. After staring at the carpet for a minute or two, he lifted his head, his eyes black and brilliant.

"I don't like that look," Julian said warily. "You had the same look that day you put tadpoles in the vicar's soup."

Amanda laughed. "But he must have been very young!"

"He was twenty," Julian said with an aggrieved expression.

"I'm not wanting to play mischief, Julian," Jack assured him. "I'm just thinking about our cousin, Jamie, in Edinburgh."

"That wastrel? Why?"

Jack grinned. "Charlotte has a soft spot for wastrels. She liked me well enough, didn't she?"

"But perhaps she's learned her lesson," Julian suggested repressively. "You will remember . . . she liked me, too. I can't imagine what you're thinking trying to shackle Charlotte to that devil-may-care Scotsman!"

Undeterred, Jack continued, "As soon as Amanda and I get settled at Ferndale after Christmas, I'm going to write to Jamie and invite him to come down in the spring to stay with us in London during the Season. I'll introduce Charlotte to Jamie, then step back and see what happens. That's all I'll do! The rest will be up to the two of them."

"Really, Jack!" Julian scoffed. "If you have turned matchmaker, you are doing a very shabby job of it. Charlotte and Jamie will *not* suit."

"But Julian," said Sam, stroking the back of his neck. "You did not think you and I would suit, either."

Julian slightly inclined his head. "That's true. However—"

"What can it hurt to introduce them to each other?"

"Sam, I promised—"

"But Jack didn't promise."

Although he had some grave misgivings about sanctioning Jack's matchmaking scheme, Julian was forced to relent. He could not deny that Charlotte, despite her reserve, liked Montgomery men. And he likewise could not deny that unlikely matches made some of the happiest of unions. He and Sam were a prime example of that.

"All right, brat," Julian said with grudging good humor and an affectionate squeeze of Sam's knee. "I see your point."

"Then it is settled," Jack said triumphantly. "Next spring Jamie Montgomery and Charlotte Batsford will meet."

Sam and Amanda smiled across the room at each other. Their eyes told all. If Charlotte had a chance to love and be loved by a Montgomery man, she'd be a fool not to give it one more try.

Now, how did that quote go? Ah, yes. . . . Third time was the charm.

Avon Romances—
the best in exceptional authors and unforgettable novels!

WICKED AT HEART   **Danelle Harmon**
78004-6/ $5.50 US/ $7.50 Can

SOMEONE LIKE YOU   **Susan Sawyer**
78478-5/ $5.50 US/ $7.50 Can

MIDNIGHT BANDIT   **Marlene Suson**
78429-7/ $5.50 US/ $7.50 Can

PROUD WOLF'S WOMAN   **Karen Kay**
77997-8/ $5.50 US/ $7.50 Can

THE HEART AND THE HOLLY   **Nancy Richards-Akers**
78002-X/ $5.50 US/ $7.50 Can

ALICE AND THE GUNFIGHTER   **Ann Carberry**
77882-3/ $5.50 US/ $7.50 Can

THE MACKENZIES: LUKE   **Ana Leigh**
78098-4/ $5.50 US/ $7.50 Can

FOREVER BELOVED   **Joan Van Nuys**
78118-2/ $5.50 US/ $7.50 Can

INSIDE PARADISE   **Elizabeth Turner**
77372-4/ $5.50 US/ $7.50 Can

CAPTIVATED   **Colleen Corbet**
78027-5/ $5.50 US/ $7.50 Can

Avon Romantic Treasures

*Unforgettable, enthralling love stories,
sparkling with passion and adventure
from Romance's bestselling authors*

SUNDANCER'S WOMAN *by Judith E. French*
77706-1/$5.99 US/$7.99 Can

JUST ONE KISS *by Samantha James*
77549-2/$5.99 US/$7.99 Can

HEARTS RUN WILD *by Shelly Thacker*
78119-0/$5.99 US/$7.99 Can

DREAM CATCHER *by Kathleen Harrington*
77835-1/$5.99 US/$7.99 Can

THE MACKINNON'S BRIDE *by Tanya Anne Crosby*
77682-0/$5.99 US/$7.99 Can

PHANTOM IN TIME *by Eugenia Riley*
77158-6/$5.99 US/$7.99 Can

RUNAWAY MAGIC *by Deborah Gordon*
78452-1/$5.99 US/$7.99 Can

YOU AND NO OTHER *by Cathy Maxwell*
78716-4/$5.99 US/$7.99 Can

Discover Contemporary Romances at Their Sizzling Hot Best from Avon Books

JONATHAN'S WIFE   *by Dee Holmes*
78368-1/$5.99 US/$7.99 Can

DANIEL'S GIFT   *by Barbara Freethy*
78189-1/$5.99 US/$7.99 Can

FAIRYTALE   *by Maggie Shayne*
78300-2/$5.99 US/$7.99 Can

WISHES COME TRUE   *by Patti Berg*
78338-X/$5.99 US/$7.99 Can

ONCE MORE WITH FEELING   *by Emilie Richards*
78363-0/$5.99 US/$7.99 Can

HEAVEN COMES HOME   *by Nikki Holiday*
78456-4/$5.99 US/$7.99 Can

RYAN'S RETURN   *by Barbara Freethy*
78531-5/$5.99 US/$7.99 Can